Praise for *The First Lady and the Rebel*

"Historical fiction at it best: A unique, intimate view of a character we thought we knew. The Civil War comes to life through two sisters on opposite sides, one the first lady of the not-so United States. And through it all, a fascinating family saga. I learned a lot and loved this book."

—Karen Harper, *New York Times* bestselling
author of *American Duchess*

"Susan Higginbotham's *The First Lady and the Rebel* is a meticulously researched and powerfully written account of the complicated and compelling relationship between the Todd sisters. Higginbotham's two female protagonists are bonded by blood and love, but pulled apart by war. Set against the sweeping backdrop of our nation's Civil War, this is the tragic and true story of human hearts both fierce and fallible, of deeply mixed loyalties, and of the imperfect but inspiring individuals who were asked to do the unimaginable. Moving and enlightening."

—Allison Pataki, *New York Times* bestselling
author of *The Accidental Empress*

"Susan Higginbotham has done it again—crafted a richly detailed novel that immerses readers in America's Civil War. *The First Lady and the Rebel* explores the tragic story of a family and a nation torn apart, while shedding light on rarely reported events in the personal life of Abraham Lincoln. Mary Todd Lincoln, the President's wife, and her sister, Emily Todd Helm, are devoted to their husbands and to each other, yet find themselves on opposite sides of the conflict as they face overwhelming grief and loss. The novel presents a devastating time and place rendered so vividly you'll feel as if you'd lived through the war yourself. Higginbotham's painstaking and extensive research is evident from the engaging first chapter to the novel's moving conclusion. For those who like their historical novels based on real people, this book is a must-read."

—Amy Belding Brown, author of *Flight of the Sparrow*

ALSO BY SUSAN HIGGINBOTHAM

The Traitor's Wife
Hugh and Bess
The Stolen Crown
The Queen of Last Hopes
Her Highness, the Traitor
Hanging Mary

The
FIRST LADY
and the REBEL

The

FIRST LADY
and the REBEL

A NOVEL

Best wishes t Karen,

SUSAN HIGGINBOTHAM

sourcebooks
landmark

Published by Sourcebooks Landmark, an imprint of Sourcebooks
P.O. Box 4410, Naperville, Illinois 60567-4410
(630) 961-3900
sourcebooks.com

Library of Congress Cataloging-in-Publication Data

Names: Higginbotham, Susan, author.
Title: The First Lady and the rebel / Susan Higginbotham.
Description: Naperville, Illinois : Sourcebooks Landmark, [2019]
Identifiers: LCCN 2019001134 | (trade pbk. : alk. paper)
Subjects: LCSH: Lincoln, Mary Todd, 1818-1882--Fiction. | Helm,
    Emilie Todd, 1836-1930--Fiction. | Presidents' spouses--Fiction. |
    GSAFD: Biographical fiction.
Classification: LCC PS3608.I364 F57 2019 | DDC 813/.6--dc23 LC record
available at https://lccn.loc.gov/2019001134

Printed and bound in Canada.
MBP 10 9 8 7 6 5 4 3 2 1

↪ 1 ↩

MARY

OCTOBER 1839 TO NOVEMBER 4, 1842

The man she intended to marry had yet to learn about their future together, but she had already made up her mind.

It was a pity, though, that she had been so bedraggled when they first saw each other, shortly after Mary arrived at her married sister Elizabeth's house to pay an extended visit of the sort that was hoped by families to end in matrimony for the unmarried sister and quite often did. The trip from Mary's home in Lexington, Kentucky, to Elizabeth's in Springfield, Illinois, had taken over two weeks, and had involved nearly every means of transport known to man—rail, boat, coach, and even a stretch on foot when the coach hit a muddy patch. Mary had arrived at her sister's house tired and out of sorts, and eager to take a nap and freshen up. Instead, she had found that Elizabeth, whose house drew anyone of any importance in Springfield, had company: their cousin John Todd Stuart and his law partner. So: a roomful of lawyers, who could be either the dullest people in existence or the most fascinating, depending on what they chose to speak about. Hoping for the latter, Mary had repaired her coach-worn appearance as best she could and entered the room.

"Cousin!" John Stuart kissed her cheek, then shook hands with her father, who had been her escort on the journey. "We were just leaving, and I'm sure you're glad of it after your long trip. We'll stop by once you're settled in. You didn't meet Mr. Lincoln here on your last visit, did you?"

"No," Mary said. She gazed at the stranger in the room, a man of about thirty years of age who somewhat awkwardly extended his hand to her. "I would have remembered Mr. Lincoln."

He was certainly not a forgettable person. He was tall, well over six feet, a trait that Mary, at five feet two, usually found off-putting in a man. With this man, however, she scarcely cared that she had to tip her head up to look at him, for his face, sharp-edged and topped by a thatch of ill-tamed black hair, was well worth the effort. It was not a handsome face by any means, but after years of enduring the good-looking and vacuous young men of Lexington, Mary had concluded long ago that handsomeness was overrated. This man had character in his face—character and intelligence. She had never seen the like.

But she could not simply stand there staring at Mr. Lincoln as if she were a practitioner of physiognomy. "I have heard of you, Mr. Lincoln, many times. Weren't you the leader of the effort to get the state capital moved here?"

Ninian Edwards, Mary's brother-in-law, broke in before Mr. Lincoln, who had appeared at a loss for what to do after releasing Mary's hand, could reply. "Miss Todd will talk politics like a man if you allow her."

"Why, yes I will," said Mary. "It is unladylike, I grant you, but if we feel the effects of politics as much, if not more so, than you gentlemen, shall we not be allowed to take an interest in such a weighty subject? But you have not allowed Mr. Lincoln to answer my question, Brother Ninian."

"It was the work of many, Miss Todd," Mr. Lincoln said. His voice was not deep, as Mary had expected, but peculiarly high-pitched, though Mary, on reflection, found it not to be displeasing. "But we have to be off, as Mr. Stuart says."

"Well," said Mary. "Those many should be quite pleased with themselves, for Springfield has improved very much since I was here last. I expect it will be a regular metropolis when I next visit."

Mr. Lincoln nodded, then all but fled from the Edwardses' parlor.

∽⊘∼

"You quite overwhelmed the man," her sister Elizabeth said as she showed Mary to her room a little while later. "He scarcely says boo to us women in Springfield who have known him for some time, much less a complete stranger."

"I find him fascinating." Mary began to unpack her trunk. In Lexington, a slave would already have accomplished that task, but it was clear that in Springfield she would have to fend for herself.

"Five, six words, and you find him fascinating?"

"He has *mind*, Elizabeth. I can tell that."

"Oh, *mind*." Elizabeth snorted. "Well, he needs that, because he certainly does not have breeding. Did you not see how he was dressed? He must throw his clothes on in the pitch-darkness."

"I was not looking at his dress. I hope he comes back here soon so I can."

"He will; he's here quite often, but if you want to hold a conversation with him, you'll need to be prepared to do the talking yourself—if you're a woman, at least. With the men, he can tell stories and idle time away for hours. But tell me, how is everyone at home?"

"Oh, the same. Our stepmother sends us her kindest regards, not to mention her vast relief at having one less stepdaughter to plague her. Ann is as trying as ever, although she cheered up marvelously when I left upon finally getting to claim our room as hers. The little ones are driving Mammy Sally to distraction, and the baby is squalling as loud as he ever was. Levi's habits do not improve." Somewhat awkwardly, Mary shook out the gown she had just removed from her trunk. "Oh, and Emily was nearly kidnapped. The mite wandered off—probably as tired of the baby squalling as the rest of us—and a passing couple was so taken with her beauty, they took her home and kept her there until their minister happened to come by and impressed upon them that they were doing wrong! She is a lovely little thing." Settling her chemises into a drawer, Mary asked in her most casual tone, "When do you think Mr. Lincoln will call?"

"Soon," said Elizabeth firmly. "Now, go lie down. You must be exhausted. Probably Mr. Lincoln won't appear nearly as fascinating to you when you've had some rest."

Mary sighed but did not argue. She looked around the room, which had been occupied by her second oldest sister, Frances, until her marriage just a few months before, and saw that her bed had been turned down, but not with much care. White servants, who she had learned from Elizabeth tended to do exactly as they pleased, would take some getting used to, just like the mud that filled the mostly unpaved streets of Springfield and that had slightly contaminated her dress despite her best efforts.

The mattress she sank into was of excellent quality, as was everything in her sister's household—no surprise, since Ninian Edwards was a former governor's son, and his house, perched upon a hill at a slight distance from the heart of the town, was one of the best in Springfield. From her father, however, who told her everything, Mary had learned that all was not well with her brother-in-law, who was finding it hard to pay some of his bills. But the entire country had been in the doldrums due to the bank panic of two years before. Now that Springfield was the new capital—thanks in large part to this Mr. Lincoln—perhaps things would turn around for her brother-in-law.

Her last visit to Springfield had been a short one, and had served its purpose well of allowing Mary to get a respite from a house full of half siblings, all of whom had inherited the Todd temper in varying degrees, and her stepmother. (Not that Mary was completely unsympathetic to Mrs. Todd, saddled with the task of raising the children from her husband's first marriage while bearing her own children at almost mechanical intervals.) This visit was different: with Frances married, it was time for Mary, the next sister in line, to do the same, especially as she was nearly twenty-one—by no means at the age where society would declare her doomed to spinsterhood, but still at a point of life where she had to be thinking of her prospects.

She had utter confidence that she would find a husband. Although it was true that suitors had not exactly been lining up by her father's study in Lexington, Mary had never given any of the men there a thought, much less any encouragement. She considered them shallow; no doubt they believed her to be peculiar, with her habit of saying what she thought and her unladylike interest in politics. But what did it matter? Springfield, small but pushing, was where her future lay. In Lexington, men lounged; in Springfield, they strove. Those were the sort of men that caught her fancy.

And none of them, she suspected, strove as much as Mr. Lincoln.

It was foolish for her to think, on such short acquaintance, that he was the husband for her. But while she didn't know him, she did know of him. She knew that her cousin, a fine lawyer, had taken him on as a junior partner, which he would hardly do if the man didn't have promise. She knew that Mr. Lincoln had led the group of legislators who had battled to move the Illinois capital to Springfield—no mean undertaking considering how unpromising the city had looked just a couple of years ago. (Even today, as Mary's stagecoach had pulled up alongside the new American House Hotel, a contingent of hogs had been near the door to greet the passengers.) And while he might not have breeding, the fact that he was received in her brother-in-law's parlor showed that he had other qualities, for Ninian Edwards would not let just anyone into his fine house. And it had taken something to get in the legislature in the first place.

What might such a man accomplish with her as a wife? Mary settled to sleep, smiling at the possibilities.

∽℘∼

But Mr. Lincoln did not come to the Edwards house the next day, nor the day afterward. Mary asked her sister and brother-in-law about him, only once or twice, so not as to seem overly interested, but they could say little except that he was a busy man who did not socialize much in the evenings.

She had plenty of time, anyway, Mary thought. No point of rushing into these things.

In the meantime, she visited her sister Frances, now Mrs. Wallace, who was boarding with her husband in the Globe Tavern. Four dollars a week bought the newlyweds a room, with meals included and the cacophony of coaches coming and going. "Granted, it's not what I was accustomed to," Frances said, waving Mary to a seat in the corner that served as the couple's sitting room. "But it's better than I expected. I was in tears when Dr. Wallace told me we would be living in a boardinghouse."

"I can see why," Mary admitted. The room was clean, with all the requisite furnishings, and Frances had been in it long enough to add some of her own touches, but the comforts that Mary and her sisters were accustomed to from their home in Lexington and their sister Elizabeth's home—a floor gleaming with polish, silver on the sideboards, servants within call—were missing. "Still, at least you don't have to cook or clean."

Frances leaned forward. "Actually," she said in a low voice, "I do help out occasionally. There are so few women here at the moment, and I would be frightfully bored when Dr. Wallace is gone if I do not."

"Goodness," Mary said. She was an expert seamstress, having decided some years ago to acquire the art of fine sewing rather than to trust others to emulate the fashion plates she so admired, but cooking and cleaning were tasks that she was quite happy to leave to the servants, white or black. She repressed a shudder.

She had evidently not repressed it well enough, though, for Frances said, "Sister, if you marry a man like that Mr. Lincoln, you may find yourself doing such tasks."

"Who said that I planned to marry him?"

"Well, Elizabeth said you were interested, and you do have a way of getting what you set your mind on."

"Fair enough. But I've only seen him once, and for all I know, he may not improve upon acquaintance."

"He's agreeable enough," Frances said, almost coquettishly.

"Why, do you know him?" Mary's eyes widened. "He did not *court* you, did he?"

"No. Mr. Edwards spoke of him so much, I asked him to invite him over, and we walked out together once or twice. He appeared to enjoy my company, but he put forth no effort into putting our acquaintance on a higher level, and when Dr. Wallace took an interest in me, that was that."

Mary nodded, concealing her inward sigh of relief.

It would *not* have done to be the second Todd sister of choice.

In December, the legislature met in Springfield for the first time, its members traveling by coach because the railway had not yet come to town and meeting wherever a body of men could squeeze in because the capitol building had yet to be completed. The pigs were no less intrusive, but they had to share the muddy streets now with the state's politicians. The legislators filled the American House, spilling over to the parlors of the Globe Tavern, where Frances found her slumbers sometimes being interrupted by the sound of brawling politicians.

With the legislature had come the rain, which for days upon end alternated between downpours and drizzles, occasionally mixing with a few bedraggled snowflakes. Because venturing upon the streets would have been the ruination of their gowns and slippers, those ladies who could afford to stay inside did so, sending their servants to do their marketing.

Mary could not have endured this had she not found a new friend: Mercy Levering, who had come from Baltimore to stay with her brother, Lawrason Levering, who lived next door to the Edwardses. Mary took to Mercy instantly: the young women were of an age, both were from more established cities than Springfield (although Mary had to cede Baltimore's superiority to Lexington in that respect), and both were from aristocratic families. Even better, Mercy had quickly acquired a suitor, a lawyer named James Conkling, and could safely appreciate Mr. Lincoln's virtues without aspiring to him herself.

But even Mercy's company had begun to pale after a week of rain, and Mary was itching to get back to town. That was when Mary, having dashed from her house to Mercy's, spied a pile of shingles on the porch, left there, she supposed, by some workman. "Mercy! I've an idea. Remember how Sir Walter Raleigh spread his cloak for the queen to cross over? Well, we haven't a knight, more's the pity, but we do have our own frontier way of managing."

"Whatever do you mean?"

Mary held up a shingle. She tossed it in front of her, then stepped primly onto it. "See? We'll throw the shingles down before us, and our feet will never touch the muck."

"You can't be serious."

"I most assuredly am. Can you seriously bear one more day cooped up inside?" Mary nodded in the direction of the pianoforte. "You can buy some more music," she said coaxingly.

Mercy sighed, but she had been bemoaning the lack of new music just the day before. "Oh, I suppose. But if we catch a chill and die, I'll never forgive you."

They each grabbed a pile of shingles and set off on the short walk to town, Mary's face alight with adventure, Mercy straggling along as if being led to slaughter. For two or three blocks, the scheme worked well enough, but by the fourth block, the shingles were as muddy as the streets themselves, and more than one citizen leaned out of his or her window to stare at the spectacle of the two finely dressed young ladies hopping from one shingle to another. When they finally reached civilization—Monroe Street, with its sidewalk and shops—they tossed their filthy shingles aside and rushed into a bookstore, where Mary bought the latest novel and Mercy, the latest song. By the time they exhausted the shops an hour or so later, a drizzle was replenishing the mud, and the air had a chill.

"I've had enough adventure for one day," Mercy said firmly as they left. "No more shingles. We can find my brother, or Mr. Edwards, to give us a ride home in his carriage."

"Or Mr. Conkling. But we'll have to wait until they leave their offices."

"That can't be helped."

"Wait!" Mary waved to a passing drayman. "Here's a way to get home."

"Mary, are you mad?"

"No, I'm cold and tired and want to get to the warmth of my parlor. Mr. Hart"—she smiled at the drayman, who tipped his hat—"will be delighted to be of service to us. Won't you, dear sir?"

"Most certainly, Miss Todd."

Mercy picked up her skirts and fled. "I'll stop by tomorrow," she called. "My brother would be furious if I got into that thing!"

"What a rude word for such a fine dray," Mary said as Mr. Hart helped her as best he could into the vehicle. "Shall we be off, sir?" A collection of boys were gaping at her, and she majestically waved her hand as she fancied Queen Victoria must. "To home!"

With a lurch that nearly sent her sprawling into the mud, Mr. Hart obliged.

Capital city or not, Springfield was still a small, tittle-tattle town—even more so now that the legislators were here to add to the goings-on. So Mary was not entirely surprised to hear on Tuesday—a dry day with a strong wind, all the better to drive gossip from house to house—that her adventure on the dray was known to all and sundry, to the amusement of all except for Elizabeth, whose steely silence indicated that she was in complete possession of the details.

"I didn't tell a soul," Mercy protested when Mary came over that afternoon. "I wouldn't have needed to, though. Such a spectacle needed no help from me. And if there's a soul who doesn't know about it, the cotillion will remedy that."

"Cotillion?"

"Oh, yes, some gentlemen are organizing a ball, as it's been so dreary and the men are in need of civilizing. Why, Mr. Edwards is on the committee. Your sister said nothing to you?"

"Not a thing."

"Dear, you had best sweeten her up, then." Mercy could not help but smirk. "Especially since your Mr. Lincoln will be there. Or I assume he will, as he is on the committee as well."

"He will?" Mary rose. "I must get a new gown."

"Oh, I wouldn't bother; they say he never notices what women wear. But"—Mercy snickered—"you might capture his attention if you arrive in your dray."

⁕

Mary arrived at the American House on the day of the cotillion not in a dray, but in her brother-in-law's carriage. As the ladies in their finery hurried into the suite that had been converted into a dressing room for the occasion, Mary watched with amusement as the younger matrons, who had entered clutching squirming bundles to their chests, briskly nursed the contents of the bundles before they handled them off to the girls who had been hired to watch them for the evening. "Don't mix them up," they called as the girls spread out a line of sleeping babies on the bed.

It would be pleasant to be married, but there was no need to rush into anything, she decided as she pinched some color into her cheeks. Goodness knew there were enough children back in her father's house in Lexington to look after if she were so minded.

Following her sister into the ballroom (meekly, for Elizabeth was still silently indignant about the dray incident), Mary admired the room, ablaze with candles and decked with greenery as a herald of the Christmas season. Standing by the doorway were the men who had organized the cotillion. Though Ninian and some of the others were tall men, one nonetheless towered over them: Mr. Lincoln. In his black suit, he was nattier than he had been when Mary had last met him. As did the other men, he greeted the ladies in turn as they filed into the room.

Then he saw Mary. His face twisted into a grin, he slapped his knee, and he began to laugh so hard, he wheezed. "A…dray!" he finally managed. "A dray! There's Miss Todd, the girl who rode in a dray."

"Yes," Elizabeth said freezingly. "That is my sister, who rode in a dray. Come along, Mary."

But Mr. Lincoln would have none of it. He straightened up and wiped his eyes. "Funniest…thing…I…ever…saw," he gasped. "There I was, making some notes at my desk, and who should I see coming down the street but Miss Mary Todd, in all her fine feathers, riding in that dray. I tell you, it made my day, Miss Todd. Made my week. Made my month! The finest sight I've ever seen in Springfield. Miss Todd, I want to dance with you in the worst way. Will you oblige?"

Unable to muster a reply, Mary handed him her dance card, and Mr. Lincoln neatly inscribed it. "First on the list! I can't wait, Miss Todd."

He did indeed, as Mary was fond of telling others in years to come, dance with her in the worst way. Mary had danced with awkward men and boys before, especially at Madame Mentelle's school, where as a boarder she had helped her teacher's sons learn the terpsichorean art, but she could not keep her slippers clear of Mr. Lincoln's enormous feet. This was so even though Mr. Lincoln was more focused on his feet than on Mary, who wondered wistfully if he even noticed her new gown, sprigged with blue flowers that matched her eyes, or the very becoming arrangement of her thick, dark hair.

Though she had had little patience when the swains of Lexington paid her their empty, trite compliments, she would not have taken such pretty phrases amiss coming from Mr. Lincoln. But even if Mr. Lincoln was inclined to give her such tributes, they had had no chance for conversation, because even if the dance had lent itself to it, talking and dancing simultaneously was completely beyond her partner's powers. So she had to settle for the pleasant sensation of his large hand clasping hers as she twirled around whenever her partner remembered to let her do so.

Mr. Lincoln seemed pleased enough with his performance, however—after all, Mary was still standing and had all ten toes intact—and managed a gallant bow as the number ended. He would have lingered by Mary's side to talk after she limped off the dance floor, but Mary, knowing the proprieties of such matters (and finding that Elizabeth had only just begun to thaw after the dray incident), gently reminded him that she was engaged for the next dance, and several thereafter.

Yet when she was claimed by her next partner, Mr. Stephen Douglas, who danced so well that Mary scarcely noticed his almost comically small stature, Mary found herself looking around the room for Mr. Lincoln. It was almost worth hazarding her slippers once more.

Though Mr. Lincoln had not paid much attention to her gown, which so enticingly displayed her shoulders and a hint of bosom, the other bachelors in the room apparently did, so Mary was engaged for the entire evening. As this was her first ball in Springfield, normally she would have been gratified by this, but her mind was on Mr. Lincoln and, when she could manage it discreetly, her eyes as well. She was able to learn through her observations that he did not drink, though he made no point of his abstemiousness but stood laughing amid his companions, some of whom had clearly overindulged in spirits. This pleased Mary; though no Kentucky girl expected men to avoid liquor entirely, she disliked drunkenness. If she shared any trait of her stepmother's, it was the way they both watched her brother Levi anxiously at gatherings, counting his drinks and praying that he would not pass beyond the stage of amiable intoxication.

Mr. Lincoln was not dressed badly, although his sleeves and pantaloons were a bit too short, and there was nothing in the cut of his garment to recommend his tailor. What a proper wife could do for him in that regard!

Elizabeth glided behind her, nearly causing her to drop the cup of punch she held. "Do stop staring at Mr. Lincoln," she hissed in French, continuing a habit the sisters had found useful on a number of occasions. "If it makes you feel better, though, he has asked to call tomorrow, and I have granted his wish. You may gaze at him all you like then."

∽℘∽

Mr. Lincoln bounded into the parlor the next afternoon, on time and not showing any signs of fatigue or dissipation, although the cotillion had still been going on when Mary and the Edwardses had left in the small hours. When he had taken his seat on a horsehair sofa beside Mary, she said, "Now, Mr. Lincoln, you really must tell me all the ins and outs of how you moved the legislature to Springfield. There is ample time for it today, and I insist."

"I will obey, Miss Todd, but tell me: What got you interested in politics?"

"Goodness, Mr. Lincoln, I hardly know. It almost seems as if I have always been. But if I had to assign a cause—and if you ask, I must"—Mary smiled in a manner she knew would show a dimple—"my mother died when I was quite young, and I felt the loss very keenly. You know how a parent wishes to indulge a child in such a situation."

"Well, no," Mr. Lincoln said dryly.

"A *girl* child, then, Mr. Lincoln. In any case, I liked to sit with my father when he was at home, and he would allow me to remain in the room for an hour or two while he talked to his friends, on the condition that I remained absolutely quiet. Naturally, their conversations would turn to politics, and as I could do nothing but listen, I did, and learned a great deal. And what great men I had to learn from! Henry Clay among them."

"Henry Clay? Why, he is my hero, Miss Todd. And you know him?"

"Indeed she does," Elizabeth, who had been knitting on the matching sofa across the room, put in. "Why, she made a perfect nuisance of herself one day at his house."

"I did not; he was charmed." Mary glared at her sister, then turned to Mr. Lincoln. "When I was quite a young thing, you see, I took it in my head to ride my new pony to Ashland, his estate, and show it to him. Who in the county was a better judge of horseflesh? Well, he was entertaining some gentlemen, but being the soul of courtesy, he kindly invited me in, and I had a simply delightful time listening to them.

When there was an opening in the conversation—I did not interrupt, Elizabeth, as everyone insists—I told Mr. Clay that my father thought he, Mr. Clay that is, would someday be the president, and that I would dearly like to live in the White House myself."

"I wonder what Mrs. Clay thought of that, sister."

"Goodness, I wasn't proposing to *marry* Mr. Clay. That would be shocking. I was merely stating a fact. In any case, Mr. Clay assured me that if he were ever president, I would be one of his first guests. And as far as I know, the invitation still stands, so I took it downright personally when he lost the nomination this year."

As Mary and Mr. Lincoln began bewailing Mr. Clay's loss, Elizabeth yawned once, then twice, and soon found an excuse to slip out of the room, leaving the pair to move to the subject of the relocation of the capital and, gradually, an inch or two closer together. They were still chattering away—or to be precise, Mary was chattering and Mr. Lincoln was listening—when the sounds and smells of dinner being prepared began to intrude upon their conversation, followed by Elizabeth's reappearance. "Mr. Lincoln, we would be delighted to have you stay to dine with us."

"Thank you, Mrs. Edwards, but it's going to be a busy day tomorrow. Got to do a little work tonight." He stole a look at Mary. "I hope I might call again on— I mean, at this house."

"Of course," Elizabeth said.

∽◦∾

From that day on, Mr. Lincoln appeared at the Edwards house every few days, taking the same place beside Mary. Sometimes they would talk politics; other times they would take a book from Ninian Edwards's well-stocked (if not exactly well-thumbed) library and have one read it to the other.

He knew far more about her than she did about him; all the scant details of his family she had garnered from others. His mother had died when he was young. He had not been exactly poor as a child but had never been comfortable either; his father had moved from place to place, looking for a propitious place to settle but never quite finding it. Like Mary, he was a Kentuckian, but the log cabin of his birth might have been separated from the gracious house of Mary's birth by an ocean. He had started out doing manual labor and had somehow wandered into New Salem, where he had blundered into co-owning a store, which had foundered when his partner had died of drink. With some fellows from New Salem, he had served in the Black Hawk War, which in a way had been his making, for it had brought him into contact with Mary's cousin John Stuart, who had encouraged him to read the law and eventually had taken him on as a partner. And, in all that, he had found his way into politics.

Anything more, she would have to pry out of him, she supposed.

Were they courting? Goodness, she wasn't sure even of that! He had the regularity of a lover, for certain, but not the mannerisms of one, and while he sat as close to her on the sofa as her skirts would allow, that was the only liberty he took, if it could be called that. Not that she wanted him to behave in an ungentlemanly manner, but a kiss, or even some hand-holding, would have been welcome. She had consulted Mercy, her guide to all things involving courtship (neither of her sisters would really do under the circumstances), and Mercy had agreed that something a little more should be happening. Why, her dear James had left her positively flustered the other day.

Surely Mr. Lincoln didn't find her unattractive, did he? Mary looked at herself in the mirror critically. She would never credit herself with beauty, but with her perfect complexion and her bright-blue eyes, there was certainly nothing in her face to make a man avert his.

So far, most of their meetings had been in the Edwardses' parlor, but not long after Christmas, the snow turned the rutted, homely streets into glistening white paths. Everyone on the Hill, as the Edwardses' neighborhood was called, bundled up and went for sleigh rides. As such things were done best seated in pairs, the single young men of the city were of course invited on these outings, and Mr. Lincoln, perhaps through Mercy's help, ended up being paired with Mary. The chill in the air allowed Mary to move a little closer to him without being forward, but that was the only progress they made, even though it would have been perfectly harmless for him to put his arm around her to keep her from falling out when the driver began to go a wee bit too fast.

"Good clean exercise," he had said when he handed her out— almost as an afterthought, for it was apparent that he had grown up around women who were used to doing for themselves. "Wasn't that fun, Miss Todd?"

Mary, who had spent the entire ride holding her muff in a way that invited him to slip his hand inside to join hers, had been hard-pressed not to scowl. "Delightful."

Then the legislature adjourned and Springfield's lawyers began riding the circuit, traveling from town to town to try cases in front of equally itinerate judges. "You must find that dreary, Mr. Lincoln," Mary said one evening before her companion was to depart.

"Not at all, Miss Todd. I love it. We lawyers all travel about together—judges too—and go at each other like cats and dogs in court. Then when we're done for the day, we lounge about and swap tales."

"I suppose the married lawyers don't take their wives." Too late, Mary hoped that Mr. Lincoln did not think she was insinuating anything.

Mr. Lincoln, however, was too busy recalling the pleasures of the circuit to care. "No, Miss Todd, it's not a place for ladies. The roads can be awful, the lodgings aren't always the best, and, well, we men can be a little rough."

"Perhaps you need some civilizing influences from the ladies."

"I wouldn't want to be the lady who tried." He rose, just as Elizabeth made one of her rare glides into the room. It was a wee bit depressing, Mary reflected, to have a chaperone with so little to chaperone. "I'll see you in a few weeks, miss."

If this was a courtship, at least no one could call it a rushed one.

She could understand, however, why courtship might not be the first thing on Mr. Lincoln's mind, for 1840 was an election year, with the Whig candidate, General William Henry Harrison, trying to unseat President Martin Van Buren. A Democrat had snidely remarked that

Harrison, who was not in the spring of youth, would be content to sit in his log cabin with a pension and a barrel of hard cider. The jibe had backfired, for Harrison had seized upon it, dubbing himself the "log cabin and hard cider" candidate of the people, though his origins were far from humble.

Springfield was in the thick of the election. The Whigs poured into town for their state convention in June, filling the streets with men sporting coonskin caps and pushing barrels of hard cider, the contents of which they were all too ready to consume. Mary, overcoming her chagrin that Henry Clay had not won the Whig nomination the year before, did her part to welcome the visitors, waving her handkerchief as they processed into the city, adorned with banners that she had helped sew.

Mr. Lincoln, who himself was running for reelection to the Illinois House of Representatives, did his part in extolling Harrison's virtues. Even as she sat enthralled by his speech, Mary had to admit it was all a bit absurd, because Harrison, the scion of a wealthy Virginia family, had certainly not been born in a log cabin, and while he might have spent some time in one when he moved west, it most likely was not a terribly uncomfortable one. But Mr. Lincoln made it all sound quite plausible.

Among the visitors the convention brought to Springfield was Judge David Todd, Mary's uncle. Naturally, he called to see his nieces, and after a couple of hours taking tea (no hard cider for a change) said, "Why don't you accompany me back to Missouri, Miss Todd, and stay a couple of months? Your cousin Ann would be delighted with your company."

Mary readily agreed, for she loved travel, wearisome as it could be. Besides, her closest friend, Mercy, was back in Baltimore now, so the company of a young lady of her own age would be particularly pleasant and…well, perhaps her absence might be just what was needed to get Mr. Lincoln thinking more about her. So when Mr. Lincoln turned up a few days later and took his accustomed place, Mary said, "I will be taking to the circuit myself tomorrow, to Missouri, to visit Judge Todd and his family."

"How long will you stay, Miss Todd?" He frowned slightly.

"I do not know. I am told they live in a charming city." She smiled. "Perhaps I shall be tempted to change my residence permanently, sir."

"But you will miss all the goings-on here," Mr. Lincoln said almost reproachfully.

Mary gave an elegant shrug. "What will be will be."

"Well…" He scooted slightly closer to her and leaned forward. "Mary?"

Instinctively, Mary tipped her head a little bit backward, preparing for his kiss. Would it be an awkward one? Sadly, unlike dancing, she had no basis for comparison when kissing was concerned.

"Would you like me to send you the Springfield newspapers?"

Mary tipped her head forward again. "That would be very kind of you, Mr. Lincoln." She hoped she was not gritting her teeth.

∽◉↝

Mr. Lincoln did send the papers as promised—the Springfield paper and the *Old Soldier*, the latter issued by the Harrison campaign. To her surprise, she also received the Democratic paper, the *Hickory Club*— certainly not something that Mr. Lincoln would have sent her. Her suspicions about its origins were confirmed a day or so later when Stephen Douglas sent her a letter. It was a pleasant, chatty letter, without an iota of romance in it, but it left her with the distinct impression that the writer would not be averse to such a development, if she encouraged it.

Did she wish to? Certainly Mr. Douglas was agreeable enough, and ambitious as well. Much to his credit, he did not stare at Mary as if she were a talking dog when she ventured to make a political observation. And whereas Mr. Lincoln often forgot the little politenesses to which ladies were accustomed, such as fetching lemonade at parties and bringing some candy or flowers when he visited, Mr. Douglas never did. Nothing led her to believe that she could not live happily enough with him. But…

His were not the only letters Mary received. A widower by the name of Edwin Webb, who had been another visitor to the Edwards house, wrote her a charming epistle, not so subtly advertising his merits as a husband, which were certainly considerable in the material way, although he left out the facts that he was some twenty years older than Mary and the father of two young children. Mary had not much enjoyed being a stepdaughter, and was even less inclined to assume the role of stepmother, so she sent a polite reply and hoped the matter ended there.

There was yet another suitor, this one in Missouri: Mr. Patrick Henry, who bore the name of his famous grandfather and did not allow the connection to be forgotten. He had wealth, talent, and good looks—everything except for humility. Mary decided she would have to forego the chance to bear the great-grandchildren of a patriot.

So with these three unsatisfactory strings on her bow, she returned in September to Springfield. Mr. Lincoln had won his own reelection the month before, but with the presidential election drawing near, was campaigning for Harrison and had no time to savor his victory. Nor did he have time to spend in the Edwardses' drawing room, so Mary saw him only when he gave speeches in public. This was just as well, she had to admit, for a summer lazing around in the Missouri heat, dining at her aunt's groaning table, and taking afternoon siestas had left her more than a little plump, and she would prefer Mr. Lincoln not to see her in this Falstaffian state.

At last, Election Day arrived, and then ensued the long wait while the various states made their returns. Harrison lost Illinois. Would he meet a similar fate in other states? As the days passed, Mary took to visiting her friend Eliza Francis, a lady of middle age whose husband, Simeon, published the Springfield paper, the *Sangamon Journal*. If there was news to be had, her friend would have it.

As she walked toward the Francis house on a chilly November afternoon, Mr. Lincoln's tall figure raced toward her. "Miss Todd! We've won! Harrison will be the next president."

Mary squealed and clasped Mr. Lincoln's hand. He started but did not break free. Instead, he stood smiling down at her. "I was on my way to bring you the news," he said.

"Really? I thought I had been quite forgotten these last few months."

"No."

"I am most gratified to hear that."

"It's strange. As soon as I heard the news, I knew I had to tell you straightaway to get the full enjoyment out of it."

Still holding hands, they began walking—not toward the Francis house, not toward the Edwards house, but purely aimlessly. Mr. Lincoln took his hat off his head and stared into it. Then he said to the hat, "Marry me."

"What?"

"Was I unclear? I want to marry you. To live as man and wife."

"You've never even kissed me."

"Is that a prerequisite?"

"Most women would think so."

"Well, then." Mr. Lincoln clapped his hat back onto his head, pulled her against him, and stooped.

He was not an awkward kisser, nor was he in a hurry. Nor was Mary, even as she reflected on the splendid show the pair of them were putting on.

"Now," Mr. Lincoln said when he at last straightened up. "Now, Molly, will you marry me?"

His use of this familiar form of the name was as good as another man's getting upon his knees. "Yes," said Mary. "Absolutely."

When they stopped kissing and began to work out the details, they decided to keep their engagement secret, as neither liked the idea of being the subject of the town's gossip. Besides, Mr. Lincoln told her, it might have to be a long engagement as he could not support Mary in the style to which she had become accustomed. "Or anything close," he added.

"I don't expect a fine house, or a carriage, or anything like that."

"But you do expect a house."

"Well—"

"And you'd have to do without servants. How many slaves does your father have?"

"Well, there's Mammy Sally… She's getting up there, poor thing, and Peter, and…twelve. Of course, our family is large, so… But I do almost everything for myself at my sister's house, except to cook and clean, of course. But I could learn to do those things!"

Mr. Lincoln glanced at Mary's hands, clad in immaculate kid gloves. "We'd best wait," he said dryly.

∾ℯ∽

Soon after Mary's engagement, Miss Matilda Edwards, a cousin of Ninian's, came from Alton, Illinois, on an extended visit to Springfield. She and Mary, Elizabeth was fond of pointing out, were creatures of entirely different styles: Matilda was blond, ethereal, and tall, while Mary was brunette, plumpish, and short. And it soon became clear that male Springfield, in the winter of 1840–41, preferred Matilda's style to Mary's.

Night after night, the drawing room filled to receive male callers, ostensibly to see both girls, but in reality to gaze at Matilda. Joshua Speed, the genteel Kentuckian who had left his plantation home behind to open a general store in Springfield, and who at least when compared to Mr. Lincoln was a virtual Casanova, was the worst of all. He would plant himself in an armchair, tip his head back, and float amongst the heavens as Miss Edwards played and sang in what a woman knew, and surely any rational man would have to admit, was a slightly croaking voice.

When Mr. Speed came, his best friend and lodger, Mr. Lincoln, came as well. Mary was grateful at first for this—it allowed her the opportunity to spend some time with her fiancé without attracting the notice of her sister—but as December wore on, even Mr. Lincoln's eyes began to turn in Miss Edwards's direction ever so slightly.

It would have been deeply satisfying to dislike Miss Edwards for this, but as best as Mary could tell, Matilda was perfectly unconscious of the havoc she was wreaking among the male hearts of Springfield.

She received each and every one of her callers with the same bland, sweet smile and, when they departed, settled down to her tract or her knitting with no sign of wishing they would return. Only once did Mary see her blush, and that was when Mary caught her rereading a letter in the bedroom they now shared. The envelope bore the name of Newton Strong, the gentleman who had escorted her to Springfield.

Had Mary and Matilda been rivals, they would have been very miserable indeed, for not only did they receive visits together, they received invitations together, including one from John Hardin, a connection of Mary's who asked the young women to visit him and his wife in Jacksonville over Christmas. Lest Springfield's eligible bachelors lose the opportunity of mooning over Matilda for a few days in December, they were invited too.

"I do hope you will remember you are a Todd," Elizabeth informed Mary as she packed.

"What on earth does that mean?"

"Mr. Lincoln will be there, will he not? I see him with you when he's here; I hear the gossip about the two of you. He should have made his intentions clear by now, even written to our father. I know that where he comes from men sometimes get it backward; they get a child on a girl and then marry her. He needs to know you're not that kind, and you need to remember it yourself."

"For heaven's sake!" Mary stamped her foot for good measure. "Mr. Lincoln has been nothing but gentlemanly toward me. More so, I must stay, than certain men I could name when they are in their cups."

"Who? Mary, if any man has behaved disrespectfully to you, you must let Mr. Edwards know."

"I'll not pass on tales that may be mere malicious gossip, Sister. And I will thank you to do the same with Mr. Lincoln."

In fact, she knew of no such ill behavior by any visitor to her sister's house. But it was delicious to see Elizabeth worry.

∽◦∾

The Hardin house was stuffed full of humanity. Mary and Matilda found themselves sharing a bed with Mr. Hardin's pert little sister, Martinette, visiting from Kentucky—yet another girl in search of a husband, Mary supposed. "The three M's," Martinette said as they settled into their bed. Crowded as it was, Mary had no complaints as it was freezing outside and chilly inside even with a fire. "Matilda, could you scoot over just a bit? Think of it, we could be one of the poor men having to share a bed with Mr. Lincoln." Martinette giggled. "But I bet some ladies wouldn't mind that."

Matilda, who was pious, let out a disapproving noise, and Mary preserved a judicious silence until Martinette moved to her next topic. "My brother has a surprise for us tomorrow."

"Oh, will you tell us what it is?"

"No, as it wouldn't be a surprise then," Martinette said predictably.

After everyone consumed a hearty breakfast the next morning, Sarah Hardin rose, two metal objects in her hand. "It's freezing outside. So what is it perfect for?"

"Staying by the fire," Mary suggested.

"No, my dear, ice skating! It's the rage in England; the queen loves it. Remember the delightful scene where Mr. Pickwick goes ice skating?"

"And falls in, my dear," John Hardin said.

"That's when he's sliding, not skating, and our men have tested the pond. An elephant could walk over it, they swear. Now, I have plenty of skates for anyone who's daring enough to try. Who is?"

"We are!" said Mr. Webb's son and daughter in unison.

"Well, I certainly am," said Orville Browning.

"And so am I!" Mary lifted her hand, then turned to Mr. Lincoln. "If you will assist me, sir."

Sarah Hardin winked, anticipating Mr. Lincoln's answer. "These skates will fit even your feet, Mr. Lincoln."

With this settled, the party bundled up and walked to the pond. Martinette, who had been on skates before, managed a pretty turn or two on the ice, while the Webb children—the two sweet objections, as Mary had dubbed them—fell down as often as they stood up, but shrieked joyously the entire time they did so. Matilda did not venture onto the pond, perhaps to the disappointment of the men who would have welcomed a glimpse of her stockinged legs, but did the next best thing by standing by the pond, looking her most fetching with her cheeks rosy from the cold and her dainty hands snuggled inside a muff.

Her arm in Mr. Lincoln's, Mary shuffled onto the ice. Awkward on a dance floor, Mr. Lincoln proved startlingly sure-footed on skates, and with him to prop her up, Mary grew daring to enough to glide forward. And what a treat, to have an excuse to lean against him! If only the sweet objections did not insist on skating so close to him—for children adored Mr. Lincoln—it would have been perfect.

Then a terrible shriek filled the air, and Mary and Mr. Lincoln turned to see Matilda Edwards's golden head slipping below the ice.

No human being had ever been rescued so quickly, Mary was to reflect later. In seconds, every male inhabitant of the Hardin house collected around the dainty little hole into which poor Matilda had slipped. Even Mr. Lincoln released Mary and with two long glides was at the scene, leaving Mary to capsize onto her bottom and, unable to right herself without assistance, to crawl ignominiously to the edge of the pond. By the time she reached it, the men already had Matilda free and were bearing her to the house. There was nothing for Mary to do but pry off her skates, herd the Webb children, quite forgotten by the adults, off the pond, and grimly follow the procession.

Sarah Hardin wasted no time putting Matilda to bed and dosing her with brandy. As far as Mary could tell, she was none the worse for wear, except perhaps for the effects of the brandy, which sent her fast asleep, but the party was dampened none the less for it. John Hardin said that he wished he had never bought the blasted skates. Martinette, who turned out to be the culprit who had persuaded Matilda to step onto the ice, was so lugubrious in bewailing her guilt that she too had to be helped to bed. Mr. Browning hoped that Matilda was not from consumptive stock. And Mr. Lincoln said nothing, but stared mournfully out the window.

It was like a funeral without a corpse.

In the late afternoon, Matilda came downstairs. If anything, she looked prettier after her ordeal. Bundled up in the most comfortable chair, she accepted mug after mug of hot cocoa from a penitent Martinette as the men praised her courage and the women urged her to stay by the fire so she would not catch cold. Mr. Lincoln's pained face broke into a smile, and he regaled the crowd with his best stories, at which Matilda laughed gently as befitted an invalid.

So when the stony-hearted Mr. Webb, who said he had had several plunges into the ice as a boy and had lived to tell about them, turned his attention to Mary, what else could she do but talk to him? She'd always liked him perfectly well; it wasn't his fault that he did not set her heart to fluttering. Still, when the party broke up for the evening (Matilda being helped up the stairs, although she hardly needed it), Mary lingered in the parlor, hoping that Mr. Lincoln might want a word with her, but he followed the men to his sleeping quarters, and Mary went in silence to her own bedchamber.

The men returned to Springfield the next day to attend the legislature, but Mary and Matilda lingered a couple of days in Jacksonville, hoping for snow and a sleigh ride. As the former never came, they rode back by coach to Springfield, for the tiny train that puttered its way to Jacksonville once each day had not yet been extended to the fledgling capital.

On New Year's Day, 1841, Mary was sitting in the parlor when she heard a knock at the front door, followed by the appearance of Mr. Lincoln. "Why, I wish you a happy New Year, sir. And"—she lowered her voice and smiled—"what a better way to start a new year than by planning a wedding? I've been reading cookery books and am growing quite domesticated."

"Mary—"

"Now, I know you consider me a spoiled creature, but really, sir, you underestimate us Todd girls. Why, my sister Mrs. Wallace is still lodging in the Globe Tavern, and she never complains of the quarters, even after becoming a mother! We have the capacity to make do, sir."

"Mary—"

"I am sure you don't want a grand ceremony; I don't want one either. Just a few friends and family—"

"We can't do this. We can't marry."

"Why on earth not?" Mary shot up to her full five foot two. "Has Mr. Edwards forbid it? The nerve! I am of age, and I will marry whom I please. Why, we'll elope!"

"No, Mary. It's not him. It's me. I can't marry you."

Mary sat back down. "You're in love with Matilda Edwards," she said flatly.

"No. I've hardly spoken a word to her."

"When did that stop anyone?"

"Be that as it may, I'm not in love with her. I'm not in love with anyone else."

"You are angry that I paid so much attention to Mr. Webb the other night. Maybe I was flirting a wee bit. The deceiver deceived! I meant no harm, truly. He was the only person not acting ridiculous about Matilda, and he is a perfectly agreeable man, and—"

"It's not Webb. I like Webb. Why would you being friendly to him distress me? Mary, it's me. I can't marry you. I can't marry anyone."

Mary reviewed all the reasons a man might not marry—a loathsome disease, unnatural behavior, financial distress—and decided to focus on the least frightening one. "Mr. Lincoln, I told you again and again that I don't expect to live in high style."

"I can keep a wife. It's me. Mary, will you listen to me? Every time I think of marriage, my blood runs cold. I'm not ready. I don't know if I ever will be, but I do know that I'm not ready now."

"Do you love me?"

Mr. Lincoln gazed at her for a long time. "I don't know," he said. "You're pretty, and you're smart and lively, but—"

"Then end it."

He began pacing around the room. "But we were engaged. I made a promise. Perhaps—"

Lawyer that he was, no doubt he was worried that she might sue him for breach of promise to marry—not that she would humiliate herself by taking the witness stand as a spurned bride. "End it," she repeated. "I will not hold you to a promise that you do not wish to keep. I will release you from our engagement. I will even put it in writing."

She went to the desk, supplied with ink and paper as if awaiting such an occasion, and scrawled something—anything—to the effect of what she had told Mr. Lincoln, then held out the finished product to him. Evidently, it satisfied his lawyer's mind, for he took it and stuffed it into his coat pocket.

"I didn't want to hurt you, Miss Todd."

"Yet you managed that quite competently." She turned away, conscious of the tears beginning to run down her face. "I did not write this in the letter, but know this: my feelings for you have not changed. Should you come to your senses and recognize how good we would be for each other, I will be here."

"Oh, Mary!"

He pulled her on his knee and kissed her as passionately as he had kissed her when he had proposed marriage. It was she who disengaged herself, marched to the parlor door, and flung it wide open.

"You have this all backward, Mr. Lincoln. Goodbye."

Of course, she cried all night. Who wouldn't? She refused dinner, claiming indisposition, and when poor Matilda came bearing a plate of food, she threw it across the room. Though she did wait until Matilda had left, at least.

What could she do? Springfield, and especially her own little circle, was too small for her and Mr. Lincoln's estrangement to go unnoticed, and while few if any might have suspected their engagement, Mary had no doubt that word would go out soon over it being broken. But she would have to brave it out, because going back to Lexington was unthinkable. Her sister Ann would take her place in Springfield—something she had been hinting at in her letters already—and Mary would return to her maiden's bedroom a confirmed spinster, growing peculiar and set in her ways as her younger half sisters sprouted up and began attracting suitors. She might as well start teaching school, acquire a multitude of cats, and be done with it.

In Springfield, at least she had some possibilities. Not that any of them meant anything to her.

Of course, after bathing her eyes the next morning and picking up the broken crockery, she had to tell Elizabeth. "You know, I really don't think the two of you would have been happy together," Elizabeth said. Was she fighting back a smile? "Mr. Lincoln is certainly a talented lawyer, and it's admirable how far he's come in life, but he's just not your sort, Mary, and will never be. That would have become all too apparent when you began entertaining—if he could even give you a suitable home in which to entertain. He's…well, he's a *plebian*, my dear. And, Mary, there's something else that's always made me wary. Have you ever seen him go to church? Certainly he goes to none that any of our circle attends. I have given him the benefit of the doubt, thinking he might be a member of some primitive sect, but he never speaks of going anywhere. I fear he is a nonbeliever."

"Oh, pshaw! He is a spiritual man, and that is what counts. And as for his origins, they are the only thing common about him. I can see great things in him."

"You certainly are eager to defend a man who treated you so shabbily."

"I won't have anyone speaking ill of my future husband. For he will be, when he comes to his senses."

She had spoken reflexively, but really, what other explanation could there be other than some peculiarity in Mr. Lincoln's character? It was another reason—indeed, the best reason—to remain in Springfield. When he returned to normal, she would have to be on the spot.

As January wore on, it became apparent that Mr. Lincoln was suffering dreadfully. The day after he ended (or, as Mary liked to think of it, suspended) their engagement, he failed to turn up for a vote at the legislature, and by mid-January, he had collapsed entirely, taking to his bed as if he, not Mary, had been the spurned one. Elizabeth, who made it her business to keep current with the gossip about Mr. Lincoln, informed Mary that he was all but a lunatic and that only Joshua Speed and Dr. Anson Henry, who was both Mr. Lincoln's friend and a physician, were allowed to tend to him. They would not even trust him around his dinner knife, for fear that he might end it all then and there.

While Mr. Lincoln lay confined in his bladeless room, visitors trooped to the Edwards house, eager to see the two young ladies who had brought him to his ruin. In one version of events, poor Matilda's stony heart had laid Mr. Lincoln low; in another version, Mary's coquettishness had made him, literally, insanely jealous. For either lady to leave town or even to refuse company would have driven the gossips into a frenzy, so they sat side by side in the drawing room smiling grimly, chattering inanely about any subject they could find that was as far from Mr. Lincoln as possible.

After about a week or so of this, Mr. Lincoln was seen once again in the streets of Springfield, looking pale and thin and gloomy but acting, everyone agreed, perfectly sane. The gossip receded, and life went back to normal—except that Mr. Lincoln no longer appeared at the Edwardses', or scarcely anyplace else that he was likely to meet Mary, which meant in essence that he avoided any social gathering where ladies might be present. In turn, Mary avoided the places where she might run into him, such as the homes of his married friends. Yet she made it her business to keep informed of his doings. She felt his sorrow from afar when President Harrison, whom he had worked so hard to elect, fell sick on the day of his inauguration in March and died just a month later. All for naught!

She felt less compassion for her former betrothed, however, when Elizabeth, always eager to pass on such things to her, informed her that Mr. Lincoln, who took his meals at the home of William and Eliza Butler, had taken an interest in Eliza's young sister, Sarah Rickard. At the time Mary had arrived in Springfield, Sarah had been a mere girl in pantalettes, but in the past year her hems had dropped and she had developed a noticeable bosom. "He's even taken her to see *The Babes in the Woods*," Elizabeth told her. "The first time he's been seen in female company."

"The Butlers are good friends of his, and they took good care of him while he was...indisposed. He eats with them every day. No doubt he thinks of the child as a little sister. Look at what he took her to. A nursery tale!"

Still, Mary kept a close eye on the girl as she sashayed around town, swishing her long skirts and wearing brooches that drew the eye to her fine new bosom. It was a relief to see her drooping not at all when Mr. Lincoln left in the summer to visit Joshua Speed, who had returned to his family's Kentucky plantation after the death of his father, although Mary also felt indignant on Lincoln's behalf. Did not the silly chit appreciate him?

The months wore on. Mr. Lincoln returned, by all accounts more cheerful—not that Mary saw that in person. Mercy Levering returned to Springfield, married her beau James Conkling, and promptly turned into a staid matron. Matilda Edwards, having turned down several proposals on the grounds that the grooms were too dissolute, returned to her home in Alton, from which in due time she announced her upcoming marriage to Mr. Strong. The little train that chugged to Jacksonville finally made its way to Springfield.

Back in Lexington, Mary had acquired two more half sisters, little Elodie in 1840 and little Kitty in the fall of 1841. Mary thought of going to Lexington to see them, but decided against it. When she came back, it would be as Mrs. Abraham Lincoln, not as Miss Mary Todd.

Not that Mr. Lincoln was cooperating, she had to acknowledge as 1841 turned into 1842, and yet more of her friends tumbled into matrimony—the latest being Joshua Speed, now firmly settled on his Kentucky plantation. Men still called on her, but to talk, not to court. Even Mr. Webb had given up.

Then, as summer began to descend upon Springfield, her friend Mrs. Francis invited her to spend the evening with "just a few friends," as she put it. This suited Mary well enough as she was beginning to tire of large gatherings, and what other parlor in Springfield smelled so pleasantly of newsprint? But when she arrived, she found herself the only person present, other than her hostess. "Am I frightfully early? Did I mistake the time?"

"No. You're quite right."

She led Mary to the parlor and began to chat, but her usual lively conversation seemed strained. And where were the other guests? Then a knock sounded, and Mrs. Francis sprang up, even though she had a servant to answer her door. After a moment, she reentered, leading in another guest, who came to a halt in the doorway. "Miss Todd?"

"Sir," Mary said weakly.

"Come in, come in," Eliza said. Mr. Lincoln obeyed, but remained gaping at Mary. "It is no accident that I brought the two of you here. Mr. Lincoln, sit on the sofa—yes, beside Miss Todd. There. Now, isn't this pleasant? Here's my husband, to balance things out."

A *Sangamon Journal* in his hand, Simeon Francis nodded at them as he entered the room. "How is your meddling going, my dear?"

"'Tis too early to tell, but I have hope. Look at the two of them!" She beamed at Mary and Mr. Lincoln, sitting rigidly side by side. "I don't see how they've stood to be apart all this time."

"May I ask what this is about?" Mary said.

"Yes, you may, and I'm glad one of you can speak at least. Now, look! Whatever quarrel the two of you had, you must make it up and be friends again. I know that you're fond of Mr. Lincoln, Mary, and I know that you, Mr. Lincoln, are fond of Mary. Why, you're perfect for each other. It just kills my soul to see the two of you moping apart. Oh, don't tell me that you haven't moped! Now, Sim and I will leave the room, and I expect to hear some conversation emanating from here." With a cheery wave, she departed, followed by Simeon Francis, who shrugged and gave Mr. Lincoln a sympathetic glance on his way out.

Mr. Lincoln arose and stared out the window, while Mary studied her hands. Finally, Lincoln spoke. "I've not stopped loving you. I've tried."

"Well, that's flattering, I suppose, Mr. Lincoln, but may I ask why you've tried?"

"I don't know."

"I do hope your arguments in court are more satisfactory than that."

"Lord, I've missed that tongue of hers," Mr. Lincoln said to the window.

"But you do love me, it seems? If I recall, you weren't so certain of that before."

"I do believe I'm certain of that now." He continued his survey of the street for a few minutes, then turned. "I've discussed this with Dr. Henry."

"You've made a medical case of me, Mr. Lincoln?"

"I near ran mad when I stopped seeing you. Guilt and shame. Anyway, as I told him, it's not the way I act toward women normally. I have a story to tell on myself, one that only a handful of people know of. I had a good friend in New Salem, a married lady. She had a sister in Kentucky, a handsome gal. My married friend got it into her head that I should marry said sister, and like a blockhead, I agreed. I'd met her when she paid a short visit to New Salem and liked her well enough. And my friend and her husband had been so kind and hospitable to me when I was a poor newcomer to that area... Well, I felt I'd be ungrateful if I refused. So the lady came on consignment, as it were, and she was just as I remembered, except that there was quite a bit more of her. A good thirty pounds more."

Mary sucked her breath in, wondering if she could lace her stays a little tighter. "So you rejected her?"

"No. I did as I promised. I courted her, wrote letters to her—by then I was off with the legislature—paid her visits. She had a fine face, a good wit, a good education, all the requisites. Finally, I realized it was now or never. I proposed, and she turned me down flat. Fool that I was, I proposed again, thinking perhaps she was being coy, and she turned me down as flat as a squashed frog. I should have been relieved, I suppose I was relieved, but when she said no, I almost fell in love with her then and there. A matter of wanting what we can't have, I guess."

"And perhaps not wanting what we can have?"

"I think you've hit it, Miss Todd. And so this is what I suggest: that we resume seeing each other again, but leave the question of marriage open until I can resolve my confounded doubts as to whether I can ever steel myself for matrimony."

"Mr. Lincoln, your plan is sensible, but you forget how I am placed as a woman. I cannot see you indefinitely with no hope of being your wife. Either we must marry, or we must end it. Anything else would give rise to gossip that I am your mere paramour."

"I do understand it, which is why I suggest more: that we meet secretly. Perhaps here—with Simeon and wife having meddled, how can they complain? And I suggest that by the end of the year, if we are not engaged, we end it. No need to keep polishing a bit of tin in the hope that it's going to become gold. In the meantime, should you come to prefer anyone else—and I am taking a chance there, because I am well aware that there are many who have more to offer—you are free to drop me, no hard feelings and not a word of reproach on my end."

When Mary remained silent, he said, "I'm not good at guessing what any woman is thinking, but I believe I can give it a try in your case. You're thinking that you've never heard anything less romantic in your life, that we might be discussing a mere business arrangement."

"That thought had occurred to me."

"Molly—if I may call you that again—it's because I love and respect you that I'm asking this of you. Give us time… Six months is all I ask. Time enough for me to know my mind, and time enough for you to decide whether you're making a good bargain. There I am with the business terms again, so I think I'll stop before I dig a deeper hole for myself."

"I agree to your terms, Mr. Lincoln. You are right; they do not set my heart aflutter, but I know you to be a fair and decent man, and I take them in the right spirit. But what happened to the young lady who refused you?"

"Went back to Kentucky and married quite well. So you could say she got the better of the bargain, Molly."

∽∾

The Francises agreed to make their parlor available for Mary and Mr. Lincoln's meetings. Once or twice a week or so, Mary went to visit Mrs. Francis, and Mr. Lincoln would stroll over to the newspaper office and then quite casually make his way to the Francis house next door to pay his respects to the editor's lady. For anywhere from a few minutes to a solid hour, the couple was left undisturbed. Depending upon the time they had and their mood, they talked, kissed, or did both.

If Elizabeth wondered about the new intensity of Mary's friendship for Mrs. Francis, she said nothing, nor did she comment on the fact that prospective suitors no longer flocked to the Edwards house now that Matilda had gone home. She seemed, in fact, quite reconciled to Mary becoming a permanent fixture in her house, a useful old maid who helped the children with their lessons, shared her duties as hostess, and wielded her needle to good effect.

When not secretly meeting Mr. Lincoln or old-maiding it in the parlor, Mary passed the time with a new friend, Miss Julia Jayne, who unlike most ladies shared her interest in politics. Happy as they were to spend an afternoon studying *Godey's Lady's Book*, it was the *Sangamon Journal* that was their favored reading, and never more so than that summer, when a letter from a "Rebecca" appeared ridiculing James Shields, the state auditor. He was a frequent visitor at the Edwards house, and was attentive to Mary—as he was to everyone in skirts, even the parlor maid—but labored under the hopeless liability of being a Democrat. After the appearance of the letter, he had fumed at every gathering he attended, giving the women hope that there would be a sequel to the missive. "And here it is!" Julia said, waving the newspaper in the air as she came into the parlor on a fine September day.

They spread out the paper on a table and giggled over it.

They had a sort of a gatherin there one night, among the grandees, they called a fair. All the galls about town was there, and all the handsome widows, and married women, finickin about, trying to look like galls, tied as tight in the middle, and puffed out at both ends like bundles of fodder that hadn't been stacked yet, but wanted stackin pretty bad. And then they had tables all round the house kivered over with baby caps, and pin-cushions, and ten thousand such little nicknacks, tryin to sell 'em to the fellows that were bowin and scrapin, and kungeerin about 'em....I looked in at the window, and there was this same fellow Shields floatin about on the air, without heft or earthly substance, just like a lock of cat-fur where cats had been fightin.

He was paying his money to this one and that one, and tother one, and sufferin great loss because it wasn't silver instead of State paper; and the sweet distress he seemed to be in—his very features, in the exstatic agony of his soul, spoke audibly and distinctly—"Dear girls, it is distressing, but I cannot marry you all. Too well I know how much you suffer; but do, do remember, it is not my fault that I am so handsome and so interesting."

"It's Shields to the man," Julia said. "Did I ever tell how the noxious creature tried to squeeze my hand? It was in this very house."

"It's Mr. Lincoln," Mary said.

"No, it was Shields who tried—"

"I mean Mr. Lincoln wrote this. Maybe not the first—I think that was Simeon Francis himself—but definitely this one. There's not another man in Springfield so amusing. Have you never heard him spin his yarns?" Belatedly, Mary recalled that most women did not enjoy the privilege of hearing Mr. Lincoln's tales. "Of course, I could be mistaken."

"Well, he certainly hit his mark, whoever he was. Mary, why are you grinning so?"

"I think we should join the fun. Let us compose a letter, or a poem—nay, both! I ramble so in letters, and am liable to do the same thing when writing as Rebecca. So you shall write a letter, and I shall write a poem, all to the glory of Mr. Shields."

"It would serve the coxcomb right."

Within a few days, they had composed their respective productions and handed them to a delighted Simeon Francis, who promised to run Julia's story (with which Mary had lent a hand) in the next week's issue and Mary's the week after that.

When they met the next Friday, Mr. Lincoln chuckled over Julia's contribution, which Mary had seized while it was still warm from the press. "Why, who wrote this bit of drollery?"

"Perhaps the person who wrote the piece the week before," Mary suggested archly.

"No, I did not write this—" He stopped. "I mean—"

"You mean, sir, I caught you out red-handed. You wrote the last Rebecca letter, didn't you? You cannot deny it; I know you too well."

"Well, I did, Molly. But I had nothing to do with this one before us." He studied it, frowning. "I can't guess who did."

"Perhaps you are foolishly limiting yourself to the male citizens of Springfield. After all, Rebecca is a woman."

"You mean that you wrote this?"

"No—though it was at my instigation. Miss Jayne wrote it. But I have acquired a taste for authorship myself, and next week will be my debut."

"And sadly, I will be on the circuit and won't see it fresh. You will save me a copy?"

"Certainly."

Mr. Lincoln laughed and bent to kiss her as he departed. "Poor Shields. Getting it from all sides—and both sexes. How will the poor man's vanity stand it?"

It did not, as Mary found the next week. She was in her bedroom, secretly admiring her printed verse for about the twentieth time or so (despite her anonymity, it was a fine thing to be published), when Elizabeth knocked. "Have you heard the news about that Mr. Lincoln?"

Since Mr. Lincoln had ceased to frequent the Edwards residence, he had become "that" Mr. Lincoln. Normally this annoyed Mary, but Elizabeth's smug look alarmed her. "What news?"

"James Shields challenged him to a duel, and he has accepted."

"A duel? But whatever for?" She glanced at the paper in her hand. "For these?"

"Yes, for all of those insulting pieces in the *Journal*. They say Mr. Lincoln wrote them all."

"He did not!"

"Mind you, I certainly don't approve of dueling, but what was the man thinking? In Lexington he'd been challenged after the very first piece. But if he wants to be treated as a gentleman, he must settle his disputes as one. Not that Mr. Shields is exactly what I would call a gentle—"

"Oh, for heaven's sake, who cares who is a gentleman? And why did Mr. Lincoln tell me nothing of this? I must see him." She grabbed up her skirts and hurried down the stairs, not bothering to put on her bonnet.

"Wait! Are you seeing Mr. Lincoln again? I had no ink—"

But Mary was already scurrying in the direction of Simeon Francis's house.

She had no reason, other than hope, to expect that Mr. Lincoln would be there, but there he was, engaged in a grave conversation with Simeon Francis. "Mr. Lincoln! Is it true?"

"Yes, Molly. I seem to have got myself in a heap of trouble."

Mary commenced to wailing.

"Come, come," Mr. Lincoln finally said, and led her into the parlor. "Molly, there's nothing to fear."

"But a duel! You will be shot!" She began to wail harder. "And I am the cause of it!"

"No, no, Molly. Please, woman, stop crying! The verses and Miss Jayne's letter…they irritated him, but it was my own letter that angered him the most. You've got nothing to blame yourself for."

She dabbed at her eyes, her mood switching to indignation. "And were you not going to tell me of this?"

"I got his challenge when I was out of town. I—and my friends— have been working mightily to settle with him so there'd be nothing to tell you, but he hasn't seen reason, so as you know as well as I do, I'm honor-bound to fight him."

Mary nodded grimly. Having grown up in Lexington, with its

notoriously prickly male tempers, she was well aware of the code of honor. She had hoped to see less of it in Springfield.

"But, Molly, I'm not going to get killed by Shields. Not a chance. Under the rules, I have the privilege of choosing the weapons, and I will choose broadswords, with each of us standing within a space with a plank in between us. The advantage all goes to the man with the longest reach and"—Mr. Lincoln swung his arm out—"that's me, of course. I'll do all I can to disarm him, and I have no desire to kill him."

"I am not the least concerned about the welfare of that vile man."

"Well, for my sake you should be, because I don't want him on my conscience. Molly, I can't stay. There's a chance I might get arrested if I don't leave town, so I need to get out at the crack of dawn. Besides, the broadswords I want are at Jacksonville."

"Where is this…affair…going to be?"

"Missouri, across the river from Alton."

"But won't you have to leave town if you win?" That was the practice of the bloods of Lexington, who would disappear after a duel, then turn up a couple of years later as if they had merely been on an overnight excursion. But Mr. Lincoln, without a monied family to support him, might never return from whatever new life he made for himself in exile. "What if…what if I never you see again? One way or another."

"Don't fret, Molly."

But fret she did, for three solid days until the gossip came to Springfield that at the last minute, the would-be duelists' seconds had settled the matter. Still, she would not rest secure until both Lincoln and Mr. Shields came home intact, Mr. Lincoln sheepish but in good spirits, Shields in bad spirits and so itching for a duel that he promptly challenged Lincoln's friend William Butler. Shields's second managed to avert violence, but then issued a challenge of his own. Fortunately, it too went nowhere, and the male population of Springfield remained intact.

With all this turmoil within her social circle, Elizabeth had little time to worry about Mary's relationship with Lincoln, and Mary resumed her trips to the Francis house undisturbed.

At the beginning of November, Mary sat in her hosts' parlor, reading from *Childe Harold*. Lincoln listened attentively at first, then reached in his coat pocket and pulled out a well-worn letter. Out of the corner of her eye, Mary saw him read it once, then again. Finally, he coughed. "Molly. You know Joshua Speed's been married for a few months now."

"Yes. He is doing well?"

"He's happy. He writes in this letter to tell me he is. I was afraid he wouldn't be."

"Why? Did they appear to be incompatible?"

"No, not at all. But I was worried anyway. I guess I was wondering whether a man could be truly happy in marriage, whether it would be too much of a jolt. And I was also wondering whether a man could make a wife truly happy." He stared at the letter. "He had doubts about marrying Fanny, you know. I had to keep reminding him what a fine woman she was."

"Really, Mr. Lincoln. You and he are quite peculiar."

"I know! I feel like a fool trying to explain it all to you now. You'd think it would be simple: a man meets a woman, falls in love with her, wins her affection, asks her to marry him, gets accepted, and gets to the preacher. But it wasn't for me, and if I hadn't practically pushed the man to the altar—as best as I could by mail, anyway—it wouldn't have been for Speed either. But to bring all of this to a logical conclusion, I'm asking you to marry me."

"Is this Mr. Speed's doing now, or yours?"

"All mine, Molly. All mine. Do you remember when I told you I wanted to dance with you in the worst way?"

"How could I forget?"

"Well, now I want to marry you in the worst way. I love you, Molly."

"And I you."

"So will you marry me?"

"When?"

"As soon as we can arrange it. Tomorrow or Friday. No point dillydallying further. Unless you're worried a hasty wedding will make people talk."

"It will, and it doesn't bother me in the least. I want to marry you."

"Then it's settled?" He grinned as she nodded, then, as he pulled her into his lap, he added, "I'm glad you said yes. Because after all that, it would have been mortifying if you'd said no."

∽◕↙

How efficient they were! By Thursday evening, they had picked her wedding ring, a thin gold band with "Love Is Eternal" engraved on it, arranged for room and board at the Globe Tavern (in her sister Frances's former room, it turned out), found attendants from among their very surprised friends, and engaged the Reverend Charles Dresser, whose Episcopal church Mary attended, to perform the ceremony.

What she had not done was tell Elizabeth and Ninian that she was marrying. That task she put off until Friday morning when, breakfast having been cleared, she said, "Mr. Lincoln and I are getting married. Tonight."

Elizabeth put down her coffee with a thump. "Tonight? Where?"

"Church. Mr. Lincoln is no heathen."

"No gathering afterward? No food?"

"I suppose not."

"That just won't do," Ninian said. "Marry if you wish—but marry from our house as is done among our set. Otherwise, it will seem as if you are marrying in defiance of us, which is hardly the case. Mr. Lincoln is a man of honor and acquitted himself well during the recent unpleasantness involving Mr. Shields."

So all Lincoln had had to do to gain Ninian Edwards's approval as a husband was to almost fight a duel? What if he had fought and won? Mary was on the verge of suppressing a smile when her brother-in-law said, "It would certainly be more convenient if you waited a few days, since you are to marry from this house."

"I will marry today, or not marry from this house."

"Why, have you even written to our father?"

"He will approve. And if he doesn't, I will be very sorry for it, but I am of age."

Her sister cleared her throat. "Mary, I do hope—"

"There is no reason for our haste other than the fact that we love each other and want to become man and wife without further delay."

"But how long have you been courting?"

"Since July, at Simeon Francis's house. We met there in secret."

"And you never thought fit to confide in me."

Elizabeth looked hurt—so hurt, in fact, that Mary for the first time in the conversation felt ashamed. She embraced her sister. "Dear Elizabeth, after all that happened, we felt it best to keep our courtship secret from all eyes and ears. There was no slight to you intended."

"Bother the slight to me," Elizabeth snapped. "The question is, how on earth am I to find time to do all the necessary cooking? I might be forced to send to Old Dickey's for gingerbread and beer!"

Mary could not resist. "Gingerbread is quite good enough for plebeians, I suppose," she said, and hurried out the door to find Mr. Lincoln to tell him that the wedding had been moved to the Edwardses' parlor.

∽⦿∽

The guests wouldn't have to subsist on gingerbread and beer, of course; Elizabeth was too proud of her hostessing skills for that. She set to work on one of her famous cakes, and Frances, summoned by Elizabeth for her assistance, contributed a fine ham. Mary, feeling somewhat guilty about the late notice, offered to help, but as Elizabeth thought this would be bad luck, and seeing Mr. Lincoln would also be bad luck, Mary was relegated to sitting on the sofa where she and Lincoln had spent so much time together and wondering what being a married woman would be like. Would she become as deadly serious as all of her married friends had? How many children would they have?

And of course, there was the marital act with which to concern herself. Mary had heard conflicting reports, none from good authority, about whether it was really worth the while, although she was disposed to think it would be with Mr. Lincoln, given the growing intensity of their encounters at the Francis home. Elizabeth or Frances might have been helpful, but they were far too busy with their cooking. Probably it would be unbecoming to walk to Mercy Conkling's house and solicit her views on the matter.

Oh, would the evening ever get here? She found herself reciting Juliet's speech:

> *Come, civil night,*
> *Thou sober-suited matron, all in black,*
> *And learn me how to lose a winning match*
> *Play'd for a pair of stainless maidenhoods.*

Needless to say, this was not one of the passages that she and Mr. Lincoln had read to each other.

At last, her bridesmaids—Julia Jayne, Anna Rodney, and her cousin Elizabeth Todd—arrived. Mary had surveyed her dresses and settled on wearing an embroidered muslin that also happened to be white, the color that Queen Victoria had worn to her wedding two years before and thus was especially desirable. Her bridesmaids helped Mary put it on and style her hair; then as she did not require much assistance in that regard, they allowed her to render them the same services. Meanwhile, the guests began arriving, as she ascertained from her small niece Julia, who obligingly ran up and down the stairs to report each arrival. "There is Dr. Wallace! Here come the Stuarts! There's your family, Elizabeth! There are Mr. and Mrs. Conkling!" At last, Julia poked her head in the door and cried, "And here's Mr. Lincoln!"

Mary gulped.

Presently, Ninian Edwards came up and led her and her bridesmaids downstairs, where Lincoln stood in the parlor with his own attendants, James Matheny and Beverly Powell. His necktie, which Mary had never seen entirely symmetrical, was immaculately arranged—the handiwork, she supposed, of his landlady, Mrs. Butler, who was unashamedly wiping back tears at the loss of whom she would later tell Mary was the household favorite. As for Lincoln, he looked nervous, but no more nervous than Mary herself.

The Reverend Charles Dresser began to perform the ceremony—a more formal one than their oldest guest, Judge Thomas Brown, appeared to be accustomed to, for Mary could hear him harrumphing behind her from time to time as the couple repeated their vows. Then, as Mary held out her hand, Lincoln said, "With this ring I thee wed, and with all my worldly goods I thee endow—"

"Lord Jesus Christ, God Almighty, Lincoln!" Judge Brown's voice filled the room. "The statute fixes all that!"

Evidently the judge had not sat through an Episcopalian wedding service before. Reverend Dresser struggled to maintain his composure, and Lincoln also fought to suppress a smile as he slipped the ring onto Mary's hand.

She should have been furious at Judge Brown's outburst. She should have been distressed at the rain that began to beat against the windows as if the Lord had been waiting for a cue. But what did they matter? Nothing, just as the coffee she spilled on her dress at Elizabeth's reception mattered nothing, just as the ruination of her slippers when she stepped out of the carriage in front of the Globe Tavern and into a mud puddle mattered nothing. All that mattered were the last words they exchanged as they lay entwined together later that night. "Good night, Husband."

"Good night, Wife."

∽ 2 ∾
EMILY
DECEMBER 1854 TO MARCH 26, 1856

Years before, eleven-year-old Emily Todd had watched, her lip wobbling, as her older half sister, Mary, and her husband and sons prepared to get into the carriage that would take them to the railroad station, their visit to Lexington at an end. Mary had hugged Mr. and Mrs. Todd goodbye, and then had turned with a special farewell to Emily. "Now, my dear, don't look so sad! When you are grown up, you shall visit us in our house as our special guest and stay as long as you like. Won't she, Mr. Lincoln?"

"Indeed she shall," Mr. Lincoln had said. He smiled at Emily. "We'll always have room in our house for Little Sister."

Seven years had passed, and the promise was about to be fulfilled.

∽✑∾

"Emily! How lovely you look!" Mary embraced her sister as she stepped off the train onto the platform of Springfield's depot, stalling the passengers behind her.

Abraham Lincoln gently tugged the sisters aside, then pecked Emily on the cheek. "Little Sister, it's been too long since we've seen you."

"Was the journey troublesome? How are they in Kentucky? Have you a beau yet?"

Emily laughed. "No, they are well, and no."

"I cannot wait to show you our fine carriage," Mary said as Mr. Lincoln saw to her trunk. "Not new to us—we bought it last year—but new to you. Mr. Lincoln agreed to buy one of the nicest ones Mr. Lewis had, within reason, of course. Tell me, dear, have you been to the old house lately?"

While dying of cholera a few years before, Mary and Emily's father, Robert Todd, had managed to make his will, but in his feeble state had had it witnessed by only one person instead of the requisite two. Their brother George, who got on poorly with nearly everyone in the family, had successfully challenged the will, and the gracious house in which Emily had been born had been sold instead of going to her mother. Mrs. Todd and her children had had to move to her considerably more modest family house at Buena Vista, not far from Frankfort. How Emily had cried in those first few weeks after the move, thinking of her old room in Lexington! "I don't have the heart to see someone else living there," Emily said.

Mary grimaced. "Indeed, it still makes me angry to think of it. That creature George. To think that there was a time I treated him like my own little pet. My dear, I think we must get you a new bonnet. That one does not show off your eyes as it should."

Mr. Lincoln approached with her trunk, and Emily smiled up at him. She still remembered her first meeting with her brother-in-law in 1847, five years after the Lincolns' marriage. He and Mary had visited Lexington on their way to Washington, where Mr. Lincoln was to serve in Congress. Emily had been so intimidated by his height and his craggy face that she had stepped behind her mother like a little girl. Mr. Lincoln had not laughed at her foolishness, but had shaken her hand and said, "So this is Little Sister."

As if aware of her thoughts, Mary said, "When you first met

Mr. Lincoln, he was a brand-new congressman. And now, I hope he shall be a senator."

"Now, Mother," Mr. Lincoln said, using one of his favorite forms of address for his wife, "don't count your chickens."

"I did say *hope*, Mr. Lincoln. And speaking of chickens, I have an excellent meal planned for tonight, Emily. I have come quite far in cookery since Mr. Lincoln and I were first married a dozen years ago. Why, when I read Mr. Dickens's account of poor Dora Copperfield's housekeeping, I thought he must have been peering through my kitchen window!"

Mr. Lincoln handed Emily into the carriage. It was what she had expected him to own—comfortable and well made but unpretentious. As Mary settled beside her, she said, "Now, you must not expect Springfield to be as handsome as Lexington, my dear, especially this time of year, but it has improved with time, I must say. Why, it is the same time of year I first arrived! That is propitious, I hope."

Evidently Mary assumed that Emily would find a husband in Springfield, as had all four of Emily's half sisters. But at eighteen, Emily was in no particular hurry.

Springfield was not a gracious-looking town, but it had an undeniable bustle to it. As the Lincolns' carriage passed through its streets, people waved to Mr. Lincoln, whose tall figure was unmistakable even inside the carriage, and peered at the unfamiliar lady next to his wife. "Oh, you will make quite the splash here, Emily! I count on you being the belle of the season."

Their carriage pulled onto a block lined with modest, well-kept houses and stopped in front of a one-and-a-half-story yellow cottage, tricked out handsomely with green shutters. A boy of ten sprang out— Emily's nephew Robert, known as Bob, who walked to the carriage and handed out first his mother, and then Emily, in a manner born of long practice. Knowing that he was of an age to stand on his dignity, she thanked him, careful to avoid effusiveness, and was rewarded with a smile. "How you've grown, Bob!"

"Well, I won't match Father," Bob said good-naturedly.

The door opened and out stepped a small boy, followed by a colored servant leading an even smaller boy. Those two children, Willie and Tad, were strangers to Emily, having been born after the Lincolns had last visited the Todds in Kentucky. As she admired and greeted them, she thought sadly that there should have been a fourth boy standing there: the Lincolns' second son, Eddie, who had died of consumption just months after Mary and Emily's father. Mary, who had taken to writing to Emily not long afterward, had confessed that she had nearly starved herself to death in the weeks afterward, so terrible had been her grief.

But she looked happy now, as did all the Lincolns. As they sat in the parlor and caught up on the past several years, the younger boys ran in and out, completely uncowed by their father, who beamed at them. Emily smiled to herself, remembering that back in Lexington in 1847, as the Todd family waited for the Lincolns to arrive from the depot, a young cousin of theirs had hurried into the house, fresh from the train himself. "Aunt Betsy," he had announced, "I was never so grateful to escape a train in my life. I was stuck with a couple and their brats who kept the entire train in an uproar while their father just grinned and aided and abetted their antics. I thought—" Their cousin had turned white. "Good Lord, here they are out front!"

"Why, what are you smiling at, Emily?"

"Oh, I am simply glad to be here."

"I hope it is not a beau at home you are thinking of, for I have plenty of possibilities in mind."

"Now, Mother, don't marry Little Sister off too soon. Didn't you once tell me that young ladies became so deadly serious after their marriage, it was too hard to bear?"

"Well, I hope I never did, Mr. Lincoln, and I daresay a fellow Todd would not, either. But I do agree that Emily can enjoy herself a little before she marries, even though the young men of Springfield may not agree."

Emily blushed. It was true that she had been pronounced the beauty of the family, but in the quiet of Buena Vista, no one had really been in a position to notice.

When the boys went to bed, the conversation turned to politics, a subject that alternately bored and depressed Emily. Earlier that year, Congress had passed the Kansas-Nebraska Act, allowing those two territories to decide whether or not they wished to allow slavery within their borders, and no table had been safe from the subject ever since. Mr. Lincoln was one of those who had come out against the law, and it had even led him to run for the United States Senate.

"I keep a scrapbook of all the newspapers' mentions of Mr. Lincoln," Mary said proudly. "See, this is an account of a speech Mr. Lincoln gave here in Springfield against the act. 'It is said that the slaveholder has the same right to take his Negroes to Kansas that a freeman has to take his hogs or his horses. This would be true if Negroes were property in the same sense that hogs and horses are. But is this the case? It is notoriously not so.' Mr. Lincoln was very eloquent on the subject. Mind you, I would not class him with one of those abolitionists. He merely wishes slavery not to be extended. Of course, Mr. Lincoln, you may contradict me if you wish."

"That sums it up fair enough, I guess." He winked at Emily.

Years ago, when Mary had brought Mr. Lincoln to Lexington for the first time, the Lincolns had gone to visit Mary's grandmother. Enchanted with the older sister she barely remembered from her earliest years, Emily had begged to come along, though she generally shied away from the formidable old lady, who as the mother of Robert Todd's first wife had never warmed to the second Mrs. Todd and her offspring. As they walked toward Grandmother Parker's house, they had passed W. A. Pullum's slave dealership, one of the largest in Kentucky. Emily would normally have looked away, as she had been instructed by her parents on numerous occasions, but this time she had followed her brother-in-law's gaze and saw what he saw: cages packed with miserable Negroes, awaiting auction. Some, Emily knew, would be sold to Kentucky plantation owners, but many would end up in the cotton fields of the Deep South, the fate most dreaded by a city slave.

"A melancholy sight," Mary had said.

Lincoln had stroked his chin and sighed. "Whipping post," he said, glancing at that prominent object, which fortunately was not in use at the moment.

Mr. Lincoln had looked so melancholy that Emily could not bear it. She had tugged at his hand. "We treat *our* darkies very well," she had assured him. "No whipping unless they do something really dreadful, like the time the girl held poor Alec upside down by the feet. Why, Mammy Sally takes a nip occasionally, and even so, Father would never dream of selling her south. They're really part of the family, you see."

Lincoln had looked down at her. Mustering a half smile, he had said, "Yes, Little Sister, I'm sure they are."

But he hadn't sounded all that convinced. And when her father died and the family had commenced to squabbling over his will, the slaves had been fought over as jealously as the family silver, and some had been sold. Emily had no idea where they were now. Was that how one treated family?

Not long after her conversation with Mr. Lincoln, Emily had gone into her father's study—a sacrosanct place, but something about her older sister's visit had emboldened her—and asked her father what he thought of slavery. It was clear that her father would have rather answered any other question, but he had finally said, "I've never sold a slave, except for one or two that turned violent. I've not bought one in years. I'd like to see the institution die a peaceful death. But if we rush it toward that death as the radical abolitionists would have us do, nothing good of it will come to anybody, including the slaves. And where will they go if they are set free? What can they do?"

Emily had been happy enough to leave the matter there, as she was now, and fortunately, the conversation shifted to Mr. Lincoln running for the Senate. Though no one in the Todd family had been quite so tactless as to say so, at least in her presence, Emily knew that his single term in the House of Representatives had not been a particularly distinguished one. He had come out against the Mexican War at what proved to be the precisely wrong time to do so, and his seat, once the preserve of the Whigs, had shifted to the Democrats, much to his humiliation. But it seemed that things had changed. Hoping that she was not presuming, she asked, "Do you think your chances of winning are good, Mr. Lincoln?"

Mr. Lincoln smiled. "Only a fool would take such a thing for granted, and I like to think I'm not a complete fool. But I do think my chances are fair. Still, there are some votes I must pick up, and they're not as ripe for the picking as I would hope."

"And if Mr. Lincoln is elected—and I am optimistic that the best man will prevail—you shall visit us in Washington. Ah, I see you smiling, Emily! It's true that Washington and I did not agree when Mr. Lincoln was in Congress, but I was cooped up with our dear little ones—poor Eddie!—in that boardinghouse, with the most ill-tempered men who expected the boys to be as quiet as statues, for heaven's sake, and in the dead of winter! And as we had so little money at that time, and were from the west, Washington society turned up their noses at us. But it will be different this time. We can afford pleasant lodgings, and I daresay a senator and his wife will be rather differently received than a congressman and his wife."

As the Senate election—done in those days by the state legislature rather than by popular vote—would not be held until early next year, it would be some time before her sister's optimism would be put to the test. In the meantime, the New Year came, and Emily spent it at Elizabeth Edwards's house, receiving with her older sisters the car-riages of merry gentlemen who rode from house to house, partaking of feminine smiles and refreshment and getting merrier with each stop. This day ushered in the social season, and Mary insisted there had never been a livelier one since she had come to Springfield. With four married sisters in Springfield—Elizabeth, Frances, Mary, and Ann— and some cousins as well, Emily had no shortage of invitations.

Mary superintended her dressing before these outings with as much care as if Emily had been her own daughter—more, in fact, than Emily's own mother, her hands full with the brood of rowdy boys and lively girls she had borne Mr. Todd, had ever done. On the first Sunday that Emily sat in the Lincoln pew at First Presbyterian Church, which Mary had joined after little Eddie's death due to the great kindness of the minister there, Emily watched as her sister's eyes wandered from the minister giving his sermon to the pretty face of Miss Matteson, the governor's daughter. When they walked the short distance from the church to the Lincoln home, the day being a pleasant one, Mary said, "You are much prettier than Miss Matteson, but you must have a new bonnet."

"Why, this one is practically new," Emily protested. Already Mary had bought silk for a ball gown for her.

"That may be so, but it does nothing to set off your beautiful eyes. And tell me, my dear, have you had your likeness taken?"

"No."

"Never, with that face? You astonish me. Well, tomorrow we shall order you the finest bonnet one can find in Springfield, and when it is ready, we shall have your daguerreotype made."

Mary, of course, made good on her word. Emily had been raised not to be vain, a vice her mother particularly disliked, and any con-ceit would have been mercilessly teased out of her by her brood of siblings, so she had never spent more time in front of a mirror than what was necessary to arrange herself properly. But in the privacy of the little bedroom she had at the Lincolns', she could not stop staring at the polished image of herself in its wooden case, fascinated to see herself for the first time as others must see her. What did life hold for that dark-haired, dark-eyed, pretty girl—for she was pretty, that could not be denied—with her fringed bodice, her white fan, and her new bonnet, the flowers of which the photographic artist had delicately tinted with pink? She tipped the daguerreotype back and forth as if it contained an answer that could be shaken out of it.

For the time being—Emily smiled wryly as she shut the case and stowed the daguerreotype in a drawer—life did not hold a husband, much to her sister's disappointment. The men of Springfield were agreeable enough, and some of them found their way to the Lincoln parlor, but nothing in any of them caught her heart. "Well," Mary said one day as a prospective suitor left dejectedly, having received nothing more than politeness from Emily, "you certainly won't be rushing into marriage, my dear. I suppose that's wise."

"I want to be as happy with my husband as you and Mr. Lincoln are," Emily said.

Mary pinched her cheek.

She had spoken with the goal of deflecting her sister's interest from her, but it was true that she had been studying the married couples she knew, with an eye toward her own future, and that the Lincolns did seem happy to her. They bickered sometimes, of course, or to be more exact, her sister did. Mr. Lincoln could not be broken of his habit of answering the door himself instead of allowing the servant, Mariah, to do it, especially when, as he pointed out time after time, he was closer and his arm was as capable of opening a door as Mariah's and certainly longer.

Even if he left his office on time, which happened seldom enough, he was incapable of walking directly home for supper, but would allow himself to be waylaid by anything in his path—friends, slight acquaintances, boys playing handball, girls wanting to be swung in circles, cats seeking a belly rub, dogs holding sticks—and would turn up long after the supper hour had passed. And every one of Emily's four Springfield sisters had told her the story of the day when Mr. Lincoln, immersed in thought while pulling his young son Tad in a wagon, walked on placidly after the passenger tumbled out of the wagon, impervious to the howls that sent every woman on the street rushing out her door.

"Oh my, how I lost my temper on that occasion!" Mary said as they sewed together one morning, watching the snow gently falling from the sky. "Poor Mr. Lincoln simply gave up and hurried to his office. I have driven him there more often than I care to admit, with my ill temper."

"I can't believe that."

"Nonetheless, it is true, my dear. You have not seen me at my worst, and I hope you never do. Each time I do act badly, I tell myself it will be the last time, and I hope I was right for a change."

The fine, light snow turned into a blizzard, stopping the trains and the legislators attempting to get to Springfield for the Senate election. One train had actually been stranded en route. It was laden not only with freezing passengers but with delicacies from Chicago, unobtainable in Springfield, that Elizabeth had ordered in preparation for her election-day party, and soon the former devoured the latter. "As the alternative was for them to eat each other, I don't begrudge them that," Mary said when she heard the news of the raid on the provisions. "But I do hope they remember the source of the food when they vote."

The crisis having passed, the vote was rescheduled for February. When Mr. Lincoln came to breakfast, he was somewhat better dressed than usual, which Emily thought might contribute to his look of unease. She had been part of the household long enough to dare to ask, "How many votes are you assured of, Mr. Lincoln?"

"Still forty-five, and I need fifty-one. I don't think that Shields has fifty-one either, which is a bright spot; in fact, I'm pretty certain he has fewer than I do. But there's always treachery afoot with these things."

"Now, Mr. Lincoln, you are too pessimistic," Mary said. "You've been working at this for weeks, and the stragglers are sure to go to your side."

"Well, I'm willing to be proven wrong." Mr. Lincoln rose, kissed his wife, and smiled at Emily. "But we must wait and see."

By and by, Emily and Mary, accompanied by Elizabeth, put on their best bonnets and joined their fellow women in the gallery of the statehouse. From their perch, they could see the candidates milling around as the legislators prepared to vote, Mr. Lincoln towering over them all even without the aid of his high hat. "There's General Shields," Mary said. She lowered her voice. "I must tell you about the time he and Mr. Lincoln nearly got into a duel; Mr. Lincoln will never tell you, as he does not like to be reminded of 'that fool incident,' as he calls it. But that must wait! There is Lyman Trumbull, married to my dear old friend Julia Jayne. Poor man, he's hardly picked up any support, I hear."

The first ballot came in: forty-five votes for Mr. Lincoln, forty-one for Mr. Shields, a mere five for Mr. Trumbull—Mary clucked sympathetically—and the rest for a handful of other men, including Governor Matteson. "Surely those five will migrate to Mr. Lincoln now," Emily said. "What is the point in them holding out? And if he can get just one besides that—"

Mary nodded. She tightened her grip on the railing before her.

But instead of gaining votes on the next ballot, Mr. Lincoln lost a few, and by the fourth one, Mr. Trumbull's total had increased to eleven. Ladies came and went from the gallery, but the three sisters stayed as a fifth ballot was cast, then a sixth, with Mr. Lincoln's votes climbing no higher. "When will these people come to their senses?" Mary asked.

The voting for the seventh ballot began. One by one, the legislators called out their choices, but this time, the men who had cried out "Shields!" six times over now called "Matteson!" Emily frowned, puzzled, but Mary, her face white, sat back. "They are throwing their vote to Matteson! It is the basest treachery—"

A lady turned her head, and Emily recognized the pretty face of the governor's daughter.

"Forty-four votes for Governor Matteson! Thirty-eight to Abraham Lincoln!"

Ballot number eight. Emily and Elizabeth, sitting on either side of Mary, each clasped one of her hands as the legislators called out their choices once more: forty-six for the governor, only twenty-seven for Mr. Lincoln now, and eighteen for Mr. Trumbull.

"Ballot number nine," Emily counted as the legislators, their voices wearying, again began crying out their choices. Forty-seven for Matteson, fifteen for Mr. Lincoln, and thirty-eight for Mr. Trumbull—all gained, Emily realized, from Mr. Lincoln.

She did not dare look at Mary's face, so she turned her attention to the floor, where Mr. Lincoln had risen from his seat and was intently talking to a group of men. He too had not looked up at the gallery since the first vote.

The tenth ballot began. "Trumbull!" each of Mr. Lincoln's fifteen supporters called, their voices as grim as their faces as the man who had started the balloting with five votes climbed to forty, then to fifty, and then to the needed fifty-one.

Trumbull, not Mr. Lincoln—and not Mary—would be going to Washington. Emily's eyes filled with tears of sympathy. "Mary—"

"Please, dear. Don't speak to me just now."

Emily obeyed, and they slowly made their way to the street, though not without Emily noticing with some satisfaction that the Matteson ladies looked as dejected as the Todd sisters. Mr. Lincoln was waiting for them. "Well," he said, "I told you there would be treachery."

"But how did he pick up those last votes? Those men were utterly loyal to you!"

"Because I told them to vote for Trumbull," Mr. Lincoln said quietly. "If someone besides me had to win, it should have been him instead of the others. At least he's on the right side of Kansas-Nebraska."

Mary scowled, and Emily longed to give Mr. Lincoln's free hand a comforting squeeze. As that seemed too forward, she turned toward her other sister. Elizabeth had been quiet throughout the balloting, her face expressionless, but now she looked nearly as miserable as the Lincolns. "I can't uninvite all the guests for tonight," she said so only Emily could hear her. "I shall have to have the Trumbulls be the guests of honor—but oh my, it will be awkward."

"I'm sure you can manage it," Emily said, earning a pat on her cheek.

Having given Bob Lincoln the news of his father's defeat, which he took with equanimity, they dressed in silence and then rode in the carriage to Elizabeth's. Emily's respect for her oldest sister's abilities as a hostess, already high, rose even further when she saw Elizabeth suavely greeting the Trumbulls and their supporters, including the original handful of Trumbull supporters that Mary had already dubbed "the Mighty Five." Elizabeth smiled as the Lincolns and Emily entered the room. "Mr. Lincoln, I hope you are not too disappointed about this," she said. "At least you can congratulate yourself that your principles won."

Mr. Lincoln smiled. "Not too disappointed to congratulate my friend Trumbull," he said, and moved to shake the victor's hand. Mrs. Trumbull in turn smiled at Mary, who responded with only the most frigid of nods.

"Mother, was that really necessary?" Mr. Lincoln asked, a weary edge to his voice when they had moved away.

"It was! The man had far fewer votes than you; anyone of honor would have given them to you instead of vice versa."

Emily went to bed with one fixed determination: she would not marry an aspiring politician, even one as agreeable as Mr. Lincoln. It was simply too heartbreaking.

⚬⚬

Mr. Lincoln went back to his law practice the next morning; it had been right neglected, he observed, over the past few months. Mary was less philosophical about his loss. For a solid week, she fumed about the subject to any sister within listening range—usually Emily, who after a day or so of this stole off to the company of her nephews. Bob spent the day at school, but the younger two were always ready to be amused. Her willingness to crawl on the floor with Tad and to walk Willie to the drugstore with its enticing candy display further endeared her to Mary, so much so that the latter was willing to overlook Emily's defects as a listener.

But even after both of the Lincolns had regained their spirits, Emily found herself missing Kentucky and her family there, and her mother's letters became downright plaintive. Her brothers and her sisters were constantly asking about her. And did she really mean to spend another Christmas in Springfield, far from her mother? There would be enough Christmases away from home once she married, by and by of course.

Emily could resist no more.

"I feel I've failed you," Mary said as they packed Emily's trunk, which was much fuller than it had been upon her arrival. "All the men in Springfield, and you couldn't find one to your liking?"

Emily shook her head regretfully.

"Well, perhaps there will be someone more to your liking when you come visit again," Mary said. She sighed. "If only we were in Washington. It must simply teem with eligible men."

∾

"Geometry was never my strong point," Emily's friend Mrs. Bradshaw said as they stood in the Assembly Room of Frankfort's Capital Hotel where the first ball of the season was being held, coinciding with the opening of the legislature at the beginning of the new year of 1856. "But that's a straight line if ever I saw one."

Emily had to agree as she watched Mr. Bradshaw and his companion, a stranger to her, make their way across the room to where the ladies stood talking, Mrs. Bradshaw in white silk, Emily in yellow. "Miss Todd," Mr. Bradshaw said. "Please permit me to introduce Mr. Benjamin Hardin Helm, one of our new legislators."

Mr. Helm was a tall man in his middle twenties, with a fine bearing, though his hairline gave every indication that he would be bald before his time. His face was not a strikingly handsome one, but something about it—his smile? his animated countenance when he spoke?—affected Emily most peculiarly. "I am delighted to make your acquaintance, Miss Todd. May I have a dance?"

Emily nodded, and Mr. Helm inscribed his name on the dance card she proffered. She was pleased to see that he had chosen a waltz. "Do you live here in Frankfort, Miss Todd?" he asked as he led her onto the dance floor.

"No, but not far away. I live in Buena Vista, a few miles outside out of town. I am visiting Mrs. Bradshaw."

"I was at several of these balls last year. I don't remember seeing you, and I rather think I would have."

"I was not in Kentucky. I was staying with my sister in Illinois. Her husband has a law practice there."

"And I am a lawyer myself. You can't get away from us."

"Are you enjoying the legislature?"

He smiled ruefully. "It is a humbling experience. Already I've been put in my place several times. My father warned me, but of course I thought I'd take the legislature by storm. You dance beautifully, Miss Todd."

"Is your family in politics, then?"

"Well, yes. My father was the governor here for a while."

"Oh," Emily said. How could she be so stupid?

He smiled as she blushed. "I gather you don't keep up with politics? It's a rare lady who does, I suppose. And Father was only governor for a short time. He was the lieutenant governor for John Crittenden, and when Crittenden became the United States Attorney General and resigned from the governorship, Father succeeded to his place. But he held office for only a year or so."

"Should I know what he is doing now?"

"He's the president of the Louisville and Nashville Railroad."

"Oh." Inwardly, Emily scolded herself for being so ill informed about what was passing outside of her little sphere. How ashamed Mary would be of her! Reading the newspapers had been virtually mandatory when she had stayed with the Lincolns, but she had gotten out of the habit since returning home.

Mr. Helm did not seem to mind her ignorance. Twice more that evening, he engaged her for a dance. Mrs. Bradshaw wagged her head as Mr. Helm departed, having inscribed her dance card for her last dance of the evening—etiquette, that hateful thing, requiring that she leave before the last few sets. "Three times! People will be talking."

"I know," Emily said dreamily.

She had the same dreamy feeling all through the last waltz, which she and Mr. Helm danced in nearly complete silence, looking at nothing at each other and unconscious of the crowd watching them with amused interest. Cupid often shot his darts at these assemblies, but seldom had he struck so decisively as on this occasion, and it was a fine thing for the legislators to watch their new, very earnest colleague being rendered so utterly helpless by the imp and a pair of lovely dark eyes.

Emily and Mr. Helm were still looking at each other when the music ended and the dancers around them cleared the floor. "May I fetch your cloak for you?" he asked.

It was the most romantic thing she had ever heard. "Yes."

Mr. Helm returned and carefully helped into her winter garments for the short ride to the Bradshaws' house. "We mustn't let you take cold," he said. He cleared his throat. "I happen to know that there's a train station at Buena Vista, Miss Todd. May I take the cars out there and call on you?"

∽❧∼

Her mother ran around the house, directing the servants to dust already dustless furniture and to polish silver that already shone. "One of the oldest families in Kentucky, and one of the wealthiest in Hardin County! Forty servants! We must make a good impression."

"Emily's already made a good impression," her younger sister Elodie said. "Otherwise he wouldn't be calling."

"Don't be impertinent, young lady. And is that the best you and Trudy can do with your hair?"

When Mr. Helm arrived and took his place in the parlor, it was crowded with Todds—Emily; her mother; Elodie; her brother Alec; and the youngest Todd, Kitty. If Mr. Helm was disconcerted by such scrutiny, he took it well and answered politely as Mrs. Todd quizzed him about his education, his career, and his future plans—not that she needed to ask many questions, for it was clear that she had already made some inquiries. "I understand you went to West Point, Mr. Helm."

A shade of gloom passed over Mr. Helm's face. "I did, ma'am."

"So you planned on a career in the army?"

"I did, and I was posted to Texas. But I fell ill—"

"Why, you look quite vigorous, Mr. Helm," her mother said. Emily winced.

"I have recovered my health, fortunately. But at the time, I was so miserable, and the posting so remote, that the doctor advised me to take a leave of absence and return home. I did, and after talking with Father, I decided that my talents—such as they are—would be better spent in the law, at least in a time of peace. So I went to law school in Louisville, and then to Harvard for a few months, and here I sit before you a lawyer."

"And a legislator," Mrs. Todd said suavely. She looked at Emily, who had been sitting demurely beside her while Mr. Helm was being interrogated. Perhaps, Emily thought, her mother would have been a fine lawyer as well. "Why don't you play for us, Emily?"

Dutifully, Emily took her place at the piano as Mr. Helm hastened to open the lid for her. "'Hard Times Come Again No More'?" she suggested.

"That sounds delightful, Miss Todd."

Emily began to sing. "While we seek mirth and beauty..." She could not see Mr. Helm's expression turn from polite attentiveness to genuine emotion as she sang plaintively, "There's a pale drooping matron who toils her life away."

"You are quite talented, Miss Todd," Mr. Helm said when she lifted her hands from the keyboard.

"She won every musical prize at school," Mrs. Todd informed him. "And now, we will leave you two alone to visit for a little while."

They filed out, the younger Todds looking somewhat disappointed at missing all the fun. "I was not speaking to flatter you, Miss Todd. You are genuinely a fine musician."

"I confess I would have a great deal of difficulty living in a place with no piano." Too late, she realized that her words could be taken as though she were already planning their future together. A change in subject was in short order, she decided. "Do you miss the military?"

"In some ways, but I confess to not missing my station at Fort Lincoln—"

"Why, that is the name of my favorite brother-in-law. But do pardon me, sir."

"I do not mind at all. The place was too remote, and I missed my family. Like yours, it's a large one."

"Oh, you haven't seen the half of us."

"I've seen the best." He rose. "I must go, Miss Todd. May I call Wednesday evening?"

"You may."

"Then I will." He took her hand. "And Miss Todd, if you don't mind me saying so, Wednesday cannot get here soon enough."

❦

Mr. Helm did call on Wednesday, and kept on calling, hurrying over from Frankfort as soon as his legislative duties were over for the day. Each time, he brought something with him from Frankfort—flowers, candy, sheet music. By the third visit, Emily's family left them alone in the parlor. By the fourth visit, he had kissed her goodbye. (What bliss! What heaven!) By the fifth visit, he had kissed her hello—no, it was actually Emily who had initiated that kiss, not that Hardin had minded. By the sixth visit, he had taken her into his lap. By the seventh visit, they had progressed no further than that, but Emily, lying in her bed, wondered if he had wanted to undress her half as much as she had wanted to be undressed by him.

On the eighth visit, he said, "My parents would like to meet the lady I've been writing so much about. May they visit?"

A couple of weeks later, his parents arrived. The visit must have been a success, because on the twelfth visit, Hardin—they had become "Hardin" and "Emma" to each other on that sixth visit—dropped to his knees and asked her to marry him. They had known each other for six weeks.

∾◦∾

Naturally, she said yes.

Some parental opposition (overcome, of course) would have appealed to Emily's romantic side, but such was not to be. Mrs. Todd would have summoned the minister the first day Hardin called, if it had been up to her. As for the Helms, within ten minutes of meeting Emily, they had brought out their memorabilia of Hardin—his daguerreotype from West Point, showing a serious young man not yet filled out to the handsome proportions he now bore, a drawing he had made in school, a lock of his hair. "Consider yourself fortunate that there were no cameras when I was a baby," Hardin had hissed to her.

The first person she wrote to was Mary. Her sister sent a delighted reply, praising her choice, urging her to visit Illinois on her bridal tour, and telling her not to fret herself about the marital act. But Emily hadn't been fretting about the latter at all; in fact, now that she and

Hardin were spending more time walking out together instead of sitting in her mother's parlor, they had taken advantage of their greater privacy to discuss its potential delights. She also had to disappoint her sister about the bridal tour, for with Hardin having to resume his law practice as soon as the legislative session closed, she had determined to travel the circuit with him. To this, she received a horrified reply from Mary about the dangers of bedbugs, which evidently traveled the circuit, too, and an indignant one from Elizabeth, who had all but sent out the invitations to everyone in Springfield who mattered to greet the newlyweds.

Emily remained steadfast on this matter, however, and turned her energies to assembling her trousseau, with the help of the servants and her sisters, although Emily reserved the stitching on her finest chemise—the one she intended to have Hardin take off her on their wedding night—for herself.

She was engaged in her sewing when a servant announced, "Letter for you, Miss Todd."

It was from Mary, and was—as Emily blushed to discover—full of helpful advice as to how to best enjoy the marital act, along with an enlightening discussion of how one could have one's children arrive at decent intervals if one were so inclined. This advice, which Emily's mother had certainly not followed, was so astonishing that Emily's mouth fell agape. It had not been covered at all in the book *The Young Wife* that her mother had bought for her after her engagement.

"What does Mary say?" Elodie asked.

"Oh, nothing of interest. She's still after me to visit Springfield, but I simply can't." She tucked the letter into her pocket. It needed to be reread, and reread, and then discussed with Hardin. Why, he might not even know about some of the things that Mary had mentioned.

At last, March 26 arrived. Her brother Alec walked her down the aisle of Frankfort's Ascension Episcopal Church, Emily wearing a dress of light-blue silk sprigged with pink roses. Bowing to the latest fashion, she had also donned a hoop skirt, despite the smirks of her brother, who had made a point of wondering aloud whether there would be room for the two of them to walk side by side.

The company at the wedding was not ideal, for it saddened her that her father had not lived to see her marry, and her brothers and sisters were scattered to the wind as well—her four half sisters in Springfield, Margaret in Cincinnati, Martha in Selma, and David and Sam in New Orleans. Two half brothers, Levi and George, were still in Kentucky, but Levi had not turned up for the wedding, a sign that he was likely on a spree, and George had not been invited and would not have come even if he had been. But her favorite brother held her arm, and Elodie and Kitty were there, as were most of her new family on Hardin's side—his literary sisters, his adoring younger brothers, his doting parents. As was the custom, three young slave women, chosen from around the neighborhood for their attractiveness and gentility, served as Emily's attendants, waiting on her and also serving an ornamental purpose, as they were expected to wear pretty, new frocks for the occasion.

And there was Hardin, standing proud and tall at the altar. No one could doubt that he had graduated from West Point.

They said their wedding vows and kissed decorously. Then the wedding party boarded a special train for Buena Vista, where Mrs. Todd was holding a grand reception—and where Hardin and Emily would finally become truly as one. For three hours, they danced and made merry. Alec, the scamp, had slipped her a glass of champagne, so that when she and Hardin were at last in the guest room together, she felt delightfully giddy as he pulled her into his lap, both of them stark naked, and began kissing her, moving from her lips to her throat. "You're as beautiful as Venus, Mrs. Helm."

"And you're as handsome as—" She was too distracted to think of a suitable comparison, but it hardly mattered with Hardin's lips continuing on their journey.

Long afterward, when they lay sated, Hardin said, "That started our marriage off well, my love."

"It did, indeed."

"You're sure you don't mind riding the circuit as your bridal tour? I know you've heard about its horrors from your sister Mary."

"I don't care for any of that." Emily curled closer to Hardin, if that was possible. "You can take me to any flea-bitten hotel you choose, and I will go, as long as I can share a bed with you. I will go wherever you go. Always and forever."

MARY

FEBRUARY 11 TO MARCH 4, 1861

The house on Springfield's Eighth and Jackson Street, where their three youngest sons had been born and one had died, stood empty, but that had not stopped a crowd from staring at it as Mr. Lincoln helped Mary into the waiting carriage. Mr. Lincoln gave the house a wistful look. Several years before, at Mary's urging, he had engaged a contractor to enlarge it, and although it was no match for the mansions on Aristocracy Hill, it had been more than ample to suit the needs of the Lincolns. Mr. Lincoln had never been much of a man to pay attention to his surroundings, but occasionally Mary had caught him looking at the place with something like pride. And why shouldn't he be proud? He had spent his own childhood in a succession of log cabins.

But now their home was leased to a tenant, and Mr. Lincoln would soon be in another house—the White House.

It still made Mary's head spin to think of the events that had brought her husband to the Presidency. Violence between pro-slavery and abolitionist factions in Kansas, and the Supreme Court's *Dred Scott* decision holding that colored people had no rights of citizenship, had divided the country even more than it had been over the issue of slavery, and against that backdrop, Mr. Lincoln had run for the Senate as a member of the Republican Party, which had grown out of the anti-slavery wing of the Whig Party. This time, his Democratic opponent had been Stephen Douglas, Mary's would-be beau from long ago. The two men, both fine speakers, had held a series of debates, chiefly on the slavery issue. Mr. Lincoln had failed to win the election, but his performance at the debates had brought him national attention. A speaking engagement at New York City's Cooper Union had added to his stature, and in March 1860, Mr. Lincoln had shocked the country by becoming the Republican nominee for President. Meanwhile, the Democratic Party, hopelessly split between North and South, turned up with two nominees: Mr. Douglas for the northern states and John Breckinridge, a Kentuckian, for the slaveholding states. As if three candidates were not enough, the small Constitutional Union Party had nominated John Bell. The four-way race had culminated on November 4, 1860, with Mr. Lincoln winning the election with the grace of God and the Electoral College, which had allowed him to triumph despite winning only a plurality of the popular vote. But it had been enough. As if it had happened only the day before, Mary remembered her husband banging open the door that evening as he yelled, "We are elected, Mary!"

It had nonetheless been a bittersweet victory. When accepting the Senate nomination in 1858, Mr. Lincoln had said, "A house divided against itself cannot stand," and one by one the Southern states had made good their threat to secede from the Union in the event of a Republican victory, beginning with South Carolina in December 1860, and formed what they called the Confederate States of America. Virginia and Maryland remained uneasily within the Union, as did the Lincolns' native Kentucky.

For now, at least.

Someone closed the door—bidden or unbidden, there was always someone there to do such things now, just so someone could say years in the future that he closed the President's carriage door—and Mr.

Lincoln gave the signal to depart. "I'll miss the old place," he said as the carriage began moving and the crowd begin to drift away. There would be another crowd at the Chenery House, the hotel where they were to spend their last few nights in Springfield, and most likely an even larger one when they boarded the special train that would take them to Washington. "I hope they take good care of it."

∽◎〜

"Springfield, Indianapolis, Cincinnati, Columbus, Pittsburgh, Cleveland, Buffalo, New York, Harrisburg, Baltimore, and Washington," Willie said, not for the first time. "I wish we could stay on the train the entire time."

"I am afraid that will not be possible," Mary said. "But we will certainly be on the train enough. And don't forget, there will be different trains for different legs of the journey. You will be able to compare them all."

Willie nodded and patted a small valise. "I'm going to save all the timetables for the trip in here," he said with satisfaction.

It was not like Mr. Lincoln, standing at the hotel window, to stay aloof from a conversation involving Willie, their ten-year-old, but he had had little to say for the past day or so. Mary was used to long silences on the part of her husband, but she had not undergone one like this one since that terrible day years before when little Eddie had died in their arms. "I hope, Mr. Lincoln, you are not worried over those cowards who have threatened you."

Mr. Lincoln shook his head. "No. They don't bother me."

A few weeks before, Mary had opened a letter from whom she assumed was either a well-wisher or someone wanting her influence with the President-to-be to get an appointment—there were plenty of the latter, who were trying Mr. Lincoln's patience as much as the Southern states that had been pulling out of the Union ever since the votes making her husband president had been counted. Instead, she found a crude sketch of her husband heaped with tar and feathers, with chains on his feet and a noose around his neck. "Mr. Lincoln!"

Mr. Lincoln glanced up. "Oh, yes, I get those every day," he had said almost airily, and then returned to his correspondence. Then he looked up again. "Why, that's almost a fair likeness." He rubbed his new beard, which he had started growing after the election on the advice of a young girl, Grace Bedell. "But they forgot this."

Her husband had refused to show her the threatening letters he received. "They're repetitive," he had told her, and indeed Mary had managed to peek at one once, to find that it contained little other than the word *Goddamn*, deployed in every possible iteration. The hatred made her shiver, and after that she had not pestered Mr. Lincoln about his mail.

Although Mr. Lincoln might shrug off the hatred against him— the Southerners had to hate somebody, he said, so it might as well be him—he had been less cavalier about Mary and his sons. But Bob, who had made a special trip from Harvard to join the party heading toward Washington, said he could take care of himself just fine, and Mary's vociferous arguments against waiting a few weeks before joining her husband in Washington had met with an unexpected ally in General Winfield Scott, who had advised that Lincoln would be safer from attack if his family were with him, as no Southerner worthy of the name would stoop to harm a man in front of his lady. Mr. Lincoln had not seemed fully convinced, but with the country crashing to pieces around him, he had other things to concern himself with. It had been settled that Mr. Lincoln, Bob, and other gentlemen would depart for Springfield and that Mary and the younger boys would linger behind a day, then catch up with the special train in Indianapolis.

"If you're not concerned with the threats, Mr. Lincoln, I do wish you would tell me what you are concerned with. Assuming that it is not affairs in general."

Mr. Lincoln glanced at his pocket watch. "Time to go."

Mary sighed and took the hand of Tad, soon to be eight years old, as Mr. Lincoln took Willie's. Bob, who had been watching this one-sided bickering with an amused and somewhat superior air, picked up his father's carpetbag and followed.

In the lobby, the President-elect's baggage waited to be put on the carriage. As Mary and the boys watched, Mr. Lincoln carefully roped the bags together, then wrote A. LINCOLN, WHITE HOUSE, WASHINGTON, D.C. on tags and affixed them to the luggage. Most of the luggage, in fact, was Mary's; she had gone to New York and shopped after the election. She could hardly appear at the White House in rags, could she? And the store clerks had been so accommodating when she had given her name, offering her everything on credit.

The day was rainy and cold, but that had not deterred a crowd from assembling at the Great Western Depot, where a three-car train with a bright-yellow passenger car awaited them. Mr. Lincoln stared as their sheer numbers became apparent. "Why, there's hardly a person in this crowd I don't at least recognize."

"They love you, Mr. Lincoln."

"Well, it's a pleasant change from the mail."

෴

Standing nearby was a wiry young man named Elmer Ellsworth. As the head of a militia unit known as the Chicago Zouaves, distinguished by their precision drills and their exotic uniforms, he had come to the attention of Mr. Lincoln, who had taken him into his office to read law and who had employed him in his presidential campaign. Like Mr. Lincoln, Mr. Ellsworth was a self-made man, and unlike him he was short but so handsome that as he helped move Mr. Lincoln through the crowd, more than a few young ladies forgot the President-elect to gaze at his escort. Mary's own sister Kitty had been one of the gazers when she had visited Mary after the election, but Mr. Ellsworth had a fiancée, and in any case Mary's stepmother had insisted upon Kitty returning home once the Southern states began their ridiculous foot-stamping in seceding from the Union. No one knew what Kentucky might decide, Mrs. Todd had explained, and she did not want little Kitty to be caught away from home if it did secede.

There was certainly no doubt what side Mrs. Todd would take if the war everyone was worrying about did come about, Mary thought, scowling. God forbid that her stepmother should give up her precious slaves.

When they arrived at the train, Mr. Lincoln, wincing from the pain of having shaken countless hands, bade Mary and his younger sons farewell, hopping aboard the rear platform before Willie, chagrined at being excluded from this stage of the train's journey, could protest. Then, as Mary and the boys watched with the rest, he turned to the crowd and spoke the words that he must have been mentally composing all morning. "My friends. No one, not in my situation, can appreciate my feeling of sadness at this parting. To this place, and the kindness of these people, I owe everything. Here I have lived a quarter of a century, and have passed from a young to an old man. Here my children have been born, and one is buried. I now leave, not knowing when, or whether ever, I may return, with a task before me greater than that which rested upon Washington. Without the assistance of the Divine Being, who ever attended him, I cannot succeed. With that assistance I cannot fail. Trusting in Him, who can go with me, and remain with you and be everywhere for good, let us confidently hope that all will yet be well. To His care commending you, as I hope in your prayers you will commend me, I bid you an affectionate farewell."

The crowd—many in tears—cheered, and Mr. Lincoln, his own eyes moist, turned hastily away and disappeared into the train along with all the rest. For a moment it seemed that not even the little train would summon up enough spirit to move, but then the whistle blew and the train chugged away as the crowd, umbrellas aloft, turned slowly and silently walked away.

Willie let the train pass from sight before asking, "Mother, what did Father mean about not knowing if he would come here again? The house is only rented, isn't it?"

"Just a figure of speech," Mary said lightly. But as she and the boys walked toward their waiting carriage, she was asking the same question silently to herself.

∽≈∾

Once Mary and the boys rejoined Mr. Lincoln in Indianapolis, they soon settled into the rhythm of the journey. Each time the train passed through some tiny station, there would be a crowd waiting to catch a glimpse of Mr. Lincoln, who usually obliged by coming out onto the platform and waving, sometimes even managing a hasty speech. Often they had to stop to refuel, to change locomotives, or to dine, and Mr. Lincoln would make a speech or shake hands all around. And each night, they would stop at one of the cities on their route, check into a hotel, and enjoy the hospitality of the local and state dignitaries. The crowds were attentive and receptive, and Mr. Lincoln was at his best as he spoke to them. Only the knowledge that in the South, another man, Jefferson Davis, was making his own inaugural trip marred the occasion for Mary as she listened to her husband in town after town.

Then, in Harrisburg, Pennsylvania, he came to her hotel room. In the croak his voice assumed nightly after a day of nonstop talking, he said, "Mother, you won't be pleased to hear this, and I am not pleased to be saying it, but I am going to have to take a train to Washington in secret and by myself."

"Whatever do you mean?"

"There are reports—reports based on good information—that there is a plot to attack me in Baltimore." He forestalled her shriek with a hand. "Now, that wouldn't have bothered me, as there have been threats even before we left Springfield, as you know. But this crew actually seems to have organization and a plan, and while they could prove to be completely incompetent, I would as soon not put them to the test on this occasion. I don't like to do it, because I know some will call me coward for it, but I can't laugh in the faces of those who have warned me either. So tonight, I will slip into a carriage, ride to the station, board a train, and change to a sleeper in Philadelphia, and from there go to Washington."

Thanks to Willie, Mary knew that things were not as simple as her husband described. One could not ride a train from Philadelphia straight to Washington; instead, the trains terminated at Baltimore's Calvert Street Station, after which cars traveling south had to be pulled by horses to the Camden Station a mile away. "You will be exposed to danger as much as you would be traveling with the rest of us!"

"No, because I will be traveling secretly and during the night. No one will know where I am until I arrive in Washington."

"Then I will share your danger. I will go with you."

"No, Mother. I am conspicuous enough as I am. The two of us will be even more conspicuous."

"Of course, with you pointing it out," Mary snapped. A few stops earlier, he had introduced the two of them to the crowd as "the long and short of it," and Mary had not been entirely appreciative.

"I think they would have noticed anyway," Mr. Lincoln said dryly. He ran a hand through his hair, which Mary had touched up before he dined but now showed no signs of being cared for whatsoever.

She changed her tactics. "Please, Mr. Lincoln, let me go with you. I will be no trouble whatsoever. If a disguise is needed, I will put it on."

Mr. Lincoln chuckled.

"I was not joking!"

"No, but I had an image of you dressed up as a boy or as a scullery maid. Whatever one of those looks like. And dressed up or not dressed up, what could you do to help?"

"You remember what General Scott said before we left, that the presence of your family would be the best guard against an assassination."

"Much as I respect the general, the more I think about it, the less I see his logic. Why, an assassin might delight more in taking out the whole lot of us. Mary, there's no point in batting this back and forth. Even if I were inclined to let you come, Pinkerton and the rest of them would throw a fit."

"Damn it, man, you must let me come!"

Mr. Lincoln gazed at her sympathetically, and so provokingly that she threw a hairbrush at him before he could even shake his head no. It sailed past him and narrowly missed shattering a looking glass.

"Mary, do keep your dignity." He bent and kissed her before she could launch another missile. "I will see you tomorrow afternoon in Washington."

∞℘

There was no person on earth—not even her children, not even Willie, her secret favorite and she suspected her husband's as well—she loved more than Mr. Lincoln. And there was no person on earth who could make her angrier. His infinite patience, his refusal to lose his temper with her, his inability to hold a grudge—how could she be expected to endure these things quietly?

She would tell him he should have married Matilda Edwards. "But she was too pious," he would protest. She would tell him that she could have done better, that she could have married Mr. Douglas. "I wonder what that would have been like," he would say, genuinely curious. She would become enraged over the most trivial thing—hating herself the entire time she was doing so—and he would calmly turn on his heel and go for a walk.

Only once had he lost his temper. During some quarrel, the cause of which she could not bear to remember, she had actually pursued him into their yard, waving a knife at him. She had not even realized she was holding a knife, much less intended to use it, but a neighbor had happened along, and Mr. Lincoln, catching sight of him, had grabbed Mary and shoved her into the house. "There, damn it," he had said, in a low and distinct tone she had never heard him use before to anyone, man or woman, "stay in the house and don't disgrace us before the eyes of the world." And for the entire day, she had done exactly that, weeping in her bed until he had come home from his office and she had sunk to her knees and begged for his forgiveness. Which, of course, he had given even before she had got on her knees in the first place. "Just stay away from the cutlery, Mother," he had advised, which had actually infuriated her all over again, but this time she had managed to force a smile instead.

She knew she trespassed on his good nature, that she became infuriated over trifles. Why couldn't she just *stop* herself?

But this—a threat to his life that he had actually taken seriously—couldn't be viewed as a trifle. And this time, it was the entire nation, not just herself, that was at risk. Granted, Mary didn't know precisely how she could protect him by being at his side, but she certainly could do nothing to help him with her in Harrisburg and him on a train.

Presently, a man came to the door—Norman Judd, one of Mr. Lincoln's supporters. Plainly, he had been sent as a reinforcement by Mr. Lincoln. While he explained the plan to her, as patronizingly and repetitiously as if he were conversing with little Tad, her temper broke again, and only the absence of the brush from her dressing table kept her from launching it yet again. In due time, he scurried out, but not before snapping, "Mrs. Lincoln, please do be quiet about this. Much depends on complete secrecy."

"Don't you think I know that, you fool?"

She had bellowed that, but she certainly had not let out any secrets.

As he left, she stared out the window. In the gaslight, she saw three men getting into a coach. The tallest was stooping, and he was wearing a low hat instead of his usual high hat, but there was no possibility of her not recognizing him, even if others might be fooled. She longed to open the window and tell him goodbye, to wish him a safe journey, to, above all, tell him that she loved him and had not meant anything she said. She never did! But she managed to restrain herself, even if she could not pull herself from her post at the window until long after the coach had disappeared from view.

She did not sleep at all that night, and had not expected to. The next morning, Mr. Judd knocked. Without a word, he handed her a telegram from "A. Lincoln, Willard Hotel" containing a message of one word: SAFE.

Although Mr. Lincoln had reached Washington without incident, his absence left the remaining passengers on the train in dismal spirits. The younger boys were as quiet—no, quieter—as if they were in church, and Bob pulled out one of his textbooks and began studying it, something he had not bothered to do the entire journey.

Though exhausted from her night of worrying, Mary was in better sorts than the rest. She had invited Margaret and Agnes Williams, the daughters of a prominent Pennsylvania politician, to travel with her to Washington, and she was content to relax in her upholstered chair and half listen, half sleep as the young women reviewed the all-encompassing question of what they were to wear to the inaugural ball. It was pleasant to have the well-brought-up, deferential, and yet lively Williams girls on the trip, although she wished that her younger sisters could have been there instead. But Kitty was firmly under Mrs. Todd's wing in Kentucky, and Elodie was visiting Martha, who had married a warehouse keeper, Clement White, in Selma, Alabama—an awkward place for sisters of Mary to be since the collection of rebellious states calling themselves the Confederacy had established their own capital in Montgomery. If only Emily could have come! But she had two small children and a husband who was very busy with his law practice, although Mary suspected that he, like Mr. Lincoln in his early days, was not yet making as much money as he should be. But no doubt Mr. Lincoln could find some suitable position for Mr. Helm.

"Maryland at last," Bob announced. For the first time since they had left Harrisburg, he smiled. "Let's not let these rebels dampen our spirits, shall we?" Undaunted by the fact that he, like his father, could not sing a note, he began to warble, "Oh, say can you see," and presently the entire car began to follow him in singing the tune.

When the city of Baltimore came into view, however, the car grew silent once more. Elmer Ellsworth muttered something about wishing he had brought his sword, and Bob said, "You and the young ladies had best move away from the windows, Mother."

No sooner had they obeyed than the train pulled into the station where a crowd so thoroughly covered the platform that Mary had no idea how the passengers were to exit. The train had not even halted when rough-looking men began to press at the windows and even to grab at the doors. "Where's Lincoln?"

"Trot him out!"

"Let's have him!"

"Bloody Republicans!"

"The President-elect is already in Washington," the conductor called out. "Now back off! Let these people out!"

Instead, two men suddenly barged onto the train. Never in her life had Mary been so close to such ruffian-looking creatures. Before she could scream, John Hay, a young man who had been serving as Mr. Lincoln's secretary, grabbed a cane and, wielding it to excellent effect, forced the men backward onto the platform, then bolted the door, all the while using language that Mary had not heard before. "My apologies, Mrs. Lincoln," he said when the car was secured.

"It is quite all right, Mr. Hay." The young man looked thoroughly pleased with himself, as he often did, but this time Mary shared his sentiment.

At length, the conductor and the station personnel managed to force the crowd far back enough so that they could exit, but even so, they had to walk down the platform single file, Mary's skirts brushing the train on one side and the bystanders on the other. All the while, the crowd jeered and pointed, not so much at her but at the men, but just that was quite frightening enough.

What would they have done to Mr. Lincoln if he had been on this platform? Mary shuddered.

After a pleasant luncheon with the president of the railway company, who was duly apologetic for the disrespect shown to her—not that he could help it, but Mary was gratified to get at least one apology for the ordeal of the last day—they drove to the Camden Station, where for a half hour a group of boys took turns staring into their car and pointing as if visiting a menagerie. Bob smoked a cigar, taking some considerable satisfaction in blowing the smoke out the window toward the urchins, who were finally scattered by the police. And then, at last, the train pulled out of the station and, finally, into Washington's Baltimore and Ohio Railroad Depot, where a carriage awaited them. Mary gazed at her surroundings. Washington! It had not improved in appearance since she had accompanied Mr. Lincoln there years before. The copper dome that had sat awkwardly atop the Capitol had been torn down, but its replacement had yet to be completed—an emblem, more than one wag would say in the months to come, of the sundered nature of the Union itself. The buildings sprouted haphazardly—a civic edifice here, a modest dwelling there, a mansion here—and just beyond Pennsylvania Avenue, the city's main thoroughfare, were rows of shanties, home to the city's free colored people and to the Irish. Dotted among the other dwellings were shuttered-up, forlorn-looking residences, some marked "To Let," vacated by the Southern families who had decamped Washington to join the rebels.

Presently, they arrived at the Willard. When Mr. Lincoln had served in Congress in 1847, it had been an unimpressive establishment of forty rooms, but it, like Mr. Lincoln, had come up in life, and it now covered a city block and boasted 150 rooms, separate men's and ladies' dining rooms, and its own lecture hall. The Willard brothers themselves were on hand to welcome Mary and to guide her through the lobby, dense with men reading newspapers and conferring among themselves. "We have a suite of five rooms set aside for you, madam," Joseph Willard informed her. "You won't find a more comfortable lodging in Washington."

"Not even the White House, Mr. Willard?"

Joseph Willard grinned. "Frankly, madam, I would say not. But here we are."

He knocked, and someone promptly opened the door—not a servant, but her own husband. "Now, Molly," he said as he took her into his arms while Mr. Willard hurried away. "I told you everything would be fine. Didn't I?"

❦

"'We are not enemies, but friends,'" Bob read, squinting at the paper he was holding. "'We must not be enemies. Though passion may have strained, it must not break our bonds of affection. The mystic chords of memories—'"

"Memory," Mr. Lincoln said. "I'll change that to 'memory.' Go on, Son."

"'—stretching from every battlefield, and patriot grave, to every living heart and hearthstone, all over this broad land, will yet swell the chorus of the Union, when again touched, as surely they will be, by the better angels of our nature.'"

"That is beautiful, Mr. Lincoln," Mary said.

"Well," her husband said, "I've been working on it long enough."

"Shall I read it again?" Bob asked.

"No. I'm satisfied with it at last. Just don't let me forget the thing."

He suppressed a yawn; he had arisen at five that morning, the last they would spend in the Willard. In hours, servants would pack their goods and send them to the White House. "Well," he said, "I'd like to be alone for a while before it all starts up."

Mary rose. "The next time I speak to you, Mr. Lincoln, you will be the President. I want you to know how very proud of you I am. I do wish your mother had lived to see this day. And your father."

"Yes, I do, too. Well, my mother… As for my father, I loved the man, I guess, but we were better off miles apart, I learned. I think that even today, he would still think of me as an odd duck. And he'd probably be pestering me for a job."

∽❧∾

The Willard was so crowded that, the night before, the Willard brothers, absolutely out of rooms, had borrowed hundreds of mattresses and laid them anyplace they could be squeezed in order to accommodate the spectators coming into town for the inauguration. Fortunately, an entourage of Todds had arrived in time to be given lodgings: Mary's sister Elizabeth Edwards and her two daughters, Mary's sister Margaret Kellogg from Cincinnati, and Mary's cousin Lizzie Grimsley, who, as Miss Elizabeth Todd, had been one of Mary's bridesmaids. Nothing like her married surname, she was Mary's favorite cousin. As quietly as possible, she had divorced her faithless husband not long before, and Mary trusted that a White House invitation would silence the petty-minded gossips of Springfield. Why should a woman be required to put up with what a man would never abide? She hoped that Mr. Lincoln would make her cousin a postmistress, which would allow her to live in comfort and not to be dependent upon her relations. Not that poor Mr. Lincoln had had any time to consider the matter, for since he had arrived in Washington, he had been besieged by seekers of offices great and small, who filled the hotel lobby and lined the staircase leading to Mr. Lincoln's parlor.

With the help of Cousin Lizzie and the rest, Mary dressed in a Havana-colored wool gown. She had chosen it for its simplicity, for she would be very much in the background at the inaugural ceremony, and in any case would have a chance to shine later at the ball that evening in the blue watered silk she had purchased in New York just weeks before.

In due time, the two senators who were to escort Mary and her group of ladies to the Capitol ahead of her husband arrived. As their carriage made its slow progress down Pennsylvania Avenue, Mary saw that Washington's main street was clotted with people, filling every inch of pavement, perching in trees, and lining the rooftops and upper-story windows. Some clutched carpetbags, having found no place to sleep the night before. Every species of military unit, well-armed, lined the avenue and the roofs as well. Even Mr. Lincoln, who would be riding in an open carriage with President James Buchanan, had not gainsaid their presence.

Having taken her place in the gallery of the Senate reserved for herself and other prominent ladies, Mary half watched as the incoming vice president, Mr. Hannibal Hamlin, took his oath. Years ago, she had sat in another gallery, watching as Mr. Lincoln attempted to win a seat in the Senate, which he had never managed to reach. If only she had known he was destined for higher things, she would have never wasted so much time bewailing his defeats.

Since Election Day, her sister Elizabeth and the rest of the family had been walking about in a state of perpetual surprise, still unbelieving that the man that they had thought not good enough for Mary was now the man who would have to pull the nation through this time of crisis. But Mary wasn't surprised—at least not at her core. She'd always known there was something about Mr. Lincoln.

Mr. Hamlin having finished, the room fell silent. Then dignitaries started to file in—the diplomatic corps, the justices of the Supreme Court, the House of Representatives. At last, the outgoing President, looking relieved to be done with the whole business, and the incoming one, his face impassive, entered, arm in arm. Mary had urged Mr. Lincoln, whose clothes always took on a rumpled look after being worn for more than an hour or so, to dress at the last minute, and from the neat look of his plain black suit, he had heeded her advice.

Having processed in, after some formalities, the groups processed out to the Capitol's east front, where a platform had been erected. As the Marine Band played a lively tune, Mary took her seat there along with the rest.

At last, Mr. Lincoln stepped to the platform, placed his speech upon it, and removed his hat—only to find there was no room for it on the table. Mary found herself instinctively rising until a small figure arose and, bowing, took the hat and returned to the seat. It was Senator Douglas, Mr. Lincoln's rival for the presidency and Mary's would-be suitor from those early days in Springfield.

Relieved of the burden of his hat, Mr. Lincoln reached into his coat and took out a pair of spectacles. As he slipped them on, someone yelled, "Leave them off. We want to see your eyes!"

For a moment, Mr. Lincoln fought back a smile. Then, spectacles in place, he read his speech in a clear, unfaltering voice, delivering a message of union intended more for the wavering states such as Virginia, Kentucky, and Maryland than for the crowd below him. Finishing to applause, he took the oath of office administered by the elderly Chief Justice Roger Taney—who was fortunate that there was no wind, or otherwise the frail judge would have surely been blown off the platform—and kissed the Bible.

The crowd cheered, and Mary let out a breath. For better or worse, Mr. Lincoln was now President.

In an instant, the new President was engulfed by well-wishers (and, perhaps, ill-wishers as well), shaking his hand. Even if protocol had allowed Mary to go to his side to add her congratulations, she could not have managed to press through the crowd.

At length, her escort delivered her to a closed carriage. The two Presidents, old and new, had long left in their carriage, and as Mary's carriage pulled up to the Executive Mansion, President Buchanan was already departing.

The doorkeeper, an Irishman who Mary would soon know as Edward, was ready for them. "Good afternoon, Mrs. Lincoln," he said as if she had been residing here for years.

There in the hall stood Mr. Lincoln, who bent and kissed her decorously. "Good afternoon, Mrs. Lincoln."

"And good afternoon to you, Mr. President." She sniffed. Would there be any way to rid this place of the stench of tobacco?

"President Buchanan gave me some valuable parting advice."

"Oh?"

"He told me that the right-hand well here gave better water than the left." He shook his head and looked around. "Good to know, I guess, since this will be home for the next four years."

Mary shook her head. "Don't sell yourself short, Mr. Lincoln. Eight, at least."

~ 4 ~
EMILY
MARCH 1861

D o you have your gumshoes on?" Hardin asked as they set forth
for Louisville's railway station. "It looks like rain."

Kate pointed to her feet proudly, and Emily smiled. "We both do,
darling."

"Very good."

Mary had told her that after she married, she would learn all sorts
of things about her husband. Most of the things Mary had reported
were good ones—that Mr. Lincoln, unlike many husbands, paid little
attention to how she spent the household money as long as all the bills
were paid. He'd also told her, startlingly, that he believed that while no
one should commit adultery, a woman who did so was no worse than
a man who did so. On the negative side, Mary had discovered that he
had almost no sense of color and was just as happy to see her in a white
dress as a black one—and was completely useless for telling her which
suited her better.

For Emily's part, she had learned that her husband had a decided mother-hennish quality. When she had become pregnant with Kate and he was on the circuit, he had issued so many directives about her health that Emily had begun to think he was a frustrated doctor. She was to walk out daily, except in the worst weather, but on foul days, she was to wear her gumshoes. She was to wake early and go to bed early, like the tedious maxim by Benjamin Franklin. She was, above all, not to eat green apples—advice that, when pressed, he admitted he had gained from his old mammy. Much of Emily's conduct, it seemed, would be guided by this long-dead servant.

Still, three-year-old Kate and one-year-old Dee were healthy children whose births had been easy, so perhaps there was something to be said for that advice. And Emily didn't really like green apples all that much anyway.

"Are you sure you'll be all right by yourself with the girls?"

"It's only for a short time, and Mother and Alec will be up in a day or two. You know that."

"I do, but you know how I worry."

Emily smiled. With luck, this would be their last parting for a long time.

It had been Emily's idea for Hardin to see Mr. Lincoln in Washington about a possible appointment. The men had got on well when, years before, Hardin had come to Springfield on legal business. By Hardin's account, he and Mr. Lincoln had had a long, thoughtful conversation about slavery. Mr. Lincoln had wondered whether the slaves could be settled in Liberia, but Hardin had had his doubts; freeing the slaves would devastate the economies of the rural states. Moreover, the Southerners would never consent to parting with their property without compensation, the Northern abolitionists would never consent to compensating the slave owners, and in the Deep South, where cotton ruled all, the slave owners would not even consent to compensated emancipation. All the men could agree on, respectfully, was that it was regrettable the institution had ever been introduced into the United States. Yet Hardin had come home thoroughly attached to Mr. Lincoln. "He listens to all sides of an issue—a rare trait nowadays, and one that I could stand to emulate myself. But"—he grinned—"I never saw a father so lax with his children. Those boys rule the roost."

Watching now as her husband scooped up Kate and settled her in the carriage—Dee having been left at home with her nurse, Maggie—Emily thought that the Lincoln sons were not the only children of whom that could be said.

How wonderful it would be if Mr. Lincoln could find a place for Hardin in Washington! Emily thought as they rattled toward the train station. She would have the delight of Mary's company, the girls could go to fine schools, and Washington society would be amusing as well. Or better yet, an appointment abroad. England or France might be too much to hope for, but there was a plethora of other pleasant places they could stay, for a few years at least. Russia, maybe? Emily smiled at the thought of Hardin constantly urging her to wear her furs.

They were in the station when Hardin coughed. "Emma," he said, using the version of her name he used in his most affectionate moments, "don't get your hopes up too high. Mr.—President—Lincoln may not have anything for me. And we don't see eye to eye on some things. He may not want to give me anything."

"Oh, pshaw! You know Mary would never give him any peace if he didn't. And besides, he likes you. Look at all the advice he's given you about your law practice."

"Yes," Hardin said. "He's treated me almost like a younger brother." There was a sadness in his voice.

Hardin always was pensive when they parted, although the beautiful letters he sent when he was away almost made his absence worthwhile. Emily had saved most of them, except for a few from the early days of their marriage in which Hardin had written so frankly about her physical charms that Emily had reluctantly consigned the letters to the fire as he had requested. Just thinking of some of the choicer lines made her blush, right there on the railway platform.

As the train chugged in, Kate began to bounce with excitement, distracting both parents from their conversation. Amid the passengers hurrying onto the train, Hardin lifted his daughter in his arms and kissed her goodbye, then gave Emily a passionate kiss as Kate giggled at this public display of affection between her parents.

"Write often!" Emily called as Hardin, clutching his carpetbag with one hand, waved goodbye to her with the other. "And give the President and Mrs. Lincoln my love," she called. Only when a couple of people turned to stare at her did she recall that her sentiment was very far from being universally shared in Louisville.

❧

"Where's my darling Kate? And where's my precious baby?" Mrs. Todd asked before she had even crossed the threshold of the little house Hardin had bought in Louisville after his law practice and his family began to grow. "Oh, Emily, I have the worst news."

"What is it, Mama?"

"Your sister Elodie has a suitor."

Behind their mother, Alec quirked an eyebrow at Emily, who tried to keep her face solemn. "Who?"

"A man she met at Montgomery, at the inaugural ball there. Oh, he's perfectly respectable, from an old Alabama family. He lives in Selma, where he has a good law practice, and Mr. White is acquainted with him. But he's lost his first two wives. I don't want to make a blue-beard of the man, but really..." Mrs. Todd sighed, then brightened as Kate ran into her arms and Elodie's little namesake, Dee, toddled toward her. "My grandbabies! And that's another thing. This man has two children by his first two wives. I fear he's just trying to get a stepmother for them."

This, Emily thought, struck a little too close to home. "Mama, let me show you around the house. I've made some improvements since you were last here."

"I do know your father loved me, in his way, but there's no gain-saying that he married me for his convenience, with those motherless children of his. And not one of them showing the least bit gratitude!"

If left to her own devices, Mrs. Todd would devolve to her favorite grievance, George Todd's lawsuit. "Now, Mama. Didn't Mary invite you to Washington?"

"Yes, and Martha invited me to go with them to Montgomery for *their* inaugural." Mrs. Todd shook her head, the parlous state of the country having distracted her from her own situation. "I decided I was better off going to neither. It's a topsy-turvy world."

Emily turned to her brother. "Have you thought about reading for the law like we talked about?"

Alec shook his head. "I can't settle down to anything like that with the country in the state it's in. Besides"—he grinned—"does the world really need another lawyer?"

"I think that would be lovely," Emily said mildly. It bothered her that none of her brothers, except for George the physician, had settled into any sort of profession. Levi, deserted by his wife and children, was assiduously drinking himself to death; David was running wild. Sam, at least, was respectably married and working as a clerk in Louisiana, but Emily thought he had had more potential. That left Alec for her to pin her hopes on. At least he was not dissipated like Levi.

Alec, meanwhile, was shaking his head. "Whatever's going to happen, I wish it would happen."

"Do you think there will be war?" Emily asked.

"Bound to be. The only question is when. And if there is, I'm in for it."

Emily's heart sank. "Which side?"

"Why, the South, of course. We can't let the Northern states tell us what to do." He looked at her curiously. "What's Hardin going to do if war breaks out?"

"We haven't talked of it."

Even her mother looked startled at this. "Child, how have you avoided the subject?"

Emily shrugged. "I have been hoping things would work out for the best, and that war could be avoided."

"Optimist," said Alec.

"In any case, if Mr.—President—Lincoln gives Hardin a position, the question will be decided for us." Emily allowed herself for a moment to dream of a foreign post—Rome, perhaps, or St. Petersburg—far away from all the messiness on her side of the Atlantic.

"Do you want Lincoln to give him a position?" Alec asked.

"Of course I do."

"Even if Kentucky secedes? Even with me fighting for the South?"

Emily glared at her younger brother. "I liked you better when you didn't give a thought to these things."

"Men have to."

Her mother sighed. "Mary certainly did put us in an awkward position by marrying that man. I never really did approve, you know—not that Mary or her sisters ever cared for my advice. Now, look, girls, what Grandma brought for you!"

Soon, Hardin's letters began arriving from Washington. His presidency just days old, poor President Lincoln was still beset with office seekers, and between that and the situation in the South was already beginning to look tired and worn. Mrs. Lincoln, who gave Emily her love, was appalled at the state of the Executive Mansion, which did not appear to have been cleaned since President Jackson was in residence. Hardin was not staying at the White House but at the Metropolitan Hotel (the Willard being too full, and expensive to boot). Mrs. Lincoln could have probably found him a place to sleep, but there were already grumblings in the press about the swarm of Todds in Washington, all seemingly wanting office. (If a man had said that to his face, Hardin assured Emily, he would have demanded satisfaction. Was he joking? Emily wondered.)

Julia Baker, Mrs. Edwards's married daughter, was not exactly acting like a married woman, Mrs. Lincoln was complaining; she had stayed up rather too late in the parlor, chatting with men who were not her husband. Bob Lincoln had returned to Harvard and was quite glad to be shed of Washington. The younger Lincoln boys had caught the measles but were recovering apace. Mrs. Lincoln was planning a boat excursion to Mount Vernon and had invited Hardin to come along, and he would certainly take the opportunity to visit the home of the great George Washington.

It was so pleasant and gossipy a letter that it might have been written by Mary herself. What was missing, Emily realized after she had sent her own reply letter, was any mention of politics. Or anything about what President Lincoln might have said to Hardin.

MARY

MARCH TO APRIL 1861

Though Mary had been appalled to see the shabby state of the Executive Mansion—if what was set out were the best furnishings, one could only imagine what had been discarded—Mr. Lincoln was perfectly indifferent, and the younger boys were charmed by its myriad possibilities. Within days of their arrival, they had commandeered the attic, and then naturally progressed to the roof.

Mr. Lincoln, on the other hand, was drawn to the lawn. As March bled into April and the state of the country became more dire, he could often be found there, roaming about and sometimes stopping to gaze into the night sky. Mary, knowing the man's need for solitude, generally left him undisturbed, but one evening in April, deeming that he had been out there in the chilly air too long, took to the lawn herself. "What have you been doing here for such a confoundedly long period, Mr. Lincoln?"

"Thinking, Mary. Thinking that if war is going to come, I wish it would come on. If a tooth must be pulled, do it quickly."

After South Carolina had seceded, the Confederate government had demanded that the Union abandon Fort Sumter, the federal stronghold that had protected Charleston Harbor for decades. Naturally, the request had been refused. A Union ship bringing supplies to the fort had been fired upon in January, and Mr. Lincoln had scarcely taken office when the fort's commander informed him that he would run out of supplies in six weeks. Days before, Mr. Lincoln had made the decision to resupply the garrison, knowing that to do so might provoke an attack by the rebel government, spoiling for a fight.

The ships had sailed, and now the nation waited.

Mary took her husband's hand and followed his eyes as they stared up into the stars. "Mr. Lincoln, you have done your best. If those fools are determined to fight, it will not be your fault."

"No, I'm reasonably humble, but not so much I can put the blame all on my shoulders. And I suppose that would be arrogance in its own way."

"Do wax philosophical inside. You'll catch your death of cold."

He resisted her attempts to lead him away. "No, Mary. Leave me a few more minutes."

Mary sighed, but obeyed. As she turned back to the house, she heard her husband reciting the familiar lines from *Julius Caesar*, "The fault, dear Brutus, is not in our stars, but in ourselves."

❧

The next day, someone rushed in, bearing a telegram. The rebels had begun bombarding Fort Sumter.

President Lincoln took the news calmly, as Mary had expected, while the boys promptly began measures to fortify the White House roof. In that task they found a willing adviser in the shape of Mr. Helm, who after a ridiculous show of independence had given in to Mary's demand that he move from his hotel to the White House, where he could lodge for free and enjoy the company of his wife's relations. Mr. Lincoln had been working on getting him a position commensurate with his talents, she knew, but it was a delicate matter made difficult by the presence of so many deserving Todds also wanting positions. And now Mr. Lincoln had more important things on his mind—as, apparently, did Mr. Helm, whose gloom lifted only when he was roughhousing with the Lincoln boys or serving as their engineering corps.

On Sunday, April 14, Mr. Lincoln accompanied Mary and the boys to church. It was the first time since the attack that Mary, who by custom could not pay visits but could only receive them, had been in any gathering outside the White House, and as she sat in her pew, she could feel the strange atmosphere of a Washington that was beset by excitement and by worry at the same time. She could also look around the neighboring pews and find more of them empty, deserted by Southern sympathizers.

Mr. Lincoln dutifully listened to the sermon, but she caught him surreptitiously scribbling something in a memorandum book. When they returned home—how strange to call the Executive Mansion "home"!—he closeted himself with the Cabinet and General Scott and did not emerge until early evening. "Well, we've done it," he told Mary. "Sent out for seventy-five thousand men to stop this nonsense." He stroked his beard and cleared his throat—a combination that Mary had learned meant that he was about to say something she would not like.

"Say it, Mr. Lincoln."

"Well, we're in an awkward spot here in Washington, between two states of highly dubious loyalty. Virginia could vote to secede at any hour, and Maryland's not much better."

"I am aware of those things, Mr. Lincoln. I do believe you have seen me read the newspapers from time to time."

"So if the Southerners decided to invade, we'd be ripe for it. Maybe you might want to take the boys north for a little while. Visit Bob at Harvard. Take Cousin Lizzie with you."

Mary gazed at her husband icily. "No, Mr. Lincoln. I obliged you in Baltimore. I shall not do so again."

"Well, I tried."

"If there comes a time when the boys are in danger, of course I will take them out of the city. But I won't give the rebels the satisfaction of seeing us flee before there is any need to."

"You have a point," Mr. Lincoln said. Not that it was necessary for him to acknowledge that, for Mary knew she was perfectly right.

But Mr. Lincoln had a point as well. As everyone awaited the news from the convention that had been called in Richmond to decide the secession question in Virginia, Willie and Tad, after taking their field glasses to the roof with them, reported that some residents of Alexandria, just across the Potomac, had already hoisted the rebel flag. With each day that passed with no certain news, the mood inside and outside the White House became more anxious. The job seekers began returning to their distant homes, and even while Mary made a point of riding down Pennsylvania Avenue in the handsome open carriage that had been given to the Lincolns upon their arrival in the city, to show that the President's family was still in town, others were loading their goods upon wagons and shuttering their houses.

"It's terrible," Elizabeth Keckly, Mary's colored dressmaker, told her when she came by to fit a spring dress for Mary. A former slave who had bought her freedom some years ago, Mrs. Keckly had dressed some of the most fashionable ladies of the city, including Mrs. Jefferson Davis, whose husband had been in Congress before he turned traitor and accepted the presidency of Seccessia, as Mr. Hay liked to call it. Hearing of her clientele, Mary had been only too happy to engage her when another doyenne of Washington society recommended her services. So far, Mrs. Keckly had not disappointed, and not only could she dress Mary beautifully, but she was an excellent source of news. "People are afraid there will be a shortage of food if the farmers can't get into Washington with their goods, and some are claiming that there are thousands of men in Virginia just waiting for the signal to attack."

"Surely not." But Mary could not help but think of the vile mob in Baltimore who had jeered the presidential party. Then she jumped, upending Mrs. Keckly's workbasket. "Good Lord above!"

Every bell in the Executive Mansion's elaborate system was pealing madly. Mary's first thought was that the President was furious about something and was summoning his secretaries, but such imperiousness was not like him at all. Her second thought was far more terrifying. "An attack!" she screamed and ran toward the President's office, sparing a thought to thank Providence that her dress was pinned securely.

There, she found nearly every soul in the White House gathered around a puzzled-looking president. So absorbed had he been in the map he was studying that he appeared not even to have noticed the bells until the influx into his office. "What is this? I didn't ring for anyone."

Mr. Helm grimaced. "I think I have the answer for you. Will you and Mrs. Lincoln accompany me to the attic?"

They climbed the stairs to the attic, where they were met by boyish laughter and the culprits—Tad, manning the heart of the bell system, and Willie, standing beside him, not helping but certainly not hindering either. "Father! Wasn't that a grand prank! Uncle Hardin showed us the other day how the bells worked."

"Not with this result in mind, boys."

"Yes," Tad said happily. "It was all my idea."

"I did help him get started," Willie said.

"No more attic," the President said. As ever when his sons got into mischief, he was fighting back a smile. "At least for a week. But we know everything works shipshape in case of an emergency, don't we?"

⌒◦⌒

When news from Virginia did arrive on April 18, it arrived not in single spies but in battalions, as Mr. Lincoln's beloved Shakespeare had put it. Not only had Virginia voted to secede the day before, but the secessionists there had concocted a plan to seize the arsenal at Harper's Ferry even before the vote had taken place. Then tidings came from Maryland, as if that state had not wanted to be outdone by Virginia, that the Pennsylvania Volunteers, responding to the President's call for troops, had been attacked by a mob in Baltimore while marching from one train station to another. Other states were supplying men as well, but these troops were still en route—and would have to pass through Baltimore too.

There being no place to house the bedraggled and bruised Pennsylvanians when their train finally pulled into Washington, they were quartered at the Capitol. President Lincoln hastened down the Mall to greet and thank them, and returned to the Executive Mansion with a hand aching from being shaken. "Farm boys, most of them," he told Mary. "They were in awe of their quarters with the fine carpets and the big looking glasses. I told them I felt a bit the same way myself when I was in Congress. They're fine young men. I just wish there were more than five hundred of them."

That night, all of Washington paced the floor, waiting for the rumored invasion from Virginia. Mr. Lincoln, exhausted, went to bed early, saying that he needed a good sleep to cope with a rebel horde. Sprawled across the East Room were Senator James Lane's Frontier Guards, assembled by the senator to protect the White House, while Mary's Lexington neighbor Cassius Clay, a cousin of Henry Clay and such a rabid abolitionist it was considered miraculous that he was still among the living, organized his own guard to patrol the city streets.

Unable to settle to sleep, Mary invited Mr. Helm to join her in the Red Room. "I hope the boys have not been taking too decided an advantage of your good nature, Mr. Helm."

"No, they have been a welcome distraction." He smiled, an expression Mary had not seen much on his face as of late. "And as much as I love my little girls, it's pleasant to be around boys for a change. Sometimes I feel outnumbered at home."

"As do I. But I hope nothing is weighing on your mind more than the general state of things. No ill news from Emily?"

"No, she and the girls are well. But I was very grieved to hear of Virginia's secession, and more grieved that we are heading toward war. I had hoped it could be avoided. Perhaps I was naive."

"I do pray Kentucky stays in. Do you think she will?"

"I don't dare predict anything at this point." Mr. Helm rose and took her hand. "Forgive me, Mrs. Lincoln, for sounding like an old man before my time, but I am bone tired, and I owe Emily a letter. I am going to retire for the evening. If you or the boys should need anything during the night, of course, I am at your service." He paused. "But ringing might not be the best way to summon me."

∽ᴈ∾

Soon after the Lincolns had come to Washington, Mrs. Mary Taft, the wife of the patent examiner Horatio Taft, had visited Mary, and mentioned that she had two young boys, close in age to Willie and Tad. Mary had invited the Taft boys to the White House, and they and the Lincoln boys were soon inseparable.

With the boys had come their sixteen-year-old sister, Julia. Mr. Lincoln had taken a liking to all three children, but Julia had become his pet. He once said that she reminded him of his sister, Sarah, who had died in childbirth as a young woman, but Mary wondered how much poor Sarah Lincoln Grigsby in her log cabin on the Indiana frontier could have had in common with dainty little Julia, with her bouncing curls and her Parisian French and her long-suffering airs. "Mama will still not let me wear a hoop," she announced on April 19. Washington had awakened to find its streets free of attackers, but also free of the hoped-for Northern troops, save for the Pennsylvanians. But Julia Taft clearly had her own concerns, and Mary was more than happy to put aside her own fears and listen. "She says I have to be seventeen."

"Well, my dear, you could always try what I did. When I was a child, and of course the nice crinolines we have today were yet to be invented, the ladies would sew a reed underneath their dresses, to make them hang more nicely. I longed to do the same with my own dresses, but my stepmother, reasonably enough, I suppose, thought I was far too young. So my stepmother's niece and I found a neighbor who allowed us to have some branches off her weeping willow, and when everyone had gone to bed, we lit a candle and commenced our work, sewing the branches into our dresses.

"We worked all night, and in the morning we were all dressed in our creations and ready to leave for church when my stepmother caught sight of us. She is an excitable woman at the best of times, and trust me, my dear, that was not the best of times. She told us that we would be the laughingstocks of Lexington if we turned up at church in such apparel, and ordered us to change immediately. My brothers, meanwhile, were laughing themselves sick. Naturally, I flew into a fury, and it ended with me being sent to my room in high dudgeon, where I remained for the entire day. But my dear father made it right a few weeks later by bringing us beautiful pink muslin from New Orleans, and my stepmother in a moment of kindness allowed me to direct the sewing woman as how to make it, within rea—"

"M-Mama!" Tad ran in. As always when he was excited, he could not speak coherently, and it fell to Willie and the Taft boys, on his heels, to yell, "There's been a riot in Baltimore!"

"Men were killed!"

"Trouble at Harper's Ferry!"

"We could be attacked any hour!"

Mary gasped, and Julia tried to swoon but had to settle for falling back into a chair. Mercifully, the next person to enter the room was an adult. "Mr. Helm, what is happening?"

"As the boys said, when the Sixth Massachusetts Volunteers were marching between stations in Baltimore this morning, a mob began throwing stones at them and beating the men they could catch. The volunteers fired at the mob, some of the mob fired back. A few men have been killed, and many injured. But they managed to get on the train at last."

"And Harper's Ferry?"

"Those were good tidings for President Lincoln, actually. The lieutenant in charge there, believing he could not prevail against an attack by the South, destroyed the arsenal there so it could not of any use to the Confederacy."

"And the attack?"

"There are rumors that a force is gathered at Alexandria, ready to attack the city tonight."

"We have to fortify the roof!" Tad said. He pulled on Mr. Helm's arm. "You must help us, Uncle Hardin."

"I—I must talk to your mother, Tad. But I will come to you shortly."

The four boys ran off, and at a nod from Mary, Julia reluctantly followed. When they seemed safe from another invasion by the children, Mr. Helm said, "Mrs. Lincoln, I must be leaving—the White House, at any rate, if not Washington altogether. Your husband has made me a very generous offer, and I must consider it on my own."

"A generous offer? Then surely you must take it. Do not make it unnecessarily hard on yourself, Mr. Helm. You know how fond we are of you and Emily, and how we wish to see the two of you prosper. Besides, I am certain that such an offer would make her very happy, and of course your wife's happiness should be the paramount consideration with you, as it should be with all men."

He managed a smile. "If only I could take your advice, Mrs. Lincoln."

"In any case, while you are mulling over this offer, we need you here in Washington, Mr. Helm."

Mr. Helm shook his head. "What can one man do? And with the arsenal gone, any danger is averted. In any case, my wife and daughters need me as well."

"You could send for them." But Mary knew how weak that argument was, with women and children pouring out of Washington to points north and south.

Mr. Helm didn't even bother to reply. "I will keep my promise to the boys to help them fortify the roof. And then I will leave."

In a hour or two, he returned, his carpetbag in hand. Mary had scarcely seen Mr. Lincoln since his meager breakfast that morning, but he emerged from his office to bid Mr. Helm goodbye. "Don't think I underestimate your generosity, Mr. Lincoln," Mr. Helm said.

"I do not at all. If my conscience would allow me—"

"Say nothing more of it. When you make your decision, tell me."

The men clasped hands, and Mary blew Mr. Helm a parting kiss. "Do send Emily my love, and bring her and those darling little daughters of yours to Washington when all this is past. With her beauty, she will be the belle of the town."

"Goodbye, Mrs. Lincoln. I will do that if at all possible."

He turned away down the White House lawn. When he was well out of earshot, Mary said, "Now, Mr. Lincoln, will you tell me what offer you made to Mr. Helm?"

"Later, Molly." He gave her an absent peck on the cheek. "I've got to get back to that confounded office."

∾ 6 ∾

EMILY

APRIL 1861

I n his telegram, Hardin had told her not to take the trouble to meet him at the station, but after a six-week absence, what wife would heed that advice? So when Hardin's train pulled in, Emily and the girls were there, the girls in their matching dresses Mrs. Todd had had made for them, Emily in a brand-new bonnet that she knew brought out her dark eyes. Not caring a fig for what the bystanders thought, she embraced him as soon as he stepped upon the platform. "Darling!"

Hardin kissed her and scooped up his daughters, smiling. "It's good to be home."

They walked toward Phil, their man who had been a wedding gift from Hardin's father, and the waiting carriage, Emily chattering away. "I was so worried about you with the news from Washington, and so relieved when we heard that the danger had passed. Was Mary dreadfully upset? I know she used to get upset over the smallest things in Springfield—thunderstorms and everything. Phil, doesn't Mr. Helm look thinner to you? Hardin, do you like Phil's new jacket?" They settled into the carriage, and Emily took a breath. "Well? I read in the paper that President Lincoln offered you a paymaster's job, but I know nothing about that, and you weren't kind enough to give me the details in advance. Can you tell me now, sir?"

Hardin looked at the back of Phil's neck. "We'll talk when we get home, my dear."

The talk was postponed longer than Emily would have wished, for Hardin had bought gifts for everyone, which had to be distributed. Finally, Maggie, the girls' nurse, led away her charges for their naps, and Hardin sat on the sofa beside Emily. "The President did offer me the paymaster's job, Emily. It was a kind offer, and a very generous one."

Emily clasped his hand.

"But I refused it."

"You—what?"

"Read this."

Emily stared at the letter he handed her, written by President Lincoln and offering the position as an army paymaster, which would bring with it a rank of major.

"It is more generous than you probably realize, because I would be the youngest major in the army, and the job would suit my health. And were I to choose to transfer into the cavalry, I would likely be a colonel within a year. Many men would covet this."

"And you refused it."

Hardin rose. "I wanted so badly to take this. President and Mrs. Lincoln were as kind to me in the White House as they were in their parlor in Springfield. I saw how he treated the common soldiers who came to Washington, how he shook their hands and thanked them. I saw how even under the strain he has been under, he took time to wrestle with his sons where many men in his position might have shooed them off with servants. I came away with more affection for him than I had before my visit, and my affection then was considerable. But I could not forget that his cause was not my cause, and that even if I did not directly participate in crushing the South, I would be aiding those who did.

"So I told President Lincoln I would think about his offer. He understood, and agreed. I rode over to Arlington, where Colonel Lee was kind enough to see me. He had been offered the command of the Union troops in place of General Scott, whose health no longer permits him to take the field, but he refused, and when I came, I found him in even a more dismal frame of mind than I was. I inquired about his health, and he told me that he had just resigned his commission in the army.

"I showed him the letter and told him that I was married to President Lincoln's sister-in-law. He told me that he could not advise me well in his own state of mind, but that he believed all signs pointed to a great war and he had resigned because he could not strike at his own people. And neither, my dear, can I. Even though we are in a border state, which may or may not secede, my heart is with those who have. The states cannot be dictated to by an overstrong federal government, or the republic will perish. So with that in mind, I sent Mr. Lincoln a letter refusing the commission—I could not bring myself to do it in person, and I think ill of myself for it—and I came home."

"But you went to Washington specifically to ask for a position! And this is how you treat my sister and her husband!"

"Emily, it was you who wanted me to ask for a position. I should not have agreed."

"And before you refused, couldn't you have consulted me? All these weeks I have been hoping, building these castles in the air. And then when I saw the paper... Couldn't you have told me what was in your mind?"

"I should have. You are right. I should have consulted you, too. Emily, trust me, refusing President Lincoln was the most painful thing I have ever done." He grimaced. "Except perhaps for telling you of my decision."

"Do you have any more news for me, Mr. Helm?"

"Yes." Hardin looked at his feet. "I will be going to Montgomery to offer my services to President Davis."

Emily rose to her feet and stalked downstairs to the kitchen, where

Bridgett, their Irish hired girl, was preparing Hardin's favorite meal. "Are you ill, Mrs. Helm?"

"No. Keep on with what you were doing."

She stalked back upstairs into the parlor and, ignoring Hardin's hurt-puppy look, picked up the newspaper and pretended to read it. Soon, Bridgett had prepared their supper, which they ate in near silence. After supper, Hardin cast wistful glances at the piano, which Emily ignored. At the earliest possible hour, she retired to the bedroom.

"Emily, my love—"

That morning, she had put on her loveliest undergarments, all with the thought of having Hardin take them off her. She allowed him to do so now, but he might as well have been taking them off a dressmaker's form. When he had reached her chemise, he kissed her on the cheek. "Please try to understand, Emma. If there were some way I could have accepted his offer without compromising my principles, I would have."

She lay down on her side of the bed, facing the wall. After a moment, she heard Hardin settle next to her with a deep sigh. For hours she lay there, rehearsing her grievance against him.

Somehow, she fell asleep. When she awoke, the sun was rising, and Hardin's side of the bed was empty. Pulling on a wrapper, she delved into the casket full of letters that she kept on her dressing table. Then she went into the parlor.

Hardin was smoking a cigar, something he usually did only in his small study. "I beg your pardon," he said stiffly. "Shall I move?"

"No." She sat beside him. This time, it was he who stared straight ahead as she spoke. "A wise man once wrote me something. *Eight months ago today, our fates were united for life—*"

He turned to her and stubbed out his cigar.

"*As yet we have known only the bright sunshine of life. I hope our bright future may never be dimmed by dark shadows, but if it should be otherwise ordained by an all-wise and omnipotent God; we must be prepared to bow down to his will with Christian fortitude.* We've not been tested, Hardin."

He nodded. "We've been very lucky. Our girls are healthy, and we've had no ill fortune."

"I'm terrified of what is to come."

He stroked her hair. "So am I. I wish I could take no part in it—just attend to my law practice as if our world were not falling in pieces around us. But that is not in my nature. One day our children will ask what part I took in this, and can I look them in the face and say, 'Nothing'? I cannot. Nor could I tell them that I abandoned the South because of my affection for President Lincoln. And my affection is real."

"Hardin, you know that I would never ask you to go against your conscience. You also know that my first loyalty is to you. All I ask is that you confide in me, instead of leaving me thinking that you are doing one thing when you are doing another."

"Agreed. And I am sorry I grieved you."

"When do you plan to go to Montgomery?"

"I would like a few days with you and the children first. And I will need someone to write a letter of introduction, I suppose, as I'm sure President Davis, like Mr. Lincoln, has all sorts of strangers calling upon him." He gave Emily a half smile. "Who knows, darling? Perhaps he might have a paymaster position of his own to bestow."

Emily tried to chuckle, but did not quite succeed.

❧ 7 ❧

MARY

APRIL TO JULY 1861

O n April 25, the train bearing the blue-blooded volunteers of the Seventh New York pulled into Washington, and with it, all the misery and tension of the past week vanished, as the city now had sufficient troops to defend itself against attack. President Lincoln was overheard whistling, and the boys declared their fortification of the roof a grand success in intimidating the enemy.

Only the letter the President handed Mary two days later dampened her spirits. In it, Mr. Helm graciously, yet firmly, declined the generous offer the President had made to him. "I'm not surprised," her husband said, stuffing the letter in his coat pocket where it might be found some days later. "I just wish he'd come in person, but perhaps he was afraid I would have talked him out of it. I certainly would have tried."

"He is an ingrate, Mr. Lincoln, for refusing it."

"No, he's a man of honor. Misguided honor, I must say, but honor." He sighed. "If he ever changes his mind, trust me, I'll welcome him back."

Mary shook her head in disgust. "And no thought to Emily, after I specifically asked him to keep her happiness in mind! She does not care for politics, as you must remember, but I'm sure she would have found the society agreeable here, and it would have been so pleasant to have her nearby. I was so looking forward to taking her to the opera! But she adores Hardin, and I suppose she'll support him in whatever he does. We Todd women do stand by our husbands."

"You must admit that's an admirable trait, Molly."

Mr. Helm was not her only relation to turn traitor. In due course Mary received a letter from her little sister Elodie in Selma, informing her that she had engaged herself to a Nathaniel Dawson of that city and mentioning, almost as a point of pride, that he had joined the rebel army. ("Confederate" was the term she used, of course.) Mary wrote a stern letter back to her, but she knew Elodie would only dig her heels in further, if she hadn't already married the man just to make a point.

Elodie had also taken care to let her know that no fewer than three of her brothers—David, Sam, and long-estranged George—had enlisted in the rebel army, the latter as a surgeon. Only Levi, loyal to the Union but too old and ill to be of any use to it, and Alec had stayed out of the fledgling war so far. And how long could she expect her youngest brother to avoid a fight?

Then there was her stepmother. Out of nothing but sheer civility, Mary had invited the woman and Kitty, the sole sister at home, to visit her in Washington, even though she knew a miserable time would be had by all. But Mrs. Todd had refused, saying she was needed by her own children. All of who seemed to be doing just fine on their own, if falling into full-fledged rebellion could be called that.

Mary's long-awaited trip north proved a welcome distraction from her thoughts. With Lizzie Grimsley as her companion, she traveled to Philadelphia and then New York on a mission to refurbish the White House from top to bottom. And why should she not take the opportunity to make some purchases for herself? It had been some years since the Lincolns had had to scrimp on their purchases, but the lean years of their early marriage had left her wary of spending—until now, when the owners of the grandest stores in the country rushed from their offices to welcome her personally to their retail palaces and to press their choicest wares upon her. As the wife of the President-elect, she had received something of this attention when she had gone to New York before the inaugural journey, but that was nothing as to her situation now.

Lizzie Grimsley followed bemusedly in her wake, occasionally buying a small gift to send home to Springfield, but their main companions on their trip were the reporters, who popped up at every store entrance, no matter how nondescript the party's equipage or how thick the ladies wore their veils in vain attempts to throw them off their tracks. "I will never get used to having people recording my every move," Lizzie said as they had their morning coffee in their suite at the Metropolitan Hotel the day after a particularly fruitful shopping trip. "The worst part is, I find myself dressing for the press now, lest they pronounce me dowdy."

"The papers have been very complimentary to you thus far."

"That's the rub; I feel I must keep them that way—even though I know that no one really cares what Lizzie Grimsley from Springfield puts on her back. Not even Mr. Grimsley cared, which is one of the many reasons he is no longer my husband. But if it is that bad for me, how much worse it is for you!"

"I don't mind it when they're polite about me," Mary said. "In fact, I admit I rather like it."

When they finally returned to Washington, having first gone to Cambridge to visit Bob, she could pronounce the trip an unqualified success. The New York papers had been most approving, and the Executive Mansion had benefitted hugely from her attention. She had ordered a magnificent set of Haviland china to take the place of the mismatched and chipped pieces that now sat on its tables, and indeed, the pattern charmed her so much she thought she might order a second set for her own use, minus the United States arms. Soon new carpets would grace the floor of the public rooms, topped by new chairs and sofas and shielded from the sunlight by new curtains. And

Mary had not forgotten those little touches that made a room special, such as vases, or the practical ones, such as new bellpulls.

There was much more to be done, of course. And if only Mr. Lincoln would let her refurbish his office! But so far he had stood firm, so it would most likely resemble the magpie's nest that his Springfield office had been.

Mr. Lincoln greeted her warmly at the White House and even allowed her to tell him about her purchases, although he was far more interested in hearing about Bob. He was distracted, however, because Virginia was set to ratify its decision to secede, and he and his Cabinet had determined that once that event took place, he would send Union troops to seize the city of Alexandria, just across the river from Washington. Among them would be the Lincolns' friend Elmer Ellsworth, who in April had hastened to New York to raise a force of Zouaves, which had been dubbed the Fire Zouaves since most were New York City firemen. Already they had had the delight of putting out a fire in Washington when the building next to the Willard Hotel had been ablaze, threatening its venerable neighbor.

Although Colonel Ellsworth and his men were camped some distance from the White House—on a hill near the city's insane asylum, which had produced its fair share of jokes—the colonel often rode over to the mansion to chat with President Lincoln and the boys and to see his friends from Springfield, Mr. Hay and Mr. Nicolay—and to pick up letters from his fiancée, who sent them in Mr. Nicolay's care.

As everyone in the Lincoln family was fond of the colonel, he had as much liberty within the Executive Mansion as did Willie and Tad—except that Colonel Ellsworth, unlike the boys, did not barge into the middle of Cabinet meetings and demand that the President give him his undivided attention. So Mary was not surprised when on May 22, the eve of the ratification vote, Colonel Ellsworth knocked on the door of the Blue Room. "Good evening, Mrs. Lincoln," he said. "I wanted to welcome you back from your trip."

"I am glad you came, because in my hurry leaving the city, I did not congratulate you and your men for putting out that fire. It would have been devastating to lose the Willard."

"The boys had a grand time putting it out. They've been a little restless here. Not enough to do." He grinned. "But they'll soon have plenty of excitement."

Mary was glad Bob was not there to see Colonel Ellsworth looking so sunburned and fit. When she had visited Bob, he had alluded, worrisomely, to leaving college and joining the army, as so many other young men were doing since the fall of Fort Sumter. But Mary saw no need for that just yet—if ever. And here was Colonel Ellsworth looking like a recruiting poster! Pushing that thought from her mind, she smiled at the young man. "I see you have a letter. From Miss Spafford, I presume?"

"Yes, Mrs. Lincoln, and a long-awaited one."

"You must tell Miss Spafford to write more faithfully. Why, my little sister Kitty would be happy enough to take her place, you can tell her."

"I didn't do anything to make her think… Did I, Mrs. Lincoln?"

He looked so guilt-stricken that Mary hastened to say, "No, no, I was merely jesting. Kitty has no interest in any particular young man that I know of, although I know she did admire your drilling, as did other ladies. But in any case, she is down South at the moment and likely to be attracted by some secessionist as my sister Elodie has been."

Colonel Ellsworth looked simultaneously relieved at not having captured Kitty's heart and disgusted at the thought that a rebel might steal it. He gave her a little bow. "I must be going, ma'am. The men will be wondering where I've got to."

Mary smiled again, knowing that Colonel Ellsworth's devotion to his b'hoys, as they were nicknamed, was as complete as those brawny men's devotion to their colonel. "Good night, Colonel. If I do not see you before you take Alexandria, please know my prayers are with you."

On the morning of May 24, President Lincoln came to the breakfast table with the news that in the middle of the night, eight troops of men had left Washington for Alexandria, some by boat, some by bridge. He was hopeful that the city would be taken without a fight, as many of its citizens, recognizing the city's vulnerable position, had already fled, and most important, the militia was gone as well.

Hoping to hear good news soon, Mary spent a pleasant enough morning with her plans for the refurbishment of the Executive Mansion. She was pondering over some swatches of fabric with Lizzie Grimsley when President Lincoln, who hardly ever entered the private rooms of the house this time of day, slowly walked in. Mary's surprise at his entrance gave way to alarm when she saw that that there were tears on his face. "Why, what is it?"

"Bad. Very bad. Colonel Ellsworth was killed this morning."

"You mean there was resistance after all?"

"No. None at all." Her husband wiped his eyes. "They had taken the town without incident and were walking through the streets when Ellsworth saw the Marshall House Hotel flying the rebel flag. You've heard the boys talk about that confounded flag; you can see it from the roof here plain as day through a spyglass. Anyway, Ellsworth, who was getting ready to secure the telegraph office, decided that it could wait a little while, and instead he took a small group of men and entered the hotel, then headed up to the roof and took the flag. As he came downstairs with the flag—crowing a bit, I suspect—the owner of the hotel, a rascal named James Jackson, stepped out of the shadows and shot Ellsworth straight through the heart. Just as he fell, the boy below him grabbed his rifle and shot Jackson in the face, then bayoneted him to make sure he was finished off. So there we have it, two men dead."

"Oh, Mr. Lincoln!"

"It was a foolish act, I know. The damned flag could have waited. He should have secured the place first. But how can I blame him for showing such spirit? They told me that elsewhere in the town when the Stars and Stripes was raised that there were cheers. That would have gratified our poor boy. It certainly gives me some comfort."

Lizzie had been listening to this in silent horror. "He was all his parents had, was he not?"

"Yes. His brother died not all that long ago. They are in poor health, and he was their main support. I will have to do something for them."

"Where is he now?" Mary asked.

"The Navy Yard. I have ordered that he lie in state here tomorrow before being taken to his parents in New York."

"Please, let me go see him."

The President nodded. "I'll meet you there later."

When Mary arrived at the Navy Yard, Senator Ira Harris, newly elected from New York, offered to bring the soldier who had killed Jackson to meet her. Hesitantly she agreed, and in a few moments a sandy-haired young man known as Frank Brownell, barely past boyhood and as small as Colonel Ellsworth, stood before her, toying nervously with his bloodstained suspenders as he told her the same story that the President had, but with a New York honk. As others gathered around him, he grew more animated. "The blasted flag was so big that the colonel could hardly carry it down those narrow stairs," he said, spreading his hands wide. "So he was fiddling with that, and not paying attention, when this filthy rebel steps into our path. He fired just as I saw he had a rifle. Poor Ellsworth fell down the stairs dead, just as I shot the son of a bitch who shot him. Then I ran my bayonet straight through his guts."

"Oh my," Mary said as Mr. Brownell demonstrated as best he could his bayoneting of Jackson.

"Sorry, ma'am," Brownell said meekly. "Not language for ladies, I know. I got carried away thinking about it."

"It is quite all right, Mr. Brownell, and I am glad your aim was so good. I am sure the President will see to it that you are well rewarded."

Not long afterward, the President arrived, and the two of them went inside the engine room where their young friend lay on a table, bundled in a red blanket and with the Union flag draped over his breast. Mary had seen her mother and her young son in death and had gazed into any number of caskets at funerals, but never had she seen the corpse of someone who had died violently. But Colonel Ellsworth's face, when President Lincoln gently uncovered it, was placid; only his disordered hair showed anything amiss. Instinctively, Mary reached out to smooth his dark curls and recoiled when her hand struck an area matted with blood. His or his killer's, God only knew. She hung her head and sobbed.

President Lincoln carefully replaced the blanket, paced around, and then uncovered the colonel's face once more. "My boy! My boy! Was it necessary that this sacrifice should be made?" He wiped his eyes, then straightened. "I hate to leave him alone here."

"We'll be with him all night, President Lincoln," called Corporal Brownell. "Some of us guarding the place, some of us sitting here."

"Yes, of course," the President said. He touched Colonel Ellsworth gently on the cheek, then turned to Corporal Brownell. "Tell me everything that happened," he commanded. "I want to hear it from you in particular."

∼≈∽

The next day, a funeral service was held for Colonel Ellsworth in the East Room, after which a funeral procession wended its way from the Executive Mansion to the railway depot. Mary, riding in a carriage alongside her husband and members of the Cabinet, watched as the hearse was loaded onto the car, laden with black crepe, that would take the remains home to New York.

No one, not even the President, had the heart to attend to business when they finally returned to the White House. The President shut himself in his office, the boys moped in their room, and the President's secretaries, who had been friends with Ellsworth, smoked their cigars in gloomy silence. Mary sewed for a while until she saw her mail, received that morning but forgotten until now. She sorted through the letters. Already there was a bill or two from her New York trip. A letter from her sister Elizabeth, another from a friend in Springfield. A letter from her sister Kitty, who was in Selma with Mrs. Todd visiting Martha and Elodie. Curious to hear the news about Elodie's ill-advised engagement to that rebel officer, she picked up the letter and read, after some moaning from Kitty about the dullness of Selma and complaints about the beastly hot weather, *I hear Col. Ellsworth is in Wash. Do tell him hello for me and wish him well even if he is a Yankee.*

Mary stared at the letter. Then, she reached for pen and paper, intending to break the sad news to Kitty by letter.

Suddenly, she pulled back her hand. Kitty would hear about the news in the paper, if she had not already. As a rebel, she had forfeited her right to any other notice.

In the weeks after poor Colonel Ellsworth's death, more and more soldiers filed into Washington, and Mary saw less and less of her husband, who when not meeting with his Cabinet was studying maps of the South. The best she could do was to coax him out for an afternoon carriage ride, and then only on the pretense that she required company.

Still, as spring gave way to summer, Mary found that she was enjoying Washington, war or no war, husband or no husband. On Saturday afternoons, the Marine Band played on the south lawn of the White House, which often had the effect of luring the President out on the porch, where he would stare wistfully at the flocks of gaily dressed young women picnicking on the lawn as "The Soldiers' Chorus" from *Faust* played in the background. Then, too, the Executive Mansion was looking more civilized each day, thanks to her refurbishing, and it was now a pleasure to seat herself in its rooms.

But the President had been busy in his own sphere as well, and on July 16, Washingtonians lined the streets and cheered as General McDowell and thirty-five thousand troops marched out of the capitol, destined for nearby Manassas, Virginia, the site of an important railroad junction which they planned to snatch from Confederate hands, then push on and capture Richmond, which after Virginia's secession had supplanted Montgomery as the rebel capital. Standing on the White House lawn, Mary waved a handkerchief in one hand and held a parasol in the other, for the July day was blistering hot and humid. She could not help but notice that the men were marching gamely but not in a particularly orderly manner. President Lincoln had acknowledged their greenness, but had said, reasonably enough, that the Confederate troops were just as green.

Telegrams kept the President informed of the troops' progress, and the reporters who had followed the soldiers to the field performed that service for the public. As the days passed, no one in Washington, whether a senator, an office boy, or a washerwoman, found it possible to concentrate on his or her work. Was the war about to end? Or was it just beginning?

On the morning of July 21, Congressmen and their families, the ladies bedecked in airy summer gowns and freshly trimmed bonnets, the men dapper in white suits and straw hats, headed out to Virginia in their carriages, prepared to picnic and watch what finally promised to be a battle. "You're not going with those gawkers, are you?" Mr. Lincoln asked when he heard.

"Certainly not. Such things are not my idea of entertainment." And what if one of her brothers or brothers-in-law had somehow found his way to Manassas? It did not bear thinking about, traitors or not. "I will go to church instead. Will you join me?"

The President hesitated, then grabbed his hat. "Not the day to shirk, I suppose."

She had never succeeded in figuring out exactly what her husband's religious beliefs were, although on the whole, she had decided he was a believer.

On this occasion, though, church hardly seemed worth the effort, for half the congregation was missing, having either traveled to the battle or stayed at home to await news, and the other half had their mind only partly on the Lord. Even the minister, Dr. Phineas Gurley, stumbled once or twice during his sermon, which was a good five or ten minutes shorter than usual.

When the service had finally ended and they returned to the Executive Mansion, the President hastened to the War Department, where he could read the telegraph dispatches as soon as they came in. At last, he emerged for his afternoon drive in good spirits. For a while, he said, it appeared that the Union had been losing ground, but it appeared that now the rebels were getting the worse of it.

Mary would have preferred a more scenic destination, but her husband ordered the carriage to head toward the Navy Yard, where Mary sat in the carriage and fanned herself—at least there was a breeze from the river—as the President and the commander discussed the battle. At about six, the President said, "Well, better get back," and they set off at a smart pace toward the White House.

Edward the doorkeeper's expression told them all they needed to know. Behind the door were the President's young secretaries, lined up like a miniature Greek chorus. "General McDowell is in retreat!"

"They want you at the War Department!"

"We've lost!"

"Well," the President said, replacing the hat he had just removed, "I'd best go there. Tell the boys good night for me, Mary."

He was gone until two in the morning. When he returned, it was not to bed but to his office, where the Cabinet had convened and a stream of weary battle-goers had begun to converge. Not daring to interrupt them, yet unwilling to go to bed with the world in such a state, Mary was lingering outside the office when she saw a familiar face departing from it: Robert Wilson, a visitor from Springfield who had served in the legislature with her husband at about the time when he had been courting. Not bothering with any of the niceties she would have otherwise paid a visitor, she accosted him with "Have you seen the President, Mr. Wilson?"

"I have."

"What did he tell you? Pray tell me."

Mr. Wilson sighed. "He would tell me little as I am not privy to matters of state here. But I asked him if he could tell me if the news was good or bad, and he said, in as sharp a tone as I've ever heard him speak, 'Damned bad.'"

❧

The next day, amid a drenching rain, the soldiers began returning to the city—most straggling in on foot, some heaped in carts where the living and the dead were commingled. Never had Mary, watching from the window, seen such a pitiful spectacle of young manhood. It was only a wonder that they did not have a gray-coated army pursuing them into the city, but evidently the rebels were content to stay put for now.

Following the battle, which the North would dub Bull Run after the name of a nearby creek and the South would simply call Manassas, the newspapers excoriated the President, who carried on coolly with his business while Washington fretted and drank and placed blame. He quickly appointed a young major general—George McClellan, who had campaigned successfully in western Virginia—as the head of the Military Division of the Potomac and rethought his strategy. Mr. Lincoln rode to Virginia to review those troops still in the field and came back in much better spirits. "The boys still want to fight. We just need to get them into better fighting trim," he told Mary that evening. "But enough of that. Come outside, Molly."

"The comet?"

"Yes. It's a clear night. Looks promising."

Some weeks before, a glorious comet had been spotted, and since then, nearly every night—at least before Bull Run—the President had wandered out to the White House lawn before retiring for the evening, hoping to spot it. This had not surprised Mary. Her husband was not one to rhapsodize about nature, but a few years back, she and Mr. Lincoln had visited Niagara Falls, and Mary had thought the man would never stop staring at the confluence of water and rock. So far, though, he had managed to spot the comet only a couple of times.

"They call it the war comet now, you know," he said as they arrived on the lawn. "I wish it weren't saddled with that name."

"Maybe they hope that the war will be like the comet—short-lived and glorious."

Her husband snorted. "Well, I doubt now that it will be short, and I can guarantee that it won't be glorious." He searched the sky.

Then they saw it, complete with a fine tail. As if putting on a command performance for the President, it streaked across the sky as they stared at it wordlessly.

Mary stole a look at her husband's face, illuminated by the sky. He was smiling, always a wonderful apparition to behold, and not one she had seen much lately. When the sky at last faded to starlight, he squeezed her hand.

"We'll lick them yet, Molly."

❧ 8 ❧

EMILY

MAY TO AUGUST 1861

In the middle of May, Hardin traveled to Montgomery to offer his services to President Davis, warning Emily that he might be sent off with a force of men immediately. That, and the will Hardin executed before he left Louisville, was disquieting. With his West Point education and with a letter of recommendation from Kentucky's governor, Emily was certain the Confederacy would want him in its army. But within a week or so Hardin returned, still a civilian. "I did speak to President Davis, but he thought there were enough soldiers at the moment, and that the best I could do was to return here and work to bring Kentucky into the Confederacy. I'm not a politician; my short time in the legislature taught me that. I'd as soon stick to practicing law." He gave Emily a mock glare. "Try to look displeased, dearest."

"Well, what can I say? It's good to have you home. What is President Davis like?"

"Not the most affable man I've met; if I could base my choice on personal liking, I'd be catching the next train to Washington. Rather stiff and cold, and good at making me feel rather foolish for thinking my offering my services might please him."

Emily patted his hand. "He is a foolish man. So what will you do now?"

"Practice law. As much as I can these days when no one knows what is going to happen day to day, and work with the State Guard." Following the abolitionist John Brown's failed attempt to incite a slave rebellion in Virginia in 1859, the Kentucky governor had urged that a state militia be formed to protect against similar insurrections, and the previous year, Hardin, to his great pleasure, had been chosen as its assistant inspector general. "And wait to see whether Kentucky can stay neutral. I don't think it can. To paraphrase Mr. Lincoln, it must become one thing or another. But the Guard is charged with upholding neutrality, and I will do it as long as possible."

And so he did, but over the next few weeks, he grew increasingly frustrated. The Kentucky legislature, largely sympathetic toward the Union, regarded most of the State Guard as Southern sympathizers—a fair point, Hardin conceded to Emily—and starved the militia of funds. Worse, the legislature had established a rival unit, the Home Guard, whose members were Unionists. Then the legislators required the members of the State Guard to take loyalty oaths.

Emily could gauge the growing seriousness of the situation from Hardin's cigar consumption. When he was irritated, he would retreat to the room he had commandeered as his study and smoke. On the evening of July 20, he not only smoked, but went out afterward for a long walk. "I thought perhaps you had drowned in the Ohio River," Emily said when he at last reappeared at their house.

"General Buckner quit the Guard today."

General Simon Buckner had been the man entrusted by the governor with forming the Guard; it was he who had appointed Hardin to his position. For well over a year, Hardin had been meeting with him at the Guard's headquarters at the Galt House Hotel, and Emily had occasionally invited him and his wife to dinner. "Why?"

"Why not? The legislature is doing its best to emasculate the Guard.

Questioning our loyalty at all times, keeping us short of weapons… He couldn't bear it anymore. One affront after another."

"What will he do?"

"Eventually, I suppose, he'll join the Confederate army."

"Proving the legislature right about his loyalty," Emily said archly.

Hardin mustered a grim. "Said like a true Todd. But we really have tried to uphold Kentucky's neutrality, regardless of what we feel in our hearts. I wish they gave us more credit for it."

"Hardin, are you going to resign, too?"

"I don't know. I'm thinking about it, especially as they seem bound and determined to worry us out of existence. But while I brood, a little music would be nice, my sweet."

Emily stepped to the piano, and Hardin was in good spirits when they went to bed that evening. It was Emily who lay frowning at the ceiling afterward, wondering what the future might hold.

The next evening, July 21, Hardin went to the Galt House, as he often did, to get news of the war. For several days, there had been skirmishes in northern Virginia, and as Elodie's fiancé was stationed there, the Helms had more than a passing interest in the matter. When Hardin came home, it was well past ten, and his face was at a variation with the words he spoke. "The South has had a victory, it appears."

"In Virginia?"

"Yes, at Manassas. General Beauregard's forces routed General McDowell's, they say."

"Is Captain Dawson safe?"

"I've no idea. What's come over the wires is preliminary. Go to bed, love. We'll know more tomorrow."

This was hardly conducive to a good night's sleep, but she obeyed. Early on July 22, they rode down to the telegraph office, where a crowd had gathered. Seeing the grim faces around her as the tidings Hardin had heard were confirmed, Emily realized with a jolt that without her noticing it, the tide in Kentucky was shifting from neutrality toward the North.

There was no news, good or ill, of Captain Dawson, only the

realization that the peace she had longed for was likely not at hand, with the South enjoying a victory and the North aching for revenge. She and Hardin left quickly and quietly. When they returned home, Hardin said, "I've come to two decisions. First, I'm resigning from the State Guard today. I'm sorry to do it, but it'll likely be disbanded soon anyway. The second you might guess. With this battle, more will follow, and if Kentucky declares for the Union, I cannot follow her there. So—"

"You're joining the Confederate army."

"I am, Em. I will be following my compatriots to Camp Boone."

Lying near the Kentucky-Tennessee border, Camp Boone had been established earlier that month as a recruiting camp for the Confederacy. Many of Hardin's friends from the State Guard had already made their way there. "When?"

"As soon as I can arrange my affairs at my law office and get you settled somewhere."

"And where are you going to settle me, Hardin?"

He did not notice the tone of her voice. "I was thinking you and the girls would be best at my father's. I couldn't bear it, worrying about you here in Louisville with so many Unionists about. Whereas my father's place will be quite safe, and he's on good terms with men from both sides."

"I do not want to live with your parents, Hardin."

He crinkled his brow. "I don't understand. You got along with them fine when I was riding the circuit, didn't you?"

"Yes. I like them very much."

"Perhaps you'd rather stay with your mother? She's been coming and going so much among you girls lately, I hadn't really thought about her as a possibility. But—"

"If you are leaving Kentucky, Hardin, I will leave it, too. Think of it; if Kentucky declares for the Union, you can never come back—not as long as there is a war on. How can you even think of leaving me with your parents, or my mother, with no chance of seeing you—for how long? Months? Years? And you see how people have divided here. How do you think I will be treated when you go to fight for the South?"

"I thought you would be happier with family about you."

"I have our daughters. That will have to be family enough for me while you are gone."

"Em, if you live with my parents, they will take care of everything you and the girls need. You will be perfectly comfortable there. Following me about, you will have to board. You'll be living with strangers, most likely. Money will be tight. And how will you educate the girls?"

"I can bear all that, and I am perfectly capable of educating the girls myself."

"You won't even have a piano to play on."

"And what sort of tunes would I want to play if I were a widow in all but name? Hardin, I said I would not force you to act against your conscience. You must extend me the same consideration, and not force me to act against my inclination."

"Em—"

"I promise you, if I or the girls are in danger, we will go stay with whoever you wish. And I will not let the girls go hungry or go hungry myself. But as long as we are safe, I want the three of us to be as close to you as possible."

Hardin held up his hands. "I surrender, Miss Em. Not the best start for my military career."

"A wise decision, Mr. Helm."

∽✑

Soon, they found a suitable residence for Emily—with Dr. John Pryor Ford in Nashville, a location that Hardin considered safe for her. Dr. Ford, a professor of obstetrics at Shelby Medical College, had a large, comfortable house full of his family members, so Emily would not be lonely, nor would she be exposed to the indignities of a regular boardinghouse. Dr. Ford had gone to Transylvania College in Lexington, and thus was somewhat acquainted with almost anyone of importance in Kentucky or at least his near relation.

With that settled, Hardin began wrapping up his legal affairs, and they began readying their things for storage—Hardin's law books, their wedding silver, the bric-a-brac handed down to Emily from her grandmothers. Most of it was bound for Elizabethtown, where Hardin's parents lived, but while they were still packing, the stately old couple came in person to Louisville to urge Emily to change her mind and stay with them. "Dearest," Mrs. Helm said, "do come to stay with us. I promise I won't meddle with your rearing of the children, and there will be enough society to amuse you in Elizabethtown."

Emily smiled. "It's not that at all, Mother Helm. I just want to be as close as I can to Hardin."

"You can't change a Todd's mind, Mother. I've tried."

Next to visit Louisville were Emily's mother, escorted by an unusually subdued Alec. When Mrs. Todd and the girls were out of the room, Alec said, "Em, I have a sweetheart. Miss Mary Anne Taggert."

"Oh, Alec!" Emily hugged him. "When are you to marry?"

"Not anytime soon. As soon as I can settle my affairs—"

"You're going to join the Confederate army," Emily finished.

He nodded. "Couldn't be left out of the fun, could I? That will mean all of us Todd brothers fighting for the South, except for Levi. Mary will be incensed, but that's what she gets for marrying a tyrant."

"He's not a tyrant," Hardin said. "He's a good man, and it pains me to go to war against him. I hope it will be short, and our two nations can live side by side in peace."

Alec looked so abashed that Emily ran a hand through his hair. "Don't be hard on my baby brother, Hardin."

"I liked him, too," Alec confessed. "At least as much as I remember when he and Mary visited us in Lexington. But Em was always his and Mary's pet."

"Yes, I was," Emily said sadly.

"Does Mary know you're leaving Kentucky?"

"Not yet. I haven't had the heart to write to her."

A rustle of silk proclaimed the return of Mrs. Todd, having seen the girls off for bed. "All my children will be gone," she said bleakly. "Kitty, Elodie, and Martha in Selma, Margaret in Cincinnati, David and Sam in the army, and now you are heading off to Nashville and you heading off to fight soon. Oh, I won't try to talk either of you into changing your minds; I can't blame you for wanting to follow your husband and you for wanting to fight. I'd be off somewhere myself if I were young, I guess. As it is, I'll just stay in Lexington and wait for all of you to come back."

❧

Each morning, Phil walked down to the newsstand near the railroad depot and returned with the out-of-town papers. From them, Emily learned in early August that the Lincolns had entertained Prince Napoleon. What an excellent opportunity for Mary to have practiced the French she had learned from her headmistress Madame Mentelle, a native of Paris! For a moment, sitting among her heaps of packed boxes and the furniture tagged for sale or storage, Emily indulged in a vision of herself standing in a receiving line beside her sister. She would be wearing yellow, which set off her dark eyes and her glossy black hair and which also had the merit of looking well in the gaslight. Her French was not nearly as good as Mary's, but it was passable, and surely a well-bred man like the prince would make allowances. Hardin would be there beside her, his six feet resplendent in a dress uniform…

She shook her head and pushed the newspaper away. Hardin glanced up from his own paper. "Not bad news, my love?"

"No."

❧

Finally, their house was empty, save for a few trunks that would be traveling with them—their clothing, the girls' dolls, an assortment of books, a photograph album and a few daguerreotypes, and Emily's prayer book. As Phil, who would be going off to war with Hardin, carried the boxes out to the waiting hack, Emily stared around at the bare rooms, at the wall where her piano had stood, at the mantel over which had hung photographs of the four of them. Then and there, it struck her—everything that they were giving up. Her eyes welled with tears, and before she could stop herself, she was openly weeping.

Hardin held her against him as the girls looked on, their eyes wide with distress. "Em, when this is over, I promise, we'll find an even better house."

She sniffled and straightened her shoulders. "I know," she said.

◦◦◦

Dr. Ford, their host, was there to meet them at the station in Nashville. That was encouraging, as was the size of the house, quite large enough for Emily not to feel underfoot. "An artist used to have these rooms," Mrs. Ford said as she showed the family their lodgings. "He was a lovely man, but he needed more space. Oh, you don't mind cats, do you? Dear, it still smells just a bit of oil paint, but that could just be me."

The Helms sniffed politely.

"You'll meet my daughter, Della, soon; she is out shopping. Her husband, Dr. Callender, is at the insane asylum at present. Oh, don't look alarmed, Mrs. Helm; he is not an inmate. He is merely calling there in a professional capacity. Although with the state of things these days, we may all end up there. Oh, Mr. Wood must have left some paint behind! You may want to get your little girl away from it."

Emily snatched up Kate and continued on the tour. Her spirits revived when she saw the Fords' well-stocked library, which also held a piano. Mrs. Ford followed her gaze. "Do you play, my dear? Oh, good! We must get the tuner in—if it is not past tuning at this point—and then you shall play as much as you like. I do want you to feel quite at home here while your husband is fighting the Yankees. You will whip them, of course, sir."

Hardin, who had been bending over giving the girls a quiet talking-to, looked up, startled. Mrs. Ford clarified, "The Yankees, that is."

"Oh, yes. Of course, madam."

◦◦◦

"I hope I didn't make a mistake," Hardin said that evening—their last together. The girls had long gone to sleep, and he and Emily sat on the back porch onto which their lodgings opened. "They're a bit of an eccentric family, it seems. Maybe we should look for something else."

"They're charming, Hardin, and they all seem very good-natured. That is all that counts. Though I have to admit that having two medical men in one house is daunting. At our meal I felt as if they were diagnosing us all."

Hardin smiled faintly. "I suppose I'm trying to find an excuse to stay with you longer. It's easy to talk about going off to war. Until one actually goes off to war."

She squeezed his hand, and they continued gazing up at the August sky. "Hardin! It's the comet! I've never seen one before, ever."

"Me neither. And now I'm seeing it with you."

They watched until the Nashville sky faded to a starry blue. Then Hardin said, "Promise something, love."

"Anything."

"When you see it again, stop what you're doing and watch, and think of me. And I'll try my best to do the same, whatever I'm doing. We won't be together, but at least we'll be doing the same thing."

"As if I wouldn't be thinking of you every moment of the day already, Benjamin Hardin Helm. But I promise."

He led her inside and they made love, moving languidly in the August heat. Emily had never known such exquisite pleasure, mixed with the pain of his leaving. The slight self-consciousness that she had developed over the years after the girls were born and her figure became a touch more matronly disappeared as they explored each other more freely than they ever had since their wedding night.

At dawn, Hardin said, "Don't walk me to the station, love. I'd rather remember you exactly as you are."

"Stark naked?"

"Well, as a matter of fact, yes."

He pulled some clothes on and went to the next room to bid the girls goodbye. Hugging her knees to her bare chest, Emily sat and listened, her eyes filling with tears.

"Chickens, be good for Mama and Mammy, and do everything they tell you."

"We're not chickens," Kate said.

"Well, maybe I'm a chicken," Hardin said. He clucked.

Kate giggled. "You're a good chicken, Papa."

Hardin gave a final cluck, then spoke something in a low voice that Emily could not hear. When he returned to the room, there were tears in his eyes, but he commanded himself. "Goodbye, my love. I will write as soon as I can. You have all you need for fall? The weather will change soon."

In spite of herself, Emily smiled. "Yes, Hardin."

"Well, I thought I'd ask anyway." He embraced her. "Look for the comet tonight."

"I will. Tonight, and always."

He hurried out, not daring to linger further. Emily dressed and then carried on her day as usual—teaching Kate her letters, playing with Dee, and then walking to the church to make socks for the soldiers. Only when she lay alone that night in her bed—empty of Hardin by no means for the first time, but feeling much emptier than usual—did she give way to her tears.

❧ 9 ❧

MARY

JANUARY TO FEBRUARY 1862

J ust days into the new year, Mary picked up Washington's *Daily Republican* to learn that the previous year, her half brother David, during a short and inglorious stint as the head of the military prison in Richmond, had been accused of cruelty toward his charges and had been removed from his position. Soon, other newspapers— including the most powerful paper in the country, the *New York Herald*—had chimed in with their own stories about her brother, each more mortifying than the last.

If Levi was the family drunk and George its self-made outcast, David was the family scapegrace. He had been a willful little boy, the bane of Mammy Sally's existence at the time Mary had left home for Springfield, and when she returned to Lexington a married woman, he was gone, having run off to fight in the Mexican War. Since then, he had been on adventure after adventure, showing no interest in taking a wife or settling in one place. Until now, this was the worst that could be said of him. Mary had no idea of whether he was capable of doing the dreadful things ascribed to him—slashing someone with a sword because he had not extinguished his candle at the appropriate time, shooting men just for sticking their heads out of a prison window—but even if they were only half true, he was dead to her.

She had instructed Mr. Stoddard, the young man who served as her de facto secretary, to open all letters directed to her, including those from her siblings, to stem the rumors that she was in correspondence with the rebels. But David Todd's misdeeds assured that the scurrilous talk would continue for weeks to come—months, when one considered how tightly the press clenched any bone of scandal.

It was true, Mary admitted to herself as Mrs. Keckly fitted her for her latest dress, that she had not helped matters. No, far from it. First there had been her massive overspending of the appropriation for the White House. The store owners had been so officious, and in the thrill of having such a large budget, she had simply not noticed how the small luxuries she had acquired had added up. The President had been furious. Only with the help of the new commissioner of buildings, the gentlemanly and kind Mr. Benjamin French, had Mary been able to escape the chasm into which she had fallen.

And then there had been Mr. Henry Wikoff. During the last months of 1861, he had been a fixture in the Blue Room, where Mary had established a veritable salon, most of whose members were men. (Not that women weren't welcome, of course.) How he had come to Mary's attention she scarcely remembered, but with his charm and cultivated manners, he had become indispensable, not the least because of his checkered past, which Mary mentally spelled as *chequered* because it suited him much better.

He had been kicked out of Yale—Mr. Lincoln, hearing this, had mused that it seemed on the whole a place where one might be better off staying. There were other scandals, too, involving women, the details of which were only vaguely known to Mary. Something about the pursuit of an heiress, who had proved elusive, and some affairs as well. But all of this was many years in the past, and now Mr. Wikoff was tame enough, his misspent youth only adding to his charms.

Then, just hours before President Lincoln was supposed to give his annual address to Congress, it appeared in the *New York Herald*. Soon, word went about that Wikoff had supplied a purloined copy of the speech. Naturally, Mary's name had been dragged in; there were even whispers that she had been the culprit. Though why she would do such a thing to her beloved husband, no one could explain.

"Do they really think I would betray my husband in that manner?" she asked Mrs. Keckly, who as ever listened patiently, a task made easier by her mouth being full of pins. She was wearing black, a painful contrast to the white satin dress she was fitting on Mary. Last fall, her son had been killed in combat; as Mrs. Keckly's father had been white and the father of her son had been white, the poor young man had had no difficulty passing as a white man in order to join the Union army. "Goodness knows, the man has enough to try his patience. Now, it is not altogether impossible that I showed the address to Mr. Wikoff, out of pride. I truly do not recall. Much could be avoided if the President would honor us in the Blue Room with his presence. We would be delighted to have his company, and he could forget his cares for a time." She sighed. "Oh, pardon me for moving."

Mrs. Keckly, the last of the pins removed from her mouth, ventured, "Perhaps the reception will distract him."

"I can only hope so. Of course, with Mr. Stanton and General McClellan there, it will probably turn into a discussion of the war. Mind you, I am united with the President in wishing that the general would exert himself to do something."

She had just dismissed Mrs. Keckly when the boys ran in without knocking. Tad held up a shiny quarter. "Look what we won from Secretary Seward!"

"How did you manage that?"

"We had him guess our new pet. He couldn't guess a rabbit! He guessed a dog, a bird, and even a pig."

"He did guess a rabbit," Willie said. "You just wouldn't tell him he was right until you got the quarter."

"Oh, well," Tad said. "But he didn't guess *Nibbles* the rabbit. Hey! Shall we take Nibbles to see the snow?"

"He might get lost in it," Willie pointed out. "Being a white rabbit."

"Bundle up if you do go out," Mary said. She frowned at Willie. "You look a bit peaked. Are you well?"

"I'm fine, Mother."

"All right. Do watch where you throw your snowballs; not everyone has your father's sense of humor."

The reception had been Mary's idea, to spare the President the endless series of state dinners he was expected to host during the season. Instead, she proposed, why not hold a grand, invitation-only reception that would fulfill his social obligations and provide a diversion for the denizens of Washington—at least those well-placed enough to merit an invitation? The President had agreed, albeit without an excess of enthusiasm, and seven hundred invitations had been sent out. Hundreds of others were injured at not having been invited, and some of those who had been had haughtily declined, saying that such frivolity was unsuitable in wartime. Never mind that Mary had already decreed that dancing would not be permitted, and that other hostesses in Washington had been giving their own entertainments regardless of the war.

She engaged Henri Maillard, New York's finest caterer, for the occasion, ignoring the murmurs that a Washington firm might have sufficed and her own nagging remembrance that the temptations of New York that had proven her undoing with the redecorating appropriation. Remembering past events where guests had lost their coats, or grabbed those of other guests, in the confusion of leaving, she turned part of the second floor into a cloakroom, with servants to check the guests' garments, and made bedrooms into dressing rooms where the ladies could tidy their headdresses and arrange their skirts before elegantly descending the stairs to the East Room. She called in Mrs. Keckly for a final fitting and for some alterations to her gown, which was trimmed in black in honor of the memory of the recently deceased Prince Albert.

All was in perfect readiness. And then, on the morning of February 5, Willie, who had been ailing for several days but seemed to have nothing more than a cold, awoke with a fever.

The President insisted on summoning their doctor, and Mary heartily agreed, prepared to cancel the reception if Dr. Stone found anything alarming about her son's condition. But he pronounced that Willie was suffering from nothing that a few days in bed would not cure, and Willie, always a considerate boy, protested vigorously against his parents changing their plans. So when the clock struck eight, Mrs. Keckly was fastening the back of Mary's gown as the President, whose toilette had been completed in ten minutes, strolled in. "My," he said, observing Mary's train, "the cat has a long tail tonight." He nodded at Mary's bosom, which was somewhat in evidence. "A little nearer the head might be in better style, in my humble opinion."

"In this case only, President Lincoln, your opinion is a humble one." Mary took her husband's arm. "I will check in on Willie later, Elizabeth. Thank you for agreeing to sit with our dear little boy."

"I'll check, too," the President said, his face turning grave.

❧

The caterer had outdone himself. Even the Treasury Secretary's snobbish daughter, Miss Chase, looked impressed before she remembered herself and assumed her usual look of hauteur. Every exotic creature that was edible was represented on the menu, while for those with simpler tastes, such as the President, a stack of sandwiches sat reassuringly next to the punch bowl. No sweet tooth could fail to be satisfied by the variety of desserts offered. And the edible displays! As if taking his cue from the court of Versailles, Maillard had created beehives, around which buzzed their inhabitants filled with charlotte russe. There was a ship, spun of sugar and aptly named "Union," complemented by Fort

Pickens. President Jackson's home, the Hermitage, stood, incongruously but beautifully, next to a Japanese pagoda. And for those who cared nothing about such things, but only for imbibing, there were fine wines, champagnes, whiskeys, and liquors, which were wasted on the abstentious Lincolns but seemed to satisfy a number of the men present and even a couple of the ladies.

Bob, who was on break from Harvard, kept himself busy talking to Senator Harlan's daughter, then to Senator Hale's daughter. Governor Sprague, from mill money in Rhode Island and not quite considered to have arrived at the stature of a gentleman, sampled the whiskey, then the wine, earning an icy stare from Miss Chase, the object, rumor had it, of the very wealthy governor's affections. Mrs. General Frémont looked askance at the cherry bands on Mrs. General McClellan's gown and the red-and-white feathers in her hair, hissing to a lady companion that they were the colors of secession.

All of this would have made delightful fodder for a long, gossipy letter to one of her old friends in Springfield. Instead, Mary smiled and greeted her guests until she could safely leave her post, then hurried upstairs to Willie's bedside. "He just fell asleep," Mrs. Keckly said.

"Is he better?"

"He is no worse."

Someone stepped into the room behind her: the President, having seen his own chance to slip away. Together, they stared sadly and tenderly down at their boy until his father sighed. "Better get back to our company."

They were descending the stairs when they met Bob coming toward them. "Just thought I'd say hello to Willie," he said with the studied nonchalance of the undergraduate. Despite themselves, both parents smiled.

Twice more that evening, they returned to Willie's bedside, each time to be met with the same report by Mrs. Keckly. Meanwhile, the Marine Band played merrily, its repertoire including pieces specifically composed for the occasion. Returning downstairs, Mary did her best to smile as it struck up "Mrs. Lincoln's Polka," while the younger set, constrained from dancing, compensated by putting more of a bounce to their gaits.

At last, toward dawn, the last of the guests weaved toward a waiting carriage as the White House servants gloomily surveyed the wreck left behind—overflowing spittoons, crumbs ground into the carpet, stray gloves, fans, and even a lady's headdress. Moving like sleepwalkers, Mary and the President once again climbed the stairs to Willie's room, where Mrs. Keckly sat in her accustomed place. She looked at them wearily.

"I think he's a little worse," she said, touching the boy's forehead. "I would send for the doctor again."

Willie grew steadily sicker over the next few days, then slowly began to show improvement. But just as his parents started to hope, Tad, who had been listless since his brother fell ill, began to run his own fever. Soon Willie was sicker than he had ever been.

There was encouraging news from the war in Tennessee, but Mary did not care. The papers, having described the gorgeous attire of the reception guests, the sumptuous menu, and the elegant furnishings, now turned their attention to lambasting the Lincolns, and Mary in particular, for holding such a spectacle in wartime. Mary did not care. Congress was investigating the matter of the stolen speech, and Mary did not care. Her world had shrunk to the confines of her sons' sickroom.

The President had to care about the larger world, but he left his office for the sickroom whenever possible. As Willie worsened, the President's secretaries, young enough still to take the stairs two at a time, crept quietly from room to room. The gregarious Secretary of State, William Seward, walked around with his eyes to the floor, while the stern Secretary of War, Edwin Stanton, appeared to be on the verge of tears.

Willie begged to see his best friend, Bud Taft, who came for hours to sit by his friend's bedside, sometimes outlasting even Mary. Forced by necessity to carry on a one-sided conversation with Willie, he regaled him with riddles, of which he had a seemingly endless repertoire, gained, Mary supposed, from some boys' periodical. Most of them were so hoary that Mary could remember her own brothers telling them. "Why is a raven like a writing pen?"

Willie weakly shook his head.

"They both have quills!" Bud announced in triumph as Willie mustered a faint smile.

The President stroked Willie's hair, then ruffled Bud's. "You're better medicine than anything those doctors have come up with."

Years before, Mary had lost her second son, poor little Eddie. (He had been named after the President's old friend Edward Baker, who had compounded the tragedy by losing his own life in the war the previous October.) But Eddie had never been a robust child, and although Mary had grieved his loss terribly, something had always told her that he would not stay long on this earth. But Willie, more than any of the three sons that remained to her, was the one she had thought would be the joy and comfort of her old age. Not long before he fell ill, he had told Mary that he had decided to become either a teacher or a preacher. He would have been a fine representative of either profession, but Mary had secretly hoped that he would choose the pulpit.

One more reason, she silently reminded the Lord, for Him to spare her son's life.

Thursday, February 20, dawned bright and cold. Around noon, Bud Taft made his usual pilgrimage to the White House and entered the guest room in which Willie, too sick to be kept with Tad, lay hollow-eyed and pale. Already, the newspapers had pronounced him beyond hope of recovery.

Bud looked down at his friend and took his hand. "Why would a compliment from a chicken be an insult?"

The President sighed. "I don't think he can hear you, son."

Willie stirred. "Because it would be fowl language," he said softly but distinctly. "Go home and rest, Bud."

They were the last intelligible words Willie Lincoln spoke. At five o'clock, the sun began to set over Washington, and Willie, with each of his parents holding a hand, slipped out of the world. Her husband's weeping over the lifeless form was the last thing Mary remembered before she fell insensible to the floor.

For the next few days, she remained in her bed. Save for one letter she penned, she might as well have been as dead as Willie.

On the morning of February 24, the President came to her room. For a moment, Mary came out of herself long enough to observe that he appeared to have aged four years in as many days. "Mary. Come to the East Room to see Willie."

"I don't want to."

"Don't be foolish. It is your last chance to see our boy."

Numbly, she obeyed, and allowed Mrs. Keckly to dress her in a black gown that had been made during her incapacitation. Together with Bob, she and the President entered the Green Room, its cheerful aspect obscured by the black hangings on the windows and the mirrors.

Dressed in the pants and jacket he had usually worn to Sunday school, Willie clutched a bouquet of camellias. Vaguely, Mary remembered asking that they be brought to her after the casket was closed. He was surrounded by other sprays of flowers. Nearly lost amid them was a humble nosegay. "Who brought this?"

"Bud," said Bob. "He told me he bought it from a street vendor."

"But I wrote Mrs. Taft that those boys were not to attend the funeral! I cannot bear it. Them being in this house reminds me too much of what we have lost."

The President looked at her forbearingly. "They will not attend the funeral, although since you won't be there, I don't understand why they can't be. But hearing of your letter, I could not help but feel that Bud should be allowed to see his friend for the last time. He came, and although he left in tears, I think he will be better for having come."

"The boy saw my son before I did?"

"Our son, Mary, our son." He brushed his eyes. "And, I think, in a way, everyone's son lost in this war."

"Our son, of course," Mary said. "But not everyone's. As if our boy was public property."

Her husband shook his head. "It's the only consolation I've had over the past few days, Mary. The only way I can bear this. Don't deprive me of it."

They fell silent as a fierce wind howled outside. For a good twenty minutes, the three of them stood gazing at the dead boy. Finally, the President took Mary's hand. "Come, Molly. They'll want to be getting started."

She nodded and let him lead her out of the room. Then they went their separate ways: the President and Bob to the East Room, where the funeral was to be held; Mary, to her bed.

If she never rose from it again, it would be all the same to her.

10

EMILY

FEBRUARY TO MARCH 1862

Your stays too tight, ma'am?"

Since Emily had begun to show, Maggie, the children's nurse who doubled as Emily's attendant, had taken it upon herself to stand in for Hardin, fussing in person when Hardin could do so only by post. "Think you should be eating that, ma'am?" "You hold on tight to that railing, ma'am," had been the refrain for weeks now. Emily supposed it was natural for Maggie to be so concerned with Hardin's unborn child—as Maggie's people had been in Hardin's family for generations, and her mother had been Hardin's mammy—but it could be trying. "Not at all, Maggie. I'm very comfortable, and so is the baby. Come, we'll be late for church, and there is much to be thankful for today."

Over the past few days, Nashville's emotions had swung back and forth. While the Northern papers that reached Nashville grumbled that General McClellan in the East was doing too little, the Union generals in the West had lately been doing far too much. After a gunboat battle, Hardin's old friend from the State Guard, General Lloyd Tilghman, had been compelled to surrender Fort Henry on the Tennessee River to General Ulysses S. Grant, who had moved on to Fort Donelson. For a few days, the citizens of Nashville had been on a knife's edge, because if Fort Donelson were to fall, Nashville would be the next Union prize.

But around midnight, Emily's restless sleep had been broken by shouts outside, bearing the splendid news that the Yankees had been soundly beaten and that Nashville was safe. Good as the news was, however, it could not provide her with what she most wanted to hear—tidings of Hardin, now a colonel in command of the First Regiment of Kentucky Cavalry. The previous year, his men and other troops had seized the rail-road junction of Bowling Green, Kentucky; since then, her husband had been drilling his men and scouting, but she had heard nothing from him since Fort Jackson had fallen. Indeed, she had had but one letter from him since she sent him his Christmas gifts: a warm undershirt, a dozen socks, and the news that she was expecting their third child around May.

The latest news concerning him, that the Confederates had been forced to abandon Bowling Green, came not from Hardin but from the papers, and it had not been encouraging. Still, one had to take good news when one found it, so Emily dressed for church with the festivity a victory required, choosing her best silk gown and her newest bonnet.

The weather, crisp and clear after days of wet, wind, and snow, matched the Confederacy's brighter prospects. There was a chill in the air, giving Emily the chance to bedeck herself in the furs that Hardin had bought her for Christmas in 1860—the last Christmas they had spent together.

Banishing these wistful thoughts of Hardin from her mind, she briskly walked to church with Maggie and the girls, the latter wearing matching coats and dresses and carrying their own dainty muffs in one hand, Maggie herself rather stylish-looking in a gray wool dress handed down from Emily. "Missus?"

"Yes, Maggie?"

"Something's wrong. Folks is leaving church."

"I suppose there was a service before ours."

"Ain't never been one before, ma'am."

A married couple from her congregation appeared in view, walking rapidly toward her but talking intently to each other, heedless of passersby. Only when Emily coughed did the gentleman, startling, remember his breeding and step back to allow her to pass unimpeded. "Sir, has something happened?"

"No church. It's been canceled for today."

"Canceled! Why?"

The man shook his head and hurried on as briskly as his wife's crinoline would allow.

More people, walking the opposite direction from Emily, were filling the sidewalk. None seemed inclined to allow her to pass. "We can't possibly get the girls through this mess. They'll be trampled. Let's go back home."

She could hardly recognize the streets she had just passed through. Crowds were beginning to congregate on corners, while men, white and colored alike, were rushing in and out of the fine houses, dragging trunks outside and then rushing back in for another load. She tugged at a man walking next to her. "Sir, what on earth is going on?"

"We're whipped. That's what's going on."

"Whipped?"

"That's what I said, madam. Whipped."

There was no point in asking anyone anything, she realized. Instead, she let the crowd bear her along until a young man rushed toward her, expertly threading his way through the crowds and making promiscuous use of his elbows so as to arrive at her side. Emily recognized him as a young orderly from Dr. Ford's hospital. "Mrs. Helm! Glad I found you. I have a note from Colonel Helm that someone brought by."

"Hardin!" Emily seized the note, ignoring the curses around her as she blocked the sidewalk. Its few scrawled words barely resembled Hardin's usual neat script, but she could read it well enough for her heart to sink. *Fort Donelson surrendered. You must leave town. Come see me.* "The fort has fallen? But—"

"Mrs. Helm!" another man called.

Emily turned to see Mr. Chauncey Brooks, a salt merchant from Louisville. She had known him for years; he and Emily's old schoolmaster, the Reverend Stuart Robinson, had married sisters. As his business often brought him to Nashville, he had gotten into the habit of calling on Emily when he was in town.

With the expertise of a father of a large family, he gathered each girl into his arms as the orderly guided Emily and Maggie through the throng. When they had reached Dr. Ford's, Emily asked, "What on earth is going on? We were defeated?"

He nodded. "Fort Donelson fell at dawn. Evidently General Pillow's announcement of victory was somewhat premature. But there's no doubt about it now. It's all up for Nashville with the two forts fallen: no fortifications, no defenses. All the Yankees have to do is walk in. So people are beginning to run."

"I must see my husband." She indicated the scrawled map on the letter. "He is camped here."

"That's about seven miles from here. I'll take you there and back in my carriage. I cannot offer to do more than that as I have promised it to another family wanting to leave. They will want it as soon as they pack. I'd leave your girls here, though. How easy it will be to get out there, I don't know."

She agreed, and in due course they were on their way, part of a line of overloaded carriages and wagons snaking its way out of the city. By the time they had crossed the handsome suspension bridge that spanned the Cumberland River, the weather had turned as gloomy as the general mood, and it soon began to sleet. It was then that Emily saw the men, hundreds of them, ill-clad and shivering in the rain, marching—or, more accurately, hobbling—toward them. "Our army in retreat from Kentucky," Mr. Brooks said sadly.

"Those men are Kentucky boys?"

"Many of them."

Emily dabbed at her eyes. Was Hardin, cold and miserable, at the head of such a wretched crew?

A man in a colonel's uniform was riding toward them. Impulsively,

Emily waved for him to come to her, and he obligingly rode up. "Colonel Scott, Texas Cavalry. May I be of assistance, madam?"

"My husband is Colonel Helm, of the First Kentucky Cavalry. He is camped somewhere out this way. Have you seen him?"

"Yes, ma'am, but he and his men broke camp not long ago. You won't find him there. He's heading toward Nashville with the rest of us, somewhere."

"Then we had best turn back." She sighed. "I am sorry for the trouble, Mr. Brooks."

"You're welcome to ride alongside us," said Colonel Scott. "Not that we're the best company at the moment. These boys covered twenty-seven miles yesterday in the sleet and snow, and they woke this morning with snow covering their heads. And with sore hearts." He gave Emily a curious glance. "Someone told me Abraham Lincoln's wife is a sister of yours. Is that true?"

"Yes."

"Is she loyal to the South?"

"Not at all."

"And are you?"

Emily flushed. "With my husband suffering in the sleet and snow, you should know the answer to that, Colonel Scott."

"Yes, you're right. Sorry, ma'am. It's been a rough few days. We heard the news last night—I suppose you did too—of a victory. Woke up this morning and had it snatched away. It hurts."

With Colonel Scott riding in silence beside them, they retraced their path until they approached the bridge, jammed with wagons heading out of the city and soldiers heading into the city, while another detail of soldiers was attempting to keep the two groups from impeding each other's progress. When Mr. Brooks and Emily at last reached the entrance to the bridge, a soldier said, "Ma'am, we're not letting any civilians into the city."

"But I just came from there! My daughters are there! My husband, Colonel Helm of the First Kentucky Cavalry, will be expecting to find me there!"

"I'm sorry, ma'am. General Johnson is in the city now, and he has ordered that no civilians be let in. It's a madhouse there. Now, if it was out you wanted"—he gestured at the wagons, piled high with trunks and bedding, and covered to various degrees of success with tarpaulins—"that would be a different story."

Colonel Scott rummaged in his saddlebags and emerged with pen and paper. He scribbled something, then handed it to one of his men. "Find General Johnson, and give him this. It is a request for a pass allowing you to get through, Mrs. Helm."

"Thank you, sir."

"It is the least I can do after my thoughtless words earlier, ma'am."

For an eternity, she and Mr. Brooks sat in the carriage, watching the traffic over the bridge. The wagons coming out of Nashville were becoming smaller and shabbier, and pedestrians, carrying bundles, had joined the exodus. When Emily saw that some of the bundles were small children, her eyes filmed again.

Finally, the soldier returned with the pass. After thanking him and Colonel Scott, Emily asked, "You did not happen to see Colonel Helm, did you?"

"No, ma'am."

Emily's shoulders sagged.

After the eternity it took to get over the bridge, Emily found that the city had not improved in her absence. The hire of a carriage had gone sky-high over the past few hours, judging from the bargaining she overheard as she passed through the streets, and there were a number of covetous glances at her own conveyance. Outside the banks, which had opened to allow customers to withdraw their money in preparation for refugeeing, people fiercely guarded their place in line, terrified that the bank would run out of funds before they could be admitted inside. More than a few residents, having decided it was not worth their while to flee, had started to drink instead. Only when Mr. Brooks, muttering an apology under his breath, was forced to take a detour down the street that contained Nashville's finest brothels did Emily see any signs of cheer, as a group of women with quantities of false hair laughed together outside a saloon.

At one point, they had to draw aside to let pass a contingent of soldiers from Bowling Green. Emily's hands clenched into fists as the bystanders, many of them men of an age to be serving themselves, taunted and jeered at the men in their sodden clothing and worn-out shoes. "Leaving us to the Yankees, are you? Cowards!"

"You are the cowards! Not them!" she called.

Mr. Brooks looked nervously at the gun that he carried at his side. Emily subsided, contenting herself with glaring at the spectators.

At last, they reached Dr. Ford's, where Kate ran out to greet them. "Mama! We have to go. The Yankees are going to burn the entire town! Tonight!" She frowned. "Or maybe we're going to burn the town. I forgot."

"No one is going to burn anything, Kate," Emily said wearily, gratefully sinking into a chair after a servant relieved her of her coat and bonnet. For the first time in a while, she felt the full effects of her pregnancy. "In any case, Mr. Brooks is very kindly going to the station to try to arrange a train for us. I don't know what I would have done without him today." She roused herself. "Mrs. Ford, are you leaving?"

"No, dear, we're staying right here. Dr. Ford will not desert his post at the college unless made to. It is a pity you are leaving, though I understand the necessity. Dr. Ford was so looking forward to treating you when your time came."

Shortly, Mr. Brooks appeared with the news that Mr. Stevenson, the president of the Louisville and Nashville Railroad, remembering John Helm's connection with that railway, had offered her and her family seats on his private train, bound for Chattanooga. So bidding Mrs. Ford goodbye, Emily took one last look at the cheerful parlor and, with the girls and Maggie, proceeded to the railway station. A train was pulling out, so full of humanity that Emily wondered how it moved down the track. Women and children, some standing, crammed the inside of the cars, while men stood on the railings outside the cars and in between the cars; a few daring souls even rode atop the cars.

Watching it all was a crowd, some of whose members were clutching belongings and craning their necks in hopes of glimpsing another train. Others were just there to gawk and get in the way—and were doing a fine job of it.

Somehow, the train lurched away from the station, not without a few stragglers jumping on. Emily was staring after it when she heard Kate cry, "Papa!"

Emily whipped around and in seconds was in Hardin's arms. "Darling!"

He pushed back her bonnet and kissed her vigorously, meeting with cheers from a few bystanders. When he at last released her and dropped to his knees to embrace the girls, she realized that he had grown a beard and was thinner and more muscular.

"Papa, how did you know to find us here?" Kate asked.

"Why a little bird—known as Mrs. Ford—told me."

"I should have waited for you, but I thought that you'd want us out of the city," Emily said.

"You thought right. The Yankees are nowhere near—not yet—but I'll not risk you being here." He sighed. "Poor Bowling Green. We had to burn quite a bit of it when we left."

"That wasn't nice, Papa," Kate said.

"Well, no. But we had no choice." He turned to Dee, who seemed somewhat confused about his identity. "Don't you recognize Papa under all this hair, sweetheart?"

Dee considered the matter. "I think so," she finally said.

Hardin rose, and the smile faded from his face. "I can't stay here, Emily, though there's nothing that I long for more. I made arrangements for you to take a carriage with some other ladies to Murfreesboro, but this will be more comfortable for you." He gave her waist a significant look. "Tell me, are you doing well?"

"I'm fine, Hardin. I've had a very easy time and expect no problems. Just as there were none with the girls." She smiled. "I see you checking for my rubbers."

"And be careful of green apples."

The special train pulled into the station, and the crowd gazed sullenly at it—as well they might. One car held a contingent of fine-looking horses, and another, a carriage. There were three passenger cars, two with velvet trappings and a third, Emily supposed, for the family servants. "You going to be comfortable enough?" someone yelled as Mr. Stevenson appeared, accompanied by an elegant lady and a passel of children and servants, one of whom carried a cat basket, the other of whom led a dog.

"Forgot anything?" another bystander yelled.

Hardin grimaced very slightly, and Emily wondered if he, like she, was thinking that Mr. Stevenson, who in addition to his position as the head of the railroad was a quartermaster for the army, should stay in Nashville at least until everyone had fled who was going to flee. But they could hardly complain in the face of his kindness. So she conferred her brightest smile upon Mr. Stevenson as Hardin thanked him for his consideration toward her. It was a short conversation, as her host was eager to get his journey underway.

As Hardin helped her and the others to their seats, as comfortable as anticipated, Emily turned to him. "It breaks my heart to think of you out there in the wet and cold. I wish I could share your hardships."

"Well, that's one of us," Hardin said drily. He kissed her and the children. "Nothing makes me more comfortable than knowing that you are safe. Stay in Chattanooga until I tell you to leave. Here's some money—for what it's worth. I heard prices are up."

Mr. Stevenson coughed, and Hardin gave Emily one last kiss and hurried off the train. She smiled at him and waved as the train pulled away, Hardin's face the only smiling one in a sea of frowns.

As a horse neighed at the indignity of traveling by rail, Emily settled back into her upholstered seat by its curtained window. The car was well-stocked with newspapers, and to keep her mind from running on this all-too-brief meeting with Hardin—she realized she did not even know where he was headed—she took the one Mr. Stevenson offered her. There, she learned that some days before, Mary had given a ball at the White House: *Mrs. Lincoln received the company with gracious courtesy. She was dressed in a magnificent white satin robe, with a black flounce half a yard wide, looped with black and white bows, a low corsage trimmed with black lace, and a bouquet of crepe myrtle on her bosom.... The half-mourning style was assumed in respect to Queen Victoria... The supper was set in the dining room, and is considered one of the finest displays of gastronomic art ever seen in this country. It was prepared by Maillard of New York and cost thousands of dollars.*

Thousands! What was her sister thinking, spending so much during wartime? Surely if the Confederate soldiers were shivering, the Union ones must be as well. And was it really suitable for an American to wear half mourning for Queen Victoria's husband? Emily snapped the paper shut in irritation, not reading far enough to see the brief announcement that Willie Lincoln was ailing.

But as she shut her eyes to doze and the train clacked along in the sleet and rain, she could not help but picture Mary in her marvelous gown.

No one could call the Crutchfield House hotel, located opposite the railway station, quiet, but Emily's room was well-appointed and clean. Never before, however, had she stayed in a hotel without parent or husband. She was grateful when, on Monday afternoon, Mr. Brooks sent up his card to inform her that he had arrived in town.

When she arrived in the crowded lobby, she found that Mr. Brooks had a companion, whom he addressed as Major Charles Anderson. "I would like to beg a great favor of you, Mrs. Helm. I have been given orders to prepare for the reception of as many as twelve hundred soldiers who were in at the hospital in Nashville."

"Twelve hundred!"

"Some came late yesterday, in pitiful condition, chilled to the bone after having spent hours in cattle cars... There was no other place to put them."

Emily winced.

"I am doing my best to get things ready for them. I have found buildings to serve as hospitals, made arrangements to get them from the station, even put up stands with coffee and bread at the depot so that they might have sustenance. But the men are simply lying on the floors of these hospitals. I have men making frames, and I have the material for bed sacks—but no one to cut out and sew them. The ladies in the town here have so much else to do. Mr. Brooks, who helped get some of the soldiers over to the hospital, suggested that you might be able to help while you are staying here."

"There is nothing that would make me happier." Emily glanced around the lobby. It was crowded with men and women, some waiting for rooms, others passing time between trains. "And if you bring the materials here, I believe I can find others to help as well."

Major Anderson complied, and soon Emily's hotel room was awash with brown cotton, which she cut out while the girls, under Maggie's supervision, chased each other around in the hotel yard. Each time a train arrived, Emily would walk down to the lobby, her arms laden with thimbles, needle, thread, and sacks, and circulate among the women waiting there, asking if they could lend a hand for the soldiers. Hardly anyone refused her, especially when they noticed her lack of a waist.

She had been at this for well over a week when she made her usual approach to a lady who was engrossed in a newspaper. "Of course, dear. I'll help once I finish reading what's new in Yankeedom." She pointed to the columns reprinting news from the Northern papers. "Now, here's some news! Serves her right, if you ask me."

"Serves who right?"

"Why Mrs. Lincoln, of course. See? One of her brats is dead, and the other is thought to be close to it. The Lord does punish trait—"

Emily snatched up the paper. "*Willie?*" Quickly, she read the headline announcing her nephew's death. The nephew who had been so pleased to show her his pets at Springfield, the nephew whom Hardin had roughhoused with at the White House. She threw the paper back at the woman. "That sweet boy was my nephew, and I'll hear no ill of him. Or my sister."

"Madam? You are Mary Lincoln's *sister?*"

All eyes in the lobby lit upon Emily. "I am. I am also the wife of a colonel in our army. Now are you going to gloat over a little boy's death, or help our sick soldiers?"

Meekly, the woman took the clothing and sewing utensils Emily all but threw at her. When several others had followed suit and completed their work—sewing so diligently and quietly that Emily might have been their forewoman at a factory—she retired to her room with her armload of sacks. There, she read the full account of poor Willie's demise and death—and, to her horror, the suggestion that his loss was divine retribution for Mary's extravagance. How could people be so cruel? She could not imagine how she would feel if she lost one of the girls—or, at this point, the child she was carrying. Now Mary, a devoted mother, had suffered such a loss twice. And what must Mr. Lincoln be feeling? Mary had once confided that she thought Willie was his favorite.

Sitting in her room with tears streaming down her cheeks, Emily forgot for the moment she was a Confederate and remembered only that she was a Todd.

In early March, after Emily had completed hundreds of bed sacks—it was a rare night when she did not dream of them—she had a telegram from Hardin, advising her to come to Huntsville, Alabama, where he had secured lodgings for her. Emily bade farewell to the friends she had made in Chattanooga, then, with the efficiency she was quickly developing, packed their belongings. Of course, packing was an easier business, for she had had to leave some things at Nashville, now occupied by the Union. She supposed some of her silk dresses were adorning a Yankee woman.

Having handed her key to the desk clerk and settled her bill—Hardin had been right about things being more expensive—Emily decided to wait for the train in the comfort of the lobby instead of going to the chilly depot. As she settled onto a sofa with the girls, she saw a young soldier lying on a cot, one of several that had been set up in the lobby in deference to all the sick and injured men passing through the town.

His face had the yellow-gray tinge that Emily had seen too often during her stay, the look of a man who might not have seen battle but who had been just as soundly whipped by exposure, malnutrition, and the illnesses that rampaged through the military camps. Next to him stood a couple of his friends. One had bought tobacco from the window in the lobby and was trying in vain to get his friend to chew it, while the other was tempting him with coffee. The invalid shook his head. "There's just one thing I think I could eat."

"Say the word, and we'll get it for you if it can be had."

"Yeah! We've got plenty of time."

"An apple, with just a bit of red on the side. Just like my mother has in her yard."

The companions looked gloomily at each other.

Emily reached into the lunch basket she had packed for the trip and walked to the cot. "Will this do until you get home? I am sure it cannot match your mother's, but it is a fine Southern apple."

The soldier reached for the apple with hands that moved as slowly as those of someone four times his age. Reverently, he gazed at the tinge of red. "It'll do just fine. Thank you, ma'am." He shook his head as one of the companions offered to cut it. "No. I just want to look at it."

Presently, a whistle betokened the imminent arrival of the train. Emily gathered together her small group and her belongings, then looked at the soldier on the cot. He clutched the apple, but his face was still. "Dang it, Willie," his friend said. "If you could have just held out for thirty more miles…"

"His name is *Willie*?"

"Yes, ma'am. Willie Potter. His mama didn't want him going off to war, but he went anyway. You know how it is."

"Yes." Emily reached into her satchel and pulled out a handkerchief. Daintily embroidered with her initials, it was one of the last store-bought ones she owned. She tenderly laid it over the dead man's face. "Goodbye, Willie," she said softly, and headed toward the depot.

11

MARY

MARCH 1862

Muffled from head to toe in deepest mourning, Mary entered William Stoddard's office after he called, "Come in!" in response to her knock. "Oh, Mrs. Lincoln, I am sorry. Had I known it was you, I would have seen you in."

"It is quite all right, Mr. Stoddard."

"How is Tad today?"

"Better. He is refusing to take his medicine, which the President feels is an excellent sign."

"And you, Mrs. Lincoln?"

Mary shrugged. "I am up because Mrs. Pomroy and my sister have prevailed upon me to get up." After Willie's death, Bob had telegraphed Mary's sister Elizabeth in Springfield, begging her to come to the White House to offer what comfort she could, and Elizabeth had agreed, though with a certain air of martyrdom that even Mary when mired in the deepest of grief had noticed. Of all her sisters, Emily would have been the most congenial, but... Mrs. Rebecca Pomroy, a nurse from the hospital at Columbian College, had been sent by Miss Dix, the superintendent of army nurses, to tend Tad, but Mary had needed her ministrations as well. "I suppose they are right. I cannot shut myself up forever. Life goes on."

Mr. Stoddard nodded, clearly finding this awkward. He indicated the letters on his desk. "I have just been sorting your mail, Mrs. Lincoln. Condolences here. Petitioners here."

"And letters accusing me of being a spy and a traitor here." Mary looked at the latter pile, which as usual was the tallest but was less impressive than it generally was, probably due to Willie's death. It was also due to Willie's death, she knew, that the tedious fuss over the President's speech had subsided. The charming Mr. Wikoff had decided to travel. "But what is this?"

"I wasn't sure where to put it. It's from the Reverend John Pierpont. Odd duck. Maybe you've heard of him? Old chap. Got run out of a church for being too much of an abolitionist and a temperance advocate—mind you, this was in Boston, so we're saying something. Graduated from Yale. He's written some poetry, some pamphlets, some plays. Spiritualism is his interest these days, I think. He got so fired up about the war he volunteered to serve as a chaplain with the Twenty-Second Massachusetts, but after a couple of weeks it became apparent that his health wasn't up for going on campaign, so someone—Senator Sumner, I suppose—got him a job with the Treasury Department. He sends his condolences, but he also wants to see you, so it really falls into both piles, I suppose. Very complex for a secretary, you see."

"I shall take it myself and relieve you of your difficulty, then."

"Very kind of you, ma'am." He smiled and resumed his sorting, adding one more letter, then another, to the "spy and traitor" pile.

The Revered Pierpont was a stately old man, deep into his seventies, with a long beard that reminded her of John Brown's. Idly, Mary wondered if he had grown it as a homage to the failed insurrectionist.

After offering his condolences, the reverend said, "I did have another purpose for coming, Mrs. Lincoln—in fact, it is my main purpose. I hope you will forgive me, madam, if I sound intrusive and presumptive, but the other night, I had a visitation from the spirit world, which I thought would be of interest to you."

He made it sound as if a neighbor had called. "The spirit world."

"The spirits of the dead are in regular communication with us, Mrs. Lincoln, if we will only listen. I do listen." He smiled. "At my age, they seem to find me especially congenial."

"Who visited you?"

"Why, your son Willie, of course." Mr. Pierpont took out a piece of paper from inside his coat and squinted at it; in other circumstances, Mary might have found the old gentleman's refusal to don spectacles endearing. "I took notes, as is necessary. He said he was very happy and is enjoying spending time with his grandfather—which grandfather he did not say. He was much relieved to hear of the recovery of his younger brother."

"One needn't be in communication with Willie, or anyone else, to learn those things. Everyone has a grandfather, and Tad's recovery has been in all the papers."

The old man shrugged. "Of course. I quite understand your skepticism, madam. I was a skeptic myself. I will not press the matter further, but simply advise that you leave yourself open to communication with the dear boy. He was quite engaging—but there again I am telling you nothing you do not know."

Mary brushed at her eyes.

"Now, I have read—not heard from young Willie—of your great grief, and I was wondering if I might take the liberty of reciting a poem of mine to you. It is quite old, but sadly apropos now with so many young men being lost in the war, and I have been told that some have found comfort in it."

"You may."

Her visitor smiled again. In a voice redolent of years at a pulpit, he intoned:

I CANNOT make him dead!
His fair sunshiny head
Is ever bounding round my study chair;
Yet, when my eyes, now dim
With tears, I turn to him,
The vision vanishes—he is not there!

I walk my parlor floor,
And through the open door
I hear a footfall on the chamber stair;
I'm stepping toward the hall
to give the boy a call;
And then bethink me that—he is not there!

I thread the crowded street;
A satcheled lad I meet,
With the same beaming eyes and colored hair:
And, as he's running by,
Follow him with my eye,
Scarcely believing that—he is not there!

I know his face is hid
Under the coffin lid;
Closed are his eyes; cold is his forehead fair;
My hand that marble felt;
O'er it in prayer I knelt;
Yet my heart whispers that—he is not there!

I cannot make him dead!
When passing by the bed,
So long watched over with parental care,
My spirit and my eye
Seek it inquiringly,
Before the thought comes that—he is not there!

When, at the cool, gray break
Of day, from sleep I wake,
With my first breathing of the morning air
My soul goes up, with joy,
To Him who gave my boy;
Then comes the sad thought that—he is not there!

When at the day's calm close,
Before we seek repose,
I'm with his mother, offering up our prayer,
Whate'er I may be saying,
I am, in spirit, praying
For our boy's spirit, though—he is not there!

Not there! Where, then, is he?
The form I used to see
Was but the raiment that he used to wear.
The grave that now doth press
Upon that cast-off dress,
Is but his wardrobe locked—he is not there!

He lives! In all the past
He lives; nor, to the last,
Of seeing him again will I despair;
In dreams I see him now;
And, on his angel brow,
I see it written, "Thou shalt see me there!"

Yes, we all live to God!
Father, thy chastening rod
So help us, thine afflicted ones, to bear,
That, in the spirit land,
Meeting at thy right hand,
'Twill be our heaven to find—that he is there!

Mary's eyes filled with tears. "That is lovely. Might I have a copy, sir?"

"I took the liberty of bringing one," Reverend Pierpont said, reaching into his inexhaustible pocket. "And the latest issue of *The Banner of Light*, should you wish to become more familiar with spiritualism—do pardon the folds. Tell your husband that I believe he is a blessing sent to this nation to scourge it of the horrors of slavery. And with that, madam, I will take my leave."

It was not until late that evening that Mary had a chance to read the Reverend Pierpont's newspaper. After spending a happy morning in his father's office, Tad had become lonely for Willie and had to be comforted by both parents, and Mary's sister Elizabeth, who thought that just about anything could be cured by putting a flower in a pot, had insisted that she go for a stroll in the White House greenhouses. So she had hidden the paper away. It was something of which the very conventionally pious Elizabeth would disapprove anyway. But what would she know? All four of her children were living.

Should she tell the President of the Reverend Pierpont's visit? Mary decided against it—for now, at least. Although she had not initiated the encounter, Mr. Lincoln would probably take it as evidence that she was unbalanced. Why, just a few days ago—on a Thursday, when she had simply refused to leave her bed—he had threatened, albeit in the most kind and considerate manner, to send her to the insane asylum if she did not rouse herself. She bore him no grudge for this; Willie had died on a Thursday, and since then, that day had been the hardest day of the week for each of them. Even the President had shut himself in his office and ordered that he not be disturbed, as he had the two Thursdays before that. But still, it had been mortifying to have one's own husband implying that one was a lunatic, and there was no need to give the man more fodder. But what if Reverend Pierpont's claims were not all nonsense? The old gentleman certainly seemed sane enough, if a bit eccentric. And he had not appeared to have a pecuniary motive.

She skimmed through the slightly grubby newspaper, which advertised itself as "A Weekly Journal of Romantic Literature and General Intelligence." There was a rather tedious piece of fiction, written in serial form, so that Mary would have to buy the next issue to see how it turned out. (She had to admit she was mildly curious about the matter.) Advertisements for mediums giving lectures jostled rather uneasily against perfectly conventional advertisements. The war was not forgotten, with one columnist exhorting the ladies of the Union to urge their men to do service. There were, of course, several robust defenses of spiritualism.

On page six were the messages from the dead. A young boy, whose father was fighting in the war, assured his mother that his father was fine and would send her money. A crusty Irishman, who had retained his brogue in the spirit world, advised his wife not to waste her money on prayers for him. A rebel soldier who had lost his life at Bull Run, and still bore a considerable grudge, wished to deliver a message of instructions to his son but launched into a tirade about hanging abolitionists before he could give any specifics. A young girl named Martha bore a simple message: "I have been two years a spirit. I died of fever. My father died shortly after me. My mother is left with two younger children, and she is very unhappy. I have come to tell her we did not die, but only went home, and we can come and talk with her if she wants us to."

What mother would not want that?

The next day, Mrs. Pomroy stopped in to see them. With Tad's crisis past, she had begged to be allowed to resume her nursing duties at the hospital, but Tad had grown so attached to her that she had agreed to spare a few minutes of her time each day to come see him. "I am glad to see you out of bed, Mrs. Lincoln," she said.

"I am glad to be out. Mrs. Pomroy, I know you are a widow. Do you have children?"

"A son in the army. The others are long dead."

"So you have known a mother's grief yourself."

"I have."

"How do you bear it?"

"I did not bear it well at first. I lost my children, my husband, and my home. I was in despair, until I put myself in the Lord's hands, and I have been a happy woman ever since. When the war broke out and my son enlisted, I was quite alone again, and I was at a loss as to what to do with myself. Then I spotted an ad for nurses and asked myself, *Why not?* My husband had spent much of his life as an invalid, so I could nurse just as well as I could do anything else. I prayed upon it, and then I answered the ad, and fortune brought me from Massachusetts to Washington." She hesitated. "Mrs. Lincoln, I must say that the best cure for my own grief has been ministering to those poor lads. So many of them long for their mothers."

Mary ignored this very gentle hint. "Have you ever tried to communicate with your dead?"

"Goodness, Mrs. Lincoln, why would I want to do that? We will all be reunited by and by."

"For curiosity's sake, perhaps."

"I think it best not to be curious about some things, Mrs. Lincoln."

Evidently there were two types of New Englanders, Mary decided, with Mrs. Pomroy on one extreme and the Reverend Pierpont on the other.

That night, as usual, she retired to bed alone, knowing that the President would join her late or not at all, depending on what was happening with the war. Normally, this was a grievance of hers, but tonight it suited her well. After settling into bed and hearing no signs of her husband's footfall, she raised herself up on her elbows. Quietly but distinctly (how loud did one have to be in such cases?), she called, "Willie."

No answer. She pitched her voice higher. "Willie."

Something rustled. "Willie!"

The rustling grew yet louder. Then the door opened, and a cat shot out from underneath the bed and toward the hallway. "There you are!" Tad announced. He grabbed up his pet. "Good night, Mother," he called.

"Good night, sweetheart."

Mary lay back in bed and sighed. There had to be a better way of contacting Willie than this. And if Tad were around, poor Willie wouldn't get a word in edgewise anyway.

12

EMILY

MARCH TO MAY 1862

Y ou're feeling well?"

"Perfectly well."

"Not…ill?"

"Not at all."

Alec sighed. "I wish this train wouldn't jounce so much."

She and Hardin had agreed that Selma, where her sisters Martha, Elodie, and Kitty were all gathered at the moment, would be the best place for her to have the baby, which was expected in May. Her pregnancy had been an easy one, as her other two had been, and she was anticipating no trouble. Her bachelor brother, however, too young to remember any of his siblings' births, was less sanguine.

"You'll tell me if you—"

Emily patted his arm. "Trust me, Alec. When my time comes, you will know. But you'll likely be long gone from here by then."

"I admit I'm rather happy about that."

Emily swatted her brother, but she knew what he meant. "I suppose escorting your pregnant sister isn't exactly what you dreamed of when you enlisted."

"Well, no. Though I'm glad to be of help—and it'll be fun to see the other girls as well. But a fellow wants to see the elephant."

"Elephant?"

"Battle, sister. Everyone says that something big is going to happen around Corinth, once we finally get there."

"Where's Corinth, Uncle Alec?" Kate asked. "What's there?"

"Mississippi—a state that's much more fun to pronounce than to be in, in my humble opinion. As for what's there—two railroads. One running north to south, the other east to west. We need to keep those railroads, and the Yankees want them." When Kate nodded, satisfied, he turned back to Emily. "It's frustrating. Our unit has scouted and covered the retreat from Bowling Green, but we haven't fought. Just marched and frozen ourselves stiff." He glanced down at Kate. "Now, what are you looking at, princess?"

"Your hair. It's so red in the sunlight. Almost pink."

"Kate! Don't comment on people's appearances."

"Well, it is a little hard to miss," Alec said, removing his cap so Kate could get a better look at his thrush of hair. "A little thin on top, sadly, though not as thin—ahem—as your father's. Did your mother ever tell you that your father was worried that you were going to turn out a redhead?"

"It's true." Emily smiled and ran her hand through Kate's auburn hair. "Your father was riding the circuit when you were born, and as I was worn out afterward, your grandmother Todd wrote him to give the particulars. She wasn't at all sure how to describe your hair color at the time, and your father worried that you might be another Alec."

"Was Papa there when I was born?" Dee asked.

"Yes, he wasn't traveling so much then."

Dee stuck her tongue out at Kate smugly.

"Elodie Helm!" Emily frowned at her daughter. "This traveling about has destroyed their manners," she told Alec. "They see the soldiers horsing about, and people of all descriptions coming in and out of hotels, and they pick up everything."

"I'll try to set a better example, then." Alec sat straight in his seat. In a nasal voice, he intoned, "Young ladies, do not raise your voices. This is a very respectable train, I'll have you know."

In this manner, their journey passed pleasantly. In Selma, there was more cheer to come when for the first time since the war had broken out, she was reunited with Martha, Elodie, and Kitty. If their three older full siblings—Margaret, David, and Sam—had been present, it would have been wonderful; if their mother had been there, too, it would have been perfect. Between all of them, they pieced out where the missing ones were: Margaret still in Cincinnati, their mother perhaps with her or perhaps in Kentucky, and David and Sam both heading toward Corinth. "So one way or another, when something happens, a Todd is going to be in the thick of it," Alec predicted happily.

And perhaps a Helm, too, Emily thought. She shivered.

While her brothers and her husband were preparing for God only knew what, her prospective brother-in-law, Captain Dawson, was preparing to come home. "He wants to marry as soon as he gets back," Elodie said. "He is hoping that with his year of enlistment over, he will not be asked to stay in the service, although of course he will follow the government's orders." She glanced at Emily. "I hope you do not think the worse of him for wanting to leave."

"The important thing is, do you?"

"No. I could not love a man who would not fight at all, but he has done his duty, and he has seen battle. As he wrote to me, it is time that some of those idle men enlisted instead of leaving the glories of war to others. And goodness knows it is tiresome to hear men who have not fought in the war criticize the conduct of those who do."

"You've only met him in person a few times. Do you think you'll be happy?"

"Yes. He is well thought of here, although he is not at all

gregarious—I often wonder how he managed to court me! And he writes lovely letters. Would you like to walk by his house?"

Emily agreed, as it was a fine day and Hardin was always urging her to take exercise. As they walked along, various women and girls greeted them, while other merely nodded coldly or not at all. Seeing Emily's inquiring look, Elodie said, "It's not easy being Abraham Lincoln's sister-in-law here, you know. People regularly walk up to me and tell me they hope he is captured and hanged, and expect me to respond with a smile! The worst of it was over Christmas, when someone proposed to put on a tableau portraying him as a black ape, knowing full well how peculiarly situated we Todds are and how much pain it would give us. I made a fuss about it and have been consigned to the second tier of society because of that. But I daresay when I become Mrs. Dawson, and have a house and servants, they will be more accommodating."

"No doubt."

Soon thereafter, they arrived at a gray house, well shaded by old trees. Though not ostentatious or imposing, it looked large and comfortable, with an ample porch and beautiful gardens. Elodie said, "Pretty, isn't it? I confess I thought a little more highly of Captain Dawson when I saw his house. Rather like Lizzy Bennet and Pemberley. His people often send me things from the garden, at his order."

"It's lovely." Emily thought of her and Hardin's little, lost house in Louisville and could not repress a sigh.

"I hope you will be my first visitor—and that you will have your baby there, if we are married in time. It will be more comfortable for you than in the Whites' house, which is a bit crowded. And in truth, it will be nice to have a sister in the house while I adjust to marriage. I will adjust, won't I?"

"Of course." Emily patted her sister's hand and gazed at Captain Dawson's fine house. "It is the separations that you will find difficult."

∾⃘

At the end of March, both of Emily's daughters fell ill with measles—not a serious case, but enough to make everyone in the house thoroughly miserable. Alec left them for the front, and Martha's husband, in a burst of patriotism, enlisted, even though Mr. White was far from healthy. He had signed up for ninety days, and Emily had her doubts as to whether he would manage that long, even under the best of conditions.

Still, Emily had to admit, there was a certain amount of fun in the sisters having the house all to themselves, save for Emily's and Martha's children and the servants. Kitty lined all of her older sisters up and did their hair; Emily loosened her wrapper so that it flapped around her like a tent; and Martha and Elodie gossiped to their heart's content about their neighbors in Selma and their infinite stupidity. "To hear them talk, you'd think Kentucky was barely civilized," Elodie said. "They don't know anything about our beautiful state."

"Well, someone in Huntsville asked me if Kentucky ladies kissed their horses," Emily said. "I told her that we just stroked their manes and spoke to them very sweetly."

"And they think we're all Yankee sympathizers," Kitty said. "Of course, that's because we're Todds. Though I was sad when poor Colonel Ellsworth died, so I suppose they're right as far as that goes."

"A pity all that beauty was wasted on the North," Martha said dryly.

"I was sad when poor Willie Lincoln died," Elodie said as the others nodded. "Poor mite. I wonder how Mary's bearing up. Have you heard anything from her, Emily? You always were her favorite of us."

"Not a thing. But I suppose she could hardly write to us in the South without causing a stir. And can you imagine the postmaster handing us a letter marked 'Executive Mansion, Washington City'?"

"I don't hear from anyone in Springfield anymore, either," Martha said. "Of course, I haven't tried to get a letter there, so I suppose I can't complain. All I know is what I read in the papers. And I suppose that's all they know of us."

"I wonder how Father would feel," Emily said. "The children from his first marriage on one side of this war, and the children from his second on the other. A house divided, just like Mr. Lincoln said."

"Well, you needn't quote the man," Martha snapped.

They were quiet for a while. Then Elodie stood. "Enough of this. Is Emily going to have a boy or a girl, and when? Let's lay wagers."

They could not shut out the war, however—not that they tried. Each morning, they or a servant went out and returned laden with as many newspapers as had made their way into Selma. Then, depending on that day's haul, each sister would take a paper and turn straight to the war news, which depending on the state of the telegraph lines could be days old by the time it reached Selma. "Victory at a place called Shiloh Church, not far from Corinth!" Kitty said when April was well into its second week. She skimmed down the column. "But heavy losses on both sides."

"What does 'heavy' mean?" Martha asked.

"It means we have to worry," Emily said. "Although we would do that anyway."

The next day's newspaper still spoke of a Southern victory but was far more subdued. General Sidney Johnson, the commanding general in the west, had been killed, but beyond that there was little news to be had of individual casualties.

At last, Hardin telegrammed to say that he and Alec were in Tuscumbia, Alabama, but he gave no news of anyone else dear to the sisters' hearts. A couple of days passed, and Emily, enjoying a lazy morning in bed, was awoken by Martha's screams. Wearing only her chemise, she hurried to the parlor to find her sister sobbing and clutching a telegram. "Is there bad news about Clement?"

"No. Sam. He's dead!"

Martha bent her head and sobbed as Emily studied the telegram, tears running down her own cheeks. It was from their brother-in-law Charles Kellogg, who could tell them little other than that their brother Sam had been killed at the second day of battle at Shiloh. "Could he be mistaken?"

Even in the midst of her sobs, Martha managed the scornful snort of an older sister—all the response her query deserved, Emily knew.

Of the four of them, Martha, nearest in age to Sam, had been the closest to him; he had even introduced her to her future husband, his classmate at Centre College.

As her other sisters, hearing the news, joined in the weeping, a memory came to Emily: Sam laughing at some story Mr. Lincoln had told the first time Mary had brought him and her boys to Lexington. They had all laughed, but Sam for some reason had found the story funnier than the rest. And now Sam had died fighting against the storyteller. "Do you think Clélie knows?" Emily asked as she recalled the daguerreotype of Sam's pretty wife, whom she'd never met in person. Sam's death had left her a widow with four small children. She was not alone in the world, having family in New Orleans, but still…

"No. I suppose we should make sure." Martha dully brushed at her cheek. "I'll telegraph her. How do you even break the news of something like that?"

"Perhaps they'll have suggestions at the telegraph office," Emily said. The bitterness in her voice surprised her. "They ought to be used to it by now."

"Mother!" Kitty said. "Who will tell Mama?"

Not even Martha volunteered for that task. "Let's all write to her," Emily said. "She needs to hear from as many of us as possible."

"It might be months before she receives anything," Elodie said. The letter would have to be sent via a flag-of-truce boat, unless they came across someone who had a pass to cross into the Union and could put it in the mail there. "The Northern newspapers will probably pick up the story long before that."

"We can only do our best and send her our love."

Kitty scowled. "Well, all I can say is that I hate the Yankees now. And I hate Lincoln more than any of them. I don't care how many sweets he bought for us when they visited."

"Me too," Martha said. "Not that I liked him much to begin with. Such an ugly man, and with such rustic manners. Why, Emily, what does that expression mean? Are you in labor?"

"No. I don't like to hear Mr. Lincoln spoken of in that manner. For good or ill, he is family."

"Mostly ill," muttered Martha.

Even as they donned what mourning clothes they could procure in blockaded Selma, life went on. Hardin wrote to tell them that he had been promoted to brigadier general and had appointed Alec his aide-de-camp. While the sisters were still celebrating this good news, Captain Dawson, Elodie's sweetheart, returned home, minded to marry immediately, as Elodie explained to her sisters in one of the rare moments when her fiancé was not in the Whites' parlor mooning over her. "I considered saying no, as it is so soon after Sam's death, but Sam wouldn't care, surely. He always wanted people to enjoy themselves. And Captain Dawson wants to make sure I am provided for if he is called back to war and the worst happens. And—well, he kisses as well as he writes. I was pleasantly surprised."

Emily pinched her sister's cheek. "Wait until you discover the rest."

Aided by a timely blockade run that had filled the shops with goods, the sisters were able to assemble a respectable trousseau for Elodie. They were sewing away when they heard a knock at the door. As there had been plenty of people stopping by in the past few days with the wedding preparations in hand, Emily paid no attention but went on with her sewing. Then she glanced up as a man entered the room. "Alec!" She gasped as another figure came into view. "*Hardin!*"

"Think we would miss the wedding?" Alec laughed as Emily clung to her husband. "And the birth?"

When Hardin at last stepped away from her, Emily frowned, for he was clearly in pain. "Hardin? Were you injured?"

"No." He forestalled her question. "It's…er…a condition that's been bothering me awhile. Last week, the surgeon took care of it."

"Hemorrhoids," Alec said cheerfully. "We're all family here."

"Thank you, Alec, for clearing that up." Hardin winced. "Well, it's true. The hazards of being in the cavalry."

"So he's on medical leave, and what better place to spend it than here instead of in Corinth?" Alec said. "So you can thank his nether regions for us being here."

Hardin blushed, and Emily could not repress a snicker.

The girls, who had been playing at a neighbor's house, ran in. "Papa!" Kate said. "Aunt Elodie's getting married!"

"And Mama's having a baby!" Dee said.

"And poor Uncle Sam is dead," Kate said. "But they say he got to whip some Yankees first."

"Did you bring us anything?" Dee asked hopefully.

Hardin shook his head. "There weren't any shops where I was, chickens. So I just brought myself."

"That's enough," Kate said, and Dee, after a moment of consideration, agreed.

❧

With the Whites' house now overflowing with visitors, Captain Dawson kindly invited Hardin, his family, and Alec to stay at his own fine house. "I can't tell you how good this feels after a camp bed," Hardin said as he stretched out in bed beside Emily that night. "Or how good it feels to be sharing it with you, darling." He stroked her swollen belly. "The two of you."

She smiled and settled closer to him. "I will hate to have to send you back, even though you do have that fine new rank now."

"I wish I had done more to deserve it." He sighed. "My men weren't involved in the fighting at Shiloh, as I told you. We were off on scouting duty. I sent good intelligence through—and one piece of very bad intelligence. On the first day of the battle, General Beauregard was concerned with whether General Buell was going to be able to come to the aid of General Grant. We spotted General Buell's army headed toward Decatur and telegrammed Beauregard with the good news that Buell wasn't coming to Grant's side. But our scout had seen only a portion of Buell's army. The rest of his men were moving exactly where we didn't want them to be—toward Grant.

"Beauregard sent off a telegram exulting about his victory—his force had done very well that day—and decided to suspend the fighting for that day. I'm told it was not entirely from the misinformation I'd given him, that he simply thought his men could fight no more that day, and perhaps they couldn't have. But whatever the cause, the next day our victory was lost, and our army had to pull back to Corinth."

"I'm sure it was a mistake others have made."

"Yes, it's not uncommon. But it gnaws at me to have made it and to wonder how many lives, including Sam's, were lost because of it."

"If your superiors had believed you were at fault, they would never have promoted you."

"Maybe."

"Please, Hardin! Whatever happened, you are but human, and your superiors must realize that. Let us enjoy the time we have together. Doesn't you being here with me cheer you just a little?"

He kissed her, and in a moment he was the old Hardin. "Yes, it certainly does."

On May 13, Elodie and her Captain Dawson were married at St. Paul's Episcopal Church in Selma. Elodie was lovely in her white organdy dress, the material for which had been obtained by a sympathetic merchant, and Captain Dawson beamed so much throughout the ceremony, one would have never thought him reserved. Hardin, his bleak mood cast aside, looked splendid in his general's uniform. Alec, who gave the bride away, was equally fine in his lieutenant's garb. Kitty, who along with some friends Elodie had made in town was a bridesmaid, looked charming. As for Emily, feeling every bit of her nine months of pregnancy, she did her part by refraining from going into labor during the ceremony, which from the nervous glances directed at her by some of the guests had certainly been considered within the realm of possibility.

Captain Dawson took his new bride to his plantation outside of the city, leaving the Helms in possession of their fine house and well-trained servants, all of whom assured Emily that they stood in readiness to fetch the town's best midwife, Aunty Rose, and if needed, a doctor.

Near dawn on the morning of May 18, Emily opened her trunk and untied the bundle of letters that she carried from place to place. Most of them were from Hardin, dating from his days riding the circuit, but the well-thumbed one she selected was from Mary, written when Emily was anticipating the birth of her first child. "In regard to your *expectations*," Mary had written, "I expect, ere this, that they are fully realized & that now, you are a happy, laughing, loving Mama."

This time, Mary probably didn't even know Emily was pregnant—would perhaps not even hear if she did not survive the ordeal of childbirth as every woman secretly feared. These cheering words, old as they were, would have to do.

"Em? What are you doing up this early?"

Carefully, Emily returned the letter to the bundle and turned to Hardin. "It's time to send for the midwife."

Hardin immediately obeyed and, with Aunty Rose's arrival, reluctantly retreated into the library. Despite Emily's unspoken fears, all went smoothly—even more smoothly, in fact, than her previous labors. Evidently, she thrived on refugeeing from one place to another. The sun was high in the sky when Aunty Rose held up a squalling infant. "A fine boy, Mrs. Helm."

Emily took her child and gazed at him. Then a knock sounded at the door. "Please let me in!" Hardin pleaded.

"You just tell the general to wait a minute," Aunty Rose said. "Got to get Mama looking pretty first."

"No, let him. He's seen worse."

Aunty Rose reluctantly obeyed, and Hardin rushed in. "Come meet your son," Emily said.

Hardin carefully picked up the boy, tears streaming down his face. "Would you like to name him after Sam, darling?"

"No. Maybe the next one. I want to name him after another brave man—a man who gave up everything to do what he thought was right.

A man who turned down an offer from Abraham Lincoln himself to follow his conscience. I will name him Benjamin Hardin Helm Junior."

"I'm not sure if I deserve the honor. But I thank you for it."

Emily took Ben Junior from his father. "Welcome to the world, Son," she said, smiling at the baby as he squirmed in her arms. "It's a bit strange at the moment, but it's the best one we've got."

∽ 13 ∽
MARY
APRIL TO JULY 1862

E very afternoon, if she had not found some other way to occupy her time, Mary's sister Elizabeth would pick up the *Evening Star* and spend a cozy hour or so sighing over the news of the day. On the last day of April, she had no sooner settled her skirts about her and lifted the paper when she gasped. "No!"

"What is it?" said Mary.

"'The death of Samuel B. Todd, brother of Mrs. Lincoln, is announced. He died on the battlefield, from the effects of wounds, at Shiloh, in the 7th of April action.'"

Sam! Mary had been twelve when he was born. He was the second of the sons born to Mary's father and stepmother, but his predecessor, little Robert, had died very young, and Mary could still remember the way Mrs. Todd had clutched Sam against her when she nursed him, as if daring the Lord to snatch him from her as He had Sam's brother.

She had not known Sam that well. By the time he could carry on an intelligible conversation, she had gone to board at Madame

Mentelle's, and though she had come home on weekends, he had been too engrossed with his own childish affairs to concern himself with the much older sister who breezed in on Friday, argued with Mrs. Todd on Saturday, and returned to school on Sunday evening in high dudgeon and to everyone's relief. After a few years of this, she had made her fateful trip to Springfield, and since then had seen but little of Sam. But she had kept up with his doings, as she had with those of all her siblings, and had written to New Orleans to congratulate him on his marriage, then on the births of his children. Had he chosen to support the Union, she would have been delighted to get to know him better.

But instead of supporting the Union, he had taken up arms against it—against her husband and, by extension, against Mary herself, for were not she and her husband one flesh? Seen from a purely rational point of view, there was now one fewer rebel to threaten them all.

Her thoughts were interrupted by a sniffle from Elizabeth, who was dabbing her eyes, even though she had known Sam even more remotely than Mary had. "Well, he was our brother," she said. "Rebel or no rebel. And how many children did he have? Three? Four?"

"Four, last I heard."

"Should we write to our stepmother, do you think? Oh dear, it is so awkward. He was a traitor, of course—but he's our traitor."

"You can write, certainly." Mary sighed. "I dare not; neither I nor the President would hear the end of it if I did and the press found out. But do give her my condolences."

Elizabeth nodded and soon took her place at the writing desk. As her sister's pen scratched, now and then hesitating as if the writer was at a loss for words, Mary picked up the discarded newspaper. Staring at her brother's stark, short death notice, she remembered her first visit to Kentucky with her husband and their two boys, Bob and Eddie. Seventeen-year-old Sam had come home from Centre College just to see the four of them. To his young nephews, he had made a point of calling himself "Uncle Sam," until the joke had worn stale—not that the Lincolns had minded. He'd teased Mary about her small stature, something that Mary would tolerate only from a family member, and had expressed the hope that her sons might inherit their father's height rather than their mother's. "As long as they get my lovely disposition," Mary had retorted airily, and Sam had held up his hands in mock surrender.

If only he hadn't moved to New Orleans, deep in the Deep South! If he had remained in Kentucky, he might have stayed on the Union side—not that this had stopped Alec or Emily's husband, though. Perhaps she could have written to him, encouraging him to stay loyal. But what influence would a sister she hadn't seen in years have had over him? Why, Emily's husband, Hardin, had spent weeks in the White House, on perfectly good terms with everyone, and had nonetheless refused Mr. Lincoln's offer of a position and joined the rebel army. Clearly, her influence hadn't counted for much even there.

Nothing counted for much, it seemed, against the system of slavery that had entangled those brothers and sisters who had stayed in the South. Perhaps she would be as much of a rebel as the rest of them if she hadn't cast her lot with Springfield, and most importantly with Mr. Lincoln.

"Well, I've finished," Elizabeth said. "I concluded with, *While Mary's peculiar position precludes her from sending her condolences personally, please be assured that she sympathizes with your bereavement.* I think that expresses it nicely, don't you?"

"'Peculiar position,'" Mary said. "Yes, indeed."

Willie had not yet communicated with her, but the Reverend Pierpont, who had been kind enough to return to the White House at her request, had told Mary that this was quite normal. The dead had their own pre-occupations and their own ways of doing things, and sometimes might wait for months or even years before revealing themselves. Years! Surely Willie would not be so heartless. She was quite sure, however, that his spirit was hovering near her at times, usually just before she fell asleep. Mary considered trying to contact Sam as well, but changed her mind. It was best to devote all of her energies to Willie.

Reverend Pierpont had suggested a medium and named several persons who could assist her discreetly. But like anyone else who could manage it, mediums were abandoning Washington for the summer, so for the next few months, Mary would have to rely on her own amateur efforts.

Until she had experienced her first full Washington summer the year before, she had not known just how miserable a house that otherwise was not lacking in creature comforts could be. Lexington and Springfield had been warm enough, but they lacked the capital's stifling humidity, which settled over the city like a scratchy woolen blanket in May and lifted only intermittently until well into September or even October. And the insects! Not content with the swampland that abutted the Executive Mansion, giving the air a perpetual stink, the bugs did what the rebels had never managed to do: invade the White House. They seemed particularly fond of the office of John Hay, who was heard to say he had not bargained for the position of the President's entomologist, but no one, not even the President, was slighted.

President Buchanan, hastening to leave town after his successor's inauguration, had taken a moment to extol the virtues of the Soldiers' Home, which in addition to housing retired military men contained several cottages, the largest of which made an ideal presidential retreat. The outbreak of the war had prevented the Lincolns from going there the previous summer, but this year, having ridden out to view it, they had decided to make it their summer home. As President Buchanan had assured them, it was just far enough from the White House for the air to be more pleasant, and the President could easily ride back and forth between the two places as his responsibilities demanded. And Mary, freed from the impertinent presidential secretaries and all the other attendant annoyances of a house that belonged to the American people, could mourn Willie in peace.

But she had heeded Mrs. Pomroy's advice, albeit some weeks after it was given, and begun spending more time at Washington's mushrooming military hospitals, chatting with the injured men, distributing the fruit she brought in her carriage, and making herself useful in small ways such as writing letters home for the patients. As she passed through the wards, shaking hands with men who had only one hand to offer, steeling herself not to flinch from once-handsome soldiers whose faces had been grotesquely twisted, watching men who had been the mainstay of their families struggle to do something as simple as to peel the oranges Mary offered them, she shuddered at the myriad ways war could damage or destroy a man.

Many of the patients—especially those who were illiterate, who were very young, who had come from isolated areas, or who were newly arrived in America—had no idea who she was, and Mary found that she preferred that. Such men did not wonder about her loyalty or snicker in remembrance of what they had read in the newspapers about her; instead, they gratefully accepted their grapes, lemons, and oranges, smiled wanly when she inquired about them, and looked in sympathy at her mourning garments. "Who died?" one youngster asked bluntly.

"My son," Mary answered quietly. Later, on the carriage ride home, she wondered if the boy—for he could not have been more than fifteen—had assumed that Willie died in battle. She felt a twinge of guilt, for if there was one thing that she was going to make sure of, it was that no such fate befell Bob.

Bob was much on her mind, for his vacation from Harvard was soon to begin, and she and Tad were to meet him in New York on his way from Cambridge. The President had received this plan as he did just about anything these days that was not connected with the war: with an easy acquiescence that was distressingly close to indifference. He was not even in Washington when Mary left for New York, but in Virginia, having gone there to meet with General McClellan, who after dallying endlessly and being demoted from his position as general-in-chief so that he could concentrate on the Army of the Potomac had finally moved into Virginia with the intent of taking Richmond, only to be driven back by General Robert E. Lee, the man who had chosen to side with his native Virginia after that state had seceded from the Union.

Now General McClellan, who had kept much of his army out of

battle and who had stayed safely away from the front, was demanding reinforcements, as if the President could simply conjure up tens of thousands of men upon a moment's notice. Mary had decided that the general had been put on earth solely to annoy her husband. But hadn't Mary urged him to get rid of the general? It was a pity no one heeded women's advice.

Having done all she could in that department, she left for New York in July with a clear conscience. She and Tad settled into her favorite establishment, the Metropolitan Hotel at the intersection of Broadway and Prince Street, where Bob joined them the evening after their arrival. How fine he looked, especially in contrast with his care-worn father! "What a splendid Harvard man you have become," she said. "I hope you won't find your vacation dull."

"No."

"Well, you won't be bored in New York, at any rate. We have quite an itinerary planned for us. I just wish your father could join us, but that is out of the question."

She chattered on, while Bob made a polite comment once in a while. For someone who was not much like his father, he was certainly beginning to share his most maddening trait—his ability to retreat into himself. But he had just completed his examinations, and she supposed that was a trying process.

For all his reserve, Bob was a model companion, showing her all the gentlemanly courtesies that the President, with his frontier notion that a smart woman could fend perfectly for herself, still was liable to omit even when he was around to do so. They toured the *Great Eastern*, the world's largest passenger ship, and Mary admired the first-class cabins and dreamed of the day she and her husband could sail in her to Europe, the war over and his cares behind him.

Bob had another engagement, so on the last day of their visit, Mary toured several hospitals. With dignitaries and reporters tagging along, there was no chance of anonymity, but it pleased her to convey the President's gratitude to the soldiers and to assure them that he would be there himself were it not for the war. "We'll whip them," a young, one-legged private told her stoutly. "I shot a few Rebs before they got me. I just wish I could go back out there again and get me some more."

"Dear, you've given plenty," Mary said. Fleetingly, it occurred to her that some woman might be giving fresh fruit and kind words to the man who had shot Sam, if he was not dead or on his way to kill more men.

Despite this disconcerting moment, she was in good spirits when she and her sons boarded their train. They were near Baltimore, and Tad was off pestering the porter, when Bob cleared his throat, and cleared it again. "Mother," he said finally. "I don't want to go back to school. I want to join the army."

"No. The nation needs brains, not just brawn."

"Mother, that's no reason not to enlist. When the war is over, I can go back and get my degree, just like many others. It'll be an interruption, that's all."

"Not if you lose your life, it won't be."

"Others are taking that chance. Why shouldn't I? Some senators have sons in the army. Why shouldn't the President?" When Mary remained tight-lipped, he said, "The newspapers call me a coward for not enlisting."

"So? They call me a traitor merely because of my rebel relations."

"It's different for a man, Mother. And at least a traitor can have some self-respect. A coward can't."

"But you are neither. If the newspapermen are too boneheaded to understand that, it is not your fault."

"But why can't I join? Is Father opposed?"

"No, at least not as far as I know. I am. Son, try to understand. You and Tad are all I have. If anything were to happen to you—"

"We all die, Mother. I could get sick and die tomorrow."

"What a comfort you are, Son."

"Well, I could."

"I am aware of the vicissitudes of life, Bob. But there is no need to court death."

"I don't want to court death. I just want to serve my country. Can't you understand, Mother? You went to those hospitals. I can't, because

I can't look those fellows in the face, knowing that they've sacrificed and suffered, while I'm strolling around Cambridge with my friends."

"We will revisit the subject when you graduate."

"The war might be over by then."

"I certainly hope so." Mary touched Bob's sleeve as he glared at her. "Son, look at me. Would you have me put on mourning for you when I have not even come out of mourning for Willie? Have you no heart?" She fought back tears. "I thought I would go mad after he died. Your dear father even went so far as to threaten to send me to the lunatic asylum if I did not contain my grief. Even now there are days when I just want to stay in bed and weep. Would you have me endure that again? Would you really?" Inspiration struck her. "And would you burden your father, who has so many cares, with yet another? Willie's death shattered him, although he had to put aside his grief and go on for the good of the nation. Must he do that twice?"

Bob pressed a hand to his temple. "You win, Mother." He stared out the window. "For now."

∽ 14 ∾
EMILY
AUGUST TO OCTOBER 1862

After Captain Dawson came to know Emily better, he confessed to her that the very worst part of the war, for him, was having to leave his fine library behind. Emily had struggled to repress a smile, for surely there were worse things—having one's comrades dying before one's eyes, for instance—weren't there? But as the summer wore on and she spent more time in her host's book-filled study, she had come to understand his point. She did not invade his sanctum when he was home, of course, but when he was at his law office or at court, she availed herself of his hospitality and read there for hours, sometimes by herself, sometimes with Ben ensconced at her breast.

To his credit, Captain Dawson did not have the stuffy aversion to novels that so many men did, and his shelves were well-stocked with them, including the Barsetshire novels of Anthony Trollope, which had become Emily's favorites. What a world to escape to! High churchmen, low churchmen, upstarts, wealthy widows, wide-eyed heiresses, fortune-hunters, and wastrels—all settled their affairs more or less satisfactorily without anyone getting killed. Emily could just about remember her own world being like that.

She was deep into *Framley Parsonage* when a servant knocked, a telegram in her hand. Even though such things did not necessarily portend ill—given the vagaries of the Confederate mail system, Hardin sometimes telegraphed her simply to inform her of his whereabouts—Emily took it with trepidation.

Dear Wife,

Alec was killed at Baton Rouge. I am slightly wounded. Will be up in a couple of days. Remain where you are until you hear from me again.

"Dear Lord," Emily muttered. Sam had been bad enough—but Alec! Kind, sweet Alec—how could anyone, even a Yankee, want to kill him? Three years her junior, he had been the first of the younger Todds to be born after her, and she could still remember disobeying Mammy Sally's orders and sneaking into the bedroom in which her mother had labored. It had been all quite grotesque—surely she had come into the world in some more genteel way—but the wonder of squalling little Alec had made up for it. Mama had not let her hold the new arrival, but she had let her count his fingers and toes, and she had smiled when Emily, who was an excellent counter for her age, had announced that all were present.

And now her mother had lost two sons in five months. Who would tell her? When would she find out? Emily could only hope that she heard before the newspapers did.

In the meantime, her sister—Elodie, who had adored her big brother Alec—would have to be told. Emily wiped her eyes and handed the telegram to the servant. "Take this to Captain Dawson at his office, and tell him to come home immediately. Mrs. Dawson will need him."

"Yes'm."

Emily went to Elodie's room, where, as she had suspected, Elodie, stripped down to her chemise, was fast asleep on her made bed. Having got with child almost immediately after her wedding, she had been in a state of perpetual drowsiness since. Her black ringlets clustered prettily around her face, and one hand rested protectively upon her belly. "Em?" she murmured. "Is something wrong?"

"No. Go back to sleep."

It was the coward's way out, Emily knew. But she would leave it to Captain Dawson to break the news to his pregnant wife.

∽◦∾

In the moment she read of Alec's death, Hardin's report that he was injured had almost passed her by. But now, with Elodie's sobs sounding throughout the house, Emily was left alone to absorb this piece of news. What did he mean by "slightly wounded"? A sprain? A grazing by a bullet? She telegraphed him back, begging for more details.

Instead, the next day Emily received a telegram from Captain George McCawley, who in those far-off days in Louisville had been a fellow lawyer and friend of Hardin and now was one of his staff officers. In Louisville, Hardin had often invited Mac, as he was called, to dinner. He and Hardin had loved to smoke and talk politics afterward, and each evening when Mac left, he had sung out, "Well, Emily, we solved all the nation's problems tonight." In his telegram, he informed her that Hardin, though not in danger, needed tending. Could she come to Arcola Station, Louisiana, as soon as possible?

Leaving the girls with Elodie, and hoping that their care and that of her stepdaughters would distract her sister from her grief over Alec, Emily gathered her and Ben's belongings into a carpetbag and hurried to the station with Margaret. Selma sweltered in August, and the weather grew only more oppressive as she entered Louisiana. It was a slow journey, as the train often stopped to accommodate military trains, and Ben, having hitherto been a rather quiet baby, chose that trip to assert himself so vociferously that Emily fretted about being ejected from the train.

Her time of arrival had been so uncertain that she had not attempted to send word of when she would be coming, so when she at last stepped onto the platform of Arcola, there was no one to meet her. It soon became apparent, however, that Arcola was full of refugees, fleeing real or imagined Yankees. She recognized the signs: the too-stylish gowns of the women, the rush to greet each incoming train in the hopes of hearing news, and above all, the lack of occupation on everyone's part.

Naturally, the refugees knew exactly what was happening in any given part of the small town, so it took only a single inquiry to learn that Hardin and some of the other men injured at Baton Rouge had been taken to Jefferson Hall, a plantation that was now serving as a hospital. Equally simple was finding someone to drive her there.

Someone had ridden over to Jefferson Hall and announced her impending arrival, so when her carriage pulled into the mansion's carefully graveled driveway, Captain McCawley was there to greet her. With him was Ben's manservant, Phil.

Mac was as she remembered him, slightly rumpled, with hair that did not look quite combed. His uniform, in turn, did not look quite pressed; in the old days, it had been his necktie that was askew. "Fine boy you've got here, Emily."

"What is wrong with Hardin? Is he in danger?"

"No, although he's pretty banged up. His horse fell on his leg and mashed it. He'll be on crutches for weeks—maybe months. But that's not why we sent for you. They're taking good care of him. It's more—"

"He's hurting, Miz Helm. Hurting in his leg and hurting in his heart about Master Alec. He needs you to give him some heart back." Phil bowed his head. "Sorry, sir, for interrupting."

"Phil's right, Emily. He's got a bad case of the blues. I guess I should start at the beginning. I don't know how well the news travels to you, but you knew we were at Vicksburg, under siege by the Yanks? They shelled the city night after night—the most terrifying, most beautiful thing I've seen, like a hundred Fourth of Julys rolled into one. One shell came within fifty feet of Hardin and Alec. Finally, thanks in large part to our ironclad, the *Arkansas*, the feds gave up the siege, and the order came to us to follow up by retaking Baton Rouge.

"It was a hellish march. The heat, the hunger, the disease, the fatigue—hundreds of men fell sick by the wayside and had to be taken to nearby farmhouses, and those who did make it were like the walking dead. Some men claimed that they were actually sleeping as they marched. So by the time Hardin gave the order to halt outside Baton Rouge, we were all in pitiful shape. It was late in the night, and we were to attack at dawn, so we just rested in place. We were all in fairly good spirits, considering, including your brother. One of his friends had a fine red sash that a young lady had given him, and Alec asked to wear it since the friend wasn't.

"Toward dawn, we heard shots, and suddenly horsemen came galloping toward us. Naturally, we fired back. But the horsemen were our troops—rangers who had somehow gotten ahead of us without anyone knowing. Some say that the rangers were surprised by federal troops, others that they were spooked by their own shadows. I don't know. All I know is that what resulted was sheer chaos. Hardin quickly realized what was going on and rode among us, calling on everyone to stop shooting, not caring for the danger in which he was putting himself. But it was too late. His horse reared, threw him off, and fell atop his thigh, and several men were shot, Alec among them. They carried him back to a farm, still alive, but he was insensible. He died in a few hours."

"So he was shot by our own? My poor brother!"

Mac nodded. "It's not uncommon in war, sadly. Mistakes get made by men, especially when they can hardly see and they're half-dead from fatigue. But no one can tell your husband that. Oh, he knows it on a purely intellectual level, but he still blames himself for Alec's death. He had come to grow very fond of him over the past few months, and of course, he knows how fond you and your sisters were of him. He's mired in grief and self-blame."

"It's like he's fallen in a hole, Miz Helm, and can't pull himself out without your help."

Emily looked at the men, different in such important respects but united in their affection for Hardin. "I'll do my very best."

Disease, not battle, had felled most of the men in this makeshift hospital, and Emily had to fight back nausea as she followed Phil through rooms that stank of human waste and vomit. At last, she reached a bedroom where, under a veritable temple of mosquito netting, Hardin lay on his back, his eyes shut. "I've brought a visitor for you, General," Phil said.

Hardin opened his eyes. "Emma," he said faintly.

"Yes. I'm here to take care of you."

"I'm so sorry about Alec."

"I know you are. Let me look at your leg, darling."

Phil grimaced and pulled back the sheet as Emily shuddered. Badly swollen, Hardin's leg was a palette of black, blue, and green, and while he said nothing, just removing the sheet had brought tears to his eyes. "Are you in much pain?"

Hardin shrugged and stared at the wall.

"Mac told me what happened."

"I tried to stop the shooting." More tears filled her husband's eyes. "I tried so hard."

"I know you did," she repeated.

If only she could get Hardin to Kentucky! His parents would surely be able to rescue him from whatever place he had wandered into. But of course, that was impossible, with Kentucky a Union state and Hardin a rebel. All she could do was sit helplessly by as this Hardin she barely knew wept like a small boy. Finally, when he had subsided, she said, "Mac said that these things happen in battles. Don't they?" Vaguely, she remembered something like it happening in Shakespeare, but could not remember the play.

"Yes, they do." He wiped his eyes. "I can tell myself that... I do tell myself that. My head listens. My heart doesn't. And even when I can convince myself that I wasn't responsible for his death, I see him there dying, and me not even able to drag myself to his side."

Emily did not want to court such visions herself. "Let me read some poetry to you."

He nodded apathetically, and she read from the volume of

Wordsworth she had brought, having purposely chosen a poet whose words could bring only green and beautiful England to mind instead of their own wretched land. To her relief, Hardin's face did relax as he listened, and by and by he fell asleep. Emily drew the covers around him, shuddering again at his leg, and gazed at the wreck of him.

"They've got him on some strong stuff, Miz Helm," Phil said. "Morphine. That's probably making him weepy, too."

Emily also felt weepy, but she doubted she would have the opportunity to indulge herself. She pecked Hardin on the cheek; he did not stir. "It's time for me to go back and feed Ben. I'll return in the morning." Mac had found them lodgings within walking distance of the hospital but far enough removed so as not to expose her baby to the sickness there.

When she returned, however, it was to find that Hardin was not only in low spirits, but irritable. Saying that the opiates dulled his mind, he had asked to have his dosage reduced. Knowing that Hardin liked to be in complete command of his faculties—it was the reason why he, though not a teetotaler like his brother-in-law Mr. Lincoln, drank only sparingly—Emily could not but concur. But it left her with a husband who alternated between snapping at everyone around him and desponding over Alec's death.

On the fourth day, having procured some fresh fruit for her husband and done her hair in his favorite style, she arrived at the makeshift hospital to find Phil sitting glumly underneath a tree. "He's a real bear this morning, Miz Helm, if you don't mind me saying so. Tried to get him to eat and he told me to stop being such an old woman and to leave him alone."

Emily's jaw tightened. "I'll speak to him, Phil."

Hardin was gazing listlessly out a window when she entered his room. Putting on a bright smile, she asked, "How was your night, darling?"

"I thought you'd be here sooner."

"I was feeding Ben. He was hungrier than usual."

"Oh."

The Todd temper, so long repressed, broke. "'Oh'? Is that all you can say about your son? 'Oh'?"

"I only—"

"You've not even asked about him, or the girls, or my family, or my journey, or whether I need money, or anything since I got here. Do you think I came all the way here from Selma, with a fussy, nursing baby, for my own pleasure?"

"Em—"

"Poor Phil told me you snapped at him this morning! Phil! Who's been your servant since you were a small boy, who's endured all the hardships you've endured and more, I imagine. I would not blame him if he ran off and joined up with the Yankees. I would truly not blame him."

"I'm—"

"Oh, I know you're grieving for Alec. Well, do you know something, sir? I'm grieving for him as well. I've known him all of his life, after all. I even tended him—well, once when Mammy Sally had had a nip. But do you try to offer me any comfort? Tell me some stories about him that I can cherish? No, you just indulge yourself and mope as if he were your private property when anyone with any sense knows that you didn't get him killed. *You* know you didn't get him killed. You're just being self-pitying and selfish. Well, I didn't come here for this. I'm going back to my lodgings, and if you can't amend your behavior, I'll just head on straight back to Selma." She stalked to the door, unaware of the complete silence that had descended over the house as young and old, healthy and sick, listened mesmerized to her curtain lecture, or as much of it as they could catch.

"Emma! Please. Come back. You're…you're absolutely right."

She turned. Hardin had gone so far as to try to swing his weight off his bed, and his face showed what an effort this had been. "For heaven's sake! Get back into bed."

After further effort, he did. Finally, he said, "How are the children?"

"They are well."

"How was your journey?"

"Tedious and hot."

"And your sisters?"

"Grieving, but well. Hardin, you don't have to ask me all of this now. It can wait."

"Well, I tried." Hardin forced a smile and took her hand. "To tell the truth, it's not just Alec that's got me blue. It's my own situation. I wanted so badly to at last lead my men to victory—and instead, I ended up flat on my back with a horse atop my leg. And now I'm lying here wondering if I'll ever get another chance to prove my worth. What if Baton Rouge was my last battle?"

What if it was? Emily resisted the allure of the thought of her and Hardin back in a house of their own in some city far from the war front, with Hardin practicing law. There was no dishonor in retiring from the service with an injury, and even without one in due course. After all, Captain Dawson, who had never suffered anything worse than a twisted ankle, had served his time and returned to civilian life without a murmur of disapproval by his Selma neighbors. But this was not what Hardin wanted to hear. "We can't know what the future holds. But we can do our best to get you up and about soon. Which means that you must cooperate with those taking care of you."

"I know. I'm glad you came, Emma."

"Thank Mac—and Phil—for that."

"I will, and I'll apologize to Phil. I'm ashamed of myself. I thought I was a better man than that."

He sighed and lay back. Emily studied the lines of pain in his face. "You didn't rest well last night, did you?"

"No. Aside from the pain, I worry. About my command—and about whether I can be the man I used to be with you."

"Oh, Hardin. You know I will love you no matter what. But I won't give up in that department very easily."

Hardin smiled. "I'm glad to hear that."

Emily did not work a complete amendment in Hardin. Sometimes she still caught him staring sadly into space, and he had to work to contain his grouchiness. But he did call for his portable writing desk and, most encouragingly, for newspapers and cigars, the latter of which appeared to have the happy effect of driving away the flies. Soon he was smoking and muttering at the war news as of old.

"The general just needed some generaling," Phil said.

But Hardin's fears were not without foundation. A surgeon told Emily that her husband would likely feel the effects of his injury for the rest of his life, and the leg, plagued by pain, numbness, spasms, weak spots, and odd contractions, was for the moment all but useless. Just to get Hardin sufficiently recovered to use crutches required hours of endeavor, with Phil carrying out all the surgeon's orders while Hardin fought back groans of pain and Emily watched, her eyes moist with tears of sympathy.

"I've decided to free Phil when the war ends," Hardin said after one particularly grueling day of his ministrations. "He deserves it." He sighed. "I'd free him now if I didn't worry that he'd head North and maybe even join up with the army there."

"I know I said that the other day, but do you think he'd actually do that?"

Hardin shrugged. "I need him too much to take the chance. As to what he would do—who knows? I can only guess what I might do in his place. Lying here makes one think. More, in truth, than I would like to."

That evening, Emily studied Maggie as she bathed Ben. In her middle thirties, she was a pretty woman who had had several admirers in Selma, whom she had fended off as far as Emily could tell. Had she not liked them? Or was it because she knew she was fated to be brought wherever Emily happened to take her? Would Maggie stay with her if she did not have to?

"Ma'am? Do you need anything?"

"No, I was just thinking of something. Carry on."

⁓

Hardin had come away with Alec's effects, including his journal and his last letter to his mother. Emily kept the letter unopened, trusting that some day she would be able to hand it to the intended recipient, but one day as Hardin slept, she read the journal, which Alec had thriftily kept in a pocket calendar from the year before. It did not take long. Most of the entries were jotted memorabilia of his whereabouts, but some were more personal. In one entry, Alec wrote happily that he had surprised his sisters by showing up in Selma unexpectedly. Emily remembered that day; indeed, it had been a pleasant surprise. At another point Alec had either undergone a reversal in love or was simply making an excuse to wax poetical:

> Oh, what can give a moment's joy; Why should I live?
> Oh, death I hope thy friendly home will come
> In fifty years or so.

It had come in months. Emily closed the book and stared blankly into space.

"Emma."

She turned to give the same blank look to Hardin. Then he gently gathered her to his breast, and for the first time since Alec's death, she wept herself dry.

～～

At the end of August, the grand day came when Hardin was at last able to raise himself on crutches and hobble to the veranda, where Emily had arranged a surprise for him: the girls, brought down from Selma by the Whites. "I'd have gotten up on these things days before if I'd known my pets were here," he said, smiling even as his eyes betrayed the immensity of his physical pain.

"Are you going to need those things for long?" Kate asked.

"I hope not." With Phil's help, he settled into a chair and held out his arms. "See? I can still hug you. Just be gentle with my banged-up leg there." With a daughter on each arm, he smiled up at Emily. "Next step, getting on a horse."

"Just an iron horse for now," Emily begged, and Hardin and Phil nodded as if humoring her.

Hardin's success on crutches meant that they could finally leave sultry Louisiana for Marietta, Georgia. Though packed with refugees, Marietta was healthful, located at the base of the Kennesaw Mountain and with natural springs of which Hardin could partake, and its convenience to the railroad meant that Hardin could travel quickly to his regiment when called back.

Mac had found them lodgings in the house of Jacob and Fanny Levy. As the hack took them from the station at Marietta, Emily recalled what he had told them: the family was originally from Charleston, had moved to Savannah for business reasons, and fearing the vulnerability of that port city, had moved to Marietta. They had leased a large house for the convenience of their numerous children and grandchildren who might need a refuge at any given moment but were happy to host others who were in need of lodgings. "I don't think I've ever been in a Jewish person's house," Emily had said.

Mac had laughed. "The Jewish part, I doubt you'll notice any difference. Now, the Charlestonian part... They're not noted for their humility down there."

But the old couple who greeted them at the door of a sprawling house were quite cordial, though Emily detected an undertone of sadness to them. Standing alongside them was an attractive, dark-haired woman in her late thirties, who introduced herself as Mrs. Pember. She was dressed in mourning, or what best approximated it in the South where the requisite garments, if available at all, were outrageously expensive. It was she who offered to show Emily her rooms while Hardin relaxed on the veranda with the Levys. "There are a couple of places where you may stay here, but we thought with your husband's leg, you'd want these rooms," she said, gesturing to an airy room with a smaller one adjoining.

"They're perfect."

"Captain McCawley wrote that you liked to play the piano. You're welcome to use the one in the parlor, though please don't play when Father is in his study; it distracts him, as I have been told in no uncertain terms." She glanced in amusement at Emily. "I see you looking for Hebraic decor, Mrs. Helm."

Emily blushed. "Yes."

"You'll not find any. We're the next best thing to Episcopalians; in fact, I married one. Mind you, he was hard to resist as he was the kindest man in the world."

"So you are in mourning for him, Mrs. Pember? I did not wish to pry. Was he killed in the war?"

"No. He died of consumption. Some people look at me quite indignantly when I tell them that, as if he were at fault for not having the foresight to be killed by a Union minié ball. War widows have a certain cachet that the rest of us lack."

Emily smiled, and Mrs. Pember stared at her. "Someone who doesn't clutch at her throat when I open my mouth! I do say what I think, perhaps too much at times, as I am often told."

"I am used to it. My older sister is quite outspoken, too—or used to be. I haven't seen her in person for years."

"You are estranged?"

"Not in the usual manner. She is married to Abraham Lincoln."

Mrs. Pember let out a noise that sounded very much like a whistle. "So you are one of *those* Todds! Well, that's awkward. Mind you, my sister was in a not entirely dissimilar position. She is married to a Union man, but she couldn't resist the temptation to spy for us. Earned her a spell of house arrest in Washington, and she and her husband were advised to move South. So they did, to New Orleans, and then the Yankees captured it. Just a few months ago, poor Eugenia was accused of laughing during a Union funeral procession—"

"I remember reading of that! So that was your sister!"

Mrs. Pember nodded. "She told Beast Butler that she was merely laughing at her children as they were playing on their balcony, but he detests the ladies of that city and wouldn't hear reason. So now my poor sister is a prisoner on Ship Island, and her husband is using all of his Union connections to try to set her free. I suppose you wouldn't have any pull there, would you?"

Emily shook her head. "I rather doubt it. I don't think I could even get a letter to my sister if I tried."

And what would she say if she did?

∽◉∽

They soon settled into a comfortable routine at Marietta. In the cool of the morning, Hardin would hobble around the neighborhood; in the afternoon, he would visit one of the springs. On some evenings, he and Emily would go to the Georgia Military Institute to watch the cadets' dress parade.

In July, soon after their arrival in Marietta, the newspapers brought word of a second Confederate victory at Manassas, this one led by General Robert E. Lee, fresh from a week of victories over General McClellan's troops. Even the Levys and Mrs. Pember, who had been in high dudgeon with each other about a book Mrs. Pember had not returned to its proper place, came out on the porch to read the account of the battle, the Levys looking over Hardin's right shoulder, Mrs. Pember looking over the left. Now General Lee, having put much heart into the South with his string of victories, was crossing into Maryland. There was good news for the Levys as well: their daughter Eugenia had been released to the custody of her husband. But far closer to Hardin and Emily's hearts was the news that General Braxton Bragg, the commander of the Confederacy's Army of Mississippi, had invaded Kentucky, followed by word from Mac that General John Breckinridge had been commanded to take his troops—including Hardin's former brigade—to join them.

"And I not among them," Hardin said when he heard about his comrades' impending departure for their Kentucky homes. That evening he went onto the verandah and smoked in solitude far into the night.

"He's not fit to be in the field yet," Emily said to Mrs. Pember the next morning as they sat knitting socks. "Just walking on crutches for an hour exhausts him, even though he swears he's improving."

"Well, feeling useless is a hard thing, especially in a man. It's quite bad enough for a woman. Trust me, I know."

"Why should you feel useless? I know you and your parents are helping the cause in many ways. We're helping now with these socks."

"True, but I could be doing more. I've no children. No one depends on me. I've been writing to some friends in Richmond, and I've determined to try to get an appointment as a hospital matron. Oh, I've no experience, but who does? It's not as if there's been a call for such until recently. I daresay I'm bossy enough, and I did take care of my husband very well while he was an invalid and when he was dying. And it will be a way out of here. I know our family disagreements look trifling and petty to you—they certainly do to me—but I can see no way out of them, except for leaving. I am simply not constituted to be a dependent daughter."

A servant knocked at the door. "Your husband wants you on the porch, Miz Helm."

Emily hurried in obedience to the summons. "Oh, dear."

Hardin sat astride his horse. He lifted his hat and smiled at her. "Care to saddle up, madam?"

"Hardin, how on earth did you manage to get on that horse?"

"With a great deal of help from Phil, and with Mr. Levy cheering me on." Mr. Levy nodded sunnily while awkwardly smoking a pipe (a habit he had picked up from Hardin). "Getting down is going to be the hard part, I think."

Emily sighed and turned to her host. "Do you have a sidesaddle, sir?"

The day after Hardin returned (intact) from his ride, the news arrived that General Lee's push into the Union had been halted at Sharpsburg, Maryland (the battle of "Antietam" to the Yankees), and that his Army of Northern Virginia was in retreat across the Potomac. Within a few weeks, General Bragg's forces, defeated at Perryville, Kentucky, retreated to Tennessee. General Breckinridge and his men were in sight of Kentucky when they were ordered to return to Knoxville. Southern morale, which had been heightened considerably by General Lee's summer victories, dropped precipitously. It was hard, Emily thought as she tossed aside a newspaper with its account of this latest setback, to believe that the war was only about a year and a half old.

About that time, in mid-October, a letter came for Hardin. "I've been offered a command."

"In the field?"

"No. They don't consider me recovered enough for it." Hardin glared at his crutches, standing at his beck and call. "Post duty. In Chattanooga. No doubt dealing with matters such as supplies, hospitals, loose privates, and loose women."

"But it's something, Hardin."

"Yes." Hardin picked up the letter, and a faint smile crossed his face. "It's something."

∽ 15 ∾
MARY
AUGUST 1862 TO JANUARY 1, 1863

I've bad news, Mary," the President said as he walked through the door of their cottage at the Soldiers' Home one sweltering day in early August.

There was so much of that these days that Mary was ready to take this in stride. She looked up inquiringly as her husband continued. "I received news over the wires that your brother Alec was killed outside Baton Rouge. And Ben Hardin Helm was knocked off his horse and injured." When Mary said nothing, he added, "I thought you'd want to know before the newspapers reported it."

"I do. Thank you."

"Molly, you needn't put on a show for my sake. I know you're grieved about Alec. He was a fine young man, as I recall. And I know you're worried about Hardin, for your sister's sake if nothing else."

"They made their own fates. They must live—and die—by their decisions."

The President looked at her dubiously. Then he went back to

freeing the slaves, while Mary went to the privacy of her room to weep for poor Alec, whose shock of red hair had provided so much fodder for his teasing siblings over the years, and, yes, to worry about Hardin for his sake as well as Emily's.

It was in July, while riding to the funeral of Secretary Stanton's poor little baby, another casualty of the sheer unhealthiness of Washington, that Mr. Lincoln, sharing a carriage with Secretary Seward and the Secretary of the Navy, Gideon Welles, had broached the topic of emancipation—a peculiar time to broach anything, but that was Mr. Lincoln for you. A few days later, he read a draft to his Cabinet, at which time Secretary Seward had suggested that it would be best to announce the policy after a military victory. But the gods of war had not cooperated. Late July had brought another crushing defeat at Bull Run, and while the Battle of Baton Rouge had yielded a modest Union victory, despite being so disastrous for the Todds, the public was far more focused on the eastern front.

The President had not asked Mary what she thought of his plan to free the slaves. She had had too much sense to be offended; when a couple had been married as long as the Lincolns had, a wife just gave her opinion without waiting around like a schoolgirl to be asked for it. (Not that Mary had been shy about giving her opinion early in the marriage either.) In any case, she had told him that she thought it was an excellent idea. She had learned to do for herself and to put up with the vagaries of hired girls; the South could, too.

That is, unless General McClellan handed Jeff Davis the key to Washington. When General Lee defeated General John Pope at the Second Battle of Bull Run at the end of August, General McClellan, sulking over the President's appointment of General Henry W. Halleck as general-in-chief, all but chortled with satisfaction. Mary even heard rumors that subordinates faithful to the superannuated general had let the Confederate troops have their way. Yet what did her husband do then? He put General McClellan in charge of the troops around

Washington, convinced that the general's men, who for reasons inexplicable to Mary adored him, would not fight for anyone else.

Mary didn't bother to give her husband her opinion about that. He knew it, and besides he came to the Soldiers' Home that day looking like a man who had been compelled to shoot his favorite dog. There was no point adding to his misery, especially when General Lee was doing this so well by invading Maryland. Not even General McClellan could stand idle, and on September 17 at Antietam Creek, he at last brought his forces to battle against General Lee's, driving Lee back into Virginia. Mary had not had anything resembling a military education, but it occurred to her, as well as to most everyone in Washington, that General McClellan would do well to pursue General Lee across the Potomac. He did not.

In the days to come, Mary would learn of the full horrors of that battle, which turned the green and pleasant Maryland countryside into Dante's *Inferno*. Fields that should have brought forth their crops instead were covered with the dead and dying, so many in some places that it was said that one could walk across the bodies like a carpet. Even with virtually any building in the area where a human could be laid being commandeered as a hospital, a number of the wounded found their way to Washington, their bodies in every degree of disfigurement; a few, physically unscathed but blank-eyed, ended up at the lunatic asylum upon the hill. Even Miss Clara Barton, the pioneering nurse whose fortitude was legendary (and, Mary privately believed, a bit irritating) returned to Washington from the battlefield in a state of collapse, felled by endless hours of tending to the injured and a case of typhoid.

But for all the Union's bleeding and McClellan's inertia, Antietam was a victory. "I'll tell you what I'm going to tell the Cabinet," the President informed Mary at breakfast a few days later. "I promised myself—and my Maker, if truth be told—that if we drove the rebels out of Maryland, I would issue an emancipation proclamation." He held up a few unassuming-looking sheets of paper. "That on the first day of January, in the year of our Lord one thousand eight hundred and sixty-three, all persons held as slaves within any State or designated part of a State, the people whereof shall then be in rebellion against the United States, shall be then, thenceforward, and forever free."

Years ago, Mary recalled, she had assured her sister Emily that Mr. Lincoln was not an abolitionist—as if it were a dreadful thing to be. As it was back then, she supposed, when people could still believe that if they did nothing, the slavery issue would just take care of itself. "I'm proud of you, President Lincoln."

"Well, thank you," her husband said, rising from the breakfast table. He had actually eaten everything set on his plate: a rarity these days when, if left to his own devices, he might forget to eat altogether.

"Willie would be proud. He detested slavery."

Her husband smiled faintly. "You know, I think he would be."

Although President Lincoln's preliminary emancipation proclamation—a warning to the rebellious states that their slaves would be set free if they did not rejoin the Union by January 1, 1863, which naturally the rebels ignored—garnered the usual crank letters and a few death threats, abolitionists were overjoyed. The Reverend Pierpont took the opportunity to send Mary a letter commending her husband's actions. Incidentally, he added, he knew of a respectable family in Georgetown who were well placed to help her communicate with Willie. Mary's reply led to another letter, and presently, as 1862 closed with no end to the war in sight, she was invited to a séance at the Laurie residence in Georgetown. The Commissioner of Agriculture, the improbably named Isaac Newton, who turned out to be a spiritualist, would be delighted to escort her.

A séance! Mary fingered the letter. She knew, of course, that respectable people held such gatherings; they had become only more common as the battlefields swallowed more husbands, sons, fathers, and brothers. But she was the President's wife. What would the press make of her speaking to the dead? No doubt they would assume she was speaking to the rebel dead at that, taking their advice on how the President could lose the war.

But she had yet to hear from Willie, and the day she most dreaded—the first anniversary of his death—was not far in the future. Hospital visits, travel, concerts—all could distract her, even serve a noble cause—but nothing could fill the blank that Willie's passing had left in her life.

Earlier in the week, she had told her plans to Mr. French, who had been invaluable in helping her through her embarrassing difficulties about the refurbishing budget. He had chuckled and told her that years before, he had gone to Mrs. Laurie's house out of curiosity and had conversed through his hostess, via pen and paper, with President Andrew Jackson. "He was extremely complimentary about my abilities and urged that I give all assistance in my power to President Franklin Pierce, who had just come in at the time. I think it's humbug, madam, but it seems to be a harmless enough humbug."

"Did you ever have the desire to contact your late wife, sir?" Mr. French, who had wed his second wife just weeks before, had looked shocked, so Mary quickly added, "I mean before you began courting the current Mrs. French, of course."

"No, ma'am. If Bess wanted to speak to me, she wouldn't do so through a medium. Anyway, I know she's in a better place, and I hope she knows I am happy again. It's one thing to try to engage Old Hickory, another to try to speak to someone who meant the world to you."

Mary had conceded he had a point. But his situation was far different, was it not? While in her final illness, the first Mrs. French had asked her dear friend to serve as Mr. French's housekeeper after she died, all but guaranteeing that she would end up as the second Mrs. French, as she had in due course. Her intentions could not have been clearer, so why would Mr. French need to get in touch?

At worst, the séance might be a disappointment; at best, it might be enormously comforting.

So on New Year's Eve, riding in Mr. Newton's plain carriage and swathed in the anonymity that wearing the deepest mourning afforded her, Mary made the short journey to Georgetown. She had told the President where she was going, and why. Her earlier misgivings that he would think her interest in spiritualism to be a sign of lunacy proved to be misplaced, for he in his usual manner had not attempted to dissuade her or put any restrictions upon her, but simply told her, rather incongruously, to enjoy herself.

Mary was relieved to see the respectable home, indistinguishable from the others on the block, at which the carriage stopped, although she had already known that Cranston Laurie, the paterfamilias, was employed by the post office and that it was his salary, not the séances of his wife and daughters, that supported the family. She was also relieved to be shown by a servant into a perfectly conventional parlor, complete with a framed photograph of President Lincoln hanging over the mantelpiece.

Mrs. Laurie, a tall, thin woman in a dress that was of quality material and well made but plain to the point of severity, greeted her with an expression of sympathy for her loss, then said, "You may have been told this, Mrs. Lincoln, but I share my spiritual gifts only with a select circle of friends and acquaintances. I neither desire nor accept remuneration, nor do I seek out the public eye. I tell you that so that you may rest assured I have no motive other than to be of assistance to you and your husband. I speak for many, by the way, when I say I believe that he will live in history for the proclamation he is to issue tomorrow."

"Thank you, Mrs. Laurie."

"Shall we begin?"

They settled around the table, on which sat pen and paper. As they—Mary, Mr. Newton, Mr. Laurie, and Mrs. Belle Miller, the Lauries' daughter—watched, Mrs. Laurie stared at the wall, then began writing so rapidly that Mary wondered if she had been trained in the art of writing shorthand. But the paper she thrust over to Mary was perfectly legible, though hurried. *Mother, I am here. Ask me what you like. Willie.*

Mrs. Laurie thrust the pen and paper to Mary. "You may ask him anything you like."

Of course she could, Mary almost rejoined; she was his mother. Instead, she wrote, *Are you happy?*

Yes. I spend a lot of my time with my uncles Alec and Sam. They under-stand that you cannot mourn for them. But they hope you do. They have been very kind to me.

Was this a trick? Mary wrote, *Tad misses you very much.*

I miss him too. Tell him I am happy and that he should try to make you happy.

Even for Willie, this sounded a bit priggish. Mary looked at Mr. Newton, but he was staring at the ceiling, leaving her and Willie to communicate in private. *I love you.*

I love you too, Mother. I must go, but I will come again.

Mary blinked. Had it been real? Should she have asked Willie a question only he could answer?

Having no pressing need to contact his dearly departed, Mr. Newton asked Mrs. Laurie to contact Richard III, who proved to be remarkably forthright about having murdered his nephews, and assured Mr. Newton unabashedly that he would do it again. *It was a matter of self-preservation.*

The king having taken his departure, Mrs. Laurie dropped the pen with which she had been serving as his amanuensis and pressed her hands to her temples.

"Mother is entering a trance," Mrs. Miller whispered. "Do not ask her questions; she cannot respond."

In a deep voice, not masculine but certainly not her own, Mrs. Laurie spoke. "'Tis not Master Willie; 'tis not King Richard. It is I, Edward Baker. The President is doing a fine thing tomorrow by freeing the slaves, but his Cabinet does not wish him well. All of its members should be fired."

"Why, I have often told him that!" At least, Mary reflected, the President, disgusted over General McClellan's failure to pursue General Lee's troops into the South, had finally given the general the boot the previous November.

"To win the war, he must replace these men with those loyal to him. Then, and only then, will there be a glorious victory."

Mary nodded, and Mrs. Laurie resumed staring. Gradually, her features softened, and she turned to nod at Mary. "Mrs. Lincoln, did you communicate with anyone?"

"I believe I did, yes."

"Good. Then let us have some tea and cake."

When she reached the solitude of her room, Mary stared at the paper Mrs. Laurie had given her, trying to hear Willie's voice in those few, rather stilted sentences. Might he have been more boyish, more natural, had there been fewer people around? Had death conferred more solemnity upon him than he had possessed in life? Or was it Mrs. Laurie's mediating influence? Then again, Richard III had been positively jovial toward Mr. Newton.

On New Year's Day, the President, absorbed in writing his final draft of the Emancipation Proclamation, did not ask her about her evening, and Mary, not wishing to distract from the grand occasion, did not raise the topic. Besides, there was no time. After a hasty breakfast of egg, toast, and coffee, the President read over the engrossed copy of the proclamation that had just arrived from the State Department, discovered an error, sent it back, and then dashed upstairs to dress and receive the influx of New Year's visitors. Mary stood by his side as they greeted the official visitors—the diplomatic corps, the justices of the Supreme Court, justices of the lower courts, a few Cabinet members, military leaders—and then retired when the doors were thrown open to the general public. Instead, she watched from the window as a crowd of men and women surged onto the White House grounds and arranged themselves with the greatest of difficulty into a single line, knocking gentlemen's hats askew and ladies' crinolines into all sorts of odd shapes in the process.

As she returned home late that afternoon from a drive, she saw that the Executive Mansion lawn and the surrounding streets were teeming with colored people, dressed as if for church in their finest clothes. A number of them held the *Evening Star*, waving it around like a banner. A single word from the driver parted them, and as Mary entered the door, they raised a cheer. "What on earth is happening?" she asked the doorman.

"The *Star* published a purloined copy of the Emancipation Proclamation."

She hurried up to the President's office, where her husband sat alone in the gathering dusk with his feet up on his desk and a bag of ice on his right hand. "Sorry, Molly. Old habit."

"You don't have to move."

"I wasn't going to." The President grinned up at her.

"So you signed it?"

"I did. I made a dog's breakfast of the signature, though. Too painful after shaking all of those hands at the reception. But it'll do."

She gestured at the window. "Are you going to speak?"

"I'll show myself. That's about all I'm equal to at the moment. It's been a long day." He teetered back on his chair precariously. "Did you contact Willie?"

"Supposedly. I do know it could be a fraud, although the Lauries seem quite sincere."

"Take me to one of those things someday. I'm curious. Not convinced, but curious."

"I will."

As if collapsing a telescope, the President drew his legs down from the desk and rose. With Mary following and a gaggle of other people, including Bob, Tad, and the secretaries, coming out of various doors to join the procession, he walked to the window over the north front door, the customary spot for a White House speech. There, he stared down at the crowd, an intermingling of black and white faces such as Mary had never seen in her life. As one person, then another, recognized the President, cheers went up, until the entire crowd was yelling for joy and waving their newspapers. "Come out!"

"We want to hug you!"

"God bless you!"

The President pulled open the window and bowed. Mary remained in the shadows, her eyes filling with tears of pride—and humility.

While she had been trying to connect with the dead, her husband had done this marvelous thing for the living. Although his proclamation had not ended slavery in the states that had stayed loyal to the Union, nor in certain areas under Union occupation, it had nonetheless freed thousands immediately, and would free more as the Union conquered more territory. Transforming the Union cause from a fight to preserve the Union to a fight against slavery would discourage England and France from aiding the South, as supporting the enslavers would be abhorrent to the people of those nations. And the proclamation would enable colored men, hitherto allowed to serve in the Union army only as laborers, to serve as soldiers without having to pass for white, as had poor Mrs. Keckly's son.

Today, so many bright, loving children like Willie had been saved from the chains of bondage. And in that thought, Mary felt a certain consolation that had eluded her in all of her attempts to communicate with the spirit world. Who would have guessed that the awkward young man she had met in Springfield could have transformed so many lives with a stroke of his pen?

Well, she had known he would do great things, just not in what way. There was no need to deny herself credit for that.

⚭ 16 ⚭

EMILY

OCTOBER 1862 TO FEBRUARY 1863

I n the months since Emily had last seen Chattanooga, it had changed, and not for the better. The constant movement of soldiers and wagons through the town had worn ruts in the city's roads, which filled with water when it rained and perpetually oozed mud and filth. With their homes requisitioned by the army and the general difficulty of making a living, most of the town's gentry had departed. The weather was gloomy, alternating between clouds with rain and clouds without rain, with an occasional howling wind for variety.

Emily had not been so happy since before the war began.

She, Hardin, and the children had the tiniest of cottages, but after months of living as other people's guests, they had it to themselves, and the owners had even left behind a melodeon. In the mornings, Hardin would hobble off to headquarters on his crutches, Emily walking beside him and carrying his valise and the food she had packed for him. In the evenings, they would eat at their own little table, and then would go into the parlor, where they might read a book aloud, or Emily might play the melodeon.

Their friend George McCawley and the other staff officers, quartered wherever the army could find a space for them, often spent evenings with the Helms, and sometimes Emily would invite the more presentable of the town's young ladies—that is, the ones who did not chew tobacco—to join them. When Mac came over alone, he and Hardin would usually end the evening by going into the tiny room that had been designated as the smokery, and Mac, upon leaving, would call out, "Well, Emily, we won the war for President Davis tonight."

They even had a visiting relation: Kitty, who arrived just days after they had settled into their lodgings. "I have to get back to Kentucky," she said almost as soon as she stepped across the threshold. "Elodie has her husband to keep her company now, not to mention Martha, and anyway, the baby will be taking up all of her time when it comes. I miss our mother, and she needs me."

"I can get you a pass through the lines," Hardin said. He stroked his beard. "But getting you safely into Kentucky is another matter. You'll need an escort."

"I can help," offered Lieutenant William Herr. He had happened to be passing by when Kitty arrived and had accepted Emily's invitation to stay for dinner with such alacrity, one would think the man had not had a hot meal in months.

"That would be lovely of you, Lieutenant Herr," Kitty said. She dimpled, which appeared to unman the lieutenant entirely. He managed the weakest of smiles.

As it was pleasant to see this attachment sprouting, and Hardin had nothing but praise for the lieutenant's character, Emily proposed an excursion to Lookout Mountain while they were waiting for Kitty's pass. Lieutenant Herr and Kitty simultaneously declared that they had always wanted to see the famous mountain, which was certainly news to Emily as far as Kitty was concerned, and the matter was settled.

Joined by Mac, and leaving Ben Junior full of milk with Maggie and the girls in the home of an accommodating householder at the base of the mountain, they hired horses and followed a four-mile road that had been cut into the mountain. Someone had warned

Emily not to look behind her or down, and she soon recognized the wisdom of the advice as her horse calmly plodded up turns so narrow that to lose its footing would have sent her to her death. Kitty was heard to whimper in fear now and then, but was comforted by Lieutenant Herr, who generously offered to dismount and lead her horse himself. But Kitty, like most of Lexington's ladies, prided herself on her equestrienne abilities, so she gritted her teeth until they reached the summit.

"Well?" asked Mac as they dismounted, Hardin with the careful assistance of Phil. "Was it worth it?"

Emily stared at the prospect before her—the glowing autumn leaves, the winding Tennessee River, the surrounding mountain peaks—and could only nod.

After eating a spartan picnic lunch, the six separated—Mac and Phil to explore another path, Lieutenant Herr and Kitty to collect leaves (so they said), Hardin and Emily to remain seated under some trees. "They say you can see seven states from here, if you have the right glass," Emily said as Hardin put his arm around her.

"Including Kentucky. Are you homesick for it?"

"Often, but not now. It's too beautiful up here."

"You could accompany Kitty back to Kentucky."

"I could, and I could fly to the moon. You know I haven't changed my mind. I stay with you, or as near as I can."

"I know. And I'm glad of it." He caressed her cheek as she snuggled closer to him. "Besides, I'd like to be the one who takes you back home. And I promise you, someday I will."

Kitty's pass arrived a few days later. With it and her fine collection of leaves in hand, Kitty set off for Kentucky, her pockets bulging with letters from her sisters to Mrs. Todd as well as photographs of Mrs. Todd's grandchildren. Her carriage was guarded by four of Hardin's men, including, of course, Lieutenant Herr. In due time, Lieutenant Herr, looking somewhat dejected, returned with the news that Kitty had safely crossed over the lines and had been left with a friend of the Todds, who would escort her to Lexington.

Then another visitor came to Chattanooga—the smallpox. Making no distinction between friend and foe, it could be every bit as deadly as a minié ball. Hardin promptly ordered that an office be opened where the entire population, white and colored alike, could come for a free vaccination. Emily had been vaccinated some time before, as had Hardin and the girls, so she could not set a personal example, but could only offer encouragement as Chattanoogans of all ages and stations presented themselves for the ordeal, the old ladies taking it much more philosophically than the young soldiers. "Remember, there's coffee when you're done," she called, waving a pot enticingly.

"Perhaps I could get a *pouf à l'inoculation*, as did Marie Antoinette," Emily suggested that evening. "That would encourage them."

"With an enticing gown cut down to here," Hardin mused, laying a hand on Emily's bosom. "I like that idea."

Emily snorted. "I'll stick to coffee."

About that same time, a telegram arrived from Richmond, instructing them to expect a visit from President Jefferson Davis, who was taking a tour of the western front. After a day or so of frantic preparations, the grimy city was well nigh presentable when the President's train chugged into the station. Emily had heard that President Davis was a rather cold man, but she had also heard that he had an eye for the ladies, so she was not surprised when the Confederate leader bestowed a gracious smile upon her as Kate stepped forward and proudly offered him a bouquet of flowers. "A daughter who promises to be as fair as her lovely mother," he said.

"Thank you, sir."

After commending Emily upon her homespun gown, the President turned to Hardin. "You have rendered us valuable services, General, and I hope you are recovering apace."

"Thank you, sir," Hardin said. "I am eager to return to the field."

"No doubt you are." The President glanced at Hardin's cane, which Hardin was holding in a way that made it as inconspicuous as possible.

"But"—he gave a faint smile—"it is no surprise you are a man of valor, for I expect nothing less of a fellow Kentuckian."

As the men traded more compliments—perhaps the President's reputation for frigidity was ill-deserved—Emily gazed at their visitor. She could not help but note that he looked ill and tired, a far cry from his carte de visite that could be bought at any photographer's shop. Did her brother-in-law in Washington look as careworn?

❧

For weeks, both armies had been anticipating a fight in Tennessee, and it came at last at Murfreesboro as 1862 limped to a close. Neither side could quite claim victory, but the conduct of the campaign left Hardin and Mac with much to discuss and a friend to mourn: Brigadier General Roger Hanson, who had been mortally wounded while leading his Kentuckians into battle.

"I wonder who will get poor General Hanson's command," Emily said.

Mac cleared his throat. "Your husband should. He's fit to return to the field, and he deserves it. He's done a fine job here, amid the muck."

"Why, thank you, my friend," Hardin said.

"Merely stating the truth."

"I do want it," Hardin said. "My one regret when I was promoted to general was that I had to leave my brave Kentucky men behind and take over Tennessee troops—fine men, to be sure, but it's not the same as joining with one's fellow exiles and fighting not just for states' rights, but to free our own state from Yankee rule."

"So do you think you'll get it?"

Hardin shrugged. "I've made it known to my superiors that I've recovered and am eager to return to action. But there are other possibilities. Some want to see Colonel Trabue promoted, and he has distinguished himself. Some would like to see Buckner back over the brigade, and Buckner himself has said that he would be willing, although it would technically be a demotion for him. I like to think that I have my own adherents, but the truth is, I just don't know. It all depends on their whims in Richmond, where, frankly, we in the west have always felt ourselves to be somewhat of an afterthought. And yet I believe this front is key to the war."

He pulled out the pocket map he always carried and showed Emily all manner of ways in which a victory in the west for the Confederacy could spell disaster for the Union. Emily listened, her occasional nods and murmurs lulling her husband into thinking that she was attending to his words instead of focusing on her own thoughts. Hardin, back at the front. Hardin, who has been so safe here.

⁓

A day or so later, she saw her chance to waylay Mac before he stepped into the house. "Mac, do you think Hardin is really ready to return to the field?"

"I half feared you would ask that."

"Well?"

"Speaking from my vast expertise as a doctor's brother, I'd say that he is. He can get upon his horse without help now. He doesn't seem to need the cane except when he's on an uneven surface or when he's had a long day of dealing with the smallpox."

"But he still has me carry his valise for him and walk with him to headquarters."

"Emily. Admittedly, I'm a bachelor and not qualified to comment on what guides married people, but I suspect that he still has you doing those things because he enjoys your company, and he knows it makes you happy to be of use to him."

"Oh."

"He's always going to be in some pain, I think… My brother had his leg removed when he was a boy, and he still gets twinges from it, so I suppose it's no different when the leg is actually there. I doubt he'll lose that limp entirely. But the most important part is that he wants to be back in the field. Being here is wearing on him. Oh, the part about being with you is pleasant, I know. But he's not happy sitting out a war behind a desk. Neither am I, for that matter."

"Then I will have to hope he gets the assignment he wants, and not the one I want. Which would to be remain right here."

She sighed, and Mac smiled. "It can't be easy to be a soldier's wife, Emily."

"It is not. Particularly since I married with the intention of being a lawyer's wife."

"That time will come again. Just you wait."

"I hope so." She lingered outside the door. "Do you have a sweetheart, Mac?"

"No. I was too fancy-free in Louisville to settle down to a particular young lady, and now that I'm here, I haven't the heart to let someone lose hers to me. Not that I think anyone's in danger of that."

"Oh, I wouldn't be so sure of that. I've seen some young ladies eyeing you."

"I'm tempted to eye them back, because the single state does have its mixed blessings. On the one hand, it's some comfort to know that if I fall, no one's heart will be broken. On the other, it can be a comfort to know that one is the object of some beautiful creature's prayers when one goes into battle."

"I am a poor substitute for that beautiful creature, but I hope you know that you are always in my prayers."

"That actually is a comfort, Emily. Thank you."

As they walked inside, Hardin came into the room, newspaper in hand. "Well, hello, Mac. When did you get in?"

"A few minutes ago. Your wife was interrogating me about my sweethearts, or lack thereof."

Hardin laughed. "I tried to marry you off in Louisville. Remember the charming Miss Harrison?"

"Yes." Mac smiled. "I suppose it's all for the best."

When news came in January, it was not of an appointment for Hardin, but of Mr. Lincoln's Emancipation Proclamation. Despite its secession from the Union, Tennessee still contained many Unionists, whom

Mr. Lincoln had not wanted to alienate; as result, its slaves were not included in the proclamation—not that anyone would have known that from the excited whispers of Chattanooga's colored population as they headed about their business on the first of the year.

"Mary once told me that Mr. Lincoln wasn't an abolitionist," Emily said as she and Hardin walked to his headquarters the morning after the proclamation. "I suppose he changed his mind."

"He certainly did. I don't know if it was a wise move on his part; it'll put more fight in the South—not that we are lacking in that regard—and will alienate those in North who are fighting this war merely to preserve the Union. But it is a bold move."

They parted, and Emily slogged her way through the muddy streets back to their cottage. Planning to read further about Mr. Lincoln's radical course of action, she looked around for the newspaper. "Maggie? Have you seen today's paper?"

"I'm sorry, missus. I think I threw it out."

"It is all right; I can borrow a neighbor's. Just take care in the future to make sure I have finished with it."

"Yes, ma'am," Maggie said, and resumed her housework, with her mistress quite unconscious of the fact that the newspaper with its announcement of Mr. Lincoln's proclamation was at the bottom of Maggie's trunk, carefully preserved underneath Maggie's summer clothing.

Emily's thoughts were soon distracted anyway by news from Selma, courtesy of Captain Dawson: Elodie had given birth to a boy. The news was still fresh when Hardin received a second letter from Captain Dawson. He handed it to Emily with a sigh. "I'm sorry, Emily, but this contains bad news. Elodie's baby died."

"Oh no! Poor Elodie. She will need our mother's comfort—and will not be able to get it." She read Captain Dawson's sad, simple letter, in which he told Hardin that the poor little boy had been named for Alec. "I know Captain Dawson will do his best to comfort her, but of course he is grieving as well. I should go to her and offer what help I can. Can you spare me? Hardin?"

Hardin was staring at another letter. "I'm being transferred," he said quietly. "To the Eastern District Department of the Gulf at Pollard, Alabama."

"I don't even know where that is."

"The bottom of the state, bordering Florida. It's at a major railroad junction, and there's a training camp there. The Yankees hold Pensacola, and our presence in Pollard is necessary to protect the railroads leading to Mobile and Montgomery. It's a mark of confidence, I suppose. But it's not what I hoped for."

"You will still take it?"

"Of course. Even if I had a choice in the matter, refusing would put paid to any good assignments in the future. But…"

He sighed, and Emily put an arm around him. When he arose to go to his supper, his limp seemed more pronounced.

Hardin said nothing more of his disappointment, however, and they made their arrangements to leave Chattanooga. Emily and the children would be staying in Selma. It would give Emily a chance to comfort her bereaved sister, and Hardin an opportunity to determine whether the situation in Pollard was suitable for the children and if so to arrange decent lodgings for them—if any such were to be found in the thrown-together town, Emily thought gloomily.

Emily found Elodie in adequate health but the lowest of spirits. With her own hearty brood of children, Emily could offer scant comfort, only let her sister weep as she described the pretty, perfectly formed little boy who had been her short-lived son. "I should have never named him after Alec," she said. "It was bad luck."

"That would have made no difference, sweetheart. You only meant to honor our brother. He was too good for this world, that is all."

It was hollow comfort, and Emily knew it. In the end, it was Captain Dawson, who had endured the loss of two beloved wives, who had the soundest advice. "We must give her time to find her strength. She has it."

Elodie was still subdued in February, when a letter from Hardin arrived. It was dated from Tullahoma, Tennessee, not from Pollard, Alabama. Emily frowned. Was not Hardin supposed to be in the latter place? Then she looked closer and saw the exuberant cross of the *T* and the sweeping tail of the *A*.

Hardin's pleasure breathed forth in every word she read. He had barely assumed his duties at Pollard when a telegram had arrived. On orders of President Davis, General Braxton Bragg was relieving him of his post at Pollard and ordering him to report to Tullahoma, to take over command of Hanson's brigade. What maneuverings had taken place in Richmond Hardin did not know, and did not care. He had the command he had coveted from the very start, leading Kentucky men, and he prayed that God would grant him the courage and ability to do it well. But her husband's pious hope seemed almost an afterthought in the midst of his exulting.

Hardin bubbled on. The army did not move quickly, so he had not taken over his duties officially yet, but by the time she got his letter, he probably would have. Mac would be on his staff, and so would Lieutenant Herr, if she happened to be in a position to tell Kitty. She understood, of course, that now that he was back in the field, he would have to find quarters for her off post, but until those arrangements could be made, Selma would be a fine place for her to pass the rest of the winter, if of course the Dawsons were amenable.

Elodie came up behind Emily as she gazed at the letter. "Bad news?"

"Hardin has the command he has always wanted. He'll be leading Kentucky men. In the field. And it absolutely terrifies me. Back to dreading every letter, every telegram."

"I had only a year of that. It was plenty." Elodie sighed.

"It just makes me want…to shoot something."

"Then why don't we?"

Emily blinked. "I didn't mean that literally."

"I do. You know how to shoot a pistol, don't you?"

"Why, yes. Hardin gave me one when I began having to travel on my own and taught me all about it." She smiled, remembering what a patient teacher he had been and how she had jumped back into his arms when the pistol recoiled. "I've never had to use it, though. When did you learn?"

"A friend taught me when I was paying his family a visit, while Captain Dawson was courting me. I was fed up with all the busybodies and the petty society quarrels here, and it cheered me up marvelously to point at a target and fire away. And that is exactly what I want to do now. It'll do you a world of good, too." Elodie rose. "I'll get John to get everything ready."

John quickly produced a brace of pistols, bullets, and a target, and within an hour the sisters had arrived at a secluded spot on the outskirts of the city. "This is for my baby," Elodie declared as she fired her first shot. It fell just short of the mark.

"Nice," Emily said. She gripped her own pistol. "This is for Hardin being back in the field."

"You'll do better next time. For our brother Alec. Oh, bother, missed again."

"For Sam!" Emily shook her head as her bullet sailed into a nearby tree. "They say there are women who fight dressed as men. I wouldn't make a creditable one."

"For this everlasting war," Elodie said. She nodded in satisfaction as she at last hit her target.

"I can do the same." Emily fired. "Now, will you look at that! A veritable hit!"

"But what were you firing for?"

"For the war, too," Emily said. "It deserves all the shots we can fire at it."

~ 17 ~

MARY

APRIL 1863

I n April, the President decided to go to Falmouth, Virginia, where General Joseph Hooker, currently in command of the Army of the Potomac, was encamped. It became a regular excursion, because the President's old friend and physician, Dr. Anson Henry, who had been made the Surveyor General of the Territory of Washington, had come clear across the country to visit, and the President insisted that he accompany them. "Them" because Mary and Tad were part of the party.

It was bitterly cold for April, so much so that they had barely boarded their steamer, the *Carrie Martin*, at the Washington Navy Yard when the wind began to howl and the sky grew dense with snow. Soon, the captain reported that he could not safely navigate to their destination, and they were forced to drop anchor and spend the night in a cove. But Mary, who considered herself quite a sailor, slept quite comfortably in the stateroom that had been fixed up for the Lincolns—except when she overheard Mr. Noah Brooks, a journalist who was accompanying them, muse to Dr. Henry that were the rebels so minded, they could have raided the unguarded steamer as it bobbed quietly in its cove and captured not only the President but his lady to boot.

But the snowy morning found them all in their proper places, and they steamed to Aquia Harbor. If the harbor had once been a pretty, quiet place, those days were long gone. There was barely room on the waterfront, teeming with vessels, for the *Carrie Martin* to dock. Men shouted orders and curses from vessel to land and from vessel to vessel. Warehouses, so hastily constructed that they already looked decrepit, had taken the places of trees. Nothing, however, had taken the place of the mud that oozed all around them. Still, the ramshackle buildings were vivid with bunting in honor of the President's arrival, and planks had been thrown down to create a sidewalk for Mary, a gesture she appreciated even though she still had to hike up her skirts well above her ankles to protect them from the filth.

From the profusion of American flags tacked to one freight car, Mary suspected this had been designated as the car of state, and she was soon proven right. It had been fitted up with a stove and some rough benches, and in this majestic fashion, the presidential party rode the five miles to Falmouth.

Mary had visited camps before, but none on this scale: it was a virtual metropolis, only with tents instead of buildings. Tens of thousands of people were encamped here, and over the next few days, most of them would get to see their president as he reviewed the troops.

Three tents had been erected for their party. Mary, who had not slept in one before, had not been looking forward to the experience, but when she entered the family tent, she found that it had been floored with rough wood and it contained a stove and three newly made camp beds, covered with real sheets. "Why, it's quite comfortable," she said.

"Good work," the President said, looking at the floor and the beds approvingly. "We have some skilled men here. I'll be glad when they can go back and do their work at home." His face turned melancholy for a moment, as it always did when he considered those men who would not return home, but then he smiled. "Reminds me of my childhood. There were times I would have loved a tent like this, when Pa was moving us around from place to place."

"You slept in a house with only three walls, didn't you, Pa?"

"Sometimes, until our cabin could be built, and I'm in no hurry to do it again. Give me a tent any day."

Their main host would be General Daniel Sickles. Mary had long counted him, a lawyer and a former senator, as a friend. It was a mark of President Lincoln's unorthodoxy, and his trust in her, that he had never remonstrated against the general's visits, for the general was not known for his fidelity to the marital bed. It was not a subject on which he was entirely consistent, for just a few years before, he had murdered Philip Barton Key, his wife's lover, in Lafayette Square, just steps from the Executive Mansion. An excellent legal defense had won him an acquittal on insanity grounds, and the war, coming along so opportunely, had given him a chance to redeem his damaged reputation— harmed not so much by the shooting, which given the circumstances everyone thought was perfectly reasonable, but by his reconciliation with his young wife, which everyone thought was shocking.

Mrs. Sickles, however, was nowhere in evidence, but the lull in campaigning had brought many officers' wives to the camp—and, it was whispered, another class of women altogether, for General Sickles was not the only officer known to chase crinoline. But only the respectable ladies were on hand when the Lincolns arrived.

Over the next few days, the President, riding on horseback, reviewed the troops—lines of them, on horse and on foot, stretching as far as anyone could see. Tad rode, too, on a pony, but Mary preferred the comfort of the carriage. It still afforded her the ability to see what moved her most: the respect the common soldiers paid to the President, and the respect he in turn paid to them by uncovering his head as he rode among them.

The officers' ladies also rode in the procession during the reviews, and one horsewoman in particular caught Mary's eye. She was a small woman in gray, with dark eyes and a quantity of dark hair massed under a hat on which red, white, and blue feathers waved merrily. While the other ladies' horses picked their way through the mud, hers seemed to glide over it, and although she like all of her companions rode side-saddle, she managed to give the impression that she could have ridden astride, or even bareback, if she chose. "Who is that?" Mary asked Mrs. Butterfield, whose husband, General Daniel Butterfield, was General Hooker's chief of staff.

"The Princess Salm-Salm," Mrs. Butterfield said dryly.

"The what?"

"She is an American who married a Prussian prince she met in Washington. I think she came there to visit a sister, or to find work, or some sort, and instead she found a prince. He is serving in our army."

"She handles that horse like a circus rider," Mary said, half admiringly.

"Yes, very impressive, isn't it? I've spoken to her, and she is remarkably vague about her background. I believe she had a stint as an actress, which I suppose she wishes to keep quiet now that she has a title—though what the young man's people in Prussia think of his choice of wife would be interesting to know. As for the riding, there is a rumor afloat that she actually spent time in the circus, but I suspect she is simply a farm girl."

"I suppose one could put a cow in front of her and see if she milks it." Mary sniffed as the princess and her steed passed out of view.

The next day, sore from the jouncing of her carriage, she spent the morning in her tent, which since her arrival had been fitted with a very comfortable set of chairs. She was reading *Lady Audley's Secret* and was tantalizingly on the verge of discovering what the secret was when Tad burst in. "Guess what happened?"

"I have no idea; what?"

"Father got kissed!" Tad chortled, oblivious to his mother's expression. "We went into General Sickles's headquarters, and a lady ran up to him and kissed him! And this is the best part—she was a princess!"

"Princess Salm-Salm," Mary said distinctly.

"That's right. How did you guess? Anyway, once she kissed him, some of the other ladies did the same. Father was rather embarrassed—but

I think he was a little amused, too. General Sickles said they put him up to it."

"I see. Is your father on his way here?"

"Yes, he stopped to talk to someone, but he will be here soon."

"Then why don't you go to the sutlers'? Here is some money; don't let them give things to you just because you are the President's son."

Tad happily pocketed his money and ran off. His place in the room was soon succeeded by his father. "Mr. Lincoln, is it true? You allowed that creature—and the others—to kiss you?"

"I really had no choice in the matter, Mother—"

"So it is true!"

"Mother, hear me out. She's a high-spirited young lady, that's all, a bit of a hoyden, I suppose, but harmless. They thought that I looked worried, as I am"—the President was awaiting news from Charleston Harbor, on which the Union had launched a raid—"and thought it would be a lark to steal a kiss from me. They asked General Sickles for his advice, and—well, being General Sickles, he thought it a fine idea. That's all, my dear."

"A circus rider, to kiss a president!"

"Circus rider? I hadn't heard that, but it would explain her ability to handle a horse so well. If it's true."

"I have no idea whether it's true or not, and I don't care. The nerve of the man! If I had been there, I would most certainly have given him a piece of my mind. As it is, I will leave you to tell him that I do not appreciate him turning his horde of brazen hussies loose upon you, nor do I expect to be required to have any of them in my presence."

"I'll tell him," Mr. Lincoln said. "Or at least I'll tell him some semblance of that."

"Do," snapped Mary. The disadvantage of being in a tent was that Mary could not stamp off to another room, as Mr. Lincoln so richly deserved. Instead, she closed the conversation by scowling and picking up her book, leaving the President to contemplate his and General Sickles's folly.

The circus rider wisely stayed out of public view the next day—a busy one, in which the President reviewed four corps of nearly forty thousand men, including General Sickles's Third Army Corps. This meant that the general was very much in evidence, which gave Mary an excellent opportunity to ignore him studiously. This seemed to hurt her old friend's feelings, she noted with some satisfaction. Who knew that such a roué could be so sensitive?

Mary would have found some excuse to avoid dinner in General Sickles's tent afterward, but Mr. Lincoln asked her to accompany him, and she could assent yet still snub the general. So she joined him, along with the Butterfields and a few others, and was buttering her bread in frosty silence when the President cleared his throat. "I did not realize until yesterday, General, that you are an extremely religious man."

"Really? I am not entirely sure that is the most apt description of me."

"Oh, yes. Mother tells me that you are the greatest Psalmist in the army. Indeed, she says you are a Salm-Salmist."

Mary sputtered. She held a napkin up to her lips, concealing her growing smile amid the laughter about her.

"Are we friends now?" the general asked plaintively.

"Friends." She held out her hand. "But don't you dare let that circus rider near my husband again."

❧

Two days later, they boarded the *Carrie Martin* for the return trip to Washington. The weather had become milder, and they stood on the deck for a little while, watching the Virginia shoreline fade away. Mary cleared her throat. "I will ask you this, and let the matter drop. How was the circus rider's kiss?"

"Rather like a glancing blow. It was more startling than anything."

"Does it compare favorably to this?" Mary raised her chin, and her husband obligingly bent his head to receive a buss.

"No, Molly." He grinned at her as they drew apart. "Not at all."

～ 18 ～
EMILY
MAY 1863

Although Emily had fretted about Hardin's returning to the front, her fears proved to be premature, for he and his brigade were ensconced in their winter quarters in Tennessee. Emily considered joining him at camp, but it was hardly a suitable place for the girls, who through traveling about so much were already growing rather too bold in their manners. Nor would it do for the brigade's new general to flaunt his family before those who had left their own behind in Kentucky. So Emily remained at Selma until spring, when she took the children and moved to Athens, Tennessee, where a number of officers' wives were staying. Nestled in the Smoky Mountains, the town was healthy for the children, and it was cultivated enough to support a female college.

Early in May, however, Hardin invited her to the camp so she could witness a drill competition. Bringing Ben, who had not quite been weaned, with her, she alighted at the railroad station to find Hardin waiting for her. "You're a sight for sore eyes," he said. "And so are you," he added, kissing Ben, who frowned at him. "No girls?"

"Kate has had a cold, so I left them with the Van Dykes." The Van Dykes were a wealthy family in town, whose grand house the girls had taken to immediately when the family invited them to tea. "But she wrote you a little letter. She writes quite well for her age."

"Well, that will have to suffice." Hardin grinned. "And I'm not sure how they would have taken to my tent, anyway. Or how you will, my dear. It's comfortable, but that's from a soldier's point of view."

"I've learned to sleep upright in a train, with a babe in my arms. I can sleep anywhere."

"The talents we develop in war." He pointed to a wagon, driven by Phil, who looked rather disgusted with his equipage. "Your chariot, dear!"

When they arrived at camp, Hardin's staff was there to greet her, including Mac, who gave her a brotherly kiss on the cheek, and Lieutenant Herr, who asked wistfully whether she had heard anything from Miss Kitty. (Sadly, Emily had not.) She chatted with the common soldiers as well. Most, bashful in the presence of the wife of their commander, greeted her shyly, but one grinned and said, "Ma'am, if we are the Orphan Brigade, you can be our mother."

"Orphan Brigade?"

"Yes, ma'am, that's our nickname because most of us are from Kentucky and can't go back to our homes."

"Then I shall be honored."

"That is Johnny Green," Hardin said. "You can't tell from looking at him now, my dear, but he cuts a fine figure in a crinoline. Just after I took command, the men decided to reward the kindness of the townspeople by putting on a play, and Private Green was daring enough to take on the lady's part. He was splendid."

"It took a deal of doing to get a young lady to lend me a gown," Private Green said. "Ladies down here prize what they have. But I finally got a very nice pink calico and a good hoopskirt."

"I'm sure you were fetching," Emily said. "You did give them back, didn't you?"

"Oh, yes," Private Green said. "Though there were some young ladies back home who would have liked the calico."

They moved on, Hardin greeting all the soldiers by name. He seemed to know something about each of them.

"It's plain to see that your men love you," Emily said that evening as they sat in Hardin's tent. "If I were a different sort of woman, I'd be rather jealous."

"They can be a wild bunch—they were on their best behavior with you—but I love them, too. I feel as if I've come home." He pinched Emily's cheek. "And I imagine now they are talking of what a lovely wife I have."

The next day, Emily, wearing a jaunty hat and a striped green gown, watched from a buggy as the Sixth Kentucky regiment drilled against the Sixteenth Louisiana. It was a fine May day, not yet too hot, and men, women, and children from nearby villages filled the grounds as spectators. When the judges gave their verdict for Kentucky, Emily stood up in the buggy and cheered, making an absolute spectacle of herself. But who cared? Hardin and his colonels, with their careful drilling, deserved the acclaim.

Over the next two days, two more competitions were held, with Kentucky besting Louisiana each time. On the fourth day, though, Hardin nudged Emily as she lay sleeping on a featherbed on the ground next to him—the better for him to take her into his arms at night. "Wake up, sweetheart. I'm sorry; you will have to return to Athens today."

She shot up. "What?"

"We've been ordered to move."

"Where?"

"We're bound for Vicksburg. Don't say anything to anyone; the men don't know, although I suppose they can guess."

Emily winced. While the drill competition had been going on, General Ulysses S. Grant, the man to whom Fort Donelson had fallen the year before, had been attacking Vicksburg. For days, the men in the camp had been speculating about which troops might be sent to reinforce General John Pemberton's Confederate troops in that city and when. "Do you want to go there?"

"I can think of better places than Mississippi in the summer, aside from hell in the summer, but at least there's action there. And my men are ready to fight. But you know I don't want to leave you. I never do."

"I know."

She fed Ben—would he be weaned when he next saw his father?—and listlessly dressed. It had been so easy, these last few months, to be lulled into believing that Hardin might stay in this camp forever—frustrated, no doubt, but safe.

But Hardin deserved cheerfulness from her, so she brought her emotions under command and was to all appearances in good spirits when they returned to the railroad station. They had parted so often, they each had their appointed lines, which they recited as a train came into view. "I'll let you know where we are as best I can. Have you enough money?"

"Yes, I do. I'll write every few days." Veering from her script, she added, "Please keep yourself safe."

He smiled sadly. "That never won a war, sweetheart."

∾ 19 ∾
MARY
JUNE TO JULY 1863

I forgot my cat!" Tad howled. "We can't go without him."

Mary fanned herself in the carriage. Although it was only June, the Washington heat was intense, and the very idea of going back into the White House to search for the wayward feline was intolerable, especially since the creature—an inaugural present to the boys from Secretary Seward—had the run of the grounds and might well be on a mousing expedition. "Dear, we can send someone over for it later."

"No!"

"What's the matter here?" Mr. Lincoln ambled up.

"My cat, Father! I have to have her."

"Well, then you shall," the President declared. He turned away, and within fifteen minutes returned with a cat basket, from which a fearsome howling emanated. "Keep that closed well, Son."

"I will, Pa."

They were off to the Soldiers' Home again, a welcome move, for in the White House, a gloom had settled so thickly that moving seemed the only way it could be dispelled. The previous month, the irritatingly competent General Lee had won a victory at Chancellorsville, leaving Richmond so smug that it could be felt all the way to Washington. The news, as the reporter Mr. Brooks (a quite pleasant man, unlike the rest of his ilk) later said, had turned the President's face the French gray of the wallpaper, and he had hastened to the Navy Yard to set sail again for the Union camp in Falmouth. There had been no princesses offering kisses this time, no grand reviews, just a grim talk with the defeated General Hooker. Yet Mr. Lincoln had returned to Washington in reasonably good spirits, confident that the troops were not demoralized.

And now Lee's army was back in Pennsylvania. The President, who had at first dismissed the action as a raid that would amount to little, had become more concerned as of late. Would the rebels be driven back again? Or would they penetrate even farther? Mary shivered at the very thought of it.

But at least Tad's cat was accounted for.

∽ᇰ∾

Although the President was ensconced at the White House, awaiting dispatches from General Meade in Pennsylvania, Mary decided it was worth her while to attempt to lure him from his office for a short ride. Even he had to breath fresh air once in a while.

Besides, she was curious to hear the latest news from the front.

Thanks to the army encamped by the Soldiers' Home, Tad had hundreds of men to pester, not to mention the Lincolns' staff, and chose to stay home. So on the second day of July, Mary rode out alone, enjoying the comparative coolness of the morning and the quietness of her surroundings. Each year, the road between the Soldiers' Home and the White House became a little busier, corresponding with the city's growth and the military hospitals on the route, but today few were on it. Perhaps they, like the President, were waiting for tidings of the war.

The carriage passed by Mount Pleasant Hospital, which Mary supposed would get an influx of patients if the reports from Pennsylvania proved correct. She would have to visit again soon, and perhaps arrange for some ice cream to be brought to the patients. They liked it so much, and the weather was so—

"Damnation!"

As Mary started up, the coachman, still shouting curses and clutching at the air, toppled from his perch and fell headlong to the ground, landing only inches outside the path of the horses. Then the carriage lurched and Mary was thrown back against her seat as the horses galloped pell-mell down the twisting road, the small carriage tilting back and forth crazily.

She would not wait to be smashed to smithereens. Gathering her courage and her skirts, she jumped free of the carriage and landed in a heap of silk, linen, and crinoline on the ground, striking her head.

As she lay there, dazed, men swarmed around her. "Why, it's Mrs. Lincoln! Are you hurt?"

"Yes," Mary said, not too far gone to wonder at the absurdity of the question. She struggled to sit up.

"Lie still, Mrs. Lincoln," a young man commanded. "You'll make things worse for yourself."

It hurt too much to argue, even as she wondered what fine show of leg she was putting on. If she had been twenty years younger, probably half the army would be here by now. "Please tell the President."

"We will, ma'am." The young man pressed a handkerchief to the back of her head. "A little bleeding here, but not too bad. You couldn't have picked a better place to fall. Right by Carver Hospital!"

"True."

"Don't worry, ma'am. You'll be fine. We'll bring out a litter straightaway."

Sure enough, in minutes, she was lifted carefully onto a litter and borne to the hospital, where Dr. Judson Nelson, whom Mary had met during her more conventional visits to that facility, tended her. "Some bruises and a cut," he said. "But fortunately no more. Nothing that a few days' rest can't cure."

"That is a relief. I do not wish to add to the President's concerns."

When she stood, however, she was slightly dizzy, and Dr. Nelson insisted on escorting her home himself. When she arrived (and found the coach, horses, and coachman all there as well, no worse for wear), the staff put her to bed, with much clucking and fuss. She was lying there when Mr. Lincoln hurried in. "Molly!"

"I am not much hurt, Mr. Lincoln."

"So I heard, but I wanted to see for myself." He perched on the side of the bed and held her hand.

It was almost worth getting banged up for. "I don't know exactly what happened."

"I do. Somehow the driver's seat came unbolted, and when he shifted position, it catapulted him out."

Mary frowned. "Sabotage?"

"I doubt it. Probably been working its way loose for a while. I'll have a word to make sure it and the rest of the carriages are checked over. I've never figured out why we need three here, you know."

"You have enemies, Mr. Lincoln. Perhaps they were hoping you would be in the carriage."

"Now, Molly, that's an awfully roundabout way of taking a man down. Just happenstance, I'm sure. Now let's have a look at your head. Nasty, but it looks like you'll mend fine."

He resumed holding her hand, and Mary drifted comfortably off to sleep. When she awoke, it was late in the afternoon, and her husband was pacing by the window.

"Mr. Lincoln, you may leave me. I will be fine alone."

"Well, I would like to get back to my office, it's true. The news from the front is encouraging, both in Pennsylvania and at Vicksburg."

"Then go. All that walking back and forth of yours is making me dizzy."

With an alacrity that would have been annoying had there not been a war going on, he obeyed.

∽◡∽

Taking Mary at her word, the President scarcely saw her over the next two days, although he did send her the capable Mrs. Pomroy in his stead. He was not at Mary's side, but ensconced at the Executive Mansion, when a distant crackle announced the dawn of the Fourth of July—the noisiest day in Washington's calendar and the most trying for anyone of a jumpy temperament.

"Mr. Stoddard was put in charge of the celebrations for the Fourth this year. He was worried that that man Lee's invasion might put a damper on the occasion," Mary said as cymbals crashed in the distance. She winced, more from the noise than from the ministrations of Mrs. Pomroy, who was dressing her wound, which Mary supposed seemed rather tame compared to the damage a minié ball could wreak. "It seems he needn't have troubled himself."

"Indeed no, Mrs. Lincoln. Washington has far more spirit than that. Why, my boys who are able to will be seeing fireworks tonight. And the ones who are confined to bed will certainly be able to hear them. Why, what is it, Master Tad?"

As always when Tad was excited, it took a moment for him to get the words out, but their meaning was unmistakable when he did. "We won, Mother!"

"Won what?"

"Why, Gettysburg, of course! That'll teach the rebels to try to push into the North again! Father sent out a proclamation about the victory this morning. It's all over town. It's the best Fourth of July ever!" Tad frowned. "Well, except for General Sickles. I heard he lost a leg."

The lingering chilliness Mary had felt toward the roué General vanished. "How horrid! But what wonderful news about the battle! Your father had good reports before, but you never know…"

"Mother, can I set off some firecrackers? The soldiers said they would help, but no one wants to make more noise than there is already because of your head."

Mary nodded. "Yes. And tell the soldiers they can make as much noise as they please today."

∽◠◡◠

Shortly before dusk, the President appeared, looking exhausted but smiling. "Why, Molly, I thought you'd be hiding under the bed from all this racket."

"For this, I can stand a little noise."

"Me too. Now if Meade will just pursue Lee into Virginia and clean things up for good... But in the meantime, Molly, you've been stuck in here all day. Would you care to watch some fireworks? We should be able to see some of them from here."

"I would be delighted to, Mr. Lincoln."

So when it fell dark, they went onto the grounds of the Soldiers' Home, the President carrying a camp stool that he set down for Mary with unusual savoir faire. If anything, from their fine vantage point they had too many fireworks to watch—the official display orchestrated by Mr. Stoddard, the smaller displays organized by hospitals and other organizations, and the amateur ones that Mary could only hope would not get anyone killed. "From all the reports, Vicksburg will fall soon, if it hasn't already," her husband said in between explosions. "Think any of your people are there? Your scapegrace brother David, or Hardin Helm?"

"I don't keep track of my rebel relations, Mr. Lincoln, even if it were easy to do so. You know that. But...from the little I do happen to hear, by sheer happenstance, they could well be there."

"Yes." Her husband watched as a fine explosion of color arched against the sky, then dissolved. "Well, I don't wish any of them ill, but I think they're going to take a clobbering."

∼ 20 ∼

EMILY

AUGUST TO SEPTEMBER 1863

Die, Yankee!" Kate howled, and knocked Dee's doll flat on its back with her own doll as the bystanders on the platform stared.

"Why don't you let me dress them as girls?" Emily suggested. "That would make a nice change."

Kate looked at her indulgently. "Girls can't fight," she explained.

"Then at least call a cease-fire when we get on the train. You are being far too loud."

"What's a cease-fire?"

"For heaven's sake! Just be quiet."

"Yes, Mama," Kate said meekly.

While Kate's doll had no difficulty killing Yankees, the Confederacy was not doing as well. In the East, there had been the defeat at Gettysburg, ameliorated only because Meade, the fool, had not followed up his victory. Then, on the Fourth of July, as a dessert for the Union, Vicksburg had surrendered to General Grant. Hardin's men, so eager for a fight, so well drilled, had never gotten the chance to come to the city's aid.

Emily could read his frustration in his letters. *If I could do so without lowering myself in my own estimation, I would resign. This separation from you and our children is getting to be intolerable. Yet I know I must stand it; every sense of duty requires me. Excuse me for giving way to this little weakness; it is not often that I permit such feelings to take possession of me.* And, as his men covered the Confederate retreat: *I have worried along after a fashion. Some days I am hardly able to get along, but I am unwilling to give up as long as I can get along. I fear I will not be able to stand it much longer. I am very thin and weak. I may say that I have hardly slept out of a swamp since I reached Jackson.*

How thin and weak had Hardin become to admit it? Emily had shuddered when she read the letter. Was Hardin preparing her for tidings that he had contracted an illness, perhaps the dreaded yellow fever?

But his next letter was reassuring enough: the army was in camp, situated near a pine forest and a spring with good drinking water—a fine change from the march, where he had drunk water that in the past he would not have given his horse. There was plenty of fresh fruit to be had, and he and his staff had just enjoyed a large watermelon. And best of all, he had requested leave. This was partly Emily's doing. She wanted him to help her settle in Atlanta, for there had been rumors of an enemy raid into Athens, which had also attracted a Confederate cavalry camp and had become much more crowded. But if the condition of Athens had not furnished an excuse to see Hardin, she would have found one, for she was desperate to see his condition for herself. And how much help did she really need anyway?

After nearly two years of refugeeing, she could move herself and her brood as efficiently as any army. She knew every station on every railroad route between Selma, Chattanooga, and Atlanta, and she was well on her way to knowing the timetables as well. While other ladies entered a railroad carriage and stared distractedly around, waiting for assistance, Emily could skirt pass them and push her way to an empty seat in a manner that would have scandalized her mother and prostrated her grandmothers. And she still had her pistol, which she had never had to use but was fully prepared to do.

After what Emily had begun to view as a typical railroad journey—soldiers and civilians crammed into a sweltering car, and the train having to rest on a siding from time to time to let more important military trains pass—they finally reached Atlanta, where Hardin had arranged to meet them at the Atlanta Hotel, although his train was not expected until the middle of the night.

The desk clerk showed her to her room. He had opened the door and handed her the key and was getting ready to turn away when Emily said, "Please check under the beds and the wardrobes in each room."

"Madam, there is no need for concern."

"There is probably not, but my husband has instructed me to always have someone check the rooms when I travel alone with my children."

With a shrug, the clerk entered the first room and flung open the wardrobe, revealing only a ladies' stocking, which he prudently ignored. He looked under the bed, as did Kate and Dee, and swept his hand under it for good measure. Then he opened the door to the second room, and started. Protruding from underneath the bed were a pair of man's boots, which upon closer inspection were attached to a man, whom the clerk hauled out. "What are you doing here, you varmint?"

"Having a rest," the man whimpered as the clerk dragged him upright.

"Rest outside, and don't let me catch you within a block of this hotel again. Now get along with you!" The clerk pulled the man out of the room and to the stairs, where he gave the intruder a parting kick. Rubbing his hands briskly together, the clerk returned and inspected the remaining wardrobe, then gave the first room another check. "All's clear, madam. Blessed if I know how the rascal got in, but he won't bother you again."

Shaken, Emily thanked him and sank into a chair as Maggie unpacked their belongings. When night fell and the children were asleep in their room, she found herself too nervous to go to sleep, so she changed into her nightdress and sat reading by a candle far into the night until she heard a step, a soft knock, and a voice calling quietly, "Emma."

"Hardin!" She unchained the door and fell into his arms. When they drew apart, she led him to the adjoining room, where the children and Maggie lay sound asleep.

Her husband smiled at the children, then closed the door softly and took Emily back into his embrace. In moments Hardin had denuded himself of his crisp new uniform and Emily of her robe, and they were entangled on the hotel bed. "I needed that," he said when they at last lay still. "But more than anything, I've needed you."

"You *have* grown thin, my love." She traced her finger around his shoulder blades.

"I'm better than I was. Camp Hurricane was like a resort after that march through Mississippi. Constant rain, mud, hunger—we experienced it all. And for naught. If we'd been given our chance at Vicksburg…"

"Be honest with me, Hardin. Do you really think the South has a chance?"

"I don't know, sweetheart. Some days I think it does. Other days I think it doesn't. All I know is that my men still have plenty of fight in them, and that—the finest Kentucky has to offer—is what keeps me going even when I don't think there's much left in me."

"You want to leave."

"I do. I miss my old life, and above all, I miss you and the children. My leg makes me miserable on some days, and on others I remember that it was my health that caused me to give up my commission in the first place. But I won't resign, for two reasons. One, were I to do so and the South should be defeated, it would haunt me to the end of my days, wondering what small help I might have been if I had stayed in. Two, I would never be able to look my men in the face were I to resign simply to make my own life more pleasant. So I'll stay in as long as I can drag myself up on a horse. And I'm far from being unable to do that."

"You should have added a third reason."

"What is that?"

"That you could not look me in the face either."

He hugged her tightly against him. "You're absolutely right. Except that should have been the first reason." After a long time, he said. "Do you know what I'd like to do for this leave of mine? Atlanta is a fine city. I'd like to enjoy it with you. Two weeks of pure frivolity, other than getting some lodgings arranged for you. Sort of like a second bridal tour. I think we need it."

"A second bridal tour for a couple with three children?" Emily stroked Hardin's fine beard. "I love the idea, darling."

For the next two weeks they enjoyed themselves in Atlanta. They attended the theater and concerts, walked in the park with the children, and took an excursion to Kennesaw Mountain. One day, they rode the train to nearby Marietta, where they visited the Levys and caught up with the news of Mrs. Pember, now the matron of Richmond's Chimborazo hospital. The timely arrival of a blockade runner with a cargo full of goods allowed Emily to get herself a new dress in the latest style—the blockade runner having thoughtfully procured fashion books as well—and she could not help but think what a handsome family they made as they strolled down Peachtree Street, down to Maggie in her own new calico dress. Hardin and Emily even attended a hop and, despite Hardin's slight limp, acquitted themselves quite well on the dance floor.

Far too quickly, Hardin's leave drew to an end. He settled Emily and the girls at the handsome home of Colonel William Dabney, a lawyer—a great relief to Emily, who had not wanted to worry her husband with the incident of the man in her room, but who had secretly dreaded remaining there with no male protector.

"It appears that things are heating up in Tennessee," Hardin said as he gathered his things and Emily prepared for their ritual of parting at the railway station. "I expect that's where we'll end up. Rosecrans is advancing toward Chattanooga, which we have to hold."

"I still miss it there at times."

"And the South would miss it even more. It's a scruffy little place, but it's an important scruffy little place."

They took their familiar places on the platform. Emily linked her arm through Hardin's. "Remember when you left for Washington, how full of reminders and advice you were? Do you have any for me today?"

"No." A trace of sadness came over Hardin's face before he smiled. "You don't need them anymore."

"Do you have the tobacco bag I made you, Papa?" Kate asked.

Hardin patted his pocket. "I never go anywhere without it. Well, except to church, maybe."

Dee thrust her doll in her father's face. "Say goodbye," she commanded.

Hardin obeyed, then picked up Ben, who pronounced, "Papa ride train," in a sonorous tone, and then, "Train! Train!"

"He never tires of them," Emily said.

Hardin tousled his son's head. "Look out for your mama," he said. "God bless you, Emma."

Emily blinked. Hardin was devout, as was she, but this was not his usual style of farewell. Perhaps it was the cacophony of church bells in the background, although they were merely pealing the time of day. "God bless you, too, Hardin."

He kissed her and the children and swung up on the train just as the conductor blew his whistle. Then, so quickly and gracefully that no one would have ever guessed he had hurt his leg, he swung back down, gave them each another parting kiss, and hoisted himself back on the train just as it pulled out of the station. Something kept her on the platform staring after his train until it passed out of sight.

"Again, Mrs. Helm, do accept my apologies."

"It's fine," Emily said wearily, though it really was not. A couple of weeks after Hardin had departed, she had fallen ill—no more than a severe cold, it turned out, but enough to make her thoroughly miserable for a week. Just as she had begun to feel like herself again, Mrs. Dabney had sprung the bad news on her: one of her children was coming to stay and would need the room Emily was occupying. In fact, she would really need it rather soon. Reluctant to find another hotel—for if a strange man could lurk in her room at Atlanta's best hotel, what would happen at the worst?—and with the Levys' house in Marietta full, Emily had finally found a cousin in Griffin, Georgia, Mrs. Emory, who would allow her to stay for a couple of weeks until she could consult with Hardin, who according to his last telegram was somewhere in Tennessee.

So here they were, waiting for another train, heading toward another town full of strangers.

How long could she stand this? She hated Georgia's red clay. She hated not having her own house, her own piano, the dog the girls were always begging her for. She hated not being able to get a simple letter to her mother without it passing through Mr. Lincoln's censors. She hated having to adjust herself to others' routines, to fret every time that Ben cried too loudly. And careless as she and Hardin had been in Atlanta, she might well have another child on the way. She shuddered at the thought.

"Are you not well, Mrs. Helm?" Mrs. Dabney asked.

Of course she wasn't well; who could be, living like a gypsy? "I feel quite well. The day is cooler than I expected; that's all."

"Dear me. I suppose I could find some other arrangements for my daught—"

"No, Mrs. Dabney. I have enjoyed your hospitality long enough. If I have to, I can always stay with my sister."

"Mrs. *Lincoln?*" Mrs. Dabney's eyes widened in horror, and someone turned to stare at her.

"No. Mrs. Dawson, in Selma. Or Mrs. White."

"Oh." Mrs. Dabney sighed in relief.

As Mrs. Dabney made more apologies, Emily's skirt brushed a soldier who, unable to find a seat on a bench, had simply sprawled out on the platform. "Pardon me," she said absently, and then turned, half-annoyed that the young man had not even acknowledged her apology, especially as it was really he who was at fault for obstructing the platform. Then she saw why: the man was stone dead. Dead of what, a disease or an injury, she could not tell.

Perhaps he, like her, had simply lost heart.

A year ago, she would have covered his face, alerted the station master. Now, she simply walked on.

Her spirits lifted somewhat when she reached Griffin. The Emorys were there at the station with a carriage, and as they greeted her warmly and their servants loaded her meager luggage onto it, she could almost believe that this was a family visit of the sort people had paid before the war.

The next morning, September 22, was all that could be asked for in Georgia, cool and crisp but sunny, ideal for sitting outside and chatting. After breakfast, Emily and the children joined the family on the verandah. Mrs. Emory was in the process of recounting a particularly fine piece of gossip about another cousin of Emily's when a carriage stopped in front of the house, and a man in his early twenties stepped out of it.

Emily's smile froze. Everything about the scene—the size of the carriage when such a young man would have normally been on horseback or driving a sporty phaeton, the way the man removed his hat, his solemn expression—augured ill. Mrs. Emory frowned. "Why, he's with the railway, I believe. I'm quite sure I've seen him at the station. What could he want here?" She stood and called, "May I ask what brings you here, sir?"

"I'm looking for Mrs. General Helm."

Her heart hammering, Emily rose. "I am she."

The man's face, solemn before, turned grim as Maggie, unbidden, led the girls inside. He fingered a paper he held. "I've—I've—"

Emily snatched the paper from his hand.

Atlanta Sept. 22

Mrs. Genl. Helm is in Griffin. Find her + send her up on train today. The Genl. is dead.

She swayed on the porch. Around her, the world went on just as it had before her own collapsed. Absently, she passed the telegram to Mrs. Emory, who let out a little cry. "How?" she managed to utter.

"I don't know, ma'am. But there is talk at the station about a great battle that took place near Chattanooga, with much loss of life." He waited for her to say something, but Emily was silent. "The Atlanta train will be in an hour. If you can be ready, I can put you on that."

"I can pack far more quickly than that, sir." Emily raised her chin. "Hardin said I was very efficient."

"Yes, ma'am." He gestured to the carriage. "I'll take you as soon as you're ready."

Around her, people seemed to be arguing about whether she was fit to travel. "I'm perfectly capable," she said. "People die all the time. There is a war going on, after all. Isn't there?"

No one contradicted her, and she went calmly to pack her things, only to find Mrs. Emory and Maggie packing them—very irritating, as she had a system that Maggie, though a perfect servant in all other respects, had never comprehended. Why, she wasn't even bothering to pack the pistol that Hardin had bought for her, taught her so carefully how to shoot. "Give that to me," she snapped.

"No, ma'am."

This was a level of impertinence that Maggie had never shown before. Had the whole world gone topsy-turvy? "Then I'll pack it," Emily said, and snatched it off the table. She held it to her chest, remembering Hardin's careful tutorial.

Then she let it drop from her hand and sank to the floor, weeping.

∽◦∾

Who told the girls—herself, Mrs. Emory, Maggie, or someone else entirely—Emily never recalled. All she remembered was that the entire journey to Atlanta, they clutched her tight, and she clung to them, while Ben sat on Maggie's lap, sucking his thumb as if it were his only friend.

When she stumbled out of the train at the Atlanta depot, she found

George McCawley waiting on the platform. Any hopes that Emily had retained of the telegram being mistaken were dashed by Mac's painfully neat appearance. Every hair was in place; every seam of his uniform pressed. "I'm so sorry," he said, taking her in his arms. "So very, very sorry. I'd have died in his place if I could have, to spare you."

"What happened?"

"He was killed in battle near Chickamauga Creek. You never saw a man so determined, Emily. He died a hero." He released Emily and stooped down to hug the girls, who were staring at him solemnly. "A hero," he repeated. "And we were victorious." He rose, and Emily saw that his eyes were moist. "I have been put in charge of his funeral. He is being buried in the Citizen's Cemetery here tomorrow. Assuming, of course, you have no objections to it."

Even if she had had any, she was incapable of raising them. "No."

"It's a very pretty place. I picked out his resting spot this morning myself."

"Where is he now?"

"Mrs. Dabney's. I am going to take you there. She has offered you her home for the next few days."

"Mrs. Dabney's?" Emily stared at him. Two days ago, Mrs. Dabney hadn't had room for her and her children—and now she had all of them back on her hands, along with Hardin's body. She began laughing. "I am not crazy," she said when she finally stopped. "I truly am not."

Mac took her arm. "The carriage is this way."

"Wait! Who will pay for this? I have nothing saved for that. I didn't think I would have to bury Hardin. Not for years and years!"

"The government is paying for everything, Emily. Now please come along."

Guiding her like a skittish horse, Mac at last got them into a carriage. Had he remembered their baggage? She hadn't even mentioned it. Then she looked over and saw a servant loading it. Yes—all there. "Thank you," she whispered.

Mac squeezed her hand. "I'll take care of everything."

At Mrs. Dabney's house, Mac left Emily and the children in the carriage while he went inside. "He's ready for you," he said when he returned.

He led her into the parlor, the furniture of which had been rearranged to make room for an oak casket. "Shall I leave you alone with him?"

"No. Stay." Only with someone at her side could she hope to keep herself under some semblance of control, or stay upright upon her trembling legs.

He obeyed and stood back at a respectful distance while she gazed at Hardin, dressed in the handsome new uniform he had worn when he met her in Atlanta. He looked peaceful and natural, as the newspaper reporters assured their readers in such circumstances, but "peaceful and natural" was no substitute for "living," and Emily wondered how anyone could find it the least bit comforting. She trailed her hand along Hardin's impassive cheek, then the bald forehead that she had teased him about and that she had always adored. Her tears dripped on the freshly cleaned uniform. She brushed her palm against her face and sank down onto a sofa. "Tell me how he died, Mac."

Mac sat beside her and took her hand. "We crossed the Chickamauga Creek on the evening of the nineteenth in full sight of the enemy and prepared to give battle the next day. I've never seen Hardin in better spirits. He stopped by his friend General William Preston's tent and began to recite our battle song. *We'll drive the tyrant's minions to the Ohio's rolling flood—*"

"*And dye her waves with crimson with the coward Yankee blood.* Go on."

"He was laughing, predicting that those words would be proven true in sixty days. It was a cold, starry night, and when we walked back to his tent, I saw him looking at the sky. He said that he always looked for comets on clear nights."

Emily pressed her handkerchief to her eyes.

"We took our places early the next morning. While we were waiting for orders, Hardin sat under a tree, still in a fine mood. Finally, around nine thirty the order came, and he mounted his horse. One of the men said later that he looked as cheerful as if he were going on parade. He raised his sword and told his men, 'This is the road to Kentucky!'

"And there he rode—straight into an enemy breastwork and into a hail of bullets. The right side of his brigade was separated from him and the left. Twice he was repulsed. Men falling all around him. But he would not stop, Emily. He would not stop! He rallied the men for a third go. Then he gave an order to Captain William Pirtle, and in midsentence his face changed and he slid off his horse. He'd been struck in the right lower abdomen.

"They brought him to the field hospital, and General Breckinridge ordered that I stay with him. Hardin asked if there was hope. The surgeon shook his head, sadly, and told him that there was none. So he was carried to the Widow Reed's cottage, bleeding and in great pain. He was agitated at first, and adamant that he not be given any sedatives until he saw the chaplain, but after I assured him I would not allow it, he was easier and allowed us to make him as comfortable as we could. He spent a long time with the chaplain, praying and talking, and said that he had no fear of death, that he was proud to die for his country, and that his only regret was for those he left behind." Mac's voice broke, and he ran a hand across his forehead. "I'm no good at this sort of thing, Emily."

"Neither am I."

"After the chaplain left, he allowed us to give him opiates, and then he talked for a while—mostly about you. He loved you so much, had wanted to marry you as soon as he met you, and he wished he could have left you better off. He knew you would grieve for him, but he said that you were strong and would come through the ordeal. He then talked of the poss—well, then he spoke of the children, and gave his love to them and to his family in Kentucky. I checked for news of the battle, and we talked of that. He had some kind words for me, which I'll break down if I repeat. By then he was having trouble speaking. I found a book of poetry in his jacket, so I read a little of that to him. Either because I wasn't doing Wordsworth justice, or because he was simply worn out, he said he wanted to rest.

"I gave him your photograph from his pocket, and he held that until he drifted off. Only once after that, in the early evening, did I hear him utter an intelligible word. Someone came in and told us that we had won the battle, and he opened his eyes and whispered, 'Victory.' And that was it, until midnight, when he left us." Mac rose and stood by the casket. "Know, Emily, that he was never alone. I was there almost the entire time, and Herr came, too, when he could. Others visited as well. Even when he seemed insensible, we made a point of speaking to him and grasping his hand, so as to remind him that he was with friends. I hope he knew it; I think he did."

"That gives me comfort, Mac." She rose. "I think the girls should see him. Would you help me?"

Mac nodded. Clutching their dolls and being fussed over by Mrs. Dabney and her daughter, the girls were sitting in the dining room. "I want you to see your father. Remember, all that is here is his body. His soul is with the Lord. Just like we discussed on the train." So perhaps it was she who had told the girls after all.

Kate frowned. "Does he have his tobacco bag?"

Mac coughed miserably. "Actually, I have his tobacco bag, to give to your mama."

"Then how will he smoke with no place to hold his tobacco?"

"The first thing you get when you get to heaven, Kate, is a fine tobacco bag. If you like tobacco, of course."

"And if you don't like tobacco?"

If it was possible for Mac to look more tired, he did so. "Whatever you liked, Kate. Your favorite book, maybe, or a bonnet… It's all taken care of."

Kate nodded. "Don't cry, then," she commanded Dee, who had listening to this eschatological discussion with her lip trembling.

Mac lifted Kate, and Emily lifted Dee, to stare into the casket. After hesitating, Dee timidly patted her father on the cheek, and Kate, not to be outdone, kissed him on the forehead.

"Done like brave Kentucky women," Mac said.

"We're going to get Papa some flowers," Kate announced.

"Not out of Mrs. Dabney's garden, please," Emily said. "Get Maggie to take you and buy some." As she said this, it occurred to her that she had nothing in the world besides the money in her trunk, whatever salary was due to Hardin, and some receipts he had given her in Atlanta for cotton being stored at various warehouses. And Maggie and Phil. "Where's Phil?" she asked.

"I don't know. He helped tend Hardin while he was dying, and he was quite torn up when the end came. But he disappeared after that. I suspect he's headed for Kentucky, back to his own people."

So, no Phil. Not that she ever could have sold him anyway.

Yet there was surely enough to cause her misery at the moment without thinking of her penury. She pulled out her purse and handed a bill to Kate. "Buy him some nice ones."

Swathed in widow's weeds acquired from several generous Atlanta ladies—the blockade runners had not brought in any mourning goods recently—Emily sat in the Dabneys' parlor and received condolences, most from complete strangers. That morning, she had watched, dull-eyed, as Hardin's casket was lowered into the ground. Yet she had been able to feel a swell of pride at the multitudes who had turned out to escort her husband to his resting place and at the passersby who had stopped and bent their heads in respect as the funeral cortege had passed through the city's overcrowded streets.

The man heading to her now wore a natty checked waistcoat and carried a notebook. "Mrs. Helm, I am the editor of the *Southern Confederacy*. I would like to write a tribute to your husband. Can you tell me about him?"

For the first time in days, Emily came to life, chattering away about Hardin as the newspaperman assiduously scribbled. "He turned down President Lincoln's offer of a position with the enemy military. He felt that strongly about the Southern cause, and he could not be bribed with offers of advancement." She did not mention that Hardin had sought a position and changed his mind; never in her ninety-three years on earth would she mention that. Hardin deserved better than the complicated truth.

The editor finally lifted his pen. "Is there anything else you want to tell me about your brave husband, Mrs. Helm?"

"Don't let him be forgotten."

∽◡∾

The next morning, she arose just after dawn, with the servants, dressed, and went to the garden. But someone was already there—Mac, strolling around. He started. "I'm sorry, Emily. Shall I leave?"

"No. I couldn't sleep, and I wanted a little solitude before the children awoke."

"Then I am intruding."

"No. I am glad for your being here; I don't know how I could have borne the last couple of days without you."

Mac sighed. "Then I am sorry to say what I must say next. I will have to leave today to go back to the front."

"I will miss you, but I know they need you back." She stared at the rising sun. "What will I do without him? I feel utterly lost."

"I know you do. Truth be told, I feel a little lost myself. He was my closest friend. So many nights, we smoked and talked each other out of the blues." After a moment or two, he said, "Have you decided where you're going to go? Selma, with your sisters?"

"No. Kentucky. I want my mother, and Hardin's parents should have the comfort of seeing his children."

"I suppose you'll ask Mr. Lincoln for a pass?"

"Yes. He's a kind-hearted man. I'm sure he'll give it. Mac…"

"What?"

"When you told me about Hardin's last moments, you told me what he said about me, and then you started to say something about a possibility before changing the subject. What was it?"

Mac stared at the ground. "He spoke of you remarrying. He said as young and pretty as you were, you would likely remarry, and that although he was jealous of whatever that man might be, he knew you would choose carefully and pick someone who would be good to your children. Then he half smiled and said if you had to remarry, he hoped it would be to someone that he and you already knew and loved."

"I see."

This time, Mac studied his shoes. Finally, he said, "Before I leave, I must ask you an awkward question. May I write to you?"

"Why, of course."

"Just to see how you are doing—and well, just because I consider you my friend. Except for the occasional letter from my family that gets through the flag-of-truce mail, I don't hear from anybody. It gets lonesome."

"I told you a long time ago that you were in my prayers. With your kindness to poor Hardin—and to me—it is even truer now."

⚬≥⌐

Mac left Atlanta that afternoon, with a careful farewell kiss on Emily's cheek. A few days later, Emily herself left, bound for Madison, Georgia, where Eli Bruce, a wealthy man who had often assisted the Orphan Brigade, lived with his family. He had promised Emily that she could be quite secluded in his spacious home while she made her arrangements to cross the federal lines.

After the denuded family settled into their places on the train, Ben dozed in Maggie's arms, Kate took out a sketchbook that Mac had bought her, and Dee clutched her doll to her chest and engaged in a barely audible conversation with it. The doll was dressed in mourning and looked considerably more fashionable than Emily in her own hodgepodge of black garments. The girls were being so quiet, so good, it broke Emily's heart. She put an arm around each of them. "We're going to be all right," she promised them.

"When are we going to Kentucky?" Kate asked.

"I told you, it will take a while. We can't just cross over from the South to the North, or we could get arrested. We have to get passes from the Union government. Maybe even from Mr. Lincoln himself."

"But he's a bad man," Kate said. "I heard someone at Papa's funeral say so."

"He's not a bad man. He's your uncle, remember, and he and your aunt Mary used to be very fond of me—and of your father."

"But that was before the war. Wasn't it?"

"Yes, it was." Emily gazed out the window. "But I hope that their feelings have not changed." Yet the war had changed so many things. Why should she hope that this would be any different? "Even if they no longer care for us, I hope Mr. Lincoln will be kind to us as part of his family."

"I don't feel like hoping for anything."

"Well, we must. And we will."

～ 21 ～
MARY
SEPTEMBER TO DECEMBER 1863

Every time Mary entered the vertical railway at the Fifth Avenue Hotel, she did so with trepidation, but Tad did not share her wariness, and he fairly bounced with excitement as the contraption slowly descended to the lobby with a great grinding of gears. It was not his first time on it by any means; if she would allow it, he would have spent their entire stay in New York riding up and down on it.

Along with its own newsstand, a druggist, a tailor, a lady's hairdresser, and just about anything else the traveler might desire, the hotel had its own telegraph office, and it was to there that Mary headed before she left on her day's outing, having once again survived the vertical railway. "Are there any telegrams for me?"

"Yes, madam. One just came."

Mary took it, smiling. The President had sent her several over the past few days, and it was gratifyingly clear that he missed her—as well he should, since she had been in the North since late July after recovering from her head injury. On the twentieth, he had informed her that he knew of no sickness in Washington. The twenty-first had brought the assurance that the air was so clear and cool, he would be glad to see her back. A day later, he had practically begged her to return. She had made the arrangements—but then an invitation to go by river to West Point had come, and Mary had not been able to resist an excursion on the Hudson.

As she got into the carriage, she examined the telegram. Why had he sent it to her? There was no news of him personally, no plea for her to come home, simply a report of the battle near Chattanooga, which hardly seemed necessary since the New York papers, all of which Mary could obtain in the hotel lobby, were covering it perfectly well. She read on. *We lost, in general officers, one killed, and three or four wounded, all brigadiers; while according to rebel accounts, which we have, they lost six killed, and eight wounded. Of the killed, one Major Genl. and five Brigadiers, including your brother-in-law, Helm...*

Mr. Helm! He had been foolish to reject Mr. Lincoln's very generous offer, and even more foolish to get himself killed, but Mary could not help but feel sorrow. He had gotten on splendidly with the Lincoln boys—including poor Willie!—and there was no greater mark of character than that in Mary's eyes.

And what of Emily? Where was she—in Selma with Martha and Elodie, or in some other place in the South? From her sister Elizabeth, who had heard it from Mrs. Todd after Sam's death, Mary knew that Emily had left Kentucky to follow her ill-starred husband, but that was about all she knew. What would happen to her and her daughters now? Had Mr. Helm provided for them adequately? Being a widow was surely bad enough without being an impoverished widow, too. And how terrible her grief must be! Neither of the Lincolns had ever seen the Helms together, but Emily's letters before the war cut off such missives, and Hardin's wistful references to his family during his visits to Lincolns at Springfield and at the White House had made it clear that the young spouses had loved each other dearly.

For Mary, Mr. Helm's death and Emily's bereavement shaded that beautiful autumn day with melancholy, especially at West Point, where the cadets drilled for Mary and her entourage. It had not been so very long since Mr. Helm had been in attendance there. How many of his fellow graduates had shared his fate since the war began? And how many of these young men might find themselves in a battle in the months to come? The years, even? Mary shuddered. How many more young men would the god of war consume?

ↄ৵ঽ

A servant met Mary and Tad at Washington's depot and escorted them to the President's carriage, in which sat the President himself. "Well," he said, after kissing her and rumpling Tad's hair, "I've missed the two of you awfully."

"Father, I think we need a vertical railway in the White House."

"A what?"

"A little house, that goes from one floor to another. We had one at the hotel. If we had one at the White House, Mother would never have to climb stairs."

"Well, that's thoughtful of you," Mr. Lincoln said. "But I don't know if that's in the budget. Speaking of which, Molly, I was expecting some more trunks from you."

Mary blushed. "I have exercised considerable restraint, Mr. Lincoln."

In truth, she had had most of what she had bought shipped to the White House, where it would sit contentedly in her room until the Lincolns returned from the Soldiers' Home. Mr. Lincoln would likely never even notice it.

Tad dominated the conversation all the way to the Soldiers' Home and at supper, so it was not until bedtime that when Mr. Lincoln said, "I couldn't say so in my telegram, as it wouldn't do, but that was bad news about Helm."

"It was."

"I don't mind saying that the news tore me up. Left me in tears. David Davis, who stopped by about then, will tell you that I had to turn him away and shut myself up in my office. It must have seemed foolish. After all, Helm died fighting against me. It was the sheer waste of it, I suppose. Such a promising young man, dying for what? Slavery. They can dress it up as state's rights, but it's still slavery. I wish I had been able to talk him round, back when he visited. He might still have died, I suppose—couldn't imagine him not wanting to fight—but at least he would have died for the right cause, and I could honor him."

"I suppose you have heard nothing from my sister, or about her."

"Not a thing."

"Mr. Lincoln, you know up until now, I have let the rebel branch of my family fend for themselves. But I must ask: Will you assist Emily if she needs it?"

"Why, of course." Her husband gave her a quizzical look. "Did you think I wouldn't? Provided that I can do so without any harm to the Union, I'll give her whatever help I can. All she needs to do is swallow a little of that Todd pride and ask."

∽◦∽

A couple of weeks later, Mr. Lincoln, after a day working at the White House, returned to the Soldiers' House bearing letters. "Got this from a Mr. Bruce, in Madison, Georgia," he told Mary, holding a piece of blue stationery aloft. "Your sister Emily is staying with him and wants to return to Kentucky. First, he tells me that he is sure that I will regret that Helm 'could not have survived the conflict and shared in the glories of the victory'—that's rubbing it in a little, I think, but I suppose I see his point. Then he tells me your sister is 'crushed by the blow—almost brokenhearted.' Poor, poor child. Tells me that he will meet her needs as long as she cares to remain under his roof—I am glad to hear that. She has asked him to ask me for a pass to get her across the federal lines. Of course, I will issue one—but here's the part I like best, when he tells me how to send it. In *triplicates*, underlined just in case I don't get the point, I suppose. By different boats. I'm surprised he's not asking me to deliver one to Jeff Davis personally."

"Perhaps that is for his next letter."

"Maybe. But not to be outdone, your stepmother has written to me, too. She wants to go South to fetch Emily and her children—it seems she has three now, poor thing."

"Three? I never knew she was even expecting a third!" Illogically, Mary felt a burst of indignation that Emily had not told her the news.

"A war baby, I suppose. At any rate, I will issue Mrs. Todd a pass, and Emily a pass, and with luck they shall meet at some point. I just wish my generals were as willing to get about as you Todd ladies are."

Though Mary studiously ignored it, the social event of the season— nay, the decade—was approaching: Miss Chase's wedding to Governor Sprague. As the wedding date approached, Mr. Hay grew rather gloomy. "Why, I do believe the lad is a bit upset about Miss Chase getting married," Mr. Lincoln said. "I don't blame him. I think they would have made a nice couple. Both clever and sharp, and both rather easy on the eyes. But he just couldn't get her to take to him."

"Alas, Mr. Hay is not a millionaire."

"I think you nailed it, Molly. Anyway, I thought a trip to the theater might cheer him up. What about it? *The Marble Heart* is at Ford's, with John Wilkes Booth. I've heard he's a fine young actor who promises to be as good as his older brother."

So with Mr. Hay and Mr. Nicolay in tow, the Lincolns took their places at Ford's, where the proprietor, Mr. John T. Ford, had in his usual fashion converted two small boxes into a larger one so that the presidential party could be at their most comfortable.

Though not imposing in stature, Mr. Booth, with his curly dark hair and his smoldering dark eyes, was certainly fine to look upon, which made the plight of his character, a lovesick sculptor spurned by the beautiful object of his affections in favor of a wealthy rival, all the more poignant. Mary wondered if the premise of the play might hit too close to home for Mr. Hay, but he watched the proceedings detachedly, with the impassive eye of a critic. Mr. Lincoln, on the other hand, spent the entire play leaning forward in his seat. He nodded in sympathy at all the appropriate moments, laughed at the comic interludes, shook his head sadly as Mr. Booth went raging mad, and sighed when the hero crumpled to the floor, dead of a broken heart. "Fine acting," he said.

"I thought it all rather tame," said Mr. Hay.

"Did you, now?" Mr. Lincoln looked sympathetically at his secretary. "Well, to each his own. I think I'll invite him to the White House. I'd ask to meet him now, but as wrought up as he made me, I'm sure he's worn out, too. How did you like it, Molly?"

"Very well." In fact, there had been something a little unsettling about the evening, but she could not say exactly what, and in any case she was developing one of her headaches, which had become more frequent since her carriage accident. But she would not spoil her husband's fine mood.

"If I weren't so busy, I'd try to catch him as Hamlet tomorrow." Mr. Lincoln laughed. "Did you catch him looking at me when his character was accused of favoring emancipation, and he denied it? Clever of him, very clever. Looked rather sharply at me, too, I thought."

Though Mr. Lincoln did indeed extend an invitation, Mr. Booth declined it on rather vague grounds, to Mary's relief. Mr. Lincoln, though mildly disappointed, had other preoccupations, including his upcoming trip to Gettysburg, where a Union cemetery was being dedicated, to make some appropriate remarks. "It's going to be a short speech," he told Mary. "But those are the hardest to write, I think. No room for mistakes."

"Can I go with you, Pa?"

"Only if your throat is better." Over Tad's head, the President exchanged a glance with Mary. Tad did not seem seriously ill, only a little flushed and hoarse—but had not Willie started his illness in exactly the same manner?

Tad's rasp did not improve; the best that could be said was that he was not markedly worse. Still, he roused himself sufficiently so that his howls of rage echoed through the Executive Mansion as his father's carriage left for the depot the morning of November 18 without him.

If Mary had had her way, her husband would not have left

Washington, either. He looked not only tired and careworn—Chattanooga, occupied by the Union and under siege by the rebels, was much on his mind—but downright unhealthy. How he could deliver any sort of respectable speech in such circumstances, Mary had no inkling. At least she could send him the good news, later that afternoon, that Tad was somewhat better.

She was able to send him yet another encouraging telegram the next morning. Mr. Lincoln did not reply, which was no surprise, as the public inevitably took possession of him on such occasions. Mary would have to wait up for him to learn how he had borne up, and she was still waiting when, well after one in the morning, she heard the sound of the President's carriage. "You didn't have to wait up," Mr. Lincoln said. "Watch my hand; it's sore from shaking."

"Mr. Lincoln, you look terrible!"

"Yes, I think I might have a bit of what Tad's got—or something. Anyway, my bed looks mighty good to me at the moment."

"I will send for the doctor immediately."

"No, let me get some sleep. It's nothing that can't wait."

"You were able to give your speech?"

"Oh, yes. People liked it well enough. I gave my copy to Hay, but it'll be in the papers, no doubt."

And so it was. *Fourscore and seven years ago…* Mary read her husband's words over and over, marveling over his ability to encompass so much in a speech that surely must have been delivered in less than five minutes. *We are met on a great battlefield… We have come to dedicate a portion of that field as a final resting place for those who here gave their lives that that nation might live. It is altogether fitting and proper that we should do this. But, in a larger sense, we cannot dedicate—we cannot consecrate—we cannot hallow—this ground. The brave men, living and dead, who struggled here, have consecrated it, far above our poor power to add or detract. The world will little note, nor long remember what we say here, but it can never forget what they did here.*

She carried the newspaper into Mr. Lincoln's room, where he was dressing for the day, although a sensible man would have stayed in bed.

"You're wrong about the not-long-remembering part, Mr. Lincoln," she said. "It was a magnificent speech. Here, let me get that thing for you."

Her husband stood still as she adjusted his cravat. As long as he had been wearing them, he still acted as if he were being garroted when she tied it. "Well, I hope you're right, Molly."

∽⊘∼

For a few more days, Mr. Lincoln attended to his duties, while for once, all the inhabitants of White House—Mary, the secretaries, the staff—were united, bound by their desire to see him go to bed and rest. Even Tad, bedridden himself but improving daily, pointed out that if he had to stay in bed, there was no reason that Pa should not as well.

At last, a week after his return from Gettysburg, the President allowed that he did not feel equal to rising from his bed. Soon he had a spectacular rash, and Dr. Washington van Bibb, called from Baltimore to give his advice, gave his diagnosis. "Varioloid."

"The smallpox?" Mary wailed.

"A mild case of it, it appears. But you must be confined to your sickroom, Mr. Lincoln, for the next few days, and see no one who has not had smallpox."

"Not even any office seekers?" The President managed a faint smile. "That's a shame, for now I have something I can give to everybody."

∽⊘∼

By December, the President, though thinner than ever and pale, had largely recovered, although under doctor's orders, he rested in his room daily and retired at a respectable hour. With her husband mending and Tad fully mended, Mary could turn her attention to an upcoming visit from a group of Russian officers, which would require considerable pomp. She was pondering what the evening's musical selections should be when Mr. Lincoln came in. "We are going to have a visitor, Molly. A special one."

"Another one? Who?"

"Your sister Emily."

❧ 22 ❧

EMILY

NOVEMBER 1863

After a quest dogged by delay and bureaucratic muddling on the part of the chain of command of two warring nations, the passes were in order: Emily could go North, and her mother, who had been boarding in Lexington with Kitty while her Kellogg nieces attended school in that city, could go South to get Emily and the children. With Tennessee in contention, the party would have to go to City Point near Richmond, then take a flag-of-truce ship to Fortress Monroe outside of Norfolk, under Yankee control, and proceed to Baltimore. From there, they could at last leave for Kentucky.

Her sister Martha, with her husband safely home from his brief war service, would be joining them as well. She claimed that she wanted to consult a specialist about a female problem she was having, but Emily suspected that her stylish sister was lured more by the prospect of replenishing her wardrobe in the metropolis of Baltimore.

The addition of Martha to the party, however, would be countered by a subtraction. Very early in Emily's quest to return to Kentucky, it had become clear that if Maggie came with them, it would have to be as a free woman or not at all. Freeing her was out of the question, Emily had decided. It was too much like conceding defeat. But she could not sell her either, although as an experienced nursery maid and fine seamstress, she would have fetched a fair price. Even if Maggie's people had not been with the Helm family for generations, Emily had recoiled too often as she walked by slave markets to inflict that fate upon a woman who had tended her children, and tended them well, from their infancy. Nor would she risk having Maggie fall into the hands of a man who might treat her unspeakably.

At last, Emily had determined to leave Maggie in Selma with Elodie, although Elodie and her stepdaughters already had their personal maids and hardly needed another servant. But Elodie was once again expecting. If the child thrived this time, as Emily prayed he or she would, there would be a need for Maggie's services until Emily could reclaim her servant.

Still, warning the children of the impending separation had been scarcely less difficult for Emily than telling them of their father's death—after all, for two years they had seen more of Maggie than they had of poor Hardin. And Maggie herself... She had said quietly, "I was kind of hoping to get to Kentucky, too, ma'am."

"I know, but I simply can't take you there now with things as they are. But as soon as I can manage it, I will send for you. In the meantime, you will be fine with Mrs. Dawson. You know her, and she is a kind mistress."

"Yes, ma'am. She is."

That was all that had been said on the subject. But Emily could not shake her feeling that she had not done right by the woman, especially when she saw a tear drip from Maggie's eye as the servant sat reading the Bible while the children napped. Even that was a reproach, as it had been Hardin's sister Lucinda, back in Kentucky, who had taught her and all the Helm servants to read. Not even the gowns Emily gave to Maggie—some scarcely worn, but all useless to Emily now that she was in mourning for Hardin—assuaged her guilt. Instead, Maggie in her cast-off gowns seemed to be only a darker, equally gloomy version of herself.

But then the news that her mother was on her way south cast, for the moment, all thoughts of Maggie from Emily's mind. As Mrs. Todd wanted to spend a few days in Selma with Elodie and Martha, Emily said goodbye to the Bruces in Georgia and traveled there.

Emily had not trusted herself to contain her emotions on meeting her mother for the first time in two years, especially under the present circumstances. Instead, she waited at Elodie's home while her sisters went to the depot to meet Mrs. Todd's train from Montgomery.

At last, Emily saw the Dawsons' carriage come into view. The stately figure inside—dressed in mourning like herself—had not even put both feet to the ground when Emily ran into her arms. "Mama," she said, her tears keeping her from saying more.

"My darling girl. I wish I could make it right for you; I cannot. But I am here to be useful for you in whatever way I can."

But Mrs. Todd was a grandmother as well as a mother, and when Emily at last pulled away and made an effort at composing herself, Mrs. Todd turned to beam at the girls and Ben. "Girls, do you remember Grandma? And look at this fine young man! Now, I couldn't pack much, but I did bring some presents for you."

As the servants lugged some trunks into the house, their quantity and bulk suggesting that Mrs. Todd's ideas of light packing were flexible, a colored woman stepped out of the carriage. She curtsied and smiled shyly at the children, who, standing alongside an impassive Maggie, looked warily at her as Mrs. Todd said, "Children, this is Delilah. She will be helping take care of you while…for a while."

Kate and Dee glared at the interloper, while Ben stuck his thumb into his mouth contemplatively.

Wisely, however, Mrs. Todd gave Delilah the task of opening the largest of the trunks, into which the children promptly delved. The girls squealed as they discovered their presents—a French doll and a coral necklace for each—and Ben happily dragged out anything that took his fancy, ignoring the little train and Noah's ark designated for him. With difficulty, Mrs. Todd wrested various items from Ben's possession to hand to her daughters, then nodded at Emily. "These are for you, my dear, just some nice things appropriate for your situation. You mustn't let yourself go; it will lower your spirits, and poor Hardin would want to see you looking well."

Emily stared at the pile of goods her mother had handed her—the finest mourning cloth that could be had in Lexington, jet necklace and brooch, and a black bonnet and veil to top it off—and smiled. Woman that she was, she had hated her present mourning attire, which showed all too clearly that it had been assembled in makeshift fashion.

"Tomorrow we'll go to the dressmaker's," Mrs. Todd said. She patted Emily's hand. "And I have some cod-liver oil for you to take. You look terribly run-down, poor thing."

"Yes, Mother," Emily said dutifully.

It was a blessed relief, being told what to do.

༄

That evening, as a servant helped Emily out of her petticoats and hoop and removed her corset—it being unthinkable in the Dawson household that any white person should disrobe unaided—Emily caught her mother looking closely as Emily stood revealed in nothing but chemise and drawers. She waited until they were alone to say, "I am not pregnant, Mama. I have had two bleeds as proof positive of that."

Too relieved to scold Emily for speaking so frankly, Mrs. Todd said, "I almost wish it could have been otherwise, but under the circumstances..."

"Yes, I am poor enough as is."

"What do you have?"

"A couple of hundred dollars in gold—the government was kind enough to pay me Hardin's unpaid salary in coin instead of our money—and some receipts for cotton that Hardin bought from time to time and stored in Mississippi and Georgia. If I could bring the cotton to market in the North, I would be comfortable for a while."

Mrs. Todd nodded knowingly. The need of the South for capital and the North for cotton had led to a flourishing trade in cotton between the two enemies, some of it illicit, some of it sanctioned by both the Union and the Confederate governments. Mr. Lincoln had issued a number of permits for the practice.

"You must get Mr. Lincoln to let you sell it." Mrs. Todd patted Emily's shoulder as they lay down side by side, and Emily instinctively curled closer to her mother. "And I am sure he will. You were a favorite of his, and goodness knows that after Hardin and your brothers, he owes you some decency."

"I haven't even asked you about your own sorrows, Mama."

"I am trying to bear them like a Christian, child. That is all I can do. But it is hard, especially with Alec. Sam at least left behind something of himself in his daughters. But with Alec, it is almost as if he never walked the earth. At least I know he had a decent burial. That gives me some comfort. That must suffice."

A day or so before Emily was set to travel to Richmond, a letter arrived from Mac. He had read in the newspaper of her mother's arrival in the South—the connection with Mrs. Lincoln making the various Todds' comings and goings a matter of interest in the press—and was writing in hopes that the letter would reach her before she went North. He thought she would like to know that he had survived the recent Battle of Chattanooga (he did not need to tell her the sad news of the South's loss there), and asked her if she could send the enclosed letter to his mother, as he did not know if she had gotten his last flag-of-truce letter. He missed Hardin and sometimes found himself talking to him in his head, not in a crazy manner of course. And, to tell the truth, he missed her, just as he missed his sisters. One day, he hoped, he would see her in Kentucky. In the meantime, she would always be in his thoughts, and he hoped he would be in hers.

It was a simple, straightforward, brotherly letter, but something in it made her smile, and something in it made her cry. But then, just about everything made her cry these days.

꙰

The steamer *New York* from Richmond to Norfolk was full of humanity. There were a couple of gaunt political prisoners, returning to their
homes after being exchanged for Southern counterparts; a pathetic
clutch of orphans, going to reside with relatives in the North; a few
invalids and elderly people headed for specialists or more congenial
climates; wives, mothers, and sisters come to tend their wounded; and
widows in every stage of mourning. The girls, whose travels thus far
had not included a steamer, scurried on deck among them all, and
Delilah, who thus far had stayed well in the background, displayed a
hitherto unseen force of character by periodically snatching them away
from the railing.

None too soon for Emily, who had discovered that travel by water
made her slightly queasy, the steamer docked at Fortress Monroe, and
a man in a blue uniform boarded the ship, clutching a sheath of papers.
"Loyalty oaths," he said. "Sign them, and you're free to pass on."

Their faces showing a gamut of emotions, the Southerners on the
boat took the papers, and soon the room was filled with the sound of
scratching pens. Emily stared at the paper before her.

I do solemnly swear, in presence of Almighty God, that I
will henceforth faithfully support, protect, and defend the
Constitution of the United States, and the Union of the
States thereunder; and that I will, in like manner, abide by
and faithfully support all acts of Congress passed during
the existing rebellion with reference to slaves, so long and
so far as not repealed, modified, or held void by Congress,
or by decision of the Supreme Court; and that I will, in like
manner, abide by and faithfully support all proclamations
of the President made during the existing rebellion having
reference to slaves, so long and so far as not modified or
declared void by decision of the Supreme Court: So help
me God.

"Ma'am? Isn't your pen working?"

"I cannot sign this." Emily held out the paper. "I just cannot."

"My dear child—"

"Emily, sign it, for heaven's sake."

"I have a pass from Mr. Lincoln himself. Isn't that good enough? I will do nothing to make him rue his generosity. But I cannot take this oath. My husband died fighting for the South! It would be a betrayal of him."

"Shoo, now, all of you," the officer said, waving out the oath takers. "You'll be wanting to get on your way. Ma'am, much as I sympathize with your position as a widow, I cannot let you pass through the lines without you taking the oath. You'll have to talk to General Benjamin Butler, I suppose."

"*Beast* Butler?" asked Martha.

"*General* Butler, madam. It would do you well to remember that."

"I'm not the one refusing to take the oath," Martha said pertly. "She is."

They followed the soldier to General Butler's stately headquarters. Leaving them in the parlor, he disappeared and returned with General Butler. Few Yankees, though he had impressive competition, were more loathed by Southerners. When he was the military governor of captured New Orleans, the general had ordered that women who showed contempt for the occupying soldiers would be treated as women of the town, and it was he who had come up with the idea that escaped slaves would be treated as contraband of war instead of being returned to their masters. "I understand we have a problem here," he said in a milder voice than Emily had expected.

"They want me to take the oath. I cannot."

"So I heard. Madam, without the oath, I have no power to send you on. I can certainly send you back, though. But is it really such an impossibility? All you have to do is swear to be loyal, which in a nutshell means that you aren't to commit treason. No one's asking you to cheer on the Union army or wave the flag."

"I understand that, sir, but I cannot. My husband gave his life for the South, as did two of my brothers. I have a brother fighting there still. My dearest friends are still in the South."

"All right, madam. Stop before you've convinced me that I'd be a fool to let you pass across into Union lines, even with the oath. There's but one man who can decide what to do with you, and that's President Lincoln. I'll telegraph him. You do know he's been ill, madam?"

"I'm sorry," Emily said meekly. "I really do not mean to be such a bother."

General Butler merely quirked an eyebrow. "Depending on how long it takes him to rise from his sickbed, it may take a while to receive a reply," he pronounced, and left the room.

"Darling," Mrs. Todd said, "I know this is difficult. But you really—"

"I cannot, Mother." She thought of the letter she had written to Mac just before leaving Selma. *Never will I break faith with the South or with my dear friends there…*

Mrs. Todd pursed her lips and sighed.

But sooner than anyone could have hoped, General Butler returned, flourishing a telegram, which he handed to Emily. *Send her to me. A. Lincoln.* "Looks as if you'll be paying a visit to Washington, Mrs. Helm."

Emily gulped. "It does."

"Well, you've still time to get on the steamer to Baltimore, so no harm done." General Butler ushered them to the door. Then his eye lit on Delilah, and he frowned. "You're not a slave, are you, Aunty?"

"*Servant,*" said Kate.

"I am a freedwoman," Delilah said almost tetchily. "I have *papers.*"

"All right, all right. Go, all of you, in peace. And welcome to the United States!"

∼⚭∼

At the Washington depot, Emily stood uncertainly on the platform as Kate craned her head, looking for important people. After her party had reached Baltimore, Emily had telegraphed Mr. Lincoln to inform him of her plans, but no one had told her what to do when she arrived in Washington. Did one simply ask to be driven to the

Executive Mansion? Would she need to show her pass? As she hesitated, trying to remember what Hardin had told her about his visit there, a man in his midfifties, soberly dressed, stopped before her and bowed. "Cousin Emily?"

"Why, Cousin John!" There was no sweeter sight she could have seen in the strange depot than a fellow Todd, and John Todd Stuart, who had left his native Lexington for Springfield, Illinois, years before, was every inch a Todd. "How glad I am to see you here."

"I am in Congress now, and the President thought you would like an escort, not being familiar with Washington." Cousin John turned his attention to Kate. "Now, who is this? When I last saw your mother, she was barely out of short skirts, and now look what a fine young lady she's brought with her."

"I am Miss Helm," Kate said loftily.

"Why, of course! Then let me see you to your carriage." He took Emily's arm. "I am sorry that your mother did not accompany you."

"She decided to stay in Baltimore with Martha and my younger children. Under the circumstances—"

"Ah, yes." Cousin John nodded gravely, and to Emily's relief made no further allusion to the losses that had befallen the Todds in the last year. "We'll take our time going there, so you can see the sights on the avenue. See the Capitol? The statue of 'Freedom' was added just a short while ago. One day that dome just might be finished."

Emily dutifully admired the Capitol, and then the houses, bedecked with Christmas greenery, lining Pennsylvania Avenue—the city's main thoroughfare and one of the few with proper sidewalks. As in the South, those walkways were thronged with soldiers, except that these were dressed in blue. The civilians were out in full force on the brisk Saturday afternoon as well, and Emily felt a pang to her heart as she observed the ladies' fine clothing—no homespun here—and compared it to that of the ladies of the South. Young men were in abundance, and while a few women in widow's weeds could be spotted on the avenue, they were far outnumbered by ladies in bright colors.

"It really is white," Kate said approvingly as the Executive Mansion came into view. "And big. Though maybe not as nice as President Davis's house." "I wouldn't point that out," Cousin John said dryly.

"Oh, I won't," Kate assured him. "That would be rude."

The doorman waved them in, bowing to the ladies, and Cousin John led them upstairs. "The President and Mrs. Lincoln should be in the library," he said, and called, "We're here!"

Immediately, the door opened and the couple Emily had not seen in nine years stood before her. As General Butler had told Emily, Mr. Lincoln had been ill, but Emily was still shocked to see him looking so gaunt. He resembled his Confederate counterpart in one respect: every day of the war had left its mark on his countenance, and his private sorrow had added to that as well. Mary also looked careworn beyond her years, but her beautiful dress, a fashionable half-mourning gown of silk with black-and-white stripes, topped with a black lace shawl that was too fine and sheer to be useful for anything besides decoration, caught Emily's eye, as it would that of any sentient female, before anything else.

"My dear Emily," Mary said as Emily pushed back her mourning veil. "You poor, dear child."

"Allow me," Mr. Lincoln said, and clumsily untied Emily's bonnet strings. "Welcome to Washington, Little Sister."

∾ 23 ∾
MARY AND EMILY
DECEMBER 1863

A lthough Mary had seen her share of mourning women since the war began, and had of course been in that sad state herself, it was still a shock to see Emily—so fresh, so pretty in her flowered frock and blooming bonnet when Mary had last seen her when she left the Lincolns' home in Springfield to return to her mother's house in Kentucky—clad in the deepest, dullest black. Her lips were downturned, partly from sorrow, and partly from something else that Mary found herself not wanting to analyze deeply. Defiance? Determination? Anger? But after Mr. Lincoln had helped her out of her cloak and bonnet, she came into Mary's arms with only a moment of hesitation.

"It is so good to see you, dear," Mary said. "Even under these dreadful circumstances."

"And you, too." Emily brushed at her eyes. Regaining her composure, she touched the arm of the little girl beside her, an auburn-haired sprite who in looks clearly took after her father's side of the family.

"Brother Lincoln and Sister Mary, this is my older daughter, Kate. Kate, this is Mr. and Mrs. Lincoln."

"Your uncle and aunt," Mary said with a smile.

But Kate, as was the case with most children, was staring at Mr. Lincoln. "You're tall," she announced.

"Kate! That is so rude of you. We do not comment on people's appearances."

"But true enough," Mr. Lincoln said, smiling down at his niece. "Why don't you and I find your cousin Tad? And he can show you around this big old house, including the fortifications on the roof your papa helped build a long time ago."

Kate agreed, and she and Mr. Lincoln departed, leaving Mary and Emily standing alone together for the first time in seven years. Mary touched her sister's cheek. "Sit down and let us have some tea together, dear. We have much to talk of."

Emily obeyed, her crepe dress rustling as she settled into her chair.

Mary cleared her throat. "I was very grieved to hear about Mr.—General, that is—Helm. He was very dear to us." *If only he had accepted the President's offer*, she almost said.

"And you to him." Emily fell silent as a servant came in, bearing the tea things.

"Do you like the china?"

"It's lovely."

"It ought to be; I picked it out myself. Oh, there was a fuss about that! I do admit that I overspent. But really, there was scarcely a matched table setting to be had when we arrived here."

Emily nodded. Too late, Mary reflected that in Emily's penury—for that Mr. Bruce had spoken of her being in straitened circumstances—she might find this talk of fine china offensive. But her sister said, "I'm quite sure it was necessary."

"It certainly was."

Another silence fell. Had her sister been so quiet in the past? No; the Emily in Springfield, though deferential as became her position at that time as an unmarried and much younger sister, had been quite lively. But then the pall of grief that hung around her now had not been present.

Finally, Emily cleared her throat. "I wanted to comfort you so badly when I heard of poor Willie's death," she said. "He was such a darling boy."

"There could have been very little comfort you could have offered. He was the light of our lives." Mary sighed. "Our sister Elizabeth came to stay with me afterward, and goodness knows she did her best. I have come to terms with his death as much as I ever will, but I still find myself looking for him in a room from time to time."

"I still wake some mornings thinking that Hardin is merely on campaign and will be returning on leave."

"You have suffered the loss I dread most of anything. Of course, being younger, I am likely to outlive Mr. Lincoln in the natural course of things, but were he to die before his time—it does not bear thinking about." She shuddered. "Tell me of our sisters in Selma. Did Elodie ever marry the man with all the wives?"

"You make him sound like Henry VIII." For the first time, Emily managed a smile. "They did marry, but she is only his third wife—and, I hope, his last. They seem quite happy together. They lost their first child, but she is expecting another, and I hope all will go well."

"Ah, poor mite. And Martha?"

"Martha is in Baltimore with Mama, and is, well…Martha. Kitty managed to get back to Kentucky and is there now."

"Has she a suitor?"

"One of Hardin's staff officers took an interest in her. I saw him at—at Hardin's funeral, but I do not know where he is at present."

"Well, I hope he comes through the war safely."

The war! Men off to their first battle talked of "seeing the elephant," as Mary had learned from her visits to the hospitals in the cases where the seeing had not gone well, and the war stood between her and her sister like an elephant, blocking a natural conversation. How could she wish anyone on Emily's side well, without feeling that she was thereby wishing her own side ill? With trepidation, she said, "Emily, I was also grieved to learn of Sam's and Alec's deaths. You understand I could not openly mourn for them, nor could Mr. Lincoln, but it saddened us deeply. They were fine young men, with promise of more."

"Yes."

Mary turned the topic to Elizabeth, Frances, and Ann, her three sisters in Springfield. With their husbands past fighting age and no sons in the war yet, the Springfield sisters were eminently safe topics of conversation. Unfortunately, this safeness also meant a certain dullness, which made the discussion of the ladies' doings a short one, not enlivened by Emily's monosyllables.

With a certain desperation, Mary plunged on. "Do tell me about that your new son of yours, and your daughter Dee."

At last, she had struck conversational gold. Emily reached into the pocket of her dress and pulled out a slender photograph album, large enough to hold half-a-dozen cartes de visite. "Here are the three of them. It was taken in Atlanta, during—during Hardin's last leave. Aren't they just like their father?"

Repressing a sigh—for she saw that all roads led to Hardin—Mary agreed.

❧

"This is the Prince of Wales Room, where you will be staying, my dear," Mary said, pointing to Emily's trunk, which had already found its way there. "It is named, of course, because during the previous administration, the Prince of Wales stayed here. I rather wish he had delayed his visit to America, so we could have hosted him."

"Then I am quite honored. It's lovely." In truth, there was far too much dark purple in the room for Emily's taste, even though it was lightened somewhat by yellow cords.

"Several presidents died here, as did our poor Willie." Mary's eyes brimmed with tears. "I hope you may never know such a loss, my dear."

"I pray I do not." Emily looked around the room, which seemed more funereal than ever. "Perhaps—"

"Our sister Elizabeth stayed here during her last two visits," Mary said in a more cheerful tone. "She found it quite commodious—although, being Elizabeth, she had to say it might be a bit too large for her taste."

The knowledge that her practical sister Elizabeth had slept in the room cheered Emily somewhat. "Perhaps you could call it the Todd Room."

Mary chuckled, a bit too much, as she did at every remark Emily made.

Emily knew she was not being particularly companionable. In her still-raw grief, she found it hard to withstand the force of her sister's personality, and she could also not shake the feeling that she was in hostile territory, even if the White House was an oasis in the midst of it. But Mary was exerting herself so much for Emily, despite clearly still feeling the loss of poor Willie, that Emily determined to rouse herself. "Could you show me the greenhouse?"

Mary put an arm through hers. "I would be delighted."

In the evening, a caller came for Mary—General Daniel Sickles, who entered the room with as much aplomb as a one-legged man on crutches could manage. Emily, knowing of his scandalous reputation, not to mention the fact that he had borne arms against the South, was inclined to give him a formal reception, but was surprised when he gave her an equally formal one—it not having occurred to her that he might have his own grievances. Having exchanged a few inconsequentialities with him and Mary, Emily said, "If you don't mind, Mary, I will retire. It has been a long day."

"Of course, my dear."

In her room, however, she found a visitor: Tad, playing checkers with Kate, who should have been in bed but was at least in her nightgown. "Hullo, Aunt Emily," he said, standing politely but showing no inclination to leave. "I thought I'd stop by and see Cousin Kate."

"That is very kind of you."

"Did General Sickles tell you about his leg?"

"Well, no. I understand he lost it at Gettysburg, though. A pity," she added politely.

"He gave it to the Army Medical Museum, and they say he can visit it anytime he likes."

"Really? I wonder what on earth he will say to it."

"That's a good question," Tad said. "Well, I guess I should be off. Cousin Kate is a very good checker player," he added gallantly.

"I won two games," Kate said.

"So, how do you like your cousin?" Emily asked when Tad had left the room.

"He's nice." Kate furrowed her brow as she amended her remark. "For a Yankee."

∽◎∾

The next morning, Mary showed Emily her winter wardrobe, which proved to be as purple as Emily's room. "I will wear this on New Year's," she said, indicating a purple velvet. "Do you think the color suits me?"

"Very well."

"Mr. Stewart was kind enough to give this to me during one of my visits to his store in New York," Mary said, gesturing toward a white lace shawl, so delicate that if folded, it could have passed through a wedding ring. "I could certainly not look Mr. Lincoln in the face if I had purchased it myself, for it cost a frightful amount."

"How much?" Emily asked idly.

"Two thousand five hundred."

So it was *that* shawl—a legendary garment the entire South had heard about, and condemned as an example of the North's extravagance and greed. "May I put it on?" Emily asked.

"Certainly." Mary draped the garment around Emily, who gazed at herself in the mirror. Even in her severe mourning, it looked lovely on her. Hardin would have told her so—although he had told her more than once that he preferred to see her in nothing at all. "I can scarcely even feel it on my shoulders."

"Indeed, it is that fine." Mary carefully removed the shawl and returned it to its place. "To hear the press, of course, you would think that I not only paid for it with money stolen from our army, but paid for three more just like it with money stolen from the navy. But come, let us look in this wardrobe. Now that I am out of full mourning for dear Willie, there are a few things I would like you to have."

Over the next couple of hours, they occupied themselves with this task, Emily trying on garment after garment and Mary finally falling into her favorite subject—politics in general, and in particular Mr. Lincoln's chances of getting reelected. For a while, it was almost as if they were sitting in her sister's modest parlor in Springfield, an impression that was strengthened when Cousin John Stuart Todd paid a call.

That evening, Mr. and Mrs. Lincoln went to Ford's Theater. Even if her state of deep mourning did not dictate that Emily avoid such frivolity—not to mention the unspoken desire of her host and hostess not to let it be known that a Confederate widow was their guest at the White House—Emily would have remained behind, as she disliked the curious glances at her mourning garments. Instead, as Mary had ordered the state rooms to be lit for her, she took the opportunity to wander around the White House by herself, admiring the portraits of President Lincoln's predecessors and finally concluding her tour in the Red Room with the portrait of George Washington that Dolley Madison had saved from the British. Having given it due attention, Mary turned to the piano, which Mary had ordered from Philadelphia not long after moving to Washington. It was the finest instrument she had seen, and after only a few minutes of debate, she settled in front of it and began to play, singing an accompaniment in a low voice.

"Bravo!" Tad clapped. "You play like a princess, Aunt Emily."

"I told you Mama played well," Kate said loftily.

"Well, thank you. I used to practice every day until the war began, but now I must confine my playing to whenever I can find an instrument." Emily started. "Tad, is that a *goat*?"

"Of course," Tad said as his hircine companion gazed at her. "It was getting cold outside, so Pa said, 'Bring 'em in!' So I did. The other one must be on my bed."

"Well, of course," Emily said.

"Can you play some Christmas carols, Aunt Emily?"

"Well…" Emily had tried to pay as little attention to Christmas as possible; the contrast between this year and her last Christmas, spent with Hardin and the children in their little house in muddy Chattanooga, being too painful to dwell on. But she could hardly tell that to Tad, who was being such a good host to Kate, nor really to Kate herself. "All right. But you and Kate have to sing along."

The children obliged. Soon, Mr. Hay and Mr. Nicolay, who lodged as well as worked at the White House, wandered in on the impromptu concert, and over time they were joined by others. Because Tad utterly refused to go to bed without his father being present, and it was an ironclad rule in the White House that Tad be denied nothing, the singing and playing were still going on when the Lincolns came home from the theater. "Why, I had forgotten what a musician you were, Emily," Mary said.

"A tired one," Emily said, and smiled at Tad. "But it was a pleasure."

"You've worn out your aunt Emily," Mr. Lincoln said almost reproachfully. "But I would have, too, with such sweet singing."

Emily smiled, and having kissed Mary, took Kate and herself off to bed. She was closing her door when she heard Mary's voice, "I do wish Emily would make her residence here in Washington. It is so nice having a young person here, and as pretty and accomplished as she is, with time she might re—"

Before her sister's voice could die out on its own, Emily shut the door firmly. Kate yawned. "Re what, Mama?"

"I have no idea. Go to sleep."

The next afternoon, Mr. Lincoln, who on doctor's orders was keeping a less demanding schedule while he convalesced, joined the women and the children in Mary's room. Kate had brought out her photograph album. Emily had not looked at it recently, and with some embarrassment she saw that save for a few family pictures here and there, it was a veritable Confederate gallery, with Hardin in his dress uniform taking pride of place on the first page and general upon general following him. Tad, commendably, bore this parade of Southern commanders politely. Then he brought out his own album. "Here's Papa," he said, pointing to the first page. "The President," he said slyly.

"No!" Kate sat upright, her curls shaking emphatically. "Mr. Jefferson Davis is the President. I should know… I gave him flowers. Didn't I, Mama?"

"Yes, you gave him flowers. But—"

"Mr. Davis is not the President. Papa is the President. Who lives here? Not Old Jeff."

Finding herself unable to argue the point, Kate rose to her feet. "Hurrah for Jeff Davis!"

"Hurrah for Abraham Lincoln!"

"Children!" Emily and Mary said in unison.

"Now, the two of you come up here." Mr. Lincoln easily brought each child upon his knee. As they glared at each other, he said, "I think we can agree on two things. I am Tad's President, and I am Kate's Uncle Lincoln. Can we?"

"Yes," mumbled Kate.

"Yes," said Tad. "Want to play with the goats, Kate?"

"Yes!" Kate scrambled off Mr. Lincoln's knee and followed Tad out of the room.

Mr. Lincoln shook his head. "If only the war could be settled that easily."

That evening, Mary again had callers, and Emily excused herself. She was sitting in her room, enjoying a novel by Sir Walter Scott from the well-stocked White House library, when one of the mansion's servants knocked. "Mrs. Lincoln would like to see you for a moment, please."

With some reluctance, Emily obeyed. In the library with Mary were General Sickles and another man, older than Sickles and with both legs intact. "This is Senator Ira Harris," Mary said. "You really must meet his daughter sometime—a most accomplished young lady."

"Senator Harris was asking about his old friend General Breckinridge," General Sickles said. "Knowing that you just came from down South, I thought you might have word of him."

"I have heard nothing from him since he wrote his condolences to me after my husband's death," Emily said. General Breckinridge had written of Hardin and his men, *He loved them, they loved him, and he died at their head, a patriot and a hero*, but the sour-looking senator would have no interest in hearing that. "But I am certain I would have heard if anything were amiss."

"You keep in contact with the rebels?"

"When I lived in the South, I certainly did."

Senator Harris grunted. How could Mary countenance a man who was so rude? Was he drunk? There was certainly a smell of spirits in the room.

"Well, we're whipping them," Senator Harris said. "We whipped them at Chattanooga, and I hear that they ran like scared rabbits."

"It was the example, Senator Harris, that the North set them at Manassas," Emily said coolly.

Mary coughed. "Do you hear anything from your son, Senator?"

"Yes, I believe he is well. And he fought courageously at Bull Run, Mrs. Helm."

Emily stared straight ahead.

"Well," said Mary, "I am glad to hear that. Goodness, I find it hard enough to be separated from Bob, and he is only at Harvard."

"Why is he at Harvard, Mrs. Lincoln? Why isn't in the army?"

"Sore subject there," General Sickles said to the room at large.

Mary said with admirable composure, "He would be in the army if he had his way, Senator Harris, be in no doubt about that. It is I who have insisted that he remain at college. An educated man can serve his country with more intelligent purpose than an ignoramus."

"Balderdash. The army is full of Harvard men."

"And so are the graveyards."

"So that's why you don't want him to fight? I have but one son, and he is fighting for his country." He turned to Emily. "And, madam, if I had twenty sons, they would all be fighting the rebels."

"And if I had twenty sons, Senator Harris, they would all be opposing yours." Emily stalked out of the room. Head held high, she walked to the Prince of Wales Room. She was about to lock the door when Mary pushed her way in. "Dear child, I am so sorry."

"How can you associate with such men?"

"Senator Harris is not normally rude. I fear he was a little intoxicated. And perhaps something is worrying him about his son. But his behavior toward you was inexcusable, and I told him so."

Emily wiped her eyes. "Mary, I will be leaving for Baltimore tomorrow, and then for Lexington. I cannot stay here anymore."

"Dear, don't let this one incident bother you. I assure you, he is not usually like that; if he were, I would never allow him here. Why, I would love to see you stay in Washington! You would not have to stay in this place. I could help you find a nice house, and there are fine schools here for the girls. I know, of course, that you do not want society at present, but even living quietly can be agreeable here. Why Mrs. Douglas—the second wife of my almost-beau Senator Douglas, whom you might remember me telling you about—has been his widow for over two years now, and she manages to do quite a bit of good, volunteering for all sorts of worthy causes, in our hospitals and so forth. Or Mr. Lincoln might find a job for you in the Treasury or something—"

For a moment, Emily found herself tempted, albeit not by volunteering in the Union's hospitals or working for its treasury. Had not she envisioned living in Washington at one time? But Hardin had been alive then. Now she only wanted to retire to Kentucky with her shattered little family and heal her wounds. "It is kind of you, Mary, but I never intended to stay more than a few days. It is not that man's boorishness; it is simply that Kentucky is my home. This place can never be."

∽❧∼

The next morning at breakfast, Emily turned to Mr. Lincoln just as he was leaving them for his office. "May I speak to you in private, sir?"

"Please, not so formal. But yes, we may speak." He led her away. "My office is right through this passageway. I ordered its construction myself; it saves me from being pestered more than I am already. Present company excepted, of course."

Emily settled into the chair he indicated—a cracked leather one that like the rest of the office chairs was considerably less elegant than the other furnishings in the house. "Before I left, I wanted to explain why I could not take the oath. It was not disrespect to you, but respect for my husband's memory."

"Understood. I won't make you take it, if you agree not to take advantage of my lenience."

"I would never do so."

"No, I didn't think you would. But it had to be said." He gestured toward a desk piled with paper. "I've been reading some accounts of Chickamauga, and your husband's engagement in particular. Hardin gave us a good fight, for far longer than most in his position could have managed, myself included. I hope you don't bear any anger against me for his death."

"No!" Emily looked up at him earnestly. "I regard his death—and those of my brothers—as the fortune of war and the providence of God. I don't claim to understand it, but that is how I regard it."

"Yes, that is how I feel about poor Willie. But back to Hardin. You do know that I offered him a position."

"Yes."

"I was being begged for positions from all and sundry, but I was glad to oblige in his case because I knew him to have ability, and I wanted to please him—and you and Mary. It was the best I could have offered at that time, without making any more enemies than I had already. He'd seemed eager enough for one. But he refused. Was it his friends who changed his mind? His father?"

"You wrong him, sir. It was his own conscience. He did take counsel from others, but in the end, he did what he believed was right, and he died believing that he had made the right decision, even though it cost him everything."

"Well, I did all I could to keep him on our side. I was fond of him. Very fond of him." He wiped his eye. Then he smiled, his eyes crinkling as they had so often in Springfield. "By the way, I had it from General Sickles—the man is a gossip—about the goings-on last night. I heard that you were a match for Senator Harris."

"I should not have lost my temper, but—"

"A Todd not lose her temper? As I told him, you've got a tongue like the rest of the Todds, and frankly, Harris deserved it." He chuckled, then rummaged around his desk. "Before you leave, I'll write out a paper giving you the protections of a loyal citizen. If anyone in Lexington gives you a hard time, you just show it to them."

"Thank you. You have been so kind that I hate to ask you for more, but I must. If I could get a permit to sell my cotton—"

Mr. Lincoln sighed. "I'll do my best, but you have to understand that half of the North wants a permit to sell Southern cotton, and the other half disapproves of the practice—at least until they find some cotton they want to sell. It's a delicate matter already and even more delicate if I favor a relation, especially with an election coming up. But get Hardin's will probated, as must be your first step in any case, and I'll see what I can do. I can promise nothing, but I don't intend for you to be in want. I can at least write out an order stating that when the place where your cotton is stored—Jackson, Mississippi, and Georgia, right?—comes within our lines, you shall be allowed to prove your ownership of it, and claim it."

Emily had hoped for more, but with her return to Kentucky so tantalizingly close, she was not disposed to complain.

She fetched Kate, who had spent the morning sketching their room and a couple of the state rooms. Together with the Lincolns they walked to the front portico, where a carriage stood waiting to take Emily and Kate to the depot. Mary pressed a purse into her hand—"Just a pretty little bauble, dear"—and Emily took it, guessing the intent, which would be confirmed when she opened it in the carriage and found it full of greenbacks. Beside her, Tad and Kate shook hands in farewell. "Here's President Davis for your album," Kate said.

"And here's President Lincoln for yours."

"Give my regards to our mother and the rest," Mary said with the slight hesitation she always had used in giving her stepmother that maternal epithet. She lowered her voice. "And my deepest sympathies for her losses of Sam and Alec."

"Come back and visit when you can, Little Sister." Mr. Lincoln kissed Emily on the cheek and smiled at Kate, who was frowning at his photograph as if uncertain whether she had made a fair trade. "And, Miss Kate, don't toss that photo away. I do grow on people."

Mary said, "I know you said you cannot stay in Washington, but I hope you will at least pay us a visit at the Soldiers' Home this summer."

"I am sorry, Mary. After the last couple of years, I am inclined to remain at home for a while. And the children need to settle down as well."

"True," said Mary. She sighed. "Well, promise me that you will wear that lovely bonnet I gave you. The flowers are so perfectly black, and while we are called upon to mourn our dead, we are not called upon to be dowdy. Remember that."

Emily smiled, wondering if Mary knew how much she sounded like Mrs. Todd. She embraced Mary and pecked her cheek. "I will."

❧

"I miss Aunt Emily and Kate," Tad announced a couple of hours after their departure.

"I know you do, dear," Mary said. As the months passed and Willie's death receded into the distance, she had regretted banishing the Taft boys from the White House, but there was no going back. The boys were now attending school up north, and she could hardly ask that they return to Washington for Tad's convenience—or to assuage her own guilt. Julia Taft was still in Washington, but she was far too grown up to romp with Tad, and in any case was now "out" and had several admirers to keep her occupied.

But although his cousin's return to Kentucky had deprived Tad of a playmate, Mary had not been entirely sad to see her sister leave. It had been so awkward, not wanting to say or do anything that would cause Emily to give way to her grief, and it was clear that the poor girl was grieving terribly. The best thing she could do, both for her happiness and for her security, was to remarry—after a respectable interval, of course. Underneath her mourning garb, Emily was still a very pretty woman, and surely Kentucky's blue bloods, the sensible ones who hadn't rushed out like poor Mr. Helm and joined the rebels, would notice that in due time.

It was a relief, too, that Emily had departed before the press noticed her—something it surely would have done despite Mr. Lincoln's best efforts to keep the matter quiet. A Confederate widow in the Executive Mansion—nay, a Confederate general's widow in the Executive Mansion! Mary could imagine the snide remarks, the suggestions that having invited a brigadier general's widow to sojourn there, the Lincolns might as well go up in rank and invite Mrs. Stonewall Jackson in the spring. And with the election coming up—one that Mr. Lincoln had to win, for Mary could not bear returning defeated to Springfield—the President's opponents, such as that puffed-up, do-nothing McClellan and those who wanted to end the war at any cost, would be looking for any little tidbit to use against him.

Yes, it was just as well that Emily had left.

That evening, though, Mary found herself missing the tinkle of the piano in the Red Room, where Emily had so often sneaked off during her visit. A typical little-sisterish thing to do, where anyone else would have simply asked, but a rather endearing one. And in her private sitting room, she felt the absence of her sister even more keenly. Emily, unlike a number of Todd women, was a capital listener.

Perhaps she might still manage to persuade Emily to spend some time at the Soldiers' Home that summer; in its secluded confines, the press was unlikely to notice her. By then, her grief might be less raw—and perhaps the war would be less of a painful subject once her sister had spent more time back in the Union. At the very least, she could visit after the election.

If, of course, they were still in the White House by then.

✌ 24 ✌
EMILY
JANUARY TO JUNE 1864

After the New Year began, Emily took Kitty with her as company and went to Louisville to probate Hardin's will and to see some old friends, having first brought the girls and Ben to Elizabethtown to visit Hardin's parents. The pain of their meeting was alleviated a great deal by the presence of the children, whom Emily left in virtual command of Helm Place, being waited on like potentates, romping around the grounds from daybreak to dusk, and being thoroughly fussed over by grandparents, uncles, and aunts to such a degree that Emily could only hope that they would not balk when required to return to Lexington, where the family had lodgings at the Broadway Hotel until Mrs. Todd could find a house to rent. There had been a surprise waiting for Emily at Helm Place: Phil, who had somehow made his way to Kentucky minus the aid of either the Confederate or Union government. Remembering Hardin's desire to set him free, Emily had promised him his freedom once Hardin's estate was settled. It was the least she could do, and she regretted not having done it for Maggie.

Upon reaching Kentucky, Emily had forwarded Mac's letter to his mother and his brother, who lived at the family estate on the outskirts of Louisville. A few days after her arrival in the city, Mac's younger brother, Dr. Frank McCawley, paid her a visit at her hotel to thank her. After they had chatted awhile and Emily had told him what she knew of Mac's whereabouts and his state of health, he said, "The last time I saw you, Mrs. Helm, was at a hop at the Galt House. Sixty? Early sixty-one? Anyway, you were in a yellow gown, and every man there was jealous of Hardin. God rest his soul."

"That seems ages ago, doesn't it?"

"Yes, we still have our hops, but it's not quite the same with so many of Louisville's finest gone to war. Still, it's lively enough here. We've been getting some good theater. Have you heard of the actor John Wilkes Booth? Being down South for so long, you might not have."

"I have, actually." Mr. Lincoln had spoken highly of his acting, although Mary had seemed less impressed.

"Well, he's just begun an engagement here, and the ladies are wild to see him, including Mother and my sisters. They're pestering me to take them."

"He's here?" Kitty breathed. "Ooh."

"I've an idea. Why don't we make a party of it? Any night you choose."

"I cannot—"

"Oh, come, Emily. You're past the deepest part of mourning, and this isn't England, where everyone measures the length of your veil."

"Miss Todd is right, Mrs. Helm. It's healthier in all respects to be out and about. In fact, as a doctor, I shall order you to come to the theater."

"I have been out and about," Emily said. She sighed. "Out and about, and up and down from North to South. So I suppose a little more could do no harm. But it must be something appropriate, not a farce or a comedy."

Dr. McCawley agreed, and that very night organized a theater party to see Mr. Booth in *Othello*, which was certainly tragic enough to meet Emily's criteria. To her relief, she found upon her arrival that she was not the only widow who had been tempted into a visit to the theater.

In any case, the place was so packed full of spectators that no one was likely to notice her, much less censure her.

The widowed Mrs. McCawley, a sprightly woman who appeared to be the source of Mac's short stature, leaned over as they settled into their box. "It was so kind of you to send dear George's letter, Mrs. Helm. He speaks of you and poor Mr. Helm very highly."

"He was invaluable to me, Mrs. McCawley, in my bereavement." Mrs. McCawley was smiling at her so approvingly that Emily wondered what exactly Mac might have said, but the dimming of the theater lights and the entrance of the scheming Iago soon occupied her thoughts.

Unseemly as doing so was in her present position, she could not help but admit to herself that Mr. Booth, who had darkened his face only slightly in assuming the role of the Moor, was an extremely handsome man, with a passionate, athletic style of acting that impressed her and mesmerized Kitty, who even after the curtain fell for intermission remained staring raptly at the stage. Only when hawkers began strolling through the theater, selling cartes de visite of Booth, did her sister come out of her trance. "Oh, I must have one!"

Dr. McCawley obligingly reached into his pocket and bought photographs for Kitty and his sisters—Emily, who had not yet shaken her refugee habit of traveling as little encumbered as possible, having demurred. Kitty squealed her thanks. "Dear, have you forgotten Captain Herr?" Emily hissed, only half jokingly. At Hardin's funeral, the captain had given Emily his condolences and a letter for Miss Kitty, which Emily had dutifully passed to its recipient.

"No, of course not," Kitty said stoutly. "But Mr. Booth's so beautiful."

Othello having murdered the unfortunate Desdemona with such fury that Emily had to restrain herself from crying for help, and having expressed his remorse with equal violence, the lights came up and Dr. McCawley said, "Well, ladies, I have a surprise for you. I doctored the manager here some time ago, and he's invited me to bring you backstage for a quick visit with Mr. Booth. What of it?"

Kitty could only fan herself in reply.

Mr. Booth looked exhausted when he appeared, but he managed

a gallant bow as Kitty squeaked, "I did so enjoy your performance, Mr. Booth."

"Why, thank you, Miss—"

"Miss Todd." Kitty's voice had nearly reached its normal timbre.

A faint ripple, too slight to be described as a frown, passed over Mr. Booth's face, but he said easily, his voice slightly hoarse, "Then shall I inscribe your photo that way?"

"That would be lovely."

Mr. Booth inscribed it with a flourish, gaining Kitty's prettiest smile, and then turned his attention and his charm upon the McCawley ladies. Then he glanced at Emily, standing in her widow's weeds at a remove from the rest. "The war, madam?"

"Yes." Something made her add, "My husband died fighting for the South."

There was no artifice in the look Mr. Booth gave her then. "Then he died nobly, madam. My condolences."

Though Emily had been slow to notice it in her relief at returning to Kentucky, Lexington was not the town of her youth. The city was packed with loyalist refugees who had been turned out of their homes when Tennessee was held by the South, the streets were full of Union troops, there to hold any rebellion at bay, and the hospitals literally groaned with wounded soldiers. The elegant Medical Hall of Transylvania University, closed before the war and later commandeered as a Union hospital, had burned to the ground in 1863—a calamity that appeared to be accidental, but which was still dispiriting.

Entire families had stopped speaking to each other, and when Mrs. Todd at last found a suitable house to rent, some of the ladies who once would have been quick to call stayed away. Not that Mrs. Todd cared, for she was happy to confine her acquaintance to the ladies whose men were or had been supporting the South. Indeed, she was on the best of terms with Lexington's Mrs. Henrietta Morgan, mother of the notorious Colonel John Hunt Morgan, the guerilla who had conducted raids on behalf of the Confederacy into Kentucky, Tennessee, Indiana, and Ohio, capturing Union soldiers, seizing goods, money, and horses, and diverting Union resources that could have been expended elsewhere, before his spree ended with his own capture. News of his escape from prison in November 1863 had cheered the entire South, although Emily in her preoccupation with getting home had hardly noticed it at the time. "You do know, Mama, that the Yankees are watching Mrs. Morgan's house very closely?" Emily ventured to say as Mrs. Todd packed up some preserves and set off to visit the fugitive's mother in her handsome home at Gratz Park.

"As if a couple of old friends having tea together could harm the Yankees," her mother said. She sniffed. "I just wish it could."

Though Emily prudently stayed home, Martha sometimes accompanied her mother to Mrs. Morgan's until she and her quantity of trunks finally set off for Alabama in late February, with Mr. Lincoln's permission. Soon, a rumor floated from South to North, acquiring embellishments along its journey, that Martha had managed to outfox Mr. Lincoln by smuggling to the South an officer's uniform decked with buttons that proved to be solid gold coins, valued at more than four thousand dollars. Emily knew the story to be nonsense, having helped pack the trunks herself. There had been plenty in them to delight Southern hearts—whiskey, coffee, letters, even a wedding trousseau for a wealthy bride-to-be in Richmond—and Emily had slipped in a few things for her friend Mrs. Pember, as well as letters to Mac and to a few of her lady friends. But there had been no uniform and no gold. Still, the rumor was too enjoyable, for both the South and Mr. Lincoln's opponents in the North, to die quickly, especially when Martha was invited to meet President Davis.

None of these matters had escaped the attention of Lexington's Union officials. And if truth be told, Emily had not been entirely inconspicuous herself. When she had left the South, her trunk had contained a modest amount of gold—not her own, but contributions for the welfare of the Confederate prisoners at Chicago's Camp Douglas. She had asked Mr. Lincoln for permission to convert the money into clothing and other necessities, and as he, presumably in the press of business, had not replied, she had taken this as permission to do so. Nor had she hesitated to do what she could for those captured Confederate soldiers in Lexington's hospitals, some of whom had served under Hardin. Few things made Emily happier in those days than to sit by the side of a sick man's bed and knit warm things for him while listening to tales of her husband's gallantry and kindness. She would not deprive herself, or her charges, of that pleasure because of a few Yankee glares; if anything, the glares made her hold her head higher as she went on her rounds.

In putting pen to paper, at least, Emily was more careful, especially in her letters to her sisters in Selma and to Mac, which went through flag-of-truce mail and therefore had to pass through censors. With her sisters, this was an easy enough task to accomplish as there was plenty of family news to discuss, most particularly Elodie's new and so-far-thriving baby, whose doings might bore the censors to death but posed no threat to the Union. Mac presented more of a challenge. Emily filled one letter with an account of the play, to which the censors surely could not find any objection, but the next was more difficult. Writing about the irksome state of Lexington would not do, nor would discussing the war news. So instead, she gave him news of her children's doings, followed by a description of a Kentucky spring. When Mac wrote back, he told her it brought back his home marvelously, and he hoped that his poor offering—a violet he'd found on his travels— would be a suitable return.

The violet was arranged perfectly on the page. Perhaps the censor had been as moved as Emily was by Mac's offering.

❧

As the evenings grew pleasantly warm, Lexington began holding concerts in the park, with a band playing a selection of tunes carefully chosen so as to anger neither the Confederate sympathizers nor the Union ones, or at least to anger both equally. Early in June, Emily had taken the children to one such event when she noticed a stir around the edges of the crowd, which began to thin out even as the band gamely played on. "John Hunt Morgan's back raiding in Kentucky!" someone whispered.

"And headed to Lexington, they say!"

A man growled nearby, "His men are no better than brigands. Better hide your horses and money."

When Emily reached home and questioned her mother, Mrs. Todd only smiled archly. "I hope he finds time to see his mother," she said.

"He's not coming here just to see his mother."

"No, I expect not." Mrs. Todd frowned in concentration at her knitting. Having successfully completed a maneuver, she said, "I believe they will be stopping by the government stables. They need horses."

The Union government housed hundreds of horses in Lexington, many intended for the use of the colored troops at nearby Camp Nelson. Stabled with the Yankee horses, and apparently none the worse for it, were some of the finest equines in the country, put there by their nervous owners after General Morgan's raid the year before.

"I'm quite sure they won't bother our own stables," Mrs. Todd said, reading Emily's mind. "They know where we stand."

This was not entirely reassuring to Emily. Hardin had often bemoaned the difficulties of stopping his men from plundering, and he had certainly tried. How hard General Morgan might try was unclear. And how were his men to know the Todds from anyone else in Lexington? Emily knew General Morgan but slightly, having been barely in her teens when her father's death had obliged them to sell their house in Lexington, and there was no reason for him to remember her.

So after the others had gone to bed, she remained in the parlor with her pistol on the table beside her. She was nearly dozing off when she became aware of a glow in the window that had not been there before. Running out onto the front steps, she saw the city surrounded by a ring of fire.

Two men on horses, all with an ill-fed appearance, rode by as she stood transfixed on the steps. "You're not going to use that dainty pistol on us, ma'am, are you?"

"Not if you leave my house alone."

"We'll relay that to General Morgan, ma'am. Now why don't you go back inside?"

Emily obeyed, shouting the house awake lest the fire spread. As her mother's servants scurried about, filling every possible container with water, she, Kitty, and Mrs. Todd secreted what valuables they could, making ample use of their corsets and pockets and suspending purses of money from their crinoline cages.

As the night wore on, Morgan's men continued to clatter into town. From the safety of an upper window, her view illuminated by the still-burning fires of what she later learned were the brewery and a series of emptied stables, Emily watched them smash the windows of the nearby banks and stores, then grab anything that might be of use to an army—whiskey, clothing, shoes, hats, saddles, writing supplies, money—and even a few things that were not. A storekeeper, running out to remonstrate, was kicked to the curb, while one of the few Union soldiers who had not taken refuge in Fort Clay met the unhappier fate of being shot in the chest.

Fighting back nausea, Emily turned away from the window, unable to bear any more, even if the victims were Yankees and their sympathizers. Then she heard the sound of artillery fire, whizzing from Fort Clay over the rooftops. "Into the cellar," she commanded, and the children, huddled in a corner with Delilah, obeyed as the women brought up the rear.

By early morning, the firing had ceased. The town secured for them—for a few hours, anyway—General Morgan and his main body of men rode around Lexington in grand style, many on their newly acquired Yankee horses fitted with freshly stolen saddles. The rebel ladies of the town—their bosoms adorned with long-hidden-away secession cockades and their hands waving long-folded Confederate flags—thronged into the streets, all but mobbing the general, who waved cheerily to everyone before heading to Gratz Park and his mother's house, leaving his men to accept the many offers of breakfast called out. "Maybe we should have some of them over," Kitty said.

Emily shook her head. "What if it got back to Mr. Lincoln? I dare not risk it."

Kitty was about to reply when Mrs. Todd said, "She's right, dear. She is in a delicate position with that man, and we'd best not jeopardize it."

Grudgingly, Kitty obeyed, and they went inside, following the example of Lexington's Unionists. As they sat down to their guestless breakfast, they heard a gate open and a horse whinny. "They're breaking into the stables," Kitty said flatly. "You were wrong, Mama."

"So I was," Mrs. Todd said. She sighed. "He was brought up so well. It must be the riffraff he picked up along the way."

Kate put her head in her hands. "They're going to take Queen Bess!"

"And Lord Dudley!" Dee began to sob. "If Papa were here…"

"They'll take nothing." Emily rose. "I'll be right back."

"Emily, darling!"

"Have you lost your mind?"

Ignoring the remonstrances around her, Emily hurried to her bedroom, then emerged from the house to find two men leading out a puzzled-looking Queen Bess. She lifted her pistol. "Put my horse back immediately."

"Why, of course, ma'am." The taller of the men, who did indeed look ruffianly, pointed a rifle at her. "Whatever you say, ma'am."

Despite being hopelessly outgunned, Emily stood her ground. "My husband fought and died for the Confederacy. Would you steal the horses of his widow—and of his little children?"

"'Confiscate' is the word we prefer to use, ma'am. Who was your husband?"

"General Benjamin Hardin Helm. He fell at Chickamauga leading the First Kentucky."

"Orphan Brigade?"

"Yes."

The men exchanged a glance, and still gripping the gun, Emily awkwardly unfurled the cloth she had been clutching. "This is the flag that covered his casket. Do you need more proof than this?"

"No, ma'am. I suppose not." The older of the men lifted his cap. "Put her back, Jim. There's enough other horseflesh in this town. Don't want to get on the wrong side of those boys."

Jim, who could not have been more than seventeen, obeyed. Emily winced as she observed his pinched cheeks and ragged clothes. "Now come in and have some breakfast," she commanded. "There's plenty of it."

⁕

Their raid a rousing success, Morgan and his men headed out of town shortly after that, leaving Lexington denuded of goods and horses and more divided than ever. Emily knew that it had not gone unnoticed that the Todds' stables had been spared.

A few days later, she and the children were walking home from the photographer's, having fulfilled a request by Hardin's parents for pictures of Ben and the girls, when two neighboring ladies passed by. Emily greeted them and waited to receive the usual frigid nod in return, as their sons were fighting for the Union. Instead, one asked, "Did you hear the news, Mrs. Helm?"

"I suppose not."

"Morgan has been driven out of Kentucky. His escapade here was an utter waste of time. Don't you think so, Tilda?"

Tilda merely smirked, to which Emily gave her own frigid nod. "Good day," she said. The June day, pleasant when she had set off on her errand, suddenly seemed muggy and oppressive.

Kate sighed. "Sometimes, Mama, Kentucky doesn't seem like home anymore."

"No." Emily wiped a drop of sweat from her forehead. "It doesn't."

∽ 25 ∾
MARY
JUNE TO JULY 1864

In June, President Lincoln was nominated to be his party's candidate in the 1864 election—not a mean feat, as both Secretary Salmon P. Chase, who had been intensely interested in being the Republican nominee, and General Ulysses S. Grant, who had not been interested, had both been potential rivals. This was a start, but Mary was taking no chances. Not only would a loss be humiliating for her husband and a boon to the rebel government, but it would be disastrous for Mary, whose creditors, freed of the benefits of being obliging and forbearing, would surely descend upon her. How much did she owe, anyway? Mary was not certain. Just looking through the bills made her ill.

Meanwhile, the press had renewed its tittle-tattle against her. Her shopping trip to New York in April generated the usual sniping, the usual insinuations that every bolt of silk she bought was somehow purchased with the blood of Union soldiers. (You would think she never did anything else but shop!) And there was the tedious business about her sister Martha and her golden buttons. Mary had refused to see the woman when she was in Washington pestering the President for a pass South, for unlike Emily's, Martha's traitorous husband was perfectly alive, and besides, Mary had never much liked this pert little half sister, the more so because people outside the family had often commented on their similarities. But when the story finally ran its course, the public would remember only that Martha was a sister of Mary, and a Confederate; ergo, Mary must be a Confederate sympathizer herself.

All of this would have been no more than the perpetual irritation of a buzzing fly or a barking dog had it not been the year of the presidential election. So Mary went to work. She could not control the antics of her rebel relations, and she could not stop shopping entirely, but she could reduce her debts, and she could do her best to secure her husband's reelection. With these goals in mind, she cultivated the acquaintance of some influential men, especially Mr. Abram Wakeman and Mr. Simeon Draper, and let it be known that if they put in a kind word for her with her creditors to reduce her debts, not to mention kind words to the newspaper editors of their acquaintances, she would in turn put in a kind word with the President when he decided on appointments for his second term.

All this, of course, was no more than many a man did for the sake of politics. Even Mr. Lincoln with his fine sense of probity was not entirely above it himself, as the stream of friendly articles that appeared in the press, their florid, anonymous prose coming straight from the pen of Mr. Hay, showed. But for a woman, of course, it was quite different. She wasn't supposed to politick and wasn't supposed to shop—only, apparently, to take tea with other ladies, who didn't want to take tea with her in the first place.

Mary shook her head disgustedly at the sheer injustice of it. Then she sat down and wrote a letter to Mr. Wakeman.

❧

Soon after his father secured his party's nomination, Bob graduated from Harvard, and with it renewed his request to be allowed to enlist in the army. Mary's hope that his academic career would outlast the war had not been realized, for the war had entered its fourth summer, with utterly no signs of an approaching Union victory. The best that could be said was that General Grant, now in charge of all the Union forces, was much more willing to incur casualties than his predecessors—and that summer, the casualties came in alarming numbers. Mary remained determined that Bob, however much he might desire otherwise, not be one of them.

So with a sulking Bob in tow this year, the family removed to the Soldiers' Home in July, hoping that this would not be their last summer there. By this time, everyone fell naturally into his or her usual routine: Mr. Lincoln riding back and forth to the White House; Mary visiting hospitals, going for drives, and making plans to head north to escape the heat; Tad generally getting into everyone's way and enjoying himself thoroughly. As for Bob, he soon regained his spirits, having found a diversion in Miss Mary Harlan of Iowa, whose father was in the Senate. Mary forbore from pointing out that spending time with this pretty young lady and with his male friends was surely more pleasant than getting killed or wounded in Virginia under the auspices of General Grant or marching toward Atlanta under the direction of General Sherman, as much of the Union army was doing at the moment.

It was a miserably hot summer, even by Washington standards, but it was not miserable enough to deter the rebels from making their usual summer excursion north under the command of General Jubal Early. This time, their goal was Washington itself. With most of the Union's resources engaged down south, it was not an unrealistic one, as was shown by the rebel victory at Monocacy, Maryland, a disquietingly short distance from the capital. "I'm half tempted to let them have the place," Mr. Lincoln said the next day after returning to the Soldiers' Home for the evening and relaying the news that the rebels were progressing further into the city, guarded at present by a small force augmented by a contingent of convalescent soldiers, government clerks, veterans, and quartermaster employees. "But they won't get it. Don't worry, Molly."

"How can I not worry after that note?" The day before, following the defeat at Monocacy, Secretary Stanton had sent the President a note informing him that his carriage had been followed by a stranger, and urging him to inform the guard detailed at the Soldiers' Home.

"If you hadn't been looking over my shoulder as I read, you wouldn't have seen the note, and you'd have nothing to worry about." Mr. Lincoln fanned himself with another letter. Whatever he might think of their contents, their utilitarian properties could not be denied.

"Not only do they want to take the city, they want to get hold of you."

"Could well be, but I'm not going to worry about it. If I get captured, I'm sure Mrs. White or one of your other sisters down there will put in a kind word with Jeff Davis."

Mary's only answer was to give her husband a frosty look, which did nothing to alleviate the heat.

They were sleeping side by side, as they often did here, where Mr. Lincoln's retiring hours were less eccentric than at the White House. Then they heard a banging, which, if not the rebel army, sounded like the next thing to it. "Come in," the President called. "Open the door, don't break it down."

A young soldier stuck in his head as Mary, clad in the slightest of chemises, pulled up the sheet with a squawk. "Secretary Stanton, sir, has asked that all of you return to the White House straightaway. The rebels are at Tennallytown!" Unfazed by the sight of the head of the Union in his nightshirt, he handed the President a note.

That was less than five miles from the Soldiers' Home. Mr. Lincoln read the note, adjusting his nightshirt at the same time. He nodded. "Guess we'd better humor him, Molly."

So at midnight, the presidential carriage, surrounded by enough guards to bring some comfort even to Mary, rattled back to the White House. The fear of invasion and the heat had lured many Washingtonians out to their stoops to pass the night, and Tad waved at them, although it was doubtful whether he could be seen amid the phalanx of mounted men. "It's important to keep up their morale," he explained.

"Good point," Mr. Lincoln said as Mary listened for enemy fire.

At the Executive Mansion, they repaired sleepily to their respective chambers, which in Bob's case meant climbing into bed with Mr. Hay. "You could sleep with me," Tad offered.

"No." Bob managed a tired grin. "Unless you want me to keep the rebels off."

Tad drew himself up. "I can handle them."

Despite Tad's confidence, Mary slept but little that night. By contrast, when Mr. Lincoln joined her, he looked more refreshed by sleep than he usually did, and he not only ate his meager breakfast with enthusiasm, but asked for more. Having disposed of his toast, he said, "Well, I'm going to head to Fort Stevens to see how things stand. Wouldn't want to get there late and miss Early."

Mary groaned, and her husband departed, to return in a few hours in high spirits. There had been skirmishing before the fort, but the Union troops were acquitting themselves admirably, down to the clerks manning the rifle pits, who had managed not to shoot themselves and to pick off the occasional rebel. And soon these enthusiastic amateurs would be replaced by the Sixth Corps. "Will you be going to the fort tomorrow?" Mary asked.

"Yes, unless Early gets the hint that he's not welcome here."

"Then take me with you." She crossed her arms defiantly, waiting for an argument.

The President did not give her the satisfaction of winning one. "All right, Molly."

They set off the next afternoon. Not since the earliest days of the war, when the fashionable of the city had packed their picnic baskets and rushed to Bull Run, had Mary seen Washington in such a state. Clerks sweated at their desks, pedestrians trudged along, and the streetcars toiled back and forth as usual, but all was done amid the sound of gunfire rumbling in the distance. As they neared the fort, every high place they passed was occupied by people clutching spyglasses and opera glasses, straining to catch a view of the action.

With all this, it took some time to reach Fort Stevens, erected soon after the war had begun. "See our signal corps?" the President said, pointing to men standing on an embankment waving brightly colored flags. "They're doing a fine job. Of course, I don't have the faintest idea what they're telling each other, but I suppose it's right."

"Back again, sir?" someone called as they entered the fortification.

"Oh, yes," Mr. Lincoln said. "Can't keep me away."

They passed into the fort's hospital ward, the President shaking the hands of the surgeons and speaking kindly to the patients. Then he said, "Well, Molly? Do you want to see the fighting?"

"Yes," Mary said firmly.

"Then come along, but you'll have to get on a parapet." He chuckled. "Had a bit of a scrape on one yesterday."

"A scrape?"

"Nothing to worry about. Are you game? You can stay here if you like."

Mary took a firming breath. "I am game."

Compressing her crinoline with difficulty—the fort had not been designed with such an eventuality in mind—she made her way to the parapet and stared at the expanse below her, dotted with rebels in every state of being from very much alive to very much dead. Jubal Early, she would later learn, had given up trying to take Washington after learning that reinforcements were on the way and had settled for harassing its defenders. But harassment, Mary discovered, still provided plenty of action. "Good Lord!" she sputtered. "They're shooting from that house!"

"Best get down then, Mary."

"And you should do the same! For heaven's sake, now!"

The President obeyed, but only for a moment. Soon, his curiosity had led him back to his perch, accompanied by Dr. Cornelius Crawford, a surgeon with whom he had been chatting. As Mary watched from her place of relative safety, she heard a burst of fire, just as a young officer called, "Get down, you fool!"

In unison, the President and Dr. Crawford tumbled from their perch, the surgeon batting at his leg. "I've been shot," he said. "Damn rebels. Will someone get a surgeon? I mean, another surgeon."

"Help him away," snapped the young officer. He glared at the

President, who was helping support Dr. Crawford. "As for you—good Lord, is it President Lincoln? I did not real—"

"Good work you boys are doing," Mr. Lincoln said as the officer turned perfectly white. "Keep it up." He stooped and picked up his hat, checking it for bullet holes. "No damage here. Crawford, you're not badly hurt, are you?"

"No," said Dr. Crawford, looking at his leg with admirable detachment.

"Then let's leave our friends here to their work, shall we? Good day, Captain…?"

"Holmes," muttered the captain. "Oliver Wendell Holmes. I didn't know it was you, sir. But if I had—well, we need you with us to see this through."

"A good point," Mr. Lincoln noted pleasantly.

Dr. Crawford's comrades having arrived to assist him, the President escorted Mary to the carriage, where she waited while her husband conferred with the fort's commander. "I have given the order to shell those houses on which the rebels are perching," he said as he took his place in the carriage. "It'll be getting noisy here soon, I reckon."

"Mr. Lincoln, what did you mean you were in a scrape yesterday?"

"The same thing, too curious for my own good. I was ordered to get down." He chuckled. "Though the officer yesterday was rather more polite about it. You, my dear, did rather well, considering."

"It is not an experience I wish to repeat."

Yet she realized that except for her husband's peril, she had never felt fear. Instead, she had felt strangely exhilarated, more alive than she had felt in months. With that feeling came a surge of optimism. Something about the episode—maybe the admiration mingling with mortification in the young officer's face, maybe the easy way in which Dr. Crawford and his fellow surgeons had greeted the President, maybe something completely indefinable—had given her hope.

The President could win this election yet. And, Mary thought as she rode off arm in arm with her husband, sooner or later, the Union was going to win this war.

∽ 26 ∾
EMILY
JULY TO OCTOBER 1864

O ver the course of the war, Emily had become a voracious newspaper reader. Although she had been deprived of Southern
papers recently, the Northern papers generally printed excerpts from
them, in the interest of sharing news from the enemy, and the Southern
papers did the same. Thus, it was while reading one of the Northern
papers that she read a Confederate account of a battle near Atlanta
that had occurred some days before.

The 1st Kentucky, then in reserve, was ordered to charge
them, in order to bring off the artillery and horses, which
was done in gallant style, led by the gallant and intrepid
McCawley, they closed upon on the foe, and a hand-to-hand
rencounter took place which has not been equaled during
the war; our men using the butts of their guns and pistols,
and the enemy their bayonets...

Our loss was 21 including Capt. McCawley, who Gen.

Williams says was the best staff officer he ever saw in any army.

Mac!

After Morgan's raid, Emily had written to Mac with what she hoped was an amusing and federally inoffensive story of Lexington's outrage—shared by Unionists and Southern sympathizers alike—over the appropriation by the raiders of the town's most renowned mare, Skedaddle. Morgan had sense enough to realize that some things were sacred, and Skedaddle had soon been returned to her favorite pasture, none the worse for her brief Confederate service. No reply from Mac had arrived, only this sad news.

Emily frantically scanned newspaper after newspaper, hoping that the report would be contradicted and finding it confirmed again and again. Only one new detail emerged. *Captain McCawley's remains were taken to Atlanta, for burial next to Brig. Gen. Benjamin Hardin Helm, on whose staff he had served.*

Since Mac had reported Hardin's dying remarks to her, Emily had purposely avoided thinking of what she and Mac were to each other or what they might become. It was far too soon, and the times too uncertain. Now, she could only weep and wonder what might have been, with only two certainties: Mac could have found no better resting place, and Emily had lost her dearest friend.

After Morgan's raid, General Stephen Burbridge, who was in charge of the military troops in Kentucky, announced a new policy: for every Union loyalist killed or even injured by Southern sympathizers, four guerilla prisoners would be shot in a public place. Very soon, the general proved true to his word. It would have been the talk of Lexington— except that increasingly, everyone, even those with little to say about the war, was too frightened to talk.

Levi, Emily's half brother, was at least safe to talk to during this period. In a town of hard-drinking men, he had acquired the reputation of the town drunk—not a mean feat. But diminishing health had reduced him to a state of near sobriety, and Emily, having renewed his acquaintance after returning to Lexington, had taken pity on him in his ailing and impoverished state and stopped by his hotel room with a basket of food several times a week. Unlike the other Todds who had stayed in Kentucky, Levi had remained loyal to the Union, and he often told Emily that when his health improved, he would make speeches on behalf of his brother-in-law Mr. Lincoln. Then he would surely reap the reward of a government job.

Emily had doubts about whether her brother would live to see the election, much less enjoy the fruits of patronage, nor did she want Mr. Lincoln, for all of his kindness to her, to prevail. But in Burbridge's Kentucky, she kept quiet about this.

She was walking home from Levi's lodgings at the Broadway Hotel at the end of July, soon after learning of Mac's death, when she sensed footsteps close behind her. Thinking it some self-important gentleman, she moved over slightly so he could maneuver around her billowing skirt and be about whatever business he deemed so important to mankind. Instead of passing her, though, the man, who wore a Union uniform, said, "Mrs. Helm?"

"Yes?"

"Would you care to come down to headquarters and answer a few questions? Or if not, I can call at your house."

"Questions? What questions do you want me to answer?"

"We can discuss that later."

Not wanting to worry the children, Emily said, "I'll come to headquarters."

When they reached their destination, the man ushered her to a seat and took a letter from his pocket. Emily gasped when she recognized Mac's handwriting. "What are you doing with that letter?"

"I would like to know what this man is doing writing to you. Is he a relation?"

"He is—was—a dear friend of my late husband, and myself, and he is where no one can do him harm."

"Dead, then?"

"Dead."

Her interrogator studied the letter. "It appears to be in some sort of code."

"Code? I don't know any codes. Will you let me read the letter, which should have been delivered to me in the first place?"

Gingerly, the man handed over the letter. It was written entirely from the point of view of Mac's horse. Brushing her eyes, she handed it back. "For heaven's sake! This is not code; it is Mac being amusing. I told him about Skedaddle being appropriated by Morgan's men, and I suppose that inspired him. Now, why are you reading my mail?"

"I think it would be obvious. Your husband served the Confederacy, and one of your brothers is still enlisted in its army. Another is a surgeon for the rebels. Your father-in-law's loyalty to the Union is dubious at best. You fed Morgan's men—"

"After they were kind enough to leave my horses untouched."

"They spared your horses, and not those of your neighbors. Your mother dines regularly with Mrs. Morgan. You and your sisters have provided comfort and support to the Confederate prisoners here and at Camp Douglas, and none to the Union soldiers in our hospitals."

"There are plenty to look after the Union patients! I have only done what is humane, for my late husband's sake." Emily impatiently swatted at a remaining tear. "You do know that I am your president's sister-in-law."

"Yes, madam."

"Then I will show you this." She reached into her pocket and pulled out Mr. Lincoln's protection order, which she had got into the habit of carrying since General Burbridge had taken charge. "If you continue to harass me in this matter, you will be violating his own order."

Her companion studied the order, then said crisply, "We are not harassing you, madam. Simply warning you about some of your dubious activities. You may go now." He handed her Mac's letter. "And I see no need for us to retain this, under the circumstances."

Emily snatched up the letter and stalked home.

⁓

Early in September, Emily, walking by the telegraph office, heard a commotion, followed by a cheer. A soldier ran out and shouted to his comrades, "We've taken Atlanta!"

Atlanta, the Confederacy's largest prize next to Richmond. Atlanta, where she had spent her last days with Hardin and laid him to rest. Emily needed no newspapers to tell her what a blow this was to the South; she only had to listen to the joyful cries of Lexington's Unionists as she trudged home.

In this case, though, the South's misfortunes could prove a boon to her own; with Atlanta within Union lines, and more of Georgia surely to follow, it was time to renew her quest to retrieve and then sell her cotton. She considered writing to Mr. Lincoln, but decided a personal appeal would be more suitable. Goodness knew what lies he had been told about her by Burbridge's men, although they had left her alone since her visit to headquarters.

It was late October when she arrived in Washington and secured a lodging at the Metropolitan Hotel—not wanting this time to be a guest of the Lincolns, although she could ill afford the expense until she could sell her cotton. She found a city full of good humor, both from the fine fall weather and from the most recent Southern defeat at Cedar Creek in Virginia. It did not match her own mood. Last month had marked the first anniversary of Hardin's death, and Mac's demise— along with the slow unraveling of the Southern cause for which both men had given their lives—had made the occasion yet more sad. Even General Morgan was dead, ambushed and shot by Union troops.

From her brief stay at the White House the year before, Emily knew that there were certain times when Mr. Lincoln attended to petitions, and had arranged her visit accordingly. Although it would have been an easy matter to be admitted to Mary's presence, she decided to take care of her business first. A successful outcome would put her in a better humor anyway.

With the election just days away, there were few office seekers in the crowded room where she took a seat. Instead, the room was full of her sister women, some there to beg for the lives of men sentenced to die by military justice, others to plead that their sons or husbands be allowed to come home to help with neglected farms or care for motherless children. One by one, they left the room and returned, most with tears of gratitude streaming down their faces.

At last, Emily's turn arrived, and she walked in to find Mr. Lincoln sitting at his desk, wringing out a hand aching from being grasped. "Why, Little Sister! Why didn't you tell us you were coming here?"

"Sir, I need your help desperately. If I am not allowed to secure my cotton now, it may be destroyed. I need my permit now."

Mr. Lincoln shook his head. "Why didn't you write to me? I could have given you an answer without you going to the trouble of coming here. Wasted trouble, I am sorry to say. I can't give you what you seek. Not now." He gazed at Emily's stricken face. "Unless you are willing to take the oath."

"No!"

"So I thought." Mr. Lincoln searched through a mound of papers. It was a task that looked as if it could take hours, but he found what he sought surprisingly quickly. "This is a letter I received about you, telling me that there was enough against you to arrest you but that you had foiled the effort by showing your pass from me. Giving information to General Morgan and his men. Passing messages to the South. Aiding and comforting our enemies. I wrote to Burbridge telling him that if you had in fact done these things, the pass I gave you protected you only against harassment for the mere circumstance of you being Hardin's widow, and that it would not protect you against the consequences of any rebellious actions."

"Sir, I had not met General Morgan since I was a young girl, and I never passed any message to him or his men. I have written to my sisters in Selma and to a good friend in the Confederate army, now dead, but I have told them absolutely nothing that could compromise the North—indeed, all my letters were sent through flag of truce. All I have done is feed a couple of Morgan's men, who were hungry and had spared our horses, and bring what comfort I can to Southern prisoners."

"I believe you. And the fact that you haven't been arrested tells me that

Burbridge had sense enough to see the accusations for what they were worth." He started to insert the letter back into the pile, but changed his mind and tossed it into the fire. "But the fact remains that you've refused to take the oath of loyalty, and still refuse to take it, and while you haven't worked against us, you've made it perfectly clear which side you're on. And there's your sister Mrs. White. We could have probably clapped her in prison for carrying contraband—what woman needs that many trunks? Instead, we let her pass back to the South, where she mocked us for the amusement of the rebel government. I've got a thick skin, but I'm no fool, and I also happen to want to get reelected. I've not fought this war for all this time not to see it through to the end, and I'm not going to give my enemies a feast by letting another rebel Todd pass into the South. Your cotton's kept this long. It will keep some more."

"It could be destroyed, or taken!"

"That's a chance your husband took when he invested in cotton with a war raging around him. I won't be held responsible for his gamble."

"Gamble!" Emily rose. "I will not stay to have his memory insulted."

"Not insulting him; just stating a fact. But you're right. There's no point in continuing this conversation, except to say that I want you to have your cotton, that I have every intention of helping you get it when the right time comes, and that I'll do what I can to protect it in the meantime—which may not be much at the moment." He rose. "I suppose you will be seeing Mary?"

"No. I will wait for happier circumstances. Goodbye, sir."

There was black crepe on the door of the Todds' rented house when Emily returned to Lexington, having accomplished nothing but to deplete the little that remained to her of Hardin's pay. She stared at Kitty as her sister opened the door. "What is this?"

"Levi died a couple of days ago. Mama nursed him. His funeral was held here yesterday. She's upstairs resting."

Emily hurried upstairs to her mother's room, where Mrs. Todd lay in bed. "Mama! Are you not well?"

Her mother opened her eyes. "Just very tired, my child." She sat up. "Your brother had a hard death. Delirium tremens. He had such promise when I married your father."

"And I was not here to help you, but wasting my time in Washington."

"So it did not go well? Well, there's little you could have done here, and Kitty was a great help. At least he had a lucid moment at the very end. He apologized for any wrongs he had done to me and to my children and told me that he had written to Mr. Lincoln, begging him for a loan, but heard nothing. He had pawned everything of value, including your father's watch. I shall try to redeem it so that David can have it."

"Mr. Lincoln would do nothing for him?"

"Apparently not. I had to pay for his funeral."

Emily clenched her fists. "Go back to sleep, Mama."

She left her mother and went to her own room. There, scarcely acknowledging the greetings of her children, Emily sat at a desk and began to write.

30th Oct. 1864—
Lexington. Ky—

Mr. Lincoln—

Upon arriving at Lexington, after my long tedious unproductive and sorrowful visit to you, I found my Mother stretched upon a sick bed, made sick by the harrowing and shocking death of your Brother in law, and my half Brother Levi Todd—He died from utter want and, another sad victim to the powers of more favored relations—With such a sad, such a dreadful lesson, I again beg and plead attention + consideration to my petition to be permitted to ship my cotton + be allowed a pass to go South to attend to it—My necessities are such that I am compelled to urge it— The last money I have in the world I used to make the unfruitful Appeal to you. You cannot urge that you do not know them for I have told you of them. I have been a quiet citizen and request only the right which humanity and Justice always give to Widows and Orphans. I also would remind you that your minié bullets have made us what we are + I feel I have that additional claim upon you—

Will you reply to this—If you think I give way to excess of feeling, I beg you will make some excuse for a woman almost crazed with misfortune—

Respectfully,
Emily Todd Helm

For a few minutes, after addressing the letter to "Mr. A. Lincoln, Washington City," she debated about whether to send it. Then she snatched up her bonnet and marched to the post office.

⚭ 27 ⚭

MARY

NOVEMBER 1864 TO MARCH 1865

I had a letter today," Mary told Mr. Lincoln when he emerged from his office. "My brother Levi is dead. It is sad news, but with his dissipation, I am surprised it took this long."

The letter, from her sister Kitty, could hardly be dignified as such, Mary thought. With the note, "I thought you should know this," Kitty had simply enclosed a newspaper clipping of Levi's obituary from one of the Lexington papers.

"So I just learned myself from Emily," Mr. Lincoln said. He held up a letter. "Evidently I am at fault."

"At fault! How on earth?"

"According to her, he died of utter want and destitution. I suppose his craving for liquor might have played a role, too, but she doesn't mention that. A few weeks back he sent me a begging letter, mixed in with news of Lexington and assurances that he could help get me elected." The President shook his head sadly. "He wanted a couple of hundred dollars. He did say he was ill, but also that he was getting better. I assumed that anything I sent would be used to fund his sprees, so I did nothing. Now I wish I had sent him something—maybe through your stepmother or Emily."

"If he did not know he was dying, you cannot be blamed for not knowing that he was. And he hasn't provided for his children in years. Why should you provide for him?"

"Well, I feel bad about it anyway. Your sister's also angry about her cotton."

Mr. Lincoln had told her about Emily's meeting with him. The sheer impertinence of her sister, not to even bother to call upon her! "Still? Surely my sister must understand that her silly cotton is not your first priority. May I see the letter?"

"No, it would only annoy you."

"Then I will see it." Before Mr. Lincoln could protest, Mary took it from his hand. "Why, this is outrageous! She knows as well as anyone that Levi courted his own death; what could you do? 'Your minié bullets have made us what we are.' Why, if the South had stayed in the Union, like people of sense, there would have been no need for minié bullets, yours or theirs! 'Yours' as if you did not try to keep the Union together." Mary handed the letter back to her husband. "I shall let you store this with whatever other treasonous communications you receive. Next, she'll be blaming you for starting the slave trade!"

Mr. Lincoln shrugged. "She'll come round to her senses. You Todd ladies always do."

Election Day—November 8, 1864—did not so much arrive as it did crawl. Mary had not lost her optimism that Mr. Lincoln would prevail over his Democratic opponent, General McClellan, but she also was well aware that optimism had often proved unfounded over the course of the war.

It was a dreary, rainy day. The White House was empty of nearly everyone but the family and the staff, and even Washington itself had a deserted air, as many of its men had returned to their home states to vote. Mary did not often contemplate the fact that ladies were denied this privilege, but on this day, she wished she could be at the polling place in Springfield, casting her ballot for her husband as any woman of sense would surely do.

Her frustration was shared by Tad, who, also being unable to vote, had to content himself with rallying every man of age he encountered to do so. His parents had barely breakfasted when Tad raced in and tugged his father's shoulder. "The Pennsylvania men are voting for you! Come see!"

Mr. Lincoln duly followed him, as did Mary, to a window, where they had an excellent view of the soldiers, who were stationed on the White House grounds, casting their ballots, all of which were the right color. Amid them trotted Tad's turkey, spared from the dinner table by the President. "What's he doing?" Mr. Lincoln asked. "Is he voting?"

"No," said Tad. "He's not of age."

At seven in the evening, Mr. Lincoln gathered up his umbrella and the cane that Mary insisted he carry for self-protection (when he bothered to remember it) and walked to the War Department to await election dispatches. It was so well established that the vigil was an all-male affair that Mary did not even ask to go with him: as she had in the 1860 election, she would have to await the result from the comfort of her armchair.

Presently, Mr. Lincoln sent a message: early returns were encouraging. Another hour brought a second equally promising message. By then, however, Mary needed no such dispatches. She had the crowd collecting outside, growing larger and more boisterous by the hour even as the rain poured down, to tell her all she needed to know.

Tad, whom no one had suggested sending to bed even if he had been willing, stood beside her, watching the umbrellas bobbing in front of the White House fence. "Do you think Pa won?" he said as a band struck up a tune.

"Yes," said the President behind them. "Pa won. At least, it's all but certain. And for all the work the next four years is going to be, it's a sweet victory."

Mary and Tad stepped aside as the President, giving in to the clamor of the crowd, opened the window and raised his voice. "I do not impugn the motives of anyone opposed to me. It is no pleasure to me to triumph over anyone; but I give thanks to the Almighty for this evidence of the people's resolution to stand by free government and the rights of humanity."

Mary shut her eyes in a quick prayer of gratitude. Not for herself—although the victory had certainly saved her from an onslaught of creditors. For the nation, which had chosen to pursue the war to victory rather than to conclude the cowardly peace that McClellan had proposed. For all those who had died in the Union cause. Most of all, for her husband, who had been so vilified and was now vindicated.

But was not she vindicated in a way as well? She had stood beside him all through this terrible war, through the terrible blow of Willie's death, and although she did not pretend to have borne the latter as patiently as he had, she had nonetheless borne it. She had stood with him under enemy fire. And with God's grace, they would stand through the next four years together.

∾

In January, Bob returned from Harvard Law School, where he had somewhat sullenly enrolled after his most recent appeal to enlist had failed. He came on a late train and arrived at breakfast at the last possible moment, so Mary had no chance for private conversation with him. After some strained small talk, he said, "Father, you said we could talk in your office."

"And we will." The President stood. "Excuse us, Molly."

"Can I come?" Tad said.

"No," Bob said.

"Then I'll let Tabby sit at your place," Tad said, and his cat hopped up on Bob's chair smugly.

Presently, the men appeared in Mary's sitting area. Mr. Lincoln cleared his throat. "Molly, Bob and I have arrived at an agreement. Bob still wants to see some of the war, and I no longer believe it fair to deny him his wish. So I will write to General Grant and ask that Bob be allowed to serve on his staff. I can't say for certain, but I guess he'll agree. If not, we'll try something else, but for now, that's the plan."

His expression and tone were clear: he would brook no objections. And what objection could she make? No longer could she press the need to stay at Harvard: Bob had obtained his college degree, and a degree from Harvard Law, while desirable, was not essential. After all, his father had done perfectly well as a lawyer without any higher education. Furthermore, it was not entirely a defeat for her, as her wishes had been taken into consideration. Bob would likely not see combat, although on General Grant's staff he would be far too close to the fighting in Virginia for Mary's comfort.

So there was nothing to do but say, "I hope General Grant is agreeable. He certainly should be."

Following the example of graciousness in victory his father had set two months before, Bob said, "Thank you, Mother. It does mean a lot to me, having a chance to serve."

"Then I hope you will have the chance. Will you stay for dinner tonight?"

"I'm sorry, no. I am dining with a...friend."

Plainly, he was speaking of Miss Mary Harlan, the daughter of Senator James Harlan of Iowa. Mary fully approved of the girl, who was well educated and pretty, without being so pretty as to be worrisome. She would have been quite content to let the couple do their courting in the Executive Mansion. Evidently, however, Bob with his outsized sense of privacy, which had grown noticeably over the past several years, preferred to tryst in secret, or so he thought. "Very well," she said serenely. "Give Miss Harlan my regards."

Bob blushed, and Mary felt some revenge for him insisting on entering the military.

∽

Of the gloomy days Mary had seen in Washington, President Lincoln's second inaugural day, March 4, surely ranked among the worst. The rain had scarcely let up for two days, turning the city's streets into pure muck. Mary, picking her way into her carriage with her black velvet skirts lifted as high as decency would allow, remembered that long-ago day when she and Mercy had made their way along Springfield's muddy streets with their pile of shingles. It was a pity she had not saved a few.

Pennsylvania Avenue was lined with spectators spilling out into the street, hanging precariously out of windows, and perching in trees. Mary smiled and waved at them somewhat guiltily, for the person they most wanted to see, the President, had quietly slipped over to the Capitol long before and was passing the time in signing bills. It was, the ever-cranky *New York Herald* would grumble, like seeing *Hamlet* without Hamlet. Still, Mary knew that there would be a fine parade of military troops, fire companies, and civil organizations behind her, and as every place or thing that could possibly support a flag had been bedecked with one, the cloudy day was much brightened by the red, white, and blue that flashed everywhere.

In the Capitol, she and her sons took their places; Bob, resplendent in his captain's uniform, for General Grant, of course, had acceded to the President's wish and had already assumed his duties. Finally, the President entered, looking particularly well turned out in a new Brooks Brothers suit that Mary had personally inspected before he left the Executive Mansion. He was escorted by his outgoing vice president, Mr. Hannibal Hamlin, and followed by his new vice president, Andrew Johnson.

Mary had understood why Mr. Lincoln, when seeking reelection, had chosen Mr. Johnson as his running mate, as he had served as the military governor of Tennessee and could be expected to help win the border states for Mr. Lincoln. Nonetheless, she had had vague misgivings about the man, which proved only too well founded when the new vice president wobbled upright to make his required speech. Was the man *intoxicated?*

For what seemed an eternity, Mr. Johnson rambled on about his humble origins—which, Mary thought, were all too plain now— while the President's face turned into a study of gloom, elegant and dignified Senator Charles Sumner buried his face in his hands, and Vice President Hamlin tugged gently at, then yanked, his successor's coattails. It was a vain effort, for it only encouraged the second man in the nation to remind the officials around him that they derived all their power from the people. "And I will say to you, Mr. Secretary Seward, and to you, Mr. Secretary Stanton—"

Mr. Seward managed a sardonic smile. Mr. Stanton looked murderous.

"Mr. Secretary... Who is Secretary of the Navy?"

"Welles," said the bearer of that name. "Good God in heaven."

"Welles," Mr. Johnson said firmly. "Mr. Secretary Welles. Power from the people."

At last, Mr. Johnson ran out of words and took the oath of office administered by Mr. Hamlin, who proffered the necessary Bible as if wanting to rap his successor's hand with it. Kissing the Bible as if it were a squirming baby, Johnson then attempted to administer the oath of office to the new senators, but after a few tries wisely turned the task over to a clerk and subsided into his seat.

The oaths completed without further ado, it was time to proceed to the east portico of the Capitol, overlooked by the building's fine new dome. New, too, was the Chief Justice of the Supreme Court who would administer the oath of office to the President after he gave his inaugural speech: Salmon P. Chase, replacing the ancient Justice Taney, who had died the previous year. But newest of all was what Mary sensed as she surveyed the crowd. The last time she had sat in this place, the spectators had looked restless and on edge, terrified of what the future might hold. Now, though many had suffered and many would likely suffer still as long as there were armies in the field, there was hope, even optimism, in the faces looking toward the portico.

To applause, the President entered, still natty in his suit and looking unruffled by his vice president's disgraceful exhibition. As the clapping ceased, he glanced up, followed by tens of thousands of eyes. The sun, hidden for days, had chosen that precise moment to break through. As the multitude fell silent, he spoke. "Fondly do we hope—fervently do we pray—that this mighty scourge of war may speedily pass away. Yet, if God wills that it continue, until all the wealth piled by the bondman's two hundred and fifty years of unrequited toil shall be sunk, and until every drop of blood drawn with the lash shall be paid by another drawn with the sword, as was said three thousand years ago, so still it must be said 'the judgments of the Lord are true and righteous altogether.'

"With malice toward none, with charity for all, with firmness in the right as God gives us to see the right, let us strive on to finish the work we are in, to bind up the nation's wounds, to care for him who shall have borne the battle and for his widow and his orphan, to do all which may achieve and cherish a just and lasting peace among ourselves and with all nations."

Mary, with tears in her eyes, was unequal to applauding. So, evidently, were most of the spectators.

As they dressed for that evening's reception, though, she took the opportunity to congratulate her husband on his fine speech. The President, drawing on his white gloves, winked. "So you didn't want the earth to sink beneath you this time?"

He referred to a speech he had made the previous year at a sanitary fair. It had not been one of his finer efforts, and Mary had told him so. "Really, Mr. Lincoln, I wish you would forget that unkind criticism of mine. I certainly have."

"Oh, you were probably right. I usually do value your opinion on these things."

On Monday, the Lincolns prepared to ride to the inaugural ball, Mary in her white silk gown, Mr. Lincoln fresh from the barber and dressed in evening clothes. Bob, who had overcome his aversion to the gossip of the press sufficiently to serve as Miss Harlan's escort, fell in step beside them as they proceeded to the waiting carriages. "By the way, Mother, I kept meaning to tell you. Before I came back to Washington, I was put in charge of seeing a lady to the rebel lines, and who do you think it was? Aunt Emily! She sends her regards."

"Going to see about her cotton," the President said.

"You mean you let her, after that impertinent letter?"

"Of course. I promised that I would help her if I was reelected, and it was a promise I always intended to keep."

Mary shook her head. "You put up with a good deal from we women, Mr. Lincoln."

"And Todd women in particular. Just don't make me dance tonight, and I won't complain."

"I had my one dance with you back in Springfield, and my feet still carry the memory."

"I hope it was worth it in the long run."

She squeezed his hand and looked up at him, so affectionately that next to them, Bob blushed. "It certainly was."

∾ 28 ∾

EMILY

MARCH 1865

Something about the handsome young Union captain waiting for them at Varina Landing looked familiar, but Emily could not place him until she remembered the face that had appeared so often in Mary's photograph album back at the White House. "*Bob?*"

"Aunt Emily? I was told only that I would be meeting two ladies. Not which two ladies." He embraced Emily and smiled at Mrs. Bettie Pratte, an old friend of Emily's who was traveling to Richmond to join her husband—the wives of living Confederate officers being unwelcome in Kentucky.

As Bob helped them disembark, Emily said, "Do you remember when you were a boy, and your mother was teaching you manners? She made you help me out of your family carriage, again and again, until you were quite the Lord Chesterfield."

"Well, I hope I learned my lesson well. Now, I do have to check your documents, or I'll find myself back at Harvard."

"I am glad that you were allowed to serve, even on the wrong side."

Bob had the graciousness to smile at that feeble joke.

In February, Mr. Lincoln, through his old Illinois friend Orville Browning, had granted Emily permission to come to Richmond. Mr. Browning, a former senator who had stayed in Washington as a lobbyist, had put her under the charge of General James Singleton, a fellow Illinoisan with connections to the South. Ostensibly, General Singleton was coming to Richmond to explore the possibility of peace, but as recent talks for that had stalled on the issue of reunion, everyone, in the South and North alike, assumed that he was in the Confederate capital to further his own business, and that of Emily and many others, of trading in cotton. The whole affair struck Emily as a little unsavory, but as one of its chief beneficiaries, she was hardly in a position to complain.

The steamer would not depart for Richmond until the next day, so in the meantime, a string of Yankee officers came aboard to talk with General Singleton. Remembering her unpleasant experience with General Sickles and Senator Harris, Emily dreaded their arrival. But things were quite different this time; it might have been any social gathering of officers and their wives. General Stephen Ord, a West Point graduate, made light conversation about his and Hardin's alma mater. Had Emily ever been there? She must visit some time, and the river journey to it was sublime, as Mrs. Lincoln could no doubt attest. General John Mulford, who was in charge of the prisoner exchanges as well as the steamer, brought his wife onboard to entertain the ladies so that the wait would not be too tedious. Just a few years her senior, Mrs. Mulford was interested in Emily's travels, particularly Lookout Mountain. How Emily had managed to ascend that height without fainting was beyond her. Might it be possible to go up just a little way and still have a respectable view? Or might just staying put on the lowest possible ground have its own charms?

Everyone was so pleasant, it was unsettling. Her hosts could afford to be pleasant, Emily supposed, given the state of the Confederacy these days. Atlanta, Savannah, Columbia, Charleston, Wilmington— all had fallen to the Yankees. Still, the Northerners were having the decency not to gloat in front of her, so she chatted amicably with them, surprising herself by her ability to mention Hardin in casual conversation without tears welling in her eyes.

Bob Lincoln and General Ord did not linger, but departed for Washington and Mr. Lincoln's second inauguration. "Do give your parents and Tad my regards," Emily said, pecking him on the cheek. "I was short with your father during my visit to him, and rather unkind in my last letter to him. I hope he—and your mother—will not think too ill of me for it."

"If he did, you wouldn't be here. As for Mother—well, if she is upset with you, she'll come round. Anyway, Tad's wild to see his favorite aunt again, and he usually gets his way."

"I noticed that," Emily said wryly.

The next day, General Singleton, having commandeered an ambulance, took Emily and Mrs. Pratte from their landing place to the Spotswood Hotel. Cannon rumbled in the distance as pedestrians in bright clothing sauntered by on Franklin Street, crowded with persons of all ranks, military and civilian; only when Emily alighted from the ambulance and saw the passersby close up could she see the patches on the fabric. It was, she thought, the perfect metaphor for the tattered Confederacy.

At the Spotswood, which was only a few months older than the war, the carpets had been torn up to make army blankets, and the cramped room allotted to her—one that she had won only through General Singleton's influence, as the city was full of refugees from the recently conquered towns—was barren of all furniture except for a bedstead and a rickety chair. But champagne, she was assured as she was handed her key, would be available from early in the morning. Evidently it was possible to spend one's entire waking hours in a soused state, and some of her fellow guests appeared to be trying.

◦❧◦

General Singleton having taken on the weight of Emily's business—indeed, Emily supposed her presence in Richmond to be largely superfluous, except that she might be called upon to sign some documents—Emily had considerable time on her hands. Her first visit was to Mrs. Pember at Chimborazo Hospital.

"You're looking well," Mrs. Pember said after they had embraced. "I know I shouldn't say it in your bereaved condition—and how sad I was to hear of General Helm's death!—but you are. If you're not looking to remarry, you had best guard yourself, because there is a perfect mania for weddings here, and you are far prettier than some of the brides I've seen. Oh, dear, these hospital walls are making me catty. I blame it on the hospital rats."

"Rats?" Emily tugged at her skirts.

"No, dear, not those kind, although I've seen my share of those, too. They thrive here, them and the cockroaches. No, the hospital rats are those patients who just won't get well, or who when they do, get sick again the moment they set foot back on the field. They're twice as much trouble as the men who are genuinely sick, and they plague me constantly for whiskey, although it has absolutely no medicinal effect upon them. Mind you, when it comes time to evacuate, I expect that a force much like that of your Jesus Christ will heal them."

"Do you think it will come to that—evacuation?"

"Well, officially, everything's fine, but unofficially, Rome is getting ready to fall. The government is packing up its papers in case it needs to flee, Congress has approved the use of colored troops, the white troops are deserting in droves, Mrs. Davis has sold some of her fine clothes for the cause, and President Davis has appointed a day for fasting and prayer. The fasting seems a bit redundant. So I would not linger here if I were you."

"And you?"

"I shall see it through. I'm not going to desert my patients, although a few probably wouldn't mind. But it's not something I want to dwell on too much, so I shall put you on the spot. What are you going to do when you return to Kentucky? Are you going to remain with your mother?"

"Yes. We do get along."

"That's pleasant. And she's bound to tell you how to raise your children, how to run your life in general—all good things in your case, for they will distract you from your grief."

Emily smiled. "Well, I have had a great deal of advice. As for what I will do—well, if I cannot get my cotton, or if Sherman's men have destroyed it, I suppose I will have to find something to make a living at. I can't have my mother supporting me forever."

"There is remarriage."

"It would have to be a very special man for me to make him my children's stepfather."

"Yes, you can't be too particular in that respect. And to be frank—"

"When are you not frank?"

"To be very frank, there are compensations in the single life. I could not be here, and do what I really think has been good, had I remarried as some advised me to do. As the ever-sensible Miss Jane Austen said, a single woman of good sense and good character must always be respected, and she need not be without occupations. Change 'widow' for that, and there you have it."

Soon after Emily arrived in Richmond, a member of the British Parliament, Thomas Conolly of Ireland, came to town from the swamps of North Carolina, where he had landed courtesy of a blockade runner. His own vessel, which he had hoped to use to haul cotton overseas, lay in the Bahamas being repaired, and it seemed most unlikely that he would be bringing anything back to Ireland besides himself, but this had not daunted his good humor or his predilection for cocktails and ladies. Mr. Conolly established himself at the Spotswood, and despite herself, Emily could not help being flattered that the aristocrat deemed her suitable to include in his champagne and oyster breakfasts and his strolls around town.

Naturally, Mr. Conolly was welcome in the highest society of Richmond, including the drawing rooms of President and Mrs. Davis and of Mrs. General Lee. Through him, and likely for Hardin's sake as well, Emily could have gained admission, but she was mindful of her obligations to Mr. Lincoln and knew that any such visits on her part would likely find their way to the *New York Tribune* and the other Northern papers. In any case, Mr. Conolly's recapitulation of his visits was nearly as good as the real thing. "Mr. Davis is a fine man," the Irishman said as a servant, leased from an accommodating Richmonder for his expertise with cocktails, mixed his specialty. "A noble bearing with sensible conversation. But Mrs. Davis—oh, Mrs. Davis! A viper with a vicious tongue, and I must say, one who does not appear at all sympathetic to the Southern cause."

It was what the North said about Mary, only in reverse. Emily almost wished that Mary were there to appreciate the irony.

∞

General Singleton kept Emily well apprised of his progress. "I've learned that some of your cotton is stored in Augusta, Georgia," he said as a waiter proffered Emily the inevitable champagne. "General Sherman spared that city, so it should be safe for now."

Emily waved away the champagne. "And the rest?"

"Unfortunately, some of it most likely was burned. But some may be here. General Helm was sensible; he stored it in different warehouses."

"I just wish he had told me more about his financial affairs."

"Well, I suppose he didn't want to think about the possibility of his own death. And we men aren't always the best at telling our wives what they need to know."

"You're certainly right about that."

"Well…" General Singleton brightened. "Here's a new acquaintance of mine, to save our sex from further attack. Major Ficklin, I have the honor of presenting the lady I spoke of, Mrs. Helm."

The rangy, rakish man who had approached their table took Emily's hand. In a soft, pleasant voice quite at variation with his buccaneerish appearance, he said, "My pleasure, Mrs. Helm. I understand from General Singleton that you are Mrs. Lincoln's sister."

"Yes," Emily said warily.

"Mr. Lincoln is a good man, and one well equipped to smooth

the South's transition back into the Union. I hope to meet him soon through the general here, and perhaps through you."

"Back to the Union? Are you that much of a pessimist?"

"No, normally I am an incurable optimist. But sometimes realism has to intervene, and she has. A victory would require divine intervention at this point, and while I don't profess to be a theologian, my sense is that the Lord has chosen to sit out this particular dance. So we must look to a new future, and repair our damage as best we can." He sighed. "I just hope I get to keep Monticello, but my hopes aren't high."

"Monticello? The Monticello?"

"Yes. She came up for auction a while back, and being a native of Charlottesville and in funds at the time, I bought her, to the delight of my old father. Only thing I ever did that really pleased the old man, which isn't to say that I didn't give him cause for displeasure over the years, because I certainly did. He was ailing, and my purchase allowed him to die in President Jefferson's bedchamber, which delighted him as only a dying Virginian can be delighted."

Emily snorted.

"We are an odd breed," Major Ficklin said. "But I do have a more practical side. I have cotton, bought and paid for, in Alabama, which I wish to sell in the North, all with the proper permits. Once I do that, I will return to my natural habitat, the west."

"Major Ficklin helped establish the Pony Express," General Singleton said.

"Yes, those were the days," Major Ficklin said wistfully. "Might I ask you to put a good word in for me with your brother-in-law, Mrs. Helm?"

"I hardly know you, sir," Emily said, more archly than she had intended.

"Then I must study to know you better, Mrs. Helm."

∽≈∾

Major Benjamin Ficklin did indeed spend a good amount of time with Emily over the next few days. He regaled her with tales of his adventures, all of which, rather to Emily's surprise, turned out to be true. He had fought the Mormons in the west. He had fought the red men in the west. He had fought in Mexico. He had fought briefly in the war, but having found life in camp tedious, and being plagued with asthma as well, had decided that he could serve the Confederacy just as well by running the blockade.

The day after their introduction, he pulled a sheet of paper out of his pocket. "My darling niece has given me a list of things I am to acquire for her in Washington when I go there. She is preparing for her wedding. As you have been in the North, and know what is being worn, I would dearly appreciate your advice."

"I have not been north of Baltimore, so I fear my knowledge is rather provincial. But I will do my best."

With the help of a *Godey's Lady's Book* that had made it through the blockade, Emily advised as best she could, while Major Ficklin talked of his misspent youth at Virginia Military Institute. "I was expelled when I painted a horse with zebra stripes—or was it when I set off a small explosion? In any case, I begged to be taken back—why, I don't know—and at last graduated, fourth from the bottom of my class."

"Only fourth?"

"Yes, it surprises me now that there were three men who managed to rank below me. What they did to earn that privilege, I shudder to imagine."

"I would love to know," Emily said dryly.

Having marked some suitable items as guidance for Major Ficklin's shopping, Emily handed the magazine to him. Then she frowned. "Major Ficklin, you have been in London, haven't you?" She looked closely at the excellent cut of his clothes. "I think you know more about what is fashionable than do I."

"You have caught me, Mrs. Helm. I simply enjoy the pleasure of your company. Now, don't look at me that way! Ladies are my weakness. When I see a pretty lady, I must contrive to spend time with her."

"I am the mother of three children, and a recent widow."

"Yes, I know. That is part of your charm—your unavailability. At least, I trust you are unavailable. I noticed that Irish chap writing some poetry for you."

"It was a poem about the South, and her noble cause."

"Not a love poem? I am disappointed. I had heard that he was quite the rogue with the ladies. Still, be careful around him, Mrs. Helm."

"*You* are telling me to be careful around *him*?"

"I am. I am really quite harmless."

"You have never been married?"

"No. My friends have tried their best. They keep introducing me to young ladies—most of them quite fetching—but I just cannot make up my mind to marry yet. Either there is so much else to do, or the times are so expensive to keep a young lady in the proper style."

"You could marry an older lady, one of fortune."

"Now, that is a thought. But that would preclude me enjoying the company of younger ladies, and that just won't do. Now, there is something that has been bothering me, Mrs. Helm. Your bonnet."

"My bonnet?"

"Yes. If I may just make a small adjustment—"

With trepidation, Emily handed it over to him. Major Ficklin studied it, and then switched the position of two of the black artificial flowers that adorned it. "Perfect," he pronounced, and handed it back to her.

Emily studied his handiwork and wondered how she could have possibly approved of any other arrangement of the flowers.

❧

On March 23, General Singleton was waiting at Emily's accustomed seat when she came down to breakfast. In a low voice, he said, "Let me speak to you in private, Mrs. Helm."

Emily nodded and followed him outside. When they had walked a safe distance from curious ears, he said, "We must leave this place. I have it on good authority that things are about to heat up soon, and I don't want to be trapped here. More to the point, I don't want you trapped here. Mr. Lincoln made me responsible for your safety. He was adamant on that point."

"Really?"

"Why, of course." He looked at her quizzically. "Did you think he would not be? You are his sister-in-law, after all."

Although Bob had told her that she had not lost Mr. Lincoln's affection with her foolish letter, it was good to have further proof of it. "Yes, of course. I'll go pack."

"There's still unfinished business about our cotton, of course, but that can't be helped. We'll take counsel with Mr. Browning when we return to Washington." He gave her another look. "Mrs. Helm…"

"What, sir?"

"I hope you won't be leaving a loved one here."

"What do you mean?"

General Singleton coughed. "I mean, you have been spending a great deal of time with Mr. Conolly and Major Ficklin. I fear that you might have developed an attachment to one of them. Being but young still—"

Emily laughed. "Mr. Conolly has confided in me about his love troubles. He is rather fond of a young lady here, whose parents do not approve of his morals. Major Ficklin is not suited for a domestic life in the least. They are perfectly charming men, and I have enjoyed their company, but neither is a man I would marry, if they were inclined to ask. Which neither is."

"Well, that's good." He looked unconvinced, though. Emily could not blame him, because she too had been surprised to find herself enjoying these last few weeks in Richmond. It had even been amusing to receive the attentions of Mr. Conolly and Major Ficklin, knowing that their hearts were not at risk and that hers was still in Hardin's keeping.

She had no time to ride out to Chimborazo Hospital, and had to settle for sending Mrs. Pember an affectionate note. In the parlor of the Spotswood, Mr. Conolly lifted his cocktail in a goodbye toast and promised to make her at home should she ever find herself in Ireland. Major Ficklin adjusted her bonnet ribbons to his satisfaction. "I'll be in Washington soon myself, Mrs. Helm. I hope to see you and General Singleton there."

"Why don't you go with us now?"

"Because, dear lady, I have no pass. I must cross the Potomac under cover of darkness. But the young man who rows me across is quite competent, and I've no doubt he will bring me through safely."

"Then I wish you a safe trip." She strained up and kissed him on the cheek. Hardin surely would not mind.

After she had said goodbye to her lady friends at the Spotswood—a great many of them—she and General Singleton rode to the wharf and boarded the flag-of-truce ship. As it left, Emily stared back at the receding city. What would happen to her friends there? What about the Kentuckians she had encountered, some soldiers, some civilians, who had given her letters and messages to take home with her? Might the letters packed in her trunk be the last communications from some of them? She shuddered.

General Singleton was looking back as well. He shook his head. "I believe that this will be the end, and that it will be ugly, Mrs. Helm. You're best far away—but I know it pains you to leave."

"It does. My own cares seem very small by comparison. I feel that I am leaving my friends to their fates."

Midway through her journey, Emily gazed out of her well-appointed stateroom and saw a steamer heading south, the *River Queen*. The name was familiar; Emily had heard of it in some connection with Mr. Lincoln. It was then, as if obliging her by removing all possible doubt, that she saw standing on the deck the unmistakable figure of her brother-in-law, staring at the moon. If she had been on the deck, she might have been able to call out to him, but what could she have said? A thank-you for the kindness he had done her in allowing her to come south, and the kindness he was doing her in taking her safely north? A reproach for the destruction that he, through his generals, had wreaked upon the South and its people, and would wreak further? As Emily struggled with her emotions, Mr. Lincoln, unconscious of his audience, remained searching the heavens and was still doing so when his vessel finally drew out of Emily's view.

It was just as well, Emily supposed, that they had missed the opportunity to speak. Better to wait until another time, when she could find the right words to say to him, when they could come together as family, not as conqueror and vanquished.

Never did it occur to Emily that this was the last time she would see him alive.

∽ 29 ∾
MARY
MARCH 1865

E veryone seems to think I need to go to City Point," Mr. Lincoln said toward the end of March. "Bob has telegraphed to invite me, and so has General Grant. So I guess I'll go, although I think it's a plot to get me to rest. Are you in on it, Molly?"

"No," Mary answered truthfully. "But I certainly agree with the conspirators, if a conspiracy exists." While the papers had praised the President's inaugural speech, they had also noted his worn-out appearance, and Mary, happening one day to look at a photograph of him from his first days in office, had actually started at the contrast between that and the man who stood before her.

"Well, you're invited, too, and Tad. It'll be good to take a look at the front, at any rate."

Mary gladly agreed, and on March 23, they drove to the Sixth Street wharf and boarded the *River Queen*, a steamer that the President had used for an abortive peace conference at Hampton Roads, Virginia just weeks before. When they arrived the next evening at City Point, the hamlet near Petersburg that had become General Grant's head-quarters, the Lincolns found waiting for them not only Bob and the general, but Mrs. Grant.

Ideally, Mary should have taken to Mrs. Grant when the two first met the year before, for they had much in common. Both were from the west—Mrs. Grant hailed from Missouri. Both were from slaveholding families; indeed, Mrs. Grant had traveled with her enslaved nurse until rather embarrassingly late in the war. Both had had to overcome some familial opposition to their marriages. Both, for a time, had enjoyed a less comfortable standard of living as wives than they had enjoyed as daughters. Both were married to extremely busy men.

Aside from that, Mrs. Grant was an agreeable woman: she was even-tempered and, though somewhat shy at first meeting, was quite forthcoming upon further acquaintance without being overly talkative. And while she was a few years younger than Mary, she could not be called handsome, being afflicted with a difficulty of her right eye that gave her a perpetual squint and marred what would have otherwise been a pleasant, if not a pretty, face.

So all told, Mary should have liked Mrs. Grant. She did not, and she knew perfectly well why. It was not that if General Grant won the war, he would likely be nominated for the presidency, although that certainly did not help matters. No, it was the adoring way the general looked at his cross-eyed wife, the almost comical way he indulged her. Even allowing her to take her slave from post to post was the result of his reluctance to see her deprived of any of the comforts she had enjoyed under an equally indulgent father.

Mary knew Mr. Lincoln loved her, of course. But was she as utterly necessary to him as Mrs. Grant was to the general? That she could not help but wonder at, and even to doubt.

Still, she managed a smile when Mrs. Grant was shown into the room of the *River Queen* that served as her parlor. Then Mrs. Grant plopped onto the sofa next to her, and Mary's smile froze. Over the past four years, she had grown accustomed to people waiting to be invited to sit beside her, and there was no shortage of chairs in the parlor.

Mrs. Grant noticed her frown, as might any sentient person. "I'm afraid I crowd you," she said meekly.

"Not at all," Mary said, far too sweetly. With some satisfaction, she observed Mrs. Grant's discomfort until the woman at last found an excuse to move.

∽◎∽

The next morning, Mary awoke to good news: while everyone on the *River Queen* was sound asleep, the rebels had attacked Fort Stedman, scarcely ten miles off from City Point, but had been beaten back.

While the President went ashore to confer with General Grant at his headquarters, Mary stayed behind on the deck, marveling at the activity about her. The siege of Petersburg and General Grant's need to set up a headquarters and a supply center had transformed this quiet place where the James and Appomattox Rivers met. Now the manor that overlooked the rivers was occupied by the Union quartermaster and his staff, its lawn dotted by tents and cabins, its slaves run off or serving in the Northern army. Ships from the North converged upon City Point at all times, bringing with them anything an army might need—except for bread. It was cooked on-site, and the scent from the bakery was almost strong enough to compensate for the unpleasant smells created by the convergence of too many men and beasts in too small a space.

City Point had its railroad, too, which the Lincolns, the Grants, and a host of others boarded late in the morning to travel to General Meade's headquarters. As the little train bumped and chugged along, Mary stared out at her surroundings. Ancient trees shielded stately mansions with open doors and gaping windows, abandoned by their aristocratic inhabitants. Where were they now? Refugeeing somewhere, no doubt. One of the few war-related topics that Emily had broached on her visit to Washington had been her grief at having to leave behind her little house in Louisville. Mary had not thought much of it at the time—after all, she had left behind her home as well—but now she felt a twist of pity for those that the war had compelled to wander, even if they had brought it upon themselves. And what of those who had nothing to return to but ruins? Or who would return as little better than ruins themselves?

Then she gasped. Lying near the tracks was the body of a soldier, clad in blue, inches away from another body in butternut. "For goodness's sake, bury them!" she whispered. The words had just escaped her mouth when the train turned a curve and she saw a whole mass of dead, wounded, and dying men strewn around the field, some close enough for her to see the agony on their faces. Here and there lay scraps of Union and rebel uniforms—but no, they were not mere cloth but parts of men who had set out that morning young and vibrant and whole. She turned away, terrified of what she might see next.

Mr. Lincoln was staring at the bodies as well. "I did warn you, Molly, that we might catch sight of something like this."

"Yes, you did," Mary said. "But I hadn't realized it would be so close." How on earth did anyone survive these battles with his sanity intact? And what images to fill the dying moments of those who had not survived them, like her brothers and Emily's husband! Mary shuddered.

Fortunately, they soon reached the station at Globe Tavern, from which they would ride to General Meade's headquarters. A few horses had been put on the train, and General Grant offered the President his choice between Cincinnati, a large chestnut gelding, and Jeff Davis, a black pony. Knowing that Cincinnati was the general's favorite, Mr. Lincoln chose Jeff Davis, who was ill-suited for a man of his height. "He looks ridiculous on the mount," Mary said as she and Mrs. Grant settled into their ambulance.

"I will make certain that the general insists that he have Cincinnati henceforth," Mrs. Grant said. "Usually it is I who rides Jeff Davis." She giggled. "My, that does sound vulgar, doesn't it? But he is a fine pony. He came from the plantation of Jefferson Davis's brother. He was in rather poor shape when the army captured him, but the general has a wonderful way with horses, and now he has a splendid gait." Mrs. Grant giggled again. "The pony, that is. But really, doesn't General Grant sit his horse beautifully?"

Mary had little to say in response.

For a couple of hours, the men toured the battlefield while Mary and Mrs. Grant visited patients in the hospital tents. Mary had always been kind and attentive to these sick and wounded men, but now that she had so directly glimpsed the horrors they had seen, she marveled at those who were able to summon a smile when she approached them, and understood those who could not.

When they at last reboarded the train, now augmented by several cars bringing the wounded to City Point, all were pensive over the sights of the day. Captain John Barnes, a naval officer whose vessel, the *Bat*, had shadowed the *River Queen* on its voyage in order to protect the Lincolns, had joined the landlubbers on the excursion to the front, and had made himself useful by helping to succor the injured as they awaited transportation to the hospitals. "I came across this red-headed rebel boy—I mean a boy, fourteen at best and I suspect closer to twelve—lying on his back amid a heap of bodies, begging for his mother. I couldn't see any injury on him, so I asked him what the matter was, hoping I might be able to get him on his feet and walk him back to headquarters and to one of our lady nurses. He turned his head to show me, and I saw the most ghastly head wound I've seen. He died then and there, just from the effort."

"The poor little thing," Mary and Mrs. Grant said, almost in unison.

"That's who they've been reduced to sending into battle," Mr. Lincoln said. "Children." He shook his head. "It can't end soon enough. And yet there are people who claim we enjoy this."

The next day, the President decided to review some ships and General Ord's Army of the James. This would entail a journey down the James River to Aiken's Landing, a route that to Mary's relief would spare them the horrors of the previous day. As the *River Queen* was the most commodious vessel, the Grants joined the Lincolns onboard for the voyage, as did General and Mrs. Ord. Another general's wife! But at least Mrs. Ord did not try to crowd Mary off her own sofa.

In fact, the water part of the trip was excellent. As they passed through the pontoon bridge that General Sheridan was using to cross the James, the President admired the engineering, while Tad and young Jesse Grant snickered at the sight of some soldiers bathing on the bank and not leaving a great deal to the imagination. From there they proceeded to the USS *Malvern*, where Admiral David Porter surprised them all by providing an excellent luncheon, far better than anything Mary had had on land recently. Even the President appeared to notice what he ate.

At Aiken's Landing, Mary, Mrs. Grant, General Grant's aide Captain Adam Badeau, and an additional escort, Lieutenant Colonel Horace Porter, settled into an ambulance, and the other men got on the horses that had traveled on the *River Queen*. This time, the President rode Cincinnati. Captain Barnes, who again was among the party, accepted the offer of a horse, to the accompaniment of much jesting about sailors being unused to riding. "I'll have Mrs. Ord look after you," General Ord said to Captain Barnes, nodding at his wife, who though not an extraordinarily pretty woman did cut a nice figure in a riding habit.

As their ambulance set off, Mary could not help but think that Mrs. Ord had the better of the bargain. The road was a corduroy one, the logs that formed it having been laid with little regard to uniformity of size, so their conveyance, not intended for comfort in the best of circumstances, jolted and bounced while at the same time traveling at the pace of a weary snail. No self-respecting horse would follow it, and Captain Barnes and Mrs. Ord soon drifted away, as, of course, had the President and General Grant.

Mary perceived that if they did not pick up the pace, the review would start without her. "Can't the driver hurry?"

Lieutenant Colonel Porter frowned. "Actually, I think he's taken a wrong turn."

"Perhaps, sir, you should have kept him on the right path," Mary snapped.

Mrs. Grant exchanged a sympathetic look with her husband's aide. "This terrain is so swampy, one part of it looks just like the other to— Ouch!"

Their bonneted heads slammed up against the roof of the ambulance, and for a moment, the contraption lurched so much that it appeared that it would fall over into the muck. "Mrs. Lincoln! Mrs. Grant! Are you hurt?"

"No," said Mrs. Grant. "Just shaken. But my bonnet!" She took it off and stared at it ruefully. "At least it's not my best one. Mrs. Lincoln?"

Mary still sat stunned from the impact, which seemed to have revived the pain from the injury she had received before Gettysburg. She blinked. "Yes. Please stop and let me out of this conveyance immediately."

"Mrs. Lincoln, you will ruin your clothing, and get there no faster," Lieutenant Colonel Porter said with maddening practicality. "Why, I think we've got past the worst of the road anyway."

Most reluctantly, Mary acceded, and the ambulance continued on its forlorn way. Then at last, the assembled troops, white and colored, came into view, as did the reviewing party. "A noble sight," Mrs. Grant commented.

But Mary hardly gave them a glance. Her gaze was fixed on the President's top hat, followed at too close a distance by a lady's hat.

Well. It was reasonable that the review had started without her, Mary supposed; the President and the troops simply couldn't stand there staring at each other while waiting for Mary's tardy entourage. But for a lady to be prancing on horseback by her husband's side in front of the cream of the Union army, as if she had some right to be there, while Mary was stuck in this sorry vehicle? As her head throbbed beneath her crushed bonnet, her anger rose. "Who is that woman, and how dare she personate me!"

"No one could impersonate you, my dear Mrs. Lincoln," Captain Badeau said.

"She must leave his side immediately. She has no business there whatsoever!"

Mrs. Grant doing her own very fair personation of a member of the Signal Corps, the lady—Mrs. Ord—spotted her and immediately rode over to the ambulance, followed in due time by Captain Barnes. "Mrs. Lincoln! Mrs. Grant!" Mrs. Ord held out her free hand. "I am terribly sorry that we were separated from you, but my horse is quite spirited, and—"

"How dare you ride beside the President!"

Captain Barnes said, "Mrs. Lincoln, Mrs. Ord meant no harm. If there is any fault at all, it is mine. When we reached the troops, we had to go somewhere, and Mrs. Ord asked me whether I thought it would be proper for us to join the reviewing column. Not being sure of the army etiquette, I asked a staff officer, and he told me to come right along. So we did, until Mrs. Grant signaled to us just now."

"Had I seen you earlier, I would have come over straightaway," Mrs. Ord added. "I am most sorry. But in any case, I was not close to the President at all. General Grant, my husband, and others were at his si—"

"Are you calling me delusional, you strumpet?"

"Strumpet!" Mrs. Ord's lip wobbled, and then she actually burst into tears. "I will not stay here to be insulted so. Strumpet!"

"I will escort you to City Point," Captain Barnes said with a mix of gallantry and relief. "Come."

With a parting sniffle, Mrs. Ord accepted the offer, and the two rode off, Mrs. Ord's horsemanship not affected by her emotions.

"Let us ride over there now," Mrs. Grant said, breaking the silence.

"You presume to give orders now, Mrs. Grant?"

"For heaven's sake!"

"I am not so mistaken to see what you are aiming at, Mrs. Grant. You want to be in the White House, do you not?"

"I am quite satisfied as a general's wife, Mrs. Lincoln."

Mary tossed her aching head. "Oh, you had better take it if you can get it. It is very nice."

"Drive on," Captain Badeau said. "Quickly."

"Oh, there you are, Molly," the President said when their ambulance finally reached the reviewing column.

"Yes," Mary said, gritting her teeth. "There I am."

"Would you tell me what in the devil this is all about?"

It was near midnight on the *River Queen*, back in harbor at City Point. There had been an awkward dinner with the Grants, followed by an awkward visit from Captain Barnes—well, not a visit. Mary had insisted that the man leave his quarters at the *Bat* and give a full account of the goings-on with Mrs. Ord. "I made it quite clear at dinner. General Ord's wife personated me. I cannot understand why a man who would humiliate me in that manner should be kept on in his position."

"You seriously expect me to get rid of a perfectly good general, just before our push into Petersburg, because of some silly quarrel with a woman I didn't give a second glance to?"

"Well—"

"You dragged poor Captain Barnes out of his bed for this."

"Well—"

"You forced me to endure a meal, listening to you rant about this nonsense, with General Grant and his staff looking on, probably wondering why I didn't take you in hand."

"Well—"

"I don't understand this, Mary."

Hearing him use her given name, instead of "Molly," was like having him slap her in the face. She flinched and started to speak, but he went on talking. "In our twenty—"

"Twenty-two!"

"Dang it, woman, I was going to say, twenty-two years of marriage, I have never once thought of being with another woman. Not once! In that time, I have let you have men and boys stay the night in Springfield when I was away because you were terrified of staying alone. Since we've been in Washington, I have let you entertain men in my absence, let them stay until all hours. I have let you travel with them, ride in carriages alone with them. Some of these were men with reputations I wouldn't want, like Wikoff. But I let you have your way, because I trusted you. Even after I received letters claiming I was being cuckolded. I tossed them aside with the contempt they deserved. Why? Because I trust you. And you should trust me. But when I ride out in front of thousands of people, with a lady a few feet behind me, without even paying attention to her, you carry on like a shrew."

"I do trust you! It is not that. It is…the disrespect to my position."

"I've made allowances, Mary. I know you're still mourning Willie. *I'm* still mourning Willie. I know you've lost two brothers in the war—don't tell me you don't care about those dead boys, because I know you do. I know the nonsense that's been talked about your loyalty. So I've put up with a lot. But when you toss your fits in public like you did today… Do you think I enjoy having men look on at me, pitying me?"

She shook her head.

"What got into you? I'm asking. I just don't understand."

Mary was silent, because she hardly knew the answer herself. Her envy of Mrs. Grant, the dead and dying men she had seen, Captain Barnes's pathetic story about the rebel lad—a redhead like poor Alec—begging for his Southern mama, the fatigue of traveling, the bump on her head—maybe it was those things. Or maybe it was the pent-up tensions of these four years of war that were finally being released. "I don't know. I honestly do not. But it will not happen again, Mr. Lincoln."

"I hope not." He hesitated. "Mary, understand this. A man can take a lot—except for being pitied. When that happens…"

He shrugged and left the room.

EMILY AND MARY

MARCH TO APRIL 1865

Having left Virginia just as the Lincolns were headed to that beleaguered state, Emily, newly arrived in Washington under General Singleton's protection, had little to do except to receive General Singleton's reports about his meetings with the lobbyist Mr. Browning, who was smoothing the way with Mr. Lincoln and the War Department for Emily and others to retrieve their cotton. After a few days of this, Emily decided that it was time to move on to the slightly less expensive, and more congenial, confines of Baltimore, where she would not have to put up quite so much with what had become a deathwatch for the Confederacy. Baltimore, though not as blatantly pro-Southern as it had been at the beginning of the war, still housed a number of Confederate sympathizers, and Barnum's City Hotel, as well as being spacious and comfortable (no torn-up carpets as at the poor Spotswood!), was noted for its friendly attitude toward Southerners.

Someone had misplaced Emily's room key, so while the clerk went in search of it, she occupied herself by flipping through the pages of the register she had just signed, looking for the names of any friends or acquaintances from the South who might be staying there. It was another name, however, entered with a flourish under the entries for March 25, that caught her eye. When the clerk returned, triumphantly holding her key aloft, she asked, "John Wilkes Booth? The actor?"

"The same, madam."

"Did he have an engagement here?"

"No, just a flying visit." The clerk puffed up a bit. "Mr. Booth always stays here when he is in town. He is very fond of this hotel. But acting, I don't believe he has been on the stage recently except for an engagement a short time ago in Washington. A pity, as he's always done well here in Baltimore."

"He is a fine actor; I saw him in Louisville last year. I hope to see him on the stage again one day."

"No doubt we will." The clerk motioned for a porter, who grabbed Emily's trunk. "I hope you enjoy your stay in Baltimore, madam."

Aptly enough, given her behavior there, Mary left City Point on April Fools' Day. By the time she left, there had been fewer people to embarrass herself in front of. General Grant had gone to the front, with an irritatingly sentimental parting from Mrs. Grant involving a great deal of kissing. Captain Barnes and the *Bat* were sent to take General Sherman, who had come to City Point to confer with the President and General Grant, back to North Carolina, where, Mary hoped, the captain would vanish into one of the swamps that appeared to lie across most of that benighted state. If there were any infernal generals' wives around, they kept a safe distance from Mary.

Tad had wanted to stay with his father and in the center of the action. For that very reason, Mary had been inclined to object, but feeling herself rather on delicate ground with the President, refrained from doing so. Instead, she had extracted a promise from her husband to telegraph daily, and with that and a single, dignified kiss (it was a pity Mrs. Grant was not nearby to profit from the example), departed for Washington.

Yet as soon as she arrived at the Executive Mansion, she felt an itch to be back at City Point. Perhaps she would enjoy herself more, she thought, if she collected a congenial party instead of being forced into companionship with the likes of Mrs. Grant. The cultured Senator Charles Sumner would be a fine companion, as would be the Marquis Adolphe de Chambrun, a young Frenchman who was visiting Washington in a quasi-diplomatic capacity and whose unaffected manners and admiration for the United States in general and Mr. Lincoln in particular had quickly endeared him to Mary.

She was attempting to compose an invitation to the marquis in French, and to her chagrin was having to resort to a French grammar book for assistance, when the Secretary of War was announced on the morning of April 3. Though Mary knew Secretary Stanton to have a kindly side—he was a doting father and had always been kind to Tad and poor Willie—smiles did not set easily on his face, which made the full-blown grin he wore a little alarming. "Good news, Secretary Stanton?"

"Yes. We have taken Petersburg, and the rebels have abandoned Richmond. Our men are entering the city—what's left of it. The rebels set fire to the warehouses and the armory before they left the city, and the fires spread."

Mary clasped his hand, just as the city churches began to peal their bells and a roar came from the streets. "I guess the news is out," Mr. Stanton said.

And what news the fall of Richmond, heralding the inevitable collapse of the Confederacy, was! Offices and shops closed, bands played, and the churches and taverns filled as everyone celebrated in his own way. Senator Sumner, who had been an abolitionist long before anyone else, and whom even Mary acknowledged had a rather heavy manner about him, was whistling from his favorite Italian opera when he paid a call on Mary that evening. Mr. Hay, having celebrated at the Willard, was rumored to have had difficulty finding the Executive Mansion afterward.

Secretary Seward ordered a grand illumination of Washington's public buildings for the evening of April 4. Mary, still fatigued from her journey, stayed home, but from the window she could see the men, women, and children happily traipsing from building to building, admiring the gleaming city, and the next day, the newspapers had all the details. Never had the Executive Mansion, aglow with candles, shimmered so brightly. Mr. French, who had the Capitol in his charge, had bedecked it with a transparency reading *This is the Lord's Doing, It Is Marvelous in Our Eyes* lit up from behind with gas. An illuminated ten-dollar note graced the Treasury Building. Not to be outdone by the government, Washington's merchants had lit their establishments as well, and many of the private houses had followed suit. No house, however, looked finer than that of Mr. French, whose bay window proclaimed THE AMERICAN UNION. Mary made a note to compliment him on his efforts the next time she saw him.

It was marvelous to behold, even vicariously. But she wished the President could have been there to see the city so joyous.

Emily stared at the newspaper with its taunting headline, RICHMOND FALLEN. It was what she had expected to hear, of course, but she must have held out more hope than she had acknowledged, for the news made her weep. What was next? General Lee's army was still in the field, and there was still a Confederate government, although its leaders had all fled Richmond. But she could not deceive herself. As Richmond went, so must the Confederacy.

Hardin, whose photograph was always the first thing Emily unpacked and sat on the dresser during her travels, would not want her to fall prey to despair—and neither would Emily's pride suffer her to do so. So on April 6, when Baltimore, its civic pride demanding that it respond to Washington's illumination two nights before, put on its own show of gaslight and candles, she did not draw her curtains, but pulled a chair up to the window and watched Baltimoreans gawk at the brilliance around them. For many of them, she knew, it mattered less that the Union had almost won the war than that it was almost over. Now men could pursue their professions, farm their fields, marry, and sire children without the fear of being called away to an uncertain fate. Who could blame them for rejoicing?

Still, if she never heard a band play "Yankee Doodle" again in her life, she would be quite satisfied.

༄

"*Mon Dieu,*" said the Marquis de Chambrun as their carriage passed the husks of burned-out houses, some trailing smoke.

Mary could not have said it better. Even before their party reached Richmond, they had seen plenty to presage the ruin they witnessed now: the dead horses lining the riverbanks, the debris from blown-up ships floating in the river, the flags marking the sites of suspected torpedoes, which, the captain had been overheard to say, could blow them to kingdom come if he were not careful to avoid them.

He had been careful, and their party—Mary, Senator Sumner, the charming young visitor from France, Senator and Mrs. Harlan and their daughter, and Mrs. Keckly—had arrived at the wharf and their waiting carriages safely, greeted by the cheers of the city's colored population. Two days before, President Lincoln had been the object of their adulation.

Their journey to their first destination—the house where Jeff Davis had lived—took them first through the streets that had been spared from the fires that had licked through the city after the departing rebels set ablaze anything that was likely to be of use to the Union. From these streets Mary might have supposed Richmond to be one vast slum, for only the poorest people were abroad, either clutching the rations the Sanitary and Christian Commissioners were handing out in Capitol Square or going in search of them. Only the occasional glimpse of faces peeping through the venetian blinds of elegant houses betrayed the presence of Richmond's celebrated aristocracy.

The party's approach to the heart of the city coincided with their arrival at the burned district—block after block of singed ruins in every stage of collapse. But it was the paper covering the streets that most impressed Mary. Scorched by fire, sodden by rain showers, blown about by the breeze, documents of every description—rebel banknotes, business records, government memoranda, letters that had been treasured for generations—crunched under the wheels of the carriage as it approached the columned mansion where the Lincolns' counterparts had dined, slept, celebrated, and grieved.

Mary shuddered as she looked at the portico. There, one of the Davis boys, a lad much younger than Willie, had fallen fifteen feet to the ground while playing and had died within an hour. Reading the report in the newspaper was the only time in the past four years that Mary had allowed herself to feel a glimmer of sympathy for the rebel president and his wife.

She brushed these gloomy thoughts from her mind as General Godfrey Weitzel, who had led the Union troops into Richmond 'and who now occupied the house, greeted them, overseen by Mrs. Davis's former housekeeper, Mary O'Meila, an Irishwoman whose expression showed that she had seen far too many Yankees in the last few days. Mary thought of complimenting her and the colored servants Mrs. Davis had left behind on the condition of the house, which was so immaculate as to give the impression that its mistress might be coming back at any moment. As Mrs. O'Meila's countenance remained grim, however, Mary refrained and instead toured the house, trying not to feel too terribly smug about the decidedly faded state of its red, plush furniture.

Their next visit was to the State Capital. So this was how a government looked when it collapsed, Mary realized, staring at the broken desks, the overturned spittoons, and more paper, paper, paper. With no Mrs. O'Meilas to inhibit them, Mary and the others roamed the senate chamber. "This must be where old Jeff himself sat," Senator Harlan said.

Senator Sumner nodded at Mrs. Keckly. "Madam, please take a seat here."

Mrs. Keckly, a lady who stood on her dignity, seldom smiled. But as the seamstress who had bought her own freedom from slavery settled first in Jefferson Davis's chair, and then in the chair of the rebel vice president, Alexander Stephens, she distinctly smirked.

∽☙∼

Seldom had Mary seen Mr. Lincoln in better spirits than he was when the *River Queen* prepared to return to Washington. At the farewell party held in the evening of April 8, he ordered the band to play the "Marseillaise," which he had always liked, and when the Marquis de Chambrun wistfully commented that it was banned in his country by its emperor, the President ordered it played again. "Have you heard 'Dixie'?" Mr. Lincoln asked his French guest. "It is more or less the official song down in these parts."

The marquis shook his head, and Mr. Lincoln gave another command. His foot bounced up and down as the startled band obeyed, a little rustily at first but soon growing more sure of themselves. "My, I've missed that tune these past few years."

The President's bright mood continued the next day as they steamed toward Washington. The *River Queen* carried a modest library, including a volume of Shakespeare, which the President seized and began reading to them—mainly from *Macbeth*, his favorite play, as Mary had found out early in their courtship, when he would seize a leather-bound Shakespeare from Ninian Edwards's well-stocked shelves and become so engrossed that he sometimes forgot her presence. More than once, Mary had hidden the volume, in the belief that Mr. Lincoln and she should be getting up to something more interesting, but he inevitably found it.

Really, it still astounded her that she and Mr. Lincoln had managed to get married. Mary smiled.

Mr. Lincoln was expounding on *Macbeth* like a professor. "Look how well Macbeth's torment and guilt are expressed," he said, having just killed off Duncan. "I am particularly fond of this passage:

> "*Had I but died an hour before this chance,*
> *I had lived a blessed time; for, from this instant,*

There's nothing serious in mortality:
All is but toys: renown and grace is dead;
The wine of life is drawn, and the mere lees
Is left this vault to brag of."

"You should have been a player, Papa," Tad said.

"Well, who knows? I will still have to make a living when I leave Washington." He put down his book and gazed contentedly out at the river.

They arrived in Washington around six. Mr. Lincoln made a flying visit to the White House before riding to visit the unfortunate Secretary Seward, who had been injured in a carriage accident several days before and was bedridden, though considered to be past all danger. Having sent her sympathies with the President, Mary was catching up with her correspondence when her husband came into the room at about ten that evening. "While we were on our way back, General Grant accepted General Lee's surrender."

There was nothing to say to such news; Mary didn't even try. Instead, she simply embraced him as they both wept tears of joy. Finally, the President brushed his eyes and croaked, "Well, who gets to tell Tad?"

Emily stared at the paper and the news that only a handful of people in Baltimore besides herself could care about: the rumor that Selma had been captured and burned. Were her sisters homeless? What of Maggie? Guilt scraped at Emily again, for leaving Maggie behind.

But if Selma had indeed fallen—and given the stack of dominos that now constituted the Confederacy, and the shouts outside of the newsboys proclaiming the latest news of General Lee's surrender, Emily had no reason to disbelieve the rumor—Maggie was now free. Would she return to Emily and the children? Emily did not know, and she also knew that it was not to her credit that having been mistress over Maggie all these years, she could not venture a guess.

When Washington had awoken on April 10 to the news that the President gave Mary the previous evening, a mass of joyous humanity had rushed to the White House, where Tad, commandeering the window over the door, waved a rebel flag as the crowd cheered. Mr. Lincoln had then appeared himself, promising a proper speech the next day and ordering the band to play "Dixie"—now captured property, he had joked—and "Yankee Doodle."

Once again, the White House glowed to fine account on the evening of April 11, when Mr. Lincoln stepped to the window with a handwritten speech. Mr. Noah Brooks, who was soon to replace Mr. Hay upon the latter's embarkment upon a diplomatic posting, held a candle so that Mr. Lincoln could see what he was reading, and Tad helpfully caught the pages as the President discarded them one by one. Mary, the Marquis de Chambrun, and Miss Clara Harris stood at the next window, admiring the crowd and listening to the speech.

The speech—about his plans to bring the South back into the nation—was more solemn than befitted the occasion, Mary thought. Still, she supposed it needed to be said, and she was pleased to hear her husband also speak of giving certain colored men the vote. Those words caused a few to gasp, and Mary from her fine vantage point saw two men, one dark and slightly built, the other almost hulking in appearance, go so far as to stride away in apparent high dudgeon. Normally such a sight would have irritated her, but the last few days had been so wondrous, she simply shook her head at their folly and settled back with her friends.

Lee's surrender demanded an ever-finer illumination than the fall of Richmond had occasioned, and this time, Mary was determined to see it. Mr. Lincoln being inclined to rest, she invited the newly arrived General Grant to accompany her through town—but not his wife. Not that she had explicitly excluded Mrs. Grant, mind you, but everyone seemed to understand it that way, and as the general explained upon his arrival that he had just come from seeing the illumination with

Mrs. Grant and the Stantons (but was quite happy to see it all over again), all worked out nicely.

A quiet man who eschewed small talk, General Grant proved to be good company, content to sit back and allow Mary to give her full attention to the lights—except for when the crowd noticed him and began cheering, which happened rather too often to be entirely pleasant. But still, what a fine sight it was! The Patent Office spelled out UNION in gas jets, while a clothing store inquired in the same element How ARE You, LEE? Innumerable buildings spelled out GRANT, just in case her companion had been in any danger of forgetting his name. LINCOLN was also remembered on various edifices, and a transparency of George Washington looked down benevolently from the bank bearing his name. Secretary Stanton had bedecked his house with flags of the various army units. A fifty-dollar bond graced the Treasury Building. The principal hotels glistened, as did Grover's Theatre and Ford's Theater. The Capitol was brilliantly lit, as was the insane asylum. Across the river, General Lee's Arlington House mansion, long since taken over by the Union, shimmered as if fully aware of the delicious irony of it all.

Mr. Lincoln was in bed when she returned home, but waiting for her was a bit of pleasant news: Bob was coming to Washington and would likely be there the next morning, the 14th. Whether he would be home for good, Mary did not know, but at least he was likely out of all danger, as were so many other young men now. True, there was still a rebel army in the field, led by General Joseph Johnston, but it had recently been defeated at Bentonville in North Carolina and would doubtlessly soon be following General Lee's excellent example of surrendering.

Mary plumped her pillow, remembering the words the marquis had spoken a few days before as the *River Queen* had passed Mount Vernon. He had said that one day, Springfield, Illinois, might bear a similar status in the nation's heart as the home of the man who had brought its people through this terrible civil war. (The marquis's accent had made the compliment all the more charming.) Mr. Lincoln, standing a bit apart, had been in one of his reveries, or else he would have been heartily embarrassed by such flattery. But had it been flattery? Time would tell, and in any case her husband's second term had only just begun. There was much to be done.

Still, four Aprils before, the country had been descending into war, and now peace was at hand. It would be hard work knitting the country back together, and no one could be so naive as to think the process would be an easy one, but Mary had no doubt that her husband could manage it.

And she would be at his side as he carried out this task. Smiling, Mary shut her eyes and drifted off to sleep.

⁓ 31 ⁓
EMILY AND MARY
APRIL 14, 1865, TO JUNE 1876

O n the morning of April 14, Emily received a letter from Mr. Browning, assuring her he had not forgotten her. Between Mr. Lincoln's extended absence at City Point, and the excitement of the past few days, there had been no opportunity to see him, but he intended to wait on the President that afternoon. There was every reason to think that all the necessary permits would soon be issued.

It was middling good news—"every reason to think" was not as encouraging as Emily would have once believed—but at least it was not bad news. For a Southerner in April 1865, one had to take good news when one could find it.

⁓⁓⁓

Bob indeed turned up for breakfast on the morning of April 14, sunburned and eager to recount what he had seen of General Lee's surrendering to General Grant at a place called Appomattox Court House. "We all took away a good impression of General Lee," he said, handing his father a carte de visite. "He seems a good man, and his men were obviously devoted to him."

"A good face," said Mr. Lincoln, studying the photograph. "We will need men like these in the days to come."

Mary smiled at Bob, who was tackling his breakfast with gusto. "And lawyers, too."

"Yes, it looks as if I'll be going back to Harvard in the fall," Bob said. "I'll be glad enough of it. I can say I've seen action and didn't shirk my duties, which is all I ever wanted. But for now, all I want is a haircut and a shave."

"And then perhaps a visit to Miss Harlan," Mary suggested.

"As a matter of fact, I did have that in mind." Bob grinned and downed his coffee.

"Perhaps the two of you could join us at the theater tonight. Mr. Ford invited us; Miss Keene will be the leading lady. The Grants will be coming, I expect."

"I'll think about it," Bob said.

Mary already guessed what his decision would be. Of the four of them, he was the least avid playgoer, and besides, the gossip that being seated with Miss Harlan in the presidential box would inspire would be unendurable to him. "Very well."

"I'm going to see *Aladdin* at Grover's," Tad said. "But it might be a bit tame for you. I'm getting a little old for it myself. I'm only going because it's polite to spread around our patronage."

"Indeed," Bob said. "Well, I'll think about it."

∾⦵∾

Usually it was Mary who had to hunt down the President for their carriage rides, but this afternoon, Mr. Lincoln appeared in her room at the appointed time, wearing the shawl he favored for days that were not sufficiently chilly to warrant an overcoat. "Are you ready, madam?"

"Indeed I am, sir."

He gave her his arm—really, what had gotten into the man?—and they strolled to their waiting carriage, the President handing her in with a flourish. As Mary adjusted her dress, her husband said, "I should have mentioned earlier that the Grants won't be joining us tonight. Mrs. Grant wanted to see their children in New Jersey—I certainly can't blame her—and the general gave in to her command."

"I'll find someone."

"It will disappoint Ford, I'm sure, because everyone in Washington wants to gawk at the general. But he'll get his share when he becomes president." Seeing Mary's look, he added, "I'm not going to be running for a third term, unless there's a very good reason for me to stay here, so Grant's the logical choice. I'll be more than ready to go back to my practice in Springfield."

"Springfield? I had hoped we might move to a larger place, such as Chicago, or even New York. But I will abide by your wishes."

"Abide by my wishes? What's got into you, Molly?" He winked. "But there's plenty of time to decide that. Besides, I know you'd like to travel a bit, and I would, too. I'd like to see Europe, and Jerusalem. California, too. Now, that might be a thought for when we leave here. Maybe I could run for governor."

"I must say, Mr. Lincoln, I have seldom seen you this cheerful before."

"There's cause for cheer, with the war almost over. I want both of us to be more cheerful in the future, because we have both been very miserable, between Willie's death and this war."

"I feel that I have added to your misery sometimes, as with my performance at City Point," Mary said quietly. "For that I am very sorry."

"Now, that's not cheerful talk. Come, let's just each promise to do better, and leave what's past in the past."

She agreed, and they rode on to the Navy Yard, where several monitors had been brought for repairs, and boarded the *Montauk*, which had recently seen battle at Fort Fisher in North Carolina. "Fine old girl," Mr. Lincoln said, "She's done good service."

For a while, they traipsed around the ship, save for the passages where Mary's skirts would not allow her to navigate, and chatted with her crew. Mary was much amused to meet its surgeon, Dr. George

Todd, as unlike her disagreeable, rebel surgeon brother by the same name as a man could be. When, in passing, Mary mentioned that she and the President would be going to see Miss Laura Keene perform that night, Dr. Todd said that he had been thinking of going himself.

"Oh, you ought to," Mary said. "It promises to be a fine performance."

⟁

The Lincolns returned to the Executive Mansion in plenty of time to dine and dress for the theater, but they were delayed by the arrival of some acquaintances from Illinois, and almost delayed some more when Mr. Browning turned up. "I can't see him tonight," Mr. Lincoln told the servant who announced his arrival. "We're already late. Tell him to come back tomorrow." He looked apologetically at Mary as the servant left the room. "I feel bad not seeing Browning, but if I did, we might as well not go at all, and we've promised Major Rathbone and Miss Harris to pick them up."

"Indeed, Mr. Lincoln, you should turn more people away, rather than allow them to harass you so."

"Well, there's not much I can do at this late hour to help him anyway, if it's about the cotton business. Which it undoubtedly is. By the by, I've been thinking that maybe a postmistress situation might do for Emily."

Mary, still somewhat irked at Emily for her letter of the previous year, was about to say that it had better do for the ungrateful chit, but remembering her promise earlier, said, "It would do very well, I'm sure, and it is kind of you to think of it."

Their conversation took them to Senator Harris's house at Fifteenth and H Streets, where Clara Harris and Major Henry Rathbone awaited them. It was the residence of both, as the couple were not only engaged to each other, but were stepsister and stepbrother. This circumstance struck Mary as a bit odd, much as she liked Clara—a sensible woman of thirty who shared Mary's interest in politics. Still, it certainly made for a compact family circle, and at least the couple would be well aware of each other's peculiarities by the time they married.

As Miss Harris arranged her skirt over the obliging leg of Major Rathbone, the President thanked them for accepting the invitation at such a late hour. "Change in plans," he said apologetically.

"Yes, I read that General Grant was expected to attend. It is a pity that Henry did not wear his uniform, so the crowd might not be terribly disappointed by us being there instead."

"I will try to look properly martial," the major said.

"And soon, I hope, you will be looking marital," Mary said, and her guests tittered.

The play—*Our American Cousin*, a comedy about a rustic Vermonter visiting his aristocratic English relations—was underway when their carriage arrived at the theater. Almost every self-respecting theatergoer knew the plot, so Mary knew that she would not have missed much, nor would the audience likely mind the interruption.

And what an interruption it was! As the Lincolns and their guests made their way to their seats, Miss Keene and her fellow players froze onstage, smiling, as the orchestra struck up "Hail to the Chief" and the audience, many of them in military uniform, stood and cheered. Only when the quartet settled into their seats—the President in Mr. Ford's own plush-covered rocking chair, the ladies in cane chairs, and Major Rathbone on a sofa—did the play resume.

The President watched intently, occasionally lapsing into thoughts of his own as he often did at the theater, but never missing any of the jokes, which were plentiful. Mary, not as attracted by the broad humor, kept her eyes fixed on the stage but contentedly dwelled on the fine outing she had had with her husband. When was the last time she had had such a happy afternoon? Not in months—no, not in years.

The night before, her optimistic thoughts had centered on the future of the nation, but there was cause to be hopeful on a personal level as well. Bob, having got the military out of his system, would get through law school and enter the profession, after which he was bound to marry Miss Harlan. There would be grandchildren—no substitute for dear Willie or poor, short-lived Eddie, but still a comfort and joy to her in her advancing years. As for Tad, it was really time that his education was taken in hand—he had just turned twelve—but surely with no war to distract him, he would be more inclined to settle to his lessons. He would have to do so sooner rather than later, because Mary had every intention of holding her husband to his intent to travel after he left Washington. Mary smiled at the thought of them all having an audience with Queen Victoria, who would surely be amenable to receiving the president and his family.

Of course, she would want a female companion to take with her. Her mind drifted to Emily. Despite her late disagreeableness, there was no one better to accompany her. Though in truth, Emily might well find a second husband long before that. Why, perhaps after a few more months had passed, Mary might even consider doing a little matchmaking on her sister's behalf.

She scooted her chair closer to her husband's and took his arm. Really, they were acting more like young lovers than were the real things on Mary's side—or at least Mary was. "What will Miss Harris think of my hanging on to you so?" she whispered.

The President chuckled faintly. "She won't think anything of it," he hissed.

Mary's hand was on her husband's knee when Harry Hawk, alone onstage, fulminated, "Don't know the manners of good society, eh? Well, I guess I know enough to turn you inside out, old gal. You sockdologizing old mantrap!"

Nearly drowned out by the laughter of the crowd, there was a click, then a flash. Both of them seemingly too inconsequential to upend her entire world.

Were they part of the play? Mary turned to her husband, to see if he was as bemused as she. His head drooped. She patted his forehead, and he drooped even lower. She patted the back of his head, and just as her fingers felt something warm and sticky, someone slid past her, so close that he brushed her fine black lace shawl off her shoulders. A man, wielding a knife against Major Rathbone, who had sprung out of his seat to grapple with him, then leaping out of the box.

Mary screamed. They were all screaming now—Major Rathbone,

demanding that they stop the man; Miss Harris, echoing his cry; the man, now standing on the stage and yelling something about tyrants. Four of them screamed, enacting their own terrible drama while Mr. Lincoln drooped in his chair and the audience stared like flies drenched in amber.

Then the cry went up. "What's the matter?"

Miss Harris leaned over. "The President has been shot!"

Surely Miss Harris was wrong? But there had been that flash, that click...

The rest of the theater came to life. Women shrieked, their cries melding with Mary's. Miss Keene ran onto the stage, waving for order. Men were everywhere, some thundering across the stage, some running toward the stairwells, others simply cursing and throwing their chairs about. Only one man in the entire place was still, and Mary, her screams turning to sobs, instinctively held him upright in his chair as someone began banging at the outermost door granting passage to their box. She did not dare to leave her place to open it; everything somehow appeared to depend on her holding her husband in his place.

Slipping in the blood dripping from his gashed arm, Major Rathbone, finding the door had been barred from within, struggled to remove the barrier. Succeeding, he staggered back into the box with a young man behind him. "Dr. Charles Leale, Mrs. Lincoln. Please let me examine the President."

"Do help him," Mary choked out.

Dr. Leale nodded. He felt Mr. Lincoln's pulse, and then motioned to two other men, who helped move the President to the floor. There was blood on his shoulder, and Dr. Leale knelt to examine him after one of the men cut the President's coat and shirt away, Mary felt a surge of hope. A shoulder injury could make a man faint, surely, couldn't it? Couldn't it?

There was not a mark on the President's shoulder.

With a rustle of skirts, Miss Keene entered, still in full stage attire and makeup and bearing a pitcher of water like a scepter. "Please let me assist," she said reverently.

Dr. Leale made a motion, and Miss Keene sank amid her hoops and supported the President's head on her lap as the young surgeon continued his probing, having turned his attention to his patient's head. Mary could not even muster a protest.

"Ah," said Dr. Leale said, and made a quick movement with his fingers, resulting in a trickle of blood. Instantly, the President's breathing became somewhat more natural. "A bullet wound to the head. I removed a clot, which has released some of the pressure."

"Will my husband live?"

"Madam—"

He was saved from answering by the appearance of two men, entering the box by the way of the balcony with the help of the crowd below and Miss Harris above. Mary recognized one of them—Dr. Charles Taft, the older half brother of Willie's young friends. The association did not bode well. Weeping, she watched bleakly as he and Dr. Leale conferred with the third man, who turned out to be another doctor. "Should we take him to the White House?" Dr. Taft asked.

Dr. Leale shook his head. "No. I've seen too many men with similar wounds die in army ambulances from the jouncing about. If he must be moved, it should be to someplace close by, and with great care."

"One of you three, tell me! Will my husband live?"

The three medical men looked at each other. Finally, Dr. Leale said, "Mrs. Lincoln, we will do our best. But—"

"Tell me!"

"I do not believe he will survive."

For all the threats Mr. Lincoln had received over the years, Mary had never dared to wonder what she would feel upon hearing such words. Now she knew why. "Then I wish, sir, you would do me the favor of killing me, too."

∽♥∾

The pounding on Emily's hotel door at four in the morning could mean only one thing: something had happened to the children. Not bothering to throw on a robe, she sprang up and ran to the door. "Who is it?"

"Mabel! Let me in!"

Emily undid the latch, and a pretty woman about ten years her senior ran into the room. A Baltimorean of decided Confederate leanings, Mrs. Cranford was staying at the hotel while her house was being renovated. "Lincoln's been shot!"

"Shot?"

"In the head, in a theater in Washington. He's not expected to live. They say the actor John Wilkes Booth did it."

"Booth?" Emily stared. "But I saw him act. Why on earth would he do that?" She thought of the good-natured, good-looking young man who had so cheerfully signed Kitty's carte de visite. Why would such a man do such a dreadful thing? "Surely this is a wild, foolish rumor."

Mrs. Cranford lifted the window, which Emily had shut against the chilly night air. "Listen. Look."

On Monument Square, a crowd had gathered. "Hang him!"

"Kill him!"

"Catch Jeff Davis, and string him up!"

"Kill all the rebel sons of bitches! This is their work."

"Burn that damn hotel! It's full of rebels, always has been!"

Emily slammed down the window as Mrs. Cranford began to cry. "They'll come after us! That mob will come after us, you just wait. Women, children—they'll have no mercy!"

"Now, now," Emily said. "I'm sure the authorities have a watch on this place."

She scarcely knew what she was saying, scarcely cared. Absentmindedly, she patted Mrs. Cranford's trembling hand as she tried to absorb the news. Mr. Lincoln, whom Mary loved so much. Mr. Lincoln, who had tried his best to keep Hardin on his side. Mr. Lincoln, who had loomed so large in Emily's world ever since she was a child. Dying, and after such a horrid act! How would Mary bear it? Emily tugged at Mrs. Cranford's hand. "My sister! Was she at this theater? Was she harmed?"

Mrs. Cranford sniffled. "They say she was there with him. No word that she was hurt."

But being there was harm enough. Emily shivered.

Until dawn, Mrs. Cranford wailed and fretted until Emily at last persuaded her to go to her room and rest. Alone, Emily knelt and prayed, tears streaming down her cheeks as she waited for the inevitable news that there were now two Todd sisters who were widows.

∾◡◠

The house that the President had been taken to, immediately across the street from the theater, was owned by a Mr. William Petersen, and it was a very nice house. So Mary, bewailing that Mr. Lincoln had to die in this horrid tenement, was informed by Miss Pauline Petersen, who along with the rest of the household was pressed into service to deal with the raft of unexpected visitors that arrived that terrible night. The fourteen-year-old was the only person who did not inform Mary that what was happening was God's will or beg her to compose herself, and for those things Mary was immensely grateful. "Father doesn't need to take in boarders," Miss Petersen said, handing her a cup of tea. "He just likes a little extra money."

"Very sensible of him," Mary agreed.

It was in one of those boarders' rooms that Mr. Lincoln lay, in a bed that was too short for him. Mary was allowed in the room only periodically, which later she supposed was reasonable, because each foray was worse than the last, and each prostrated her. Bob or Senator Sumner— their eyes red and swollen—or someone else would lead her in, and despite her resolution to sit quietly beside Mr. Lincoln and quietly hold his still hand, she would end up begging him to say just one word, to twitch his lips, to only open his eyes a little, to move his hand—just one finger! His worst habit in life had been his ability to shut himself off from her when he pleased, and now, in dying, his remoteness was absolute. He had not exhibited consciousness of anything since Harry Hawk had called someone a sockdologizing old mantrap.

Dr. Robert Stone, Willie's old doctor, who had been fetched shortly after the horrendous deed ("assassination" sounded so formal, so cold, to Mary), told her that he doubted the President was feeling pain;

the damage inflicted by the bullet was too great. But then why did he emit those awful moans from time to time, which made even the men around the bedside flinch? Those sounds, and the increasing distortion of her husband's beloved face, were too much for Mary. So she had submitted herself to be ordered out of the death chamber and back onto the black horsehair sofa in the Petersens' front parlor—the *gracious* parlor, she had assured Miss Petersen—where she sat and watched the night wear on. From the window, she could see the crowd that had collected in the street keeping the same watch. Her grief had become the nation's.

Though her companions—Miss Harris, who had stayed even after poor Major Rathbone, having fainted through loss of blood, had been driven home, and Mrs. Elizabeth Dixon, a senator's wife—seemed to think that she should be spared all news of what was going on, Mary had demanded otherwise. Keeping abreast of what was unfolding outside of the parlor and the bedchamber where her husband lay dying was the only way she could avoid being enveloped by panic and grief.

Mr. Lincoln's assassin had been identified as the actor John Wilkes Booth—had not Mary had a strange feeling about the man? Whether he was plain crazy, or a rabid rebel, or both, was being debated all over Washington this long, miserable night.

Booth was at large, and so was a second assassin—a young man who had barged into the home of the Secretary of State and attacked the convalescent Mr. Seward in his bed. A mishap with his gun had forced him to use a knife instead, and between the metal immobilizing the Secretary's injured neck, the intervention of the Secretary's male nurse, his sons, and his servant, and the piercing screams of the Secretary's daughter, the assassin had succeeded only in badly injuring, not killing, the Secretary, who was expected to recover. There had been dreadful rumors that all the President's Cabinet and Vice President Johnson had been attacked, but these proved false. Most of the Cabinet members, in fact, had come through the doors of the Petersen house at one point or the other to sit by the President's bedside.

Secretary Stanton had come early in the night to the deathbed, had come out with tears in his eyes, had given Mary his condolences, and then had commandeered a room in the house and set to work, investigating the crime and giving the nation periodic updates in messages he sent to the War Department to be telegraphed. For hours now, a parade of knock-kneed witnesses had come through the Petersen door to be interrogated, their answers captured in shorthand by a neighboring war veteran with not one but two artificial legs, and the secretary already had a list of Booth associates to chase down. He was particularly interested in a John Surratt.

"Why, I know him," said Miss Petersen. "Or at least I know someone who knows him, one of his mother's boarders who knows Ma and Pa. We know that horrible man Booth, too; he visited an actor who boarded here once or twice."

"You seem to know everyone, my dear." Mary put a hand to her head. "I just hope they track Booth down soon and hang him. And all of his accomplices."

"Oh, they will," Miss Petersen said confidently. "Count on that."

"Will you bring my son to me, child?"

Miss Petersen obeyed, and Bob came into the front parlor, his eyes tired and full of misery. It was close to seven in the morning. "Let me see your father again."

"Mother—"

"You will not keep me from his side!"

"I won't. But he looks much worse than he did when you saw him last. The swelling and all—"

"Take me in."

With Mrs. Dixon's assistance, Bob obeyed. Mary stepped into the room where Mr. Lincoln lay diagonally across the too-short bed. She took a single look at him and fainted dead away.

Bob kindly did not say "I told you so" when they revived her and she recovered enough to take a seat. "One word!" she begged. "Just live to speak to us once—to me and to your children!" The tears poured down her face, and instead of directing her frustration at the dying, silent man, she yanked out a chunk of her own hair.

It was too much for Secretary Stanton, who had joined the crowd around the bed. "Get her out of here," he snapped.

No one countermanded his order, and Mrs. Dixon gently helped Mary to her feet. "Come, madam."

She would never see him alive again, she knew; by now the doctors were simply watching with the rest of them. "I have given my husband to die," she said flatly as Mrs. Dixon led her away.

Twenty minutes later, Bob and their minister, Reverend Gurley, came to tell her that she was correct.

It was nine before she could manage to leave the house for the waiting carriage. First, though, she called little Miss Petersen to her and handed her the brooch she had worn to the theater. "Take this, child. You were very kind to me."

"I can't, Mrs. Lincoln."

"Of course you can, and you must. Keep it as a remembrance." She had formed an ill opinion of Mr. Petersen—who had disappeared and left his children and boarders to tend to their unexpected guests—so she added, "Don't tell anyone you have it. It is yours and nobody else's."

"Yes, ma'am. Thank you. I'm sorry about Mr. Lincoln. I watched him come into the theater tonight, and he looked so fine."

Mary sighed, trying to replace the image she had of the man on the bed with one of Mr. Lincoln in his Brooks Brothers suit (ordered at her behest) and silk hat. "He did."

As Bob, Mrs. Dixon, and the Reverend Gurley led Mary out the door, she paused on the steps leading from the Petersens' house onto Tenth Street. Looming across the street was the theater, surrounded by an armed guard—more than once, the crowd had threatened to burn the playhouse to the ground. Never again would she set foot in this place, or in any other theater. "That awful house," she sobbed, losing the composure she had managed to attain. "That awful, awful house."

～☙～

Barnum's Hotel and most other establishments in Baltimore were swathed with black crepe, so they blended in with the leaden sky.

Although it was pouring rain, the streets were full of people wandering aimlessly around, some of them talking quietly, some of them weeping.

Emily had to squeeze through a mass of them waiting outside the telegraph office. She filled out her message: *Would it be agreeable to sister Mary to have me with her. Answer immediately to Barnum Hotel.*

The clerk started. "To Robert Lincoln? *That* Robert Lincoln?"

"Yes. He is my nephew." Seeing doubt in the man's eyes, she added, "I am a sister of President Lincoln's widow."

It was the first time since Fort Sumter that she had accorded her brother-in-law his title.

The clerk pushed back the money she offered him. "No charge."

Bob, or someone in the White House acting for him, sent a short reply: Mrs. Lincoln was seeing no visitors. Emily waited until Monday for another message. Receiving none, she packed her belongings and left for Washington.

Booth was still at large, as was Secretary Seward's attacker. Soldiers, their weapons conspicuous, boarded the cars, questioned everyone, and stared into everyone's faces, including the ladies', just in case the assassins might have donned bonnets and crinolines. It was with considerable relief that Emily stepped off the train in Washington.

Her first stop, after she checked into the Metropolitan Hotel, was at the office of Senator Browning. "What are you doing here?"

"Calling upon you," Emily snapped.

"I apologize; that wasn't a gentlemanly welcome, but you shouldn't be here. Neither should anyone else associated with the rebellion. Do you remember Major Ficklin from Richmond?"

"How on earth could I forget him?" Emily smiled; the major had been kind enough, upon crossing illicitly into Washington, to send her some papers related to her cotton that she had left at her hotel. "Is he still here in Washington?"

"Yes. He's in Old Capitol Prison. He was arrested yesterday."

"No! What on earth for?"

"Suspected of conspiring with Booth, what else?"

"He would never do that! Why, he spoke highly of President Lincoln. I cannot believe he had a hand in this awful business."

"Neither do I, but that's where we are. Stanton's not the monster some say he is, but he's got a job to do, and he's going to do it without gloves. And that's where you come in. You're the widow of a man who died fighting for the South. Mr. Lincoln once mentioned a rather unpleasant letter you wrote to him, in which you showed that you bore a grudge against—"

"That foolish letter! I was grieving for so many people at the time."

"You've recently been in Richmond, where some think the assassination was cooked up. Then you went to Baltimore, where Booth lived as a boy and which he seems to have visited recently as well. You've been friendly with Ficklin, who sent you papers."

"Perfectly legitimate papers!"

"And I would be willing to bet that when you were down South, you accepted letters from people, some of them near strangers, to pass along to their friends to Kentucky. Am I right?"

"Yes, of course. I mailed them when I got to Washington."

"Do you know what was in them?"

"Of course not. But I'm sure they were all harmless."

"Probably. But put these things all together, and you could easily wind up in Old Capitol yourself on suspicion. Until Booth and his gang are caught, tried, and hanged, everyone is game for Stanton's net. And that includes you. Go back to Kentucky, and stay there quietly. I'll do what I can about your cotton—though I warn you that President Johnson is a very different man than President Lincoln—and I'll see to it that your name doesn't get dragged publicly into this. I'll do what I can for Major Ficklin as well. Someone who's faced down danger as much as he has isn't going to be much the worse for a spell in prison."

Emily sighed, but found she could make no arguments against Mr. Browning's advice. "Have you seen my sister?"

"Mrs. Lincoln is seeing no one. I stopped by there this morning. You're not thinking of going there, are you?"

"Yes. That was my main purpose in coming to this city."

"I wouldn't risk it."

"I have to. She is my sister, and this is the worst thing that has ever happened to her. To any woman, almost." Emily rose. "Good afternoon, Mr. Browning. Thank you for your time."

✑

Washington was every bit as crepey as Baltimore and festooned with "Wanted" posters for Booth and the unnamed assailant of Mr. Seward. As she walked to the Executive Mansion, Emily took some comfort in the fact that the description of the latter bore no resemblance to Major Ficklin, or to anyone else she knew.

Bearing Mr. Browning's words in mind, she did not ask at the White House for Mary, but for Bob. It was Tad, however, who ran into her arms. "Aunt Emily!"

"Tad." She hugged him tight. "I cannot tell you how sorry I was to hear about your father."

"It was horrible," Tad said simply. "Someone announced at *Aladdin* that he had been shot, but someone else said it was just a wild rumor and we shouldn't be worried. But then I learned that it was true."

"What a dreadful way to learn the news."

Tad nodded. "I miss him. But I will see him in heaven if I am good, and I am trying to be better. Anyway, Bob is busy, but he should be here shortly. Father's in your old room until they move him to the East Room for the public viewing tomorrow, and then the funeral on Wednesday. Would you care to see him? Bob says that the embalmer did a fine job."

"I would be honored."

Tad led Emily to her former lodgings. There on a table lay a figure draped in a sheet, which Tad carefully lifted to reveal his father's face. Emily took her nephew's hand and gazed at the remains of the man she had met when she was a mere girl and he seemed to her to be the tallest being in the universe.

His first words to her, spoken when she was a child, had been gentle. "Little Sister." And her last words to him had been harsh. Oh, why couldn't she have at least lifted her hand in a friendly greeting that last time she saw him?

"Don't cry, Aunt Emily. You'll make me start."

Emily nodded and brushed her tears away as Tad gently replaced the sheet. As they left the room, her companion said, "Don't tell Mother that I brought you in there. She doesn't like even me coming in there."

"She hasn't seen him?"

"No, and she won't. She won't go into his old room, or even her old room. She hardly sees anyone. But maybe she'd like to see you. I'll bring you to her."

"Tad, if she doesn't want—"

"Come along!"

Emily had planned to broach a meeting with Mary delicately, through Bob. But since it seemed to be what Tad wanted, she let him tug her along.

Mary had taken up residence in a small room into which a single bed had been moved. "Here's Aunt Emily to see you," Tad announced to a figure underneath the covers.

Mary sat up. "Get out."

"But, Mother…"

"Run along, Tad. I will join you in a few minutes." Tad obeyed, while Emily looked at her sister with horror. Mary's eyes were mere slits from crying, and her nightgown was far from fresh.

"Did I not tell you to get out?"

"I only wanted to give you my condolences, Mary, and to see if there was anything I could do for you."

"You only wanted to gloat over my husband's death. You and your rebels wanted this! Do you think I am so naive as to think that that vile creature Booth acted alone? Jeff Davis himself is responsible for this. I know it!"

"If he is, he should be tried and hanged. Anyone involved with this murder should be." Emily looked around the room. With its multitude of windows, it should have been light and airy, but all the blinds were

shut and all the windows closed. "Do let me open a window or two and
find a fresh nightgown for you."

"Don't you dare touch those windows."

Emily obeyed, and instead sat.

"Since you are making yourself at home, I suppose you may stay a
while."

"Thank you."

"But only for a few minutes."

"All right, Mary." Emily sat in silence for a moment before venturing, "I will be going back to Kentucky tomorrow."

"To my gloating stepmother?"

"She will not be gloating, Mary, and neither am I. It was sad news
to me. Horrid news. You must believe me."

She took Mary's hand, and her sister surprised her by not brushing
it away. "You will be remaining in Lexington?"

"I don't know. It has become unpleasant for me there. I may find
someplace else to live—someplace that has not been touched so much
by the war, and where I can make a living if I have to."

"At what?"

"Teaching music, perhaps. People will want some beauty in their
lives after all this."

"I would offer to help, but I fear I have been left a pauper."

Emily doubted this—Mr. Lincoln had always been frugal—but
wisely did not argue. Instead, she asked, "Have you given thought to
where you will live? I know it is very early—"

"Not Springfield; not without my husband. Chicago, perhaps. But I
require time to make my arrangements, though I am sure the Inebriate
believes otherwise."

"The Inebriate?"

"That creature who is now President. Such a disgrace to the office!
I would not be surprised if this house does not collapse with sheer
disgust when he moves in."

"Perhaps he will rise to the solemnity of his office."

Mary dismissed this with a snort. "In any case, I will leave when

I am good and ready. Contrary to what you may think, I have not languished in bed this entire time. I have met with Secretary Stanton about the funeral arrangements; I have discussed my husband's final resting place; I have received the occasional visitor. But I do always come back to this bed."

"Why?"

"Because I do not want to think about life without my dear husband. Because I have so many regrets that I can escape only when I sleep. So many hasty remarks I made over the years to him, so many times I trespassed upon his generous nature. But you would not understand that, I am sure, being such a perfect little wife."

"I have my own regrets."

"Really? What would those be?"

Emily swallowed as she prepared to tell Mary what she had told no one else, even her mother. "When Hardin came home on his last leave, he was in poor health, tired of the war, anxious to be at home with me and the children. I encouraged him, helped restore his spirits, and sent him back to the front in fine health—the perfect fodder for a Union minié ball. I did those things because I thought his sense of honor and duty demanded them. But what if I had not? What if I had squalled and begged and carried on, and he had resigned his commission? He would be alive today, and with me."

"Ah, well. But he would have been guilt-ridden, no doubt. And in any case, you may overestimate your power. I find that when a man gives in to our wishes, it is usually only when he had secretly wanted to do something anyway."

"Perhaps. But I will always think it might have been otherwise."

They sat in silence for a while before Mary said, "Someone—I don't remember who, there has been so much going around me—told me that the doctors saved the bullet that killed my dear husband. Such a tiny thing, he said, to change history. And then I thought of that letter you wrote to my husband. *I also would remind you that your minié bullets have made us what we are.*"

"Writing that letter is another thing I regret."

"But you were right, in one respect. Those bullets have made us what we are."

"But they can't change what we were, Mary. And I hope they won't determine what we will be in the future."

They clasped hands in silence. Finally, Emily said, "Shall I stay?"

"No. Unjust as it may be, when I look at you, I think of those rebels who killed my beloved husband. Later, it may be different. But for now…"

"Then I will leave." Emily carefully kissed her sister's cheek, then headed toward the door. When she put her hand to it, she turned. "Mary?"

"Now what?"

"I am sorry; you know that we Todds always like to have the last word. I just wanted to let you know that whatever the future holds for us, I will always honor the memory of your husband." Emily opened the door. "Goodbye, and God bless you. Bob will know where to find me if you should ever want me."

∼∽

Her sister was at last gone. Mary sighed, and then lay back down and closed her eyes.

But she would rise again soon: to keep a presuming group of Springfield citizens from burying her husband in the middle of town, without having even consulted her first. Still later, she would fight for the pension she deserved as the widow of a great man.

Then her husband's former law partner, the drunken William Herndon, took to the lecture circuit and started with his wild stories—the worst being that long before he came to Springfield, Mr. Lincoln had fallen in love with some country girl named Ann Rutledge, who died of a fever before they could marry, and that he had never loved another woman since. Yet another cruel blow was to come: the death of her beloved Tad of pleurisy at age eighteen. Who would not act a little oddly under the circumstances? It was at this low point in her life that that monster of ingratitude, that creature she had to call her oldest son, had dragged her in front of a jury and had her declared insane, then committed her to a lunatic asylum.

But Mary had fought back and gained her release on a sort of parole to her sister Elizabeth, and now she stood in the hallway of Elizabeth's home in Springfield, where everything that was good about her life had started, staring at a telegram. The court had declared her restored to reason.

Well. She could quibble with the wording—how could one be restored to what had never been lost?—and the person she would not name still had quantities of her property, which would have to be wrestled out of his grasp. But for the moment, she savored her victory. She was sane, and she had gotten a judge to admit that, for the entire nation to know.

Emily had been right in those words spoken over a decade before. The Todds did like the last word.

∽ Epilogue ∾

MAY 31, 1909

B y train, by foot, by horse and buggy, and even by motorcar, thousands of people had converged upon Hodgenville, Kentucky, for the dedication of a statue commemorating the centennial of Abraham Lincoln's birth near that sleepy town. Fanning themselves in the heat, waving Union and even Confederate flags, the spectators crowded around the sculptor Adolph Alexander Weinman's production, its base bearing the word LINCOLN, the figure concealed beneath a large American flag. With a tug of a cord, the drape would fall gracefully from the statue, or so Emily, sitting on a platform with the Kentucky governor and a host of other dignitaries, had been assured.

Beside her, the last surviving sibling of Mary Lincoln, was Bob, the last surviving son of Abraham. Their respective statuses had not been lost on the reporters of the land, and while Bob was notoriously shy of the press, Emily was generally more willing to oblige by talking about the people she'd known, most all of them long dead. People like Hardin. People like her brother-in-law the President. People like her sister Mary.

More than anyone, it was Mary the reporters wanted to know about, especially as the years passed and the stories about her grew wilder. Had Mr. Lincoln left her at the altar? (No.) Had she pillaged the White House before departing it? (Certainly not.) Had she been the unloved wife of a man whose heart lay in the grave with Ann Rutledge? (A most emphatic no.) And—albeit usually phrased more delicately—was she crazy?

That question wasn't so easy to answer. It was true that Bob had felt obliged to commit his mother to a private asylum, though she hadn't remained there long, and it was also true that Mary had acted erratically in the years after her husband's death.

But crazy? Far from it: she'd gotten poor Tad the education that had been neglected during his father's lifetime, traveled twice through Europe, wrestled a pension from the hands of a stingy government.

What she hadn't done, however, was stay in touch with Emily, although Emily had tried. Oh, there had been formal contact from Mary: a polite answer to the letter Emily sent on the anniversary of Mr. Lincoln's death, a short note in response to the letter of condolence that Emily had sent after poor Tad's death. But there had been nothing more than that, and with Mary having been dead since 1882, any reunion between the sisters would have to be in heaven.

Not that Emily was in any hurry to get there. At age seventy-two, she had her children to boss around, her old friends and her young friends, her Todd genealogical research, her United Daughters of the Confederacy work, her piano, her phonograph, her favorite baseball teams—any number of things to keep her thoroughly attached to the world.

Emily brought her wandering thoughts back to the speaker, a judge who was extolling the pioneer spirit and Mr. Lincoln's virtues. When he at last finished (Mr. Lincoln could have given half a dozen Gettysburg Addresses during that period of time), Miss Florence Howard rose to recite "The Blue and the Gray," which brought a tear to Bob's eye. Then, as a chorus of children sang "America," the master of ceremonies helped Emily off the platform and handed her the cord attached to the statue's drape.

As instructed, Emily gave the cord a vigorous yank. For a moment, she thought that she would have to try again, but then the flag fell in folds to the ground, revealing a bronze Mr. Lincoln, seated in a chair. It was a fine likeness, and Emily, lingering in place to admire it as the crowds cheered, could almost hear it saying, "Little Sister."

It was as if she'd called out to him on that steamer after all.

She had kept the promise she made to Mary that day in April 1865, she reflected as the master of ceremonies led her back to her place. *I will always honor your husband's memory.* And when that heavenly reunion between the sisters finally came, she wasn't about to let Mary forget that fact.

AUTHOR'S NOTE

Following the war, Emily moved to Madison, Indiana, where she bought a house (probably with the proceeds from at last selling her cotton), served as the organist for the Episcopalian church, and taught music. Presumably out of devotion to her husband's memory—or perhaps because she found that the independence accorded a widow agreed with her—she never remarried. In 1883, through the influence of Robert Lincoln, then the Secretary of War, Emily was appointed postmistress of Elizabethtown, Kentucky, a position she held until a change in administration in 1895. Eventually, she and her three children bought a house in the outskirts of Lexington, Kentucky, where she died on February 20, 1930, at the age of ninety-three. A favorite anecdote from that period is from a friend who stopped by Emily's house to pay a call, only to find the old lady engrossed in listening to the World Series on her radio.

Although most of her public appearances, such as at Orphan Brigade reunions and United Daughters of the Confederacy functions, were related to the war, in 1911 she welcomed the National American Woman Suffrage Association's convention to Louisville. Living as long as she did, Emily had several opportunities to vote before her death. She is buried, along with her children and a number of her other family members, in Lexington's city cemetery. Decades before, Emily had had Hardin's body moved from Atlanta to his family cemetery in Elizabethtown, where he was reburied with great ceremony.

Although the spelling "Emilie" is used in some family records and on Emily's tombstone, she signed her name as "Emily," the spelling I have therefore followed. Emily also used her maiden name, styling herself "Emily Todd Helm," unlike her sister, who was known simply as "Mary Lincoln."

Katherine Helm, Emily's oldest daughter, became a portrait painter; her portrait of her aunt Mary Lincoln, based upon photographs and contemporary descriptions of Mary, hangs in the White House. Katherine Helm also wrote one of the earliest biographies of Mary, a source still used by historians for its account of Mary's girlhood years. Of Emily's three children, only her younger daughter, Elodie ("Dee" in this book), married, and none had offspring, leaving Emily without direct descendants.

After her husband's assassination, Mary and her two surviving sons moved to Chicago. Although Abraham Lincoln had left his wife comfortably off, he had died intestate, and it took a while to settle his estate. This, and the personal debt she had run up as First Lady, led to Mary's decision to sell her elaborate dresses on the secondhand market in an effort to raise funds for herself. The "Old Clothes Sale," as it was called, humiliated Robert Lincoln and drew the scorn of the press, which had little sympathy for the widow of the martyred president. After this fiasco, Mary traveled to Europe in 1868 with Tad Lincoln, whose neglected education she took in hand. In 1871, Mary and Tad returned to Chicago, where on July 15 of that year, at age eighteen, Tad Lincoln died of a lung ailment.

After this tragic loss, Mary's behavior grew steadily more erratic—at one point, having convinced herself that Robert Lincoln was seriously ill, she hastened by rail from Florida to Chicago, only to find her perfectly healthy son at the depot. At last, in 1875, Robert Lincoln, after taking counsel with his father's old friends, decided that he had no choice but to commit Mary to a private asylum in Batavia, Illinois, which first required that she be declared insane in a public proceeding. Although Mary was accorded due process by the standards of the day—indeed, Illinois offered subjects of such proceedings more protection than other states—she was understandably furious at her son. Mary enlisted the help of James and Myra Bradwell, a husband-and-wife legal team, and soon succeeded in being released to the custody of her sister Elizabeth Edwards. Having at last been declared "restored to reason," in 1876 she again took off to Europe, remaining there until her failing health obliged her to return to Elizabeth Edwards's Springfield house in late 1880. There she died on July 16, 1882, age sixty-three, and was buried with her husband and their three deceased sons in Springfield's Oak Ridge Cemetery.

Robert Lincoln became Secretary of War in 1881. Resisting pressure to run for political office, he became the president of the Pullman Palace Car Company in 1897 and died on July 26, 1926. Throughout his life, he and his wife, Mary Harlan, remained close to Emily Todd Helm and her children. For a time following Mary's insanity trial, Robert and Mary were estranged; only in May 1881, probably through the intervention of Elizabeth Edwards, did Mary agree to see her son, after which Robert visited his mother regularly until her death. Robert's widow chose to bury him at Arlington National Cemetery, created from land that once belonged to General Robert E. Lee.

While recounting the fates of the various secondary characters in this book would be a rather lengthy affair, because I left Benjamin Ficklin languishing in prison at the close of my novel, I feel obliged to mention that he was released from the Old Capitol Prison in June 1865, having never been charged with a crime, and quickly resumed his adventurous life in the West. (For the fates of some of his fellow prisoners, see my previous novel, *Hanging Mary*.) Ironically, it was his return to the relatively sedate confines of Washington that proved his undoing: in 1871, while Ficklin was dining at his friend and partner's home in Georgetown, a fish bone lodged in his throat and ultimately caused the unfortunate man to bleed to death. Ficklin was buried in his native Charlottesville, Virginia.

As always is my practice, in telling Mary and Emily's stories, I have adhered closely to the known facts, although because Emily was a less public personage than her sister, her tale contained more gaps to be filled in by conjecture. Nonetheless, I have taken one great liberty in writing this novel: there is no evidence that Emily and Mary met at the White House following Lincoln's assassination. Emily was, however, in Baltimore on the night Lincoln was shot, and she sent the telegram to Robert Lincoln mentioned in my book the following morning. With that in mind, it struck me as plausible that Emily would have attempted to see Robert before she returned to Kentucky, and perhaps been allowed a brief visit with Mary as well. In the same vein, nothing indicates that Emily ever saw John Wilkes Booth act, much less that she or her sister Kitty met him, but Hardin's will was probated in Louisville shortly before Booth performed in that city, so it is certainly possible that Emily was there at the time. As a final defense, I should note that the source that would have likely provided Emily protection from presuming historical novelists—Emily's wartime diary—was destroyed by Emily shortly before her death.

In 1864, Abraham Lincoln wrote to Stephen Burbridge that he had heard that Union authorities in Lexington had sought to arrest Emily, but the circumstances behind the rumor are unknown, and Emily much later in life claimed (somewhat implausibly) to have been unaware that she had fallen under suspicion. As Emily's mother was heard expressing her admiration for General Morgan, Martha White is known to have visited at Mrs. Morgan's house, and the Todds likely would have been in Lexington during Morgan's raid, I took those circumstances into account while constructing my account of the episode of Emily's near-arrest.

Except for some changes in spelling, Emily's "minié ball" letter as it appears in my novel follows the original verbatim, as do the telegrams announcing Alec's and Hardin's deaths and the letter from Hardin to Emily quoted in chapter 6.

Following the death of George "Mac" McCawley, Emily wrote an emotional letter of condolence to his brother, Frank McCawley—such an emotional letter, in fact, that I came to suspect that had Mac survived the war, he might have become Emily's second husband. But that, of course, is sheer conjecture. Kitty Todd's suitor, William Wallace Herr, survived the war and married Kitty in 1866.

Emily is known to have had two slaves, Margaret and Phil. Emily left Margaret behind when she returned to Kentucky, for the reasons given here. A vague family reference to her as "faithful" suggests that she may have returned to Emily's service after the war, but the tendency of ex-Confederates to overstate the attachment of former slaves to their former masters should be borne in mind. Another family story has Phil returning to Kentucky after Hardin's death and spending his later years working as a hack driver in Louisville, where he supposedly transported the actress Sarah Bernhardt on one occasion. Incidentally, Bernhardt claimed that while crossing the Atlantic, she saved a fellow passenger from falling down some stairs; the passenger turned out to be Mary Lincoln.

Abraham Lincoln and Mary Todd did break off their engagement, for reasons that remain open to conjecture, as do the circumstances of their reconciliation.

There is disagreement about whether the young Oliver Wendell Holmes told President Lincoln to "get down, you fool," but the story was too good to ignore, as were the accounts that have Mary joining her husband upon the parapets of the fort.

For those wanting to read more about Mary, I recommend the biographies by Catherine Clinton, Jean Baker, Ruth Painter Randall, and (of course) Katherine Helm, along with *The Mary Lincoln Enigma*, a collection of essays edited by Frank J. Williams and Michael Burkhimer, and Jennifer Fleischner's joint biography of Mary and of Elizabeth Keckly. Jason Emerson has written several books dealing with Mary's insanity trial, as well as a biography of Robert Lincoln, and Justin G. Turner and Linda Levitt Turner have compiled most of Mary's surviving letters. For Emily and the other Todd siblings, the best book is *House of Abraham: Lincoln and the Todds, a Family Divided by War* by Stephen Berry. Angela Esco Elder's chapter "We Weep Over Our Dead Together" in *Kentucky Women*, edited by Melissa McEuen and Thomas H. Appleton Jr., offers a good summary of Emily's life. Together, Berry and Elder edited *Practical Strangers: The Courtship Correspondence of Nathaniel Dawson and Elodie Todd, Sister of Mary Todd Lincoln*, which as well as being interesting in its own right was helpful in providing clues to Emily's whereabouts at various times.

Emily Todd Helm's papers, consisting mainly of correspondence directed to her (including a number of quite moving letters from her husband along with the sad telegram announcing his death), genealogical material, newspaper clippings, and a few writings by Emily, are in the Kentucky Historical Society in Frankfort. A number of photographs of the Todd and Helm families, as well as Alec Todd's wartime diary, are online at the Kentucky Digital Library.

Finally, as there have been books written about nearly every conceivable aspect of the life of Abraham Lincoln, with more appearing regularly, it would be simply too daunting to list all those I found to be helpful about my personal hero. Suffice it to say that I most often turned to books by Michael Burlingame (who, it should be noted, is deeply unsympathetic toward Mary), Richard Lawrence Miller, and Harold Holzer, along with Douglas L. Wilson and Rodney O. Davis's *Herndon's Informants: Letters, Interviews, and Statements about Abraham Lincoln* and Earl Schenck Miers and C. Percy Powell's *Lincoln Day by Day: A Chronology*. My hope is that readers of my book will come to share my admiration for the man who in my opinion remains, and in all likelihood will remain for a long time, the worthiest occupant of 1600 Pennsylvania Avenue.

READING
GROUP GUIDE

1. Describe Mary and Lincoln's relationship when they first met in Springfield. What drew them together? Do you think they were a good match?

2. *The First Lady and the Rebel* centers on Mary and Emily, two sisters fighting on opposite sides of the Civil War. Describe the two sisters. How are they similar? Different? What do you think they are fighting for?

3. Have you ever been in a position where you were on separate sides of an issue from a family member or close friend? How did you bridge that divide?

4. What is Emily and Hardin's relationship like? Compare it to Mary and Lincoln's. Who do you relate to more throughout the story?

5. Why do you think Hardin refuses the position Lincoln offers him at the beginning of the novel? What is driving Hardin to separate himself, and consequently Emily, from Lincoln and Mary?

6. What is Emily's connection to the Confederate cause? Describe how she interacts with Maggie. Do you think she supports slavery, or is something else keeping her in the South?

7. Describe some of the hardships Mary faces while living in the White House. What were some of the biggest challenges she had to overcome? Do you think she comes out on top?

8. Both sisters suffer loss over the course of the story. Describe those moments. How do they manage their grief? Do you think this shared suffering links them together?

9. When Emily comes with Kate to visit the White House, how do Kate and Tad relate to each other? What do you think this says about Emily and Mary? Are the children a mirror of their relationship?

10. Describe the night of Lincoln's assassination. How does Mary deal with the tragedy? How does Emily attempt to connect with her?

A CONVERSATION
WITH THE AUTHOR

What inspired you to write *The First Lady and the Rebel*?

I've always been interested in the Lincolns, but my interest inten-
sified when I was researching and writing the first of my novels set in
the United States, *Hanging Mary*. So I decided to turn my attention
to a very different Mary! Because this First Lady has been the subject
of several historical novels, I wanted to approach her story from a
different perspective—her relationship with her relatives who sided
with the Confederacy, and with her sister Emily in particular.

**Your novel is packed with historical detail. What kind of research
did you have to do to bring this story to life?**

There is a book about nearly every conceivable aspect of Abraham
Lincoln and his family, so there was very little for me to uncover as
far as Mary was concerned. What was a challenge in her case was to
find a plausible explanation for episodes that continue to baffle historians, such as her infamous breakup with Lincoln and her peculiar
behavior at City Point.

Emily was a different matter. Although Emily has been the subject of several short biographies and is prominent in Stephen Berry's book about the Todds, not much attention has been paid to her day-to-day life during the war, other than her visit to the White House. Accessible to the press as Emily was during her later life, she proved to be very reticent about her own wartime experiences, so I had to do some digging to fill in the blanks. Many of the tidbits I discovered about her came from stray references in contemporary sources. For instance, Thomas Conolly, the Irish MP Emily meets in Richmond, mentions Emily in several of his diary entries, while Emily's attempts to secure her cotton are detailed in Orville Browning's diaries and in the voluminous evidence collected following Lincoln's assassination.

One of the first stops I made was to the Kentucky Historical Society, which holds Emily's papers. Aside from the thrill of handling documents that Emily and her family handled, it was immensely helpful in a variety of ways. For instance, it was through the correspondence addressed to Emily that I learned of her friendship with Phoebe Yates Pember, who's well known by students of the Civil War for her memoir of her nursing days but whose connection with Emily has hitherto been overlooked. That same collection holds the telegram announcing Benjamin Hardin Helm's death. The telegram's not addressed to Emily; rather, it was sent to someone else with instructions to find her and send her to Atlanta. So how did Emily get ahold of it, to preserve it with her belongings? Asking myself that question helped me write a scene in my novel.

Another scene was inspired by a letter by General Singleton, returning from his trip to Richmond in March 1865, in which he mentions passing the *River Queen*, on which Lincoln was a passenger, but not realizing it until it was too late. Since Emily was under the general's protection, she almost certainly would have been on the boat too. It intrigued me to realize how close she and Lincoln came to meeting one last time before his death.

Who do you connect with more, Mary or Emily?

Probably Mary. For one, she ended up on the right side of history as far as slavery was concerned, and her enlightened attitudes are certainly more palatable to a modern person than those of Emily, who, as far as I know, went to her grave an unreconstructed Southerner. And it's also not difficult for me to identify with an increasingly cranky middle-aged woman! On the other hand, though, in some ways, Emily was more fun to write about, because since she's not as well-documented as her sister, there wasn't the sense of history constantly looking over my shoulder that I had with Mary. And I do admire Emily's grit. One of the effects of the war that's been given more attention recently is that it forced Southern women left to manage on their own by absent or dead husbands to become more independent, and Emily is certainly illustrative of that. I don't think it was only devotion to her husband's memory that caused her to eschew a second marriage.

Did you find it difficult to bring Lincoln, a well-known historical figure, to life in a new way?

Yes, I did! Lincoln is my hero, and I constantly worried that he was coming across as a bit too perfect. It helped, however, that we see him in this novel mainly in his private interactions with Mary, some of the least recorded aspects of his life.

What drew you to this period of American history?

I've been interested in the Lincolns since I was a child, but until recently, I never had much interest in the Civil War itself, which at the schools I attended was taught pretty much as a series of battles, with little emphasis on the individuals involved. My research for *Hanging Mary* led me to read more about the stories of the people caught up in the war, and that brought me to a new appreciation of this momentous time in history and of those people who lived through it—or who didn't survive it.

When you're not writing, how do you like to spend your time?

I enjoy traveling, especially when I can combine pleasure and research; hanging out with my family; keeping our two dogs entertained; and collecting nineteenth-century photographs. The latter interest grew out of my attempts to learn more about fashions of the period. I began looking at photographs to better acquaint myself with what people actually wore, which is very different from what most films and television series set during the Civil War show them wearing. Pretty soon, I couldn't resist buying a couple, and it snowballed from there. I'm pleased to own a few of the images of Mary and of Lincoln that were widely sold in the nineteenth century; it's another neat connection to history.

ACKNOWLEDGMENTS

As many historical novelists will agree, researching a novel is often far more fun than writing it, and *The First Lady and the Rebel* was no exception. While I am sure I have forgotten some institutions, for which I apologize, I am particularly grateful for the assistance of the librarians and archivists of the Kentucky Historical Society, the Abraham Lincoln Presidential Library, the Chicago Historical Society, the Filson Historical Society, the Margaret I. King Library at the University of Kentucky, the Lexington (Kentucky) Public Library, the Jefferson County (Indiana) Historical Society, the Clements Library at the University of Michigan, the Seymour Library at Knox College, the Rubenstein Library at Duke University, the Wilson Library at the University of North Carolina at Chapel Hill, the Library of Congress, and the National Archives. All made a pleasant task even more pleasant. Nor can I leave out Colleen Puterbaugh at the Surratt House Museum's James O. Hall Research Center, who provided me with an exciting and memorable "Ficklin Day." Historian Jason Emerson kindly provided me with a copy of Emily Todd Helm's telegram sent to Robert Lincoln after President Lincoln's assassination.

Anyone researching Abraham Lincoln and his family should steer his or her browser to Roger J. Norton's Lincoln Discussion Symposium, whose members can answer almost any Lincoln-related query posed to them, no matter how obscure, and whose discussions are thought-provoking and entertaining.

As ever, I am grateful to my publisher, Sourcebooks, and its staff, especially Margaret Johnston, whose editorial suggestions proved invaluable.

During the course of completing this book, I said goodbye to three old friends, Boswell, Stripes, and Onslow, and hello to another, Emmy, who, along with Dudley, continues the invaluable canine work of keeping the mail carrier from murdering me, even on royalty check arrival days. Nor can I forget my grand-cat, Harrison, whose inscrutable air surely masks a deep interest in the Lincolns.

Finally, I would like to thank my husband, Don Coomes, and my children, Bethany Coomes and Thad Coomes, for their support and sustaining presence. This does not, of course, absolve them from reading the rest of the book.

ABOUT THE AUTHOR

Susan Higginbotham is the author of seven historical novels, including *The Stolen Crown*, *The Queen of Last Hopes*, *Hugh and Bess*, and *Hanging Mary*. *The Traitor's Wife*, her first novel, is the winner of *ForeWord Magazine*'s 2005 Silver Award for historical fiction and is a Gold Medalist, Historical/Military Fiction, 2008 Independent Publisher Book Awards. She writes her own historical fiction blog, *History Refreshed*. Higginbotham has worked as an editor and an attorney and lives in Maryland with her family.